Seven Generations

Seven Generations:

Margaret Martin

Edited by Robin Truitt

Margaret Martin Books

2015

First Printing: 2015

ISBN: 978-0-578-15999-7

Library of Congress Number: 2015904288

Margaret Martin Books
margaretmartinbooks@gmail.com

Ordering Information:
Special discounts are available on quantity purchases by educators, and others. U.S. trade bookstores and wholesalers For details, contact the publisher at the above listed address.

Table of Contents

Acknowledgements

Robin Truitt: This book was edited by the wonderful Robin Truitt. Your friendship is a great treasure.

Ed Meeks, Shoshone Tribal Member, Descendant of Yellow Beads, Todza and Onipe and member of the Yellow Bangs Clan: I cannot thank Ed Meeks enough for his time reading and adding to these stories. Mr. Meeks allowed me to be inspired by his true family stories and personal experiences, and generously shared his friendship and many hilarious jokes. Your ideas, assistance and encouragement were invaluable.

Georgia Case: Georgia read, corrected and informed the writing of this book. You are awesome, Georgia!

Steve Wheelock: Thank you for your careful reading and editorial suggestions. Your encouragement means so much to me and was very helpful!

Jan Dunbar: Thank you for reading Chapter 2 and for your kind words of encouragement.

Victoriah Arsenian: Your ideas and assistance in getting this book read by a greater audience was great! You are a true professional.

Amy Winter, Diana Witherspoon, Sharon Pearson, Joselle Vitale, Barbara White, Direlle Calica, Chris Deschene, Larry and Sally Schaff and Chris Schaff: Thank you all so much for reading parts of this book and relaying your suggestions. Your encouragement was so important to me!

Danny Abbott: I hope you are reading this up there, Danny. You know you helped inspire this book and guided it from the great beyond. You taught me what to do *and* what not to do. You were a great mentor.

Dirk Martin: Thank you for being a wonderful husband and for always encouraging me to follow my dreams.

The characters in these stories, except for historical figures such as Indian Chiefs, leaders of the Mormon Church, and elected politicians are all fictional, but the context of all the stories, and the historical events described are real.

All grammar and language "mistakes" are intentional; they reflect the characters' use of English, sometimes as a second language.

Each Generation's story can be read as a stand-alone short story. Each is told in a different voice and a different style, to best reflect the story.

All matters of Indian law, no matter how unbelievable, are true.

Family Tree of Characters

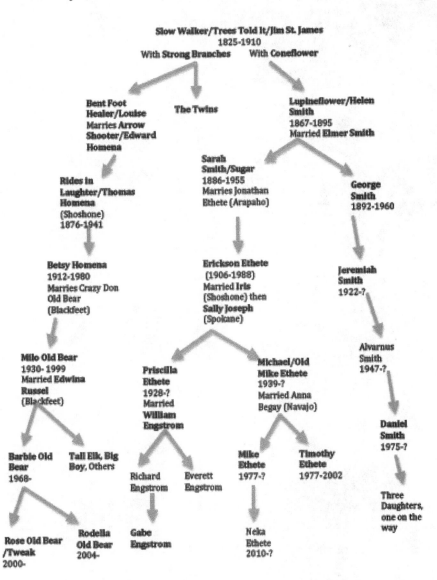

Slow Walker/Trees Told It/Jim St. James
1825-1910
With Strong Branches   With Coneflower

Bent Foot
Healer/Louise
Marries Arrow
Shooter/Edward
Homena

The Twins

Lupineflower/Helen
Smith
1867-1895
Married Elmer Smith

Sarah
Smith/Sugar
1886-1955
Marries Jonathan
Ethete (Arapaho)

George
Smith
1892-1960

Rides In
Laughter/Thomas
Homena
(Shoshone)
1876-1941

Betsy Homena
1912-1980
Marries Crazy Don
Old Bear
(Blackfeet)

Erickson Ethete
(1906-1988)
Married Iris
(Shoshone) then
Sally Joseph
(Spokane)

Jeremiah
Smith
1922-?

Milo Old Bear
1930-1999
Married Edwina
Russel
(Blackfeet)

Priscilla
Ethete
1928-?
Married
William
Engstrom

Michael/Old
Mike Ethete
1939-?
Married Anna
Begay (Navajo)

Alvarnus
Smith
1947-?

Daniel
Smith
1975-?

Barbie Old
Bear
1968-

Tall Elk, Big
Boy, Others

Richard
Engstrom

Everett
Engstrom

Mike
Ethete
1977-?

Timothy
Ethete
1977-2002

Rose Old Bear
/Tweak
2000-

Rodella
Old Bear
2004-

Gabe
Engstrom

Neka
Ethete
2010-?

Three
Daughters,
one on the
way

In Iroquois society, leaders are encouraged to remember seven generations in the past and consider seven generations in the future when making decisions that affect the people.

~ Wilma Mankiller
Elected Chief of the Cherokee Nation

One little, two little, three little Indians!
Four little, five little, six little Indians!
Seven little, eight little, nine little Indians!
Ten little Indian boys!

Nine little, eight little, seven little Indians!
Six little, five little, four little Indians!
Three little, two little, one little Indian!
No little Indian boys!

~American Frontier Folk Song

Introduction: Mr. Lou McNulty, Landman

2013

This morning, starting about dawn, I flew my small plane from my home in Central California to the airport at Riverton, Wyoming, just south of the Wind River Indian Reservation. I arrived mid-day to finish buying some oil and gas rights on that "Rez." It was a clear morning. As I started right before sunrise, I could see the California Central Valley was marked with the many fields of various greens showing one of the most abundant agricultural gardens in the world, irrigated with whole rivers brought in using human ingenuity for that purpose. Then soon I enjoyed the sunrise shining pink and peach on the East faces of the Sierra Nevada Mountain Range. On the other side, the desert valleys hadn't heated up yet so it was clear and focused. I could see how the wind and occasional rains had washed the sands and rocks into artful patterns of brown, grey, and sage greens. The signs of humanity were sparse for a while as I flew through Nevada and Western Utah, but you could see the roads cut into the landscape, evidence of mining: some old, some recent, and neat small towns. Here and there, farms bloomed green where irrigation water was available.

The Rocky Mountains had begun to rise and became stunning peaks, whose air pressure changes bounced my plane like a toy. Slowly the population had increased as I flew nearer the Great Salt Lake, sparkling wide and broad. Salt Lake City had so many homes and industries and people, many descendents of tough immigrants, clustered around. Then I skirted the corner of Idaho, over the small city of Pocatello, named after a Shoshone Chief.

Crossing into Wyoming I reflected that it is a beautiful place. From the air it still looks wild, as you can imagine it was before white men came here. But you can still notice plenty of roads, and fences and in the mountains, the patches of timber harvests. Dusty, poor looking farms show on the ground below. Cattle and horses are visible as dots. Coming in, I am again thrilled by the beauty and fresh smell in the air.

My name is Lou Mc Nulty, and I am a professional Landman. It's my job to research peoples' ownerships in land, particularly in oil and gas rights. Oil companies hire me to go meet with landowners who have rights in the resource and I negotiate to buy the rights needed.

Usually people love to get my letters and welcome me to their doors because they get a good piece of the action. In my day, I've helped lots of poor and hardworking folks living in the middle of nowhere get rich because they're sitting on oil or gas that we produce. They get fat "mailbox checks", sometimes the rest of their lives. It's a lot easier than farming and it doesn't prevent folks from running cattle or planting as they always done. It's a real good deal for everybody.

But the last piece of this job I'm finishing up now is so frustrating. Indian rights! They are the hardest job for any landman.

The whole job started out pretty typical; about fifty ownerships in Wyoming. Forty-nine of them are done. I was hoping we could go ahead without this last piece, but due to the fact that the oil is where it's at, we can't. Most of my deals were just outside of the boundary of the Wind River Indian Reservation. These were pretty standard negotiations due to the fact that most of those non-Indian landowners outside the boundaries are used to these deals and know the drill. Most already have oil money and have local lawyers who I've worked with in the past. There has been lots of oil and gas development up here and where the companies *can* do their work they already have been doing it for years.

Oil companies do a lot of work just *off* the Rez even though most of the oil is under the Rez. It's just too hard to work with the tribes so the companies just avoid them and do business with the white neighbors.

Then I had about ten deals just inside the Rez. But technically those deals were not under Indian jurisdiction because those ranches are owned by white people in what's called "fee simple estate". This means that after the reservation was formed, the government sold off these lands that used to be Indian lands to the white folks who homesteaded there. In a Supreme Court case called "Montana versus US" in 1981, the Indians lost the right to administer those lands. Even though we were still breaking treaties in 1981, it has honestly saved me a lot of work.

That case improved the property values for those ranchers, too. Since you can never predict what rules the tribes will create about the lands over and on top of what the feds require, there's a big uncertainty and nobody wants to pay fair market value for Indian controlled land. The bottom line is, nobody wants their land to be under Indian jurisdiction, probably not even the Indians, because you might get screwed if so.

My last deal, which I'm here to finish, is one I need to earn my bonus on this job. It's an Indian deal. However, it could be worse, because this deal isn't a deal for tribal "trust lands", meaning the lands owned in common by the Eastern Shoshone and Northern Arapaho tribes.

Trust land deals are actually deals with the federal government and in the end needs government signatures *and* additional expensive environmental reviews *and* you need the approval of *both* the Shoshone and the Arapaho Tribal Councils. This is because the feds hold title "in trust for the tribes". It's basically federal land and the Indians get to approve any fed deal. Getting both tribes to agree almost *never* happens because those two tribes are ancient enemies and *to this day* they spite each other at every turn while of course, screwing their people. Trust lands are about worthless even though now we know they are loaded with oil and gas, water rights, timber, coal, minerals, and all kinds of wealth. But you can't mortgage the lands, you can't sell the lands, you can't even really live on the lands unless you got everybody's permission.

Worse than that, *every dime* earned by the lands goes straight to the federal government, cause it's technically federal property. The US government is supposed to be a trustee and the Indians are the beneficiaries of the trust, just like in a rich family. After the Feds negotiate the deal with an outside company to come in and take the trust resource, they then dole money from the oil or timber or farming back to the tribe or the particular Indian. That is, if you're lucky!

There was a huge multi *billion* dollar lawsuit brought by a Blackfeet lady named Eloise Cobell who proved the government didn't do any management or accounting and cut some terrible bad deals and basically stole all the Indian's money since the 1800s. The US government can't even figure out how much it was. God knows how much money the oil and timber and mining companies stole since nobody was minding the store and they let the companies send in payments on their "honor". I imagine all those impoverished people on those dusty reservations could have used that money all those years. It's really too bad.

Anyway, thank God I don't need to jump through those hoops. I'd never see my bonus. No, my last deal on this job is on what's called an "Allotment". It's a 160-acre piece of land on the edge, but inside of the Rez. This piece of land was originally allotted to one particular Indian back in 1909. Allotments happened under the 1887 "Dawes Act". The army was trying to turn the Indians into farmers so they carved up the reservation set aside for the whole tribe and "allotted" each Indian man 160 acres. I think some of the women and children got 80 acres if they didn't have a man head of household.

Basically what happened was they originally gave about 800 Shoshones the best half of Wyoming as a reservation. By the way, it's called a "reservation" because it was originally purchased from France by Thomas Jefferson as US land in the Louisiana Purchase and when they were getting ready to homestead out the Louisiana Purchase lands to white folks they "reserved" some of the lands for federal uses, such as military forts, Yellowstone Park, and for Indians. Anyway, when they first did that they figured those Indians needed all that land for hunting and their nomad ways of life, and besides there were no white folks that far west anyway. Of course, time passed and more white folks showed up wanting that good land and they figured that 800 Shoshones (and the 800 Arapahos they later put there) didn't need half of Wyoming. So they "allotted" out lands to those Indians and were able to open up the rest of the Rez to white folks. Of course they didn't really know if the Indians could make a success of farming so the lands the Indians got were generally the poor farm lands, but at least it solved the problem on how to share those lands. The Indians are still angry, because of course this all violated the treaties.

I keep digressing but this does get complicated!

So, the rules I follow to purchase the oil rights on this allotment are different than they are for tribal trust lands and for white fee lands. Under the federal rules for allotments, I need to get at least 50% of the owners of this piece of Indian property to agree to sell, then the Bureau of Indian Affairs (I like to call it the Bureau of Ignorant Assholes) through the local BIA Superintendent, can sign on behalf of the other 50%. Problem is, who knows who the owners are? Indians didn't have regular wills or inheritance rules back in the 1800s, or even now, really, so we need to try to figure out who are all the descendents alive today of an old Indian guy named Jim St. James. And we need to figure out where those people are. It's like genealogy in reverse using impossibly ill-kept records.

People wonder why Indian tribes don't develop their resources or improve their reservations. It's because of what they call the "checkerboard" of the all these types of lands on each Rez. Yes, this same mess appears on pretty much every Indian Reservation in the United States. Can you imagine going through these steps for the each of the Fee lands, for each of the Trust lands and for each of the Allotted lands when you just want to drill a few wells? It's just not worth it to most companies, or to the tribes for that matter, to even bother.

But I have made some serious progress on my one allotment. This is thanks in part to the Mormons who kept records of almost every person in Wyoming and Utah from the early days. Funny, they thought Indians were descended from a lost tribe of Mormons called Laminites who came from Israel. So the Mormons wanted to baptize all the Indians they could, even if the Indians weren't there and didn't know they was getting baptized. It's sad and funny to think of those confused Indians who died and expected to end up at the Happy Hunting Ground but they showed up wearing tight white underwear and suits and they were expected to be singing hymns with Brigham Young in a vaulted temple for the rest of eternity!

So anyway, I have letters ready to go out to about eighty people who I believe own a piece of this allotment. Probably more than half the letters will come back as not deliverable because these Indians move around so much and most of them just have PO boxes, not addresses. I couldn't find them if I wanted. If any of them actually get the letters they probably won't answer. Why would they? They will never get all their relatives to agree to the same terms. Besides, the government will take any money that comes from the deal and put it through their "accounting system" before dividing it into eighty shares and sending it back out. The kind of money we're talking about, divided by eighty, is not enough to bother with, probably.

All this is ok for me, though because I just need to show the BIA that I made this effort and made my offer, and if I don't get responses, the BIA can then sign the deal on behalf of the Indians. The energy comany can drill all they want on that land and I'll get my bonus.

The whole thing is really screwed up and I do feel sorry for those Indian folks. It was interesting doing the research on this Jim St. James allottment. He even had another more Indian sounding name of "Trees Told It."

I like to imagine the owners of those dusty names on those old Mormon ledgers. If only we could hear their stories!

Seven Generations Margaret Martin

First Generation Trees Told It

(1825—1910)

Prologue: A Shoshone Legend

Here is how the black bear Wakini overpowered the grey grizzly bear Wakinu, making the Milky Way.

The two bears began to fight over a delicious anthill. Grey and black hair flew in all directions. Wakinu lost the fight and had to leave his home forever.

Wakinu was very sad and growled loudly. He said goodbye to the home he had always known and looked at the trees and mountains and valleys. He was blinded by his tears, and walked straight into a deep snowdrift. When he climbed out there was snow all around. His coat was white with snow and ice. His coat froze as he searched for a way out of the cold. He walked and walked, making footprints in the snow until it was night.

Then he saw a broad white trail ascending into the sky. It was beautiful. He leaped! He soared up and up, shaking the snow from his fur. He had found the bridge of dead souls on the way to the eternal hunting grounds.

All the creatures awake then looked up and saw a white trail with a big grey bear walking toward the heavens. Wakinu left behind the snow he had shaken from his coat, all along what we now call the Milky Way.

Sugar, Translator of Grandfather's Stories

My name is Sugar St. James. It is 1909 on the Wind River Indian Reservation, in Wyoming, United States of America. It is my plan to write down the stories of my Grandfather, Trees Told It, or as the white men call him, Jim St. James. He is a very great man, who I love with all my heart. He is an honored elder who is known by the people as a Buffalo Indian, or one who was around in the days of the buffalo. He is greatly respected among the New'e (as we call ourselves), or Shoshone people (as we are called by white men) or Snakes (as we are known by the hand signs).

Grandfather has many stories, for he has lived since before white men were known by the New'e. He remembers the stories of the old people, the mysteries of plants and animals, holds the knowledge of stars and many other important things that are forgotten as the people die.

My Grandfather walked and wandered throughout his life. He began among his Father's Father's people in the great deserts just over the mountains from the Pacific Ocean in what is now California, where he was born. Later, when he was about four, his parents took him as they lived among his father's mother's people, in the desert of what is now Nevada and Utah. Then after white men changed so much of Shoshone territory with their farms and sheep and cows, he lived among his mother's second husband's peoples as a buffalo hunter in what is now Idaho and Wyoming.

We are now here, on the Wind River Reservation in the new state of Wyoming. This, and those other places, are traditional New'e lands. Over his life he was a member of many different bands, all of whom had certain territories and ways of life that depended on the resources of the lands where they traveled. All those peoples he camped among were New'e, but all had very different lives. My Grandfather knows much about them all.

Despite having a crippled foot, my Grandfather walked throughout his life, from California to the deserts of Nevada and Utah, then finally into Wyoming. The desert people could not keep horses because water was very hard to find. The people needed to walk from one small water source to the next almost every day. This required Grandfather to learn to keep up with his clan. I cannot imagine the struggles he had walking all across the rocky and mountainous terrain!

But perhaps this crippled foot became a good thing when he got older. My Grandfather was allowed to sit quietly back when others made war or other mischief. He became a specialist, a skilled moccasin maker who still makes beautiful old-fashioned animal hide shoes for anyone who can trade for a special made pair for that person. They can be for any size foot, or for any use, such as for walking in an area of many cactus, or as winter warming footwear. My Grandfather says that many of the old moccasin styles are no longer needed. Some of these old styles are those for long walking (because the reservations do not permit long treks), trick horse riding (because the whites have taken many of our ponies), or for minimizing your tracks (because if we follow rules, we have no need now for tracking other Indians).

I believe my Grandfather is now 84 or 85 years old, which means he was born around 1825. To white people he looks fearsome. His face is scarred by large, deep pock-marks from a time he recovered from smallpox. His nose is big and bent and has been broken but did not heal well. This story I do not know. His hair is still long but thin at the bottom now, and gray. It is held back in a wrap of black wolf hide. Like the true Indians without white blood, he has no chin hair, and when a stray hair does appear, he is methodical to pluck it out with a wooden tweezing tool he has fashioned. His arms and legs are strong and long, and his chest is broad. His back does not curve as he holds his heart out proudly in front of him, as so few of our people do, anymore. He has such a strong heart to be able to keep from guarding it, after so much heartbreak in his life. His eyes are lively, but one must know him to be able to see what is there. At one time, he was known to be quite a comic. This I have rarely seen. Now, he is very serious in his demeanor and he is often quiet and thinking. He does not interact with white people at all which has given him a mystique and has made him more frightening to them, as if he could cast spells on them.

He speaks only in the New'e language, but I know this language well, and I also know how to talk and write in English. I sometimes translate for the Superintendent of our reservation because my handwriting is very fine and I am fluent. The Superintendent has allowed me to take old papers from the trash that are blank on the back, and writing tools, which I can use for these writings.

This writing down of stories of my Grandfather is something that I see as a gift of Story Puha, a Gift of my Grandfather's knowledge for whomever may read this someday. I do not know who that will be or what will become of these stories, but my spirit urges me to continue to do this. The stories will be better for strange readers, I think, if I tell in English some of the place names and time names. I will also tell other parts of the story so a reader will better understand. Know that Grandfather does not do this; these are my additions. I will write the stories of his life so his life remains strong after he walks away, which I fear will be soon. This grieves me, but I can hold on to him longer by writing about him.

Because these stories have no person to read them now, I will start with one story of my own. It is a great secret that my Grandfather will never tell. It is about myself, so it is my Puha to give.

My Grandfather and I have played a great trick. Oh how I am proud of this trick! It has made me powerful and strong, with Puha over the white people. They do not know that although my mother was Grandfather's daughter Lupineflower, my father was a white man named Elmer Smith and I was a Mormon until I was ten summers, but then I chose to be New'e and escaped to my true people.

My name was once Sarah Smith, and my mother was talked over to Mormon thinking and married a white man who had two other wives. My parents and the sister-wives and all my brothers and sisters lived in a Mormon town in the Cache Valley of Utah, which was, by the way, New'e traditional land. I was a very hard working girl, who was advanced beyond my classmates at school. I could read very well and could write with a nice hand. I worked on our farm and in our home for very long hours every day, except Sundays when we spent very long days at the Meetinghouse.

Even though I was born to that place, I knew that I was different. For many years, I was not allowed to know anything about being Indian, but I could feel that there was something very important in my mother's silence. I loved her very much. My father, though, was very harsh to me. He was stern and always outside working. I was punished if we did not follow his rules. It seemed I simply could not follow all those rules; it was not in my nature. But I tried. I complied. When I was bad, I was locked away in a shack by my father and whipped for my transgressions.

When I was ten years old my mother brought my baby brother and me to visit my Grandfather at this reservation. I don't know what she thought, if she was questioning her Mormon life and was going to run away, or if she was sincere in saying the trip to see her father was only a visit.

She was allowed to make this visit because she was with other Mormon people on a Mission. Despite an early agreement among Christians, this reservation was to be made Episcopalian, so we had to be cautious if we were to convert more Indians to be Later-Day Saints. Mother had been a good Mormon and I think she truly wanted to bring more Indians to this faith. I think she was also proud of my little brother and me. She wanted to show us to my grandfather to let him know how good and strong your children could become if they were Saints and lived in the Mormon way.

For me, coming to the Reservation and meeting Grandfather was coming Home. I loved my Indian relatives and began right away to learn the New'e language and to take to the way of life. Even though they were often hungry, there was love, and no whipping. The Spirit songs made sense to me. I did not want to go back to Utah. I did not care if I never saw the other sister-wives or those brothers and sisters again.

Soon after the mission came to the reservation, diphtheria broke out among the Indians and many of the missionaries also became sick. My mother was one who became ill. She was taken to the hospital at Fort Laramie along with the other sick white people. The sick Indians, of course, were left to cure themselves. I never saw Mother again, because she died on the way to the hospital.

My brother and I were staying with Grandfather while she was gone. We had also became ill with the fever, but we were treated in the Indian way by my Grandfather. We recovered. When word came that my mother had died, I begged my Grandfather to let us stay with him. He did not think it was possible, but we were lucky.

A few weeks later it was not my Father who came for us, but my oldest half-brother Thom. We found out from an Indian that brought Thom that our father had been bitten by a snake and died. Grandfather now knew that we were orphans and he decided that he would try to keep us with him.

Grandfather kept us in the lodge and told everyone we were sick. When Thom came to the camp my little brother George, who was four, ran out to meet him, so my Grandfather decided that he could only keep me. He blocked the door to the lodge and Thom decided I was still too sick to move. The next day, Grandfather sent word to Thom that I had died. When Thom came for my body, My New'e family wrapped up a small deer and some Shoshone people had a traditional funeral for me. Grandfather says Thom was very sad and I think my Grandfather hurt a little for him.

My Grandfather pretended to go on a "mourning quest" to the north part of the reservation. But really he took me away to hide out until my dark hair grew longer and my skin became brown from the sun. We had word that a group of other Shoshones had come by permission to trade from the Shoshone Reservation in Idaho.

Later when the government asked who I was, Grandfather told them that I was a relative that had come with those Indians. I was dressed traditionally like an Indian and Grandfather had tied long furs around the end of my short braids which made them look very long, and because I had become so dark and pretended not to speak much English, they believed this trick even though there was no record of me in their books. One small Indian girl is of no consequence; so no questioning continued from the white men. Many Indians knew of this trick, but they laughed behind their hands and did not speak out of respect for my Grandfather.

Soon, I went to the white school and pretended to learn to read and speak English. No one asked any questions. So now I am 24 years old and I am Sugar St. James. I am odd to be not married but I will not take a man until my days with Grandfather are done.

These are stories from my Grandfather. I will tell these stories in his voice, as close in English as I can, so you will hear his words.

Story #1 STORY PUHA

Sometimes I see my granddaughter, Sugar, look at me strangely when I tell her of my days walking on this, our Mother Earth. I do not think she understands the Way that I know and from which I talk.

I am speaking to you now in my New'e language. She is writing what I say down in white man's English. Many of the things I tell she has not heard before. I think she does not know whether I am a crazy old man to say some of these things. But I say the truth to her since she is the one who asked for these words. I am honoring her and those that will come after her. This honor is stronger than my old teaching, which was to keep these private matters private, and not to share Puha by disclosing the strong medicine in these words. Who knows what these medicines will become?

I am weak now, and older than almost all the Snake, or Shoshone, or New'e people. Even Washakie has been dead some years now. I may be the only Timbisha New'e, which is the people I was born to, that is left on this Earth. I heard that all those people from my earliest days were put in a camp guarded by white soldiers and every one was shot and buried in the desert. All these things have made my heart dark. I must struggle some mornings to get out of my skins and see the sun as I am afraid it will burn me with today's further difficulties which I am not strong enough to bear. I stay in the dark some times, not because my body is weak but because my spirit is crying.

For many years I did not know what I should do with my memories. All New'e used to know our history through stories from ancient times. They told the stories by tales and songs and prayers and dances that we shared over and over and over during the long winters of cozy times in our lodges, warmed by fires and wrapped in skins and furs listening to the drums. I now wear a bear claw necklace given to me before the death of my friend Cries in Burrow. Against my teaching, I say his name now because with the necklace, which he earned after killing two large grizzly bears with a spear, he passed to me some of his privilege to tell stories. The necklace claws are curved, and hard, like life. They now seem only harmless and beautiful but they remember power and hold the medicine of the fearsome and sacred great silver bears.

Oh the many persons that told our stories! They were my many grandfathers who had deep scars and fierce faces that would break softly into warm song tones, my many grandmothers that would make us laugh with silly tales of jackrabbit and coyote. And even little children just learning would repeat the stories, sometimes with more vivid imaginings than the old ones. These traditions were for many, their strongest Puha. But many of the memories I have are too new to be blessed with the extra Puha of long telling and repeating.

I will start to say that in our old ways some kinds of stories and songs are private possessions. Singers and tellers must earn the *right* to know them and separately they must earn the *right* to share them along. They are only passed down as gifts with purposes and obligations attached to them. I know that some Indian people will criticize me for telling these stories. I pray that I am not giving bad medicine, as there is so much medicine that has gone wrong.

I have fought within myself about whether I should tell these stories. For many years I have not told these stories since I have no medicine that has given me these rights. No songs have been sung, or bundles made to permit me to make important words. I have had no important spirit dreams honoring me with the leadership of this medicine.

So I was of two minds in telling these stories. One mind says I should not tell what I have seen. My other mind says I have seen the death of other songs and important stories and favorite words. One should never take a song belonging to another, and that if a song was given, the song carrier should be true to the song and its purposes. These songs were not all given to me, except that I have lived them. So I will claim them as mine to sing. I will pray that the New'e I now tell of and honor will be remembered for good and not for the bad of our people. I have gone to pray about this and the spirits have kept me on this Earth, so I have been given a good answer.

I will tell these stories because Sugar, and many other New'e are confused. They do not know what being a New'e is and is not. I hope these stories bless them with Puha, and give them more comfort than sadness or anger. So I will start a new story that someday maybe others will tell. I hope that my words help explain out of what roots our children will grow.

Sugar takes care of me, a broken old arrow on the ground, pointing to the past. She knows of the white world. This is good, and bad! She is even writing this down in scratches on white man's paper which is, to me, one of many new kinds of white man's medicine. She is my family and I will do as she asks, just as she does as I ask. Together, we will make these words as best as we can.

My granddaughter, is an important person. She teaches the white people the New'e, or "Shoshone" words and turns our New'e words into those that the white people put in their books. But some New'e words cannot go into books. Does the white language have a different word for the call of birds protecting eggs from the word of a call of a bird who was not protecting eggs? These words were important to a New'e, who wished to gather eggs from these birds. White men do not need these words, so the New'e words have no meaning to them. Many of these words will go away because no one needs them. These lost words make me sad.

I will tell some stories, then rest, then tell some more. I will let Sugar put them down as she wishes and according to what I have told her to do. If I am stopped by the spirits or by death, we will know that I should say no more.

Almost all of the people I have known in my life have died. I cannot begin to tell of all of them. Those that are now gone were like those words; they were people of all kinds that are not needed now in the white mans' way. There were New'e who were star tellers and locust callers and water sayers and grass listeners. One man could talk to the birds in their many languages. One woman could read the seeds of plants to know what the weather in the next year would become. So many kinds of people...gone!

Many people who lost their purposes before they lost their lives became cruel and vicious and angry and full of revenge ways, or just got drunk forever. Many who died were old ones, gentle and knowledgeable of forgotten things. Many were babies, blue frozen now below Earth or bloody inside of a wolf's belly. Many were loved by me and come often to me laughing behind their hands as I sleep or in strange times of the day... The buffalo! They are only now flies. Or rumbles deep in the ground, and echoes of sounds. All were part of New'e, the people, once. I will tell of all these things to Sugar, as I lived them and dream of them still.

I say that this is the way of all, to be born and to live and to die. New'e were not taught this strange way of white people to cherish our own beings and to worry for our fates in the other worlds or to go and live with a stranger called "the Lord". We know that we are merely part of the rocks and trees and waters and all animals and these things do not pass away. I do not grieve strongly for the passing of lives, only of people who do not sit with me now.

The New'e were more than all these people and horses and dogs and buffalo and pipes and grasses and drumming and songs blowing in the hot summer winds and biting in the cold winter gusts. The New'e were *knowledge*. We were knowledge of our true place among all beings. We knew *we* were not important, but the way of our being was of utmost honor and value. To die right! To fight unto death! To be happy through all pain! To care for our own and the Mother Earth! To commune with our spirit brothers and sisters who were always available to us! To teach the songs of the stars! To tell the secrets of the Earth sounds and insect ways! To know the spirits of the plants! To make beautiful baskets from rushes! To gather obsidian to use for arrows or to trade for shells! To know the ways of the future through ceremonies of medicine people! To sing loudly! To smell the right way to go in a coming storm! To look into a fire and see ones gone before and hear truths! To dance by fires and prepare to die in the next day in a storm, hunt or fight! To see lodges as numerous as stars along a river and know the safety of thousands of friends and hear the drums and singing and smell the smoke and horses and roasting meat of a large gathering! These things are New'e. These things are dead. For this I have cried much. I can be glad, though, that I still find myself in this place of the New'e, where my grandfathers and grandmothers have lived and died since the beginning of time.

I do not know, most of the time, when I look about this place, what I am doing here. I do not want to make the mistake of going back and being lost among old things, but I am very happy when this does happen to me. I do not have the ability to stay here, on this reservation, without going away in my mind. Because I am an old man, my spirit lives in the places and times of old. These stories of my life and those other stories I heard as a child slowly walking with the old ones are very happy for me to recall, but also they are sad, for they do not have a place here in this square wooden house, on this reservation that I can not leave. These stories live under the sky, in the wind, in the blowing grasses, in the thunder of buffalo passing like cloud shadows over hills covered with prairie grass. My spirit is sometimes still strong, so I can laugh at these scars.

I weep. I hope the sweetness of these thoughts takes me and swallows me up, for this place is too harsh in comparison to my mind place. So I will give these words and I will leave to others the responsibilities to make the right ceremonies and to know the right medicine when they hear them. Is there anyone who has this medicine now? I will pray about this.

That is all.

Story #2 STATE OF SHOSHONE

I am now in a different world from the one I lived in as a child.

Because I do not wish to begin with a complaining tongue, I will say that there are two things for which I especially appreciate the white people moving onto Shoshone lands. These things are coffee, and sugared bread. Each day I drink much coffee and begin with a warm fried bread made from flour and lard with sprinkled sugar made for me by my granddaughter. The name given to her by me is Sugar Woman because I truly love this gift.

Our people have adopted many white ways. Sometimes because these ways were good, sometimes this is without our choice. One such change that came without my wish is that I have three years ago become the owner of a place on the Earth, which white people call "land". It has boundaries that do not relate to natural places. These boundaries form a square. I have been to see this particular place one time but I do not need to go there again. This business of "land" is sacred to the white people. One of the white men sent here to do these things to us has told our people that this is how we can be rich, through land! We were always strong and rich in Shoshone places! I don't think I want this kind of wealth that comes from one small square of Mother Earth.

Before I came among white people absolutely nothing I had ever known was square. A "square" is unknown to nature and unknown to the Spirit World. I see all square things as foreign and not to be trusted.

It is my thinking that this white man strength, or "wealth" as they say, has no real worth. This land owning business is a strange experience for me; and I believe seems to have much danger. But I am a practical man, as is the New'e way. I will have this land. But I do not know why.

I am old and do not wish now to wander across many places as I did as a child and younger person. However I am deeply angry that my home is now a "Reservation" and I cannot leave this place without sneaking like a mole and risking dishonor under the "rules". To leave this place, I must ask white men and then carry a paper with their scratches that lets me go where the paper says I may go. In early reservation times we were able to ride our ponies and hunt but slowly there were more and more rules and guns with which to shoot us if we did not keep the rules. There are tales of some of our people who have died simply because they wanted to continue to wander but could not leave. Many Shoshone were given punishments and were deeply shamed for being Shoshone. I think death is better than shame.

I can say that this is Shoshone land, and I will live the rest of my life on Shoshone land. I know that many other bands and peoples suffered worse than our people because they were taken from places they were put by the earliest spirits and moved to places of strange spirits far away from their homes. I feel sometimes sad for the hated Arapahos who now live here with us, on their enemies' lands.

While some things can be brought along, many things cannot, including pride in knowing how to be strong using what you know around you. I know all these plants present here, where these rocks came from, and where I can go to pray to the right spirits. I know each stream and hillside and I can still find for you the sacred things hidden by New'e in secret places many years ago. I can take you to places where we hunted and danced and where people loved by me were left after their deaths. I know where I made my first kill and where my twin sons were born in a warm buffalo lodge during a very cold blizzard. When the stars are right, I know where to go to find the stone circles that give us Spirit messages and make us strong.

This reservation is known as the "Wind River" as the white people call the place of our reservation Wyoming. Wyoming is a state within the United States. I believe this should be the State of Shoshone with our people in charge here, but I am not a warrior and gave up the right many years ago to be a fighter for this. They now even let Arapahos live here and we must share our Shoshone Reservation with them. I see much trouble to come over this.

That is all.

{Grandfather did not want this land, which each Indian head of household is being allotted by the government. Despite his wishes, it was good that I work with the white government, and I understand their keeping of records. I made sure that Grandfather was one of the first to have an allotment, and that his allotment is fertile land, with good water. I saw many of these best areas listed on another, secret piece of paper, which were not to be allotted to Indians. You see, when the allotments are done, all the other lands will be given to homesteaders, who the railroads have brought here with promises of good land and profit. There are many of these homesteaders living right outside our reservation boundary waiting for the sign from the government that they may run on to our lands and put their stake on a piece of land that was promised to my people by United States Senate ratified treaty to be New'e land forever.

After the Indian agent had gone home one night, I stayed late so no one was looking. I put some of these best lands on the list for Indian allotments, and put some of the poor lands on the secret homesteader list. I cannot stop what is happening, but I can do small things.

I have also noted a few other records in the government books that might someday help our people. For example, I added my little brother, George Smith, as Lupineflower's son and Grandfather's grandson. Because he went back to live among the Mormon people the agency people would not call him New'e. While I will not ever see him again, I can make sure that he is listed as a Shoshone. This is my only gift to him.}

Story #3 NAMES

My white man name is Jim St. James. I have heard white men call me a Blanket Indian. I think this is because I always go about in my beautiful blanket that was an honor gift to me for something done long ago. They say "Blanket Indian" with meanness and ugliness in their mouths. They do not know how painful this is to me. Young New'e call me a Buffalo Indian. I think this is because I have been alive long enough so that I have hunted many buffalo and these young people now have only rabbits to hunt.

My New'e name is Trees Told It. I have a later story that tells of this name. Before my name was Trees Told It, my name was Slow Walker, and before that I had a name that is lost to all memory. I think that name said something about my broken foot. *{I think my Grandfather remembers this name but does not wish to tell it.}*

My people, as told about here, are also known by ourselves as New'e, and white people usually call us Shoshone, but sometimes call us Snake Indians. The hand sign for our people was the slithering of a snake. The word Shoshone means "Men who Ride" because after horses came to us, all Shoshone people had great horse medicine and they became part of us and allows our peoples to spread out in many directions to become many peoples while other tribes did not have this way.

My father's mother's people were known also as Sho-sho-go and Goshute, who lived to the east of the great salty lake. *{They traveled around the deserts of Utah and Nevada.}* Others further north and east from them were the Yamparikas, or Root Eaters. *{These bands traveled around the deserts of Eastern Oregon and Southwestern Idaho. The white men called them "Digger Indians" because they ate and sometimes drank from the roots of plants}.* New'e people were also of many other kinds, and lived across vast spaces. There were Agaiduka, or Salmon Eaters who lived along the large rivers to our north and toward the great western water (they call one of these rivers the "Snake River" after the Shoshone name in hand sign, and one of these rivers the "Columbia" after the first white man ever on Turtle Mountain. *{Turtle Mountain is what many Indian people call North America}.* Then there were the Kotsoteka and Kutsinduka, or Buffalo Eaters who used horses and hunted in the plains all around where I now sit *{These are the plains Shoshone who lived around Wyoming, Idaho, Montana and Colorado.}*

My mother's people were the Tukuduka, also known as Lemhi or Sheep Eaters who lived in what is now called the Bitterroot and Yellowstone Mountains *{They lived in more mountainous and forested areas of Wyoming and Montana}.* They have made a new government park called Yellow Stone for the enjoyment of white people out of some Tukuduka lands that have warm waters and spouting waters and colored waters.

I was born among my father's people, the Timbisha Shoshone, who lived far away towards the setting sun and near the great western water *{These were the areas in the California deserts}.* I lived there when I was very young.

The Comanches are our cousins who wore buffalo skin and horned headpieces who lived to the southeast in a place white people named "Texas" and who are the people who brought us horses. Comanches were of many different bands. They were wealthy traders and breeders and suppliers of horses to all our bands and to other tribes. They also captured many horses from other tribes, as their medicine allowed them to call the horses to them and tame them immediately. They loved mostly to fight and ride horses. I was very proud of their horse medicine. Many of our people have been part of this horse supply chain.

The white people created a group of soldiers called Texas Rangers with the sole job of killing all our Comanche cousins. Only a few of the Comanches are now left. They have a very small and dusty square of land upon which to die in a place called "Oklahoma". This name means "red man" in the Choctaw tongue even though it was Comanche roaming area. Many Indian people from as far away as the great eastern salt sea at the edge of Turtle Mountain were pushed there by soldiers with guns many years ago. I am sad that Comanches now live among their former enemies and surrounded by their current and future enemies. I am glad I am not in Oklahoma.

We have Hopi cousins who wandered for many years but now stay in villages in the desert, in a place that looks like an eagle's claw in what is now Northern Arizona. It looks like an eagle's claw because there are three connected buttes that are raised up from the desert floor to look like an eagle's talon. They grow corn and beans through ancient farm techniques in very dry and sandy lands. The white men have almost completely surrounded them by their enemies' the Dine' who originally came from vary far north in Canada but who live on what is known as the Navajo's reservation. Those Navajos are very smart and someday will fully surround the Hopi, I believe. The Hopi people keep many of our most sacred Shoshone medicines from earlier worlds.

Each of these peoples lived in whatever the Earth provided. The buffalo hunters lived in lodges or tipis made of buffalo skins and pine poles. These camps could be easily moved for hunts or gatherings. The desert people lived in dug out hillsides covered with brush and woven mats made of desert plants for shade. They would often return to the places used before. The river people lived in wooden structures sometimes called longhouses. They were semi-permanent, but women had constant work to keep the rains and snows off their families. The Hopi made permanent homes from baked mud bricks.

Some of our people are known for their war making and have gone on to die greatly in battles or to do the brutal things that all warriors are known to do. The Comanches are this way because they protect their horses and their trading and with this trading and their skill in taking buffalo, they do not need other industries. Around campfires it was common and honored to tell of the tortures of enemies by Comanche warriors. It was an honor to die in these ways, and fighting to the death is good practice, if war was decided.

Not all New'e were war-like. The Hopi were known to us as peaceful ones. They followed our spirit ordained migration the longest of all New'e. Hopis arrived at the described sacred place after many of the others of us broke off the migration path and stayed along the long route followed during the Fourth World to become other types of New'e. New'e have walked though many places and kinds of lives which are suitable to many kinds of peoples. Warring, buffalo hunting, sheep eating, salmon eating, root digging, or growing corn and beans are all good ways.

That is all.

Story #4 WHEN I WAS THE FORGOTTEN NAME

This talk will be of my father's people. I lived among them for the first part of my life and still think of those places with the most fondness and beauty.

The Timbisha, or Red Ochre people lived in the winters in a beautiful warm valley called Ko'on. *{It was also the salt valley, now called the Saline Valley in central/eastern California. Many white people could not believe Indians could live in this hot, dry place.}* White people also call places not far away "death valley" which I believe to be very stupid. It was once full of life and sustained life if one has a Timbisha mind in which to know how to live.

There were hot springs, if you knew where to find them! I remember as a small boy soaking in these warm and smelling waters. White men who stumbled in to the hot valleys during summer were frightened of this place and went away, leaving us to our lives until their lust for gold and silver rocks brought them among us to make mines and disturb the Earth people who live below.

Because my father's father was Timbisha, and my father's mother was of the Goshute people and my mother was from the north desert we lived among many different bands of different kinds of New'e during my life. We had many places and peoples to which we were welcomed.

When I was very small, our Timbisha band went very far in the summers but returned to the warm valley for the winters. We walked into the mountains to get cool when summertime came and the valley became very hot and the cool snows and mists of the tall mountains offered comfort, pinion, mesquite beans, seeds, fresh plants, game, and most precious water. These valleys had places of hot springs which we went to soak and rest.

When the weathers were right, we would often go on trips to places in the mountains to gather acorns or pine nuts. The acorns were ground and leached in water through basket for many hours into mush which was cooked by placing hot stones in the basket. We would then eat this "wewish" from this same basket.

Rabbits were our most important meat, but we sometimes hunted for deer and bear. In late fall after snows fell, men went high into the mountains to kill a ram. This was proof of manhood, and successful hunters wore the soft and shaggy fur of these rams to show their medicine. These sheep hunters made bows from the rams' horns soaked in hot springs to form the best shape.

Men and women wore on their bodies the proof of their successes. Many had headdresses or garments made of human hair, ermine skins, eagle feathers, antelope horns, chins and lips of mountain sheep, elk ivories. They were not decoration, but brought to the wearer special or animal powers and knowledge, such as the fleetness of an antelope, bravery and majesty of an eagle, fighting ability of the weasel, quiet of the sheep, and the preciousness of the small ivory that grows in the jaw of an elk.

There was an annual bear dance, which was very important. During bear dance time we would hear many stories. I heard stories of the giants with glowing eyes, and a dwarf as a master of animals. The dwarf could cause much sickness but he also helped the medicine men when they talked to him in the right way. There were monsters with teeth in their vaginas. As a child this meant nothing to me, but when I became older, it was more frightening!

White sage was very important to our prayers. It grew in up-slope facing areas where it was sometimes foggy. The smell of burned sage smoke is precious. Its scent gives me happiness to be among my people. We often traded sage with other peoples who did not have it in their homelands for shells or good foods or other things they would make.

We also gathered and traded obsidian and steatite, flint, and chert. These stones were crafted into many sharp useful things: arrows, pounding stones, and cutting knives. Our men made short hunting bows from juniper. The bows were backed by sinew and used for hunting and for games of skill. I knew how to kill a rabbit from far away by the time I was a small boy with a Timbisha bow. We gathered rushes for baskets and red ochre to paint on your skin for protection against sun and for beauty.

My Spirit Pouch, which I carry always, still contains special items from this time. These small things are greatly powerful to me.

When I lived in these areas of what is now California I remember other related people lived around us. There were the O'hya and the Kawaiisu further toward the great salt ocean, the Panamint who were semi sedentary with permanent villages and squash and beans to tend, and Vanyume who had village sites along Mohave River. All these people made beautiful twined baskets used for carrying water, leaching, winnowing and carrying food and even our babies.

Our dwellings, when we were not sleeping on sands under the stars, were conical shaped huts. Wintertime was for storytelling in these huts. We also walked to sacred places of rock art that told stories of bighorn sheep, rattlesnakes, and bees. We heard of the White Snow Creature who stayed high in the mountains and controlled many of our foods. Above all were the Creator or Tamapo Stories. Second to the Creator were the Thunderbeings. There are many other lessons of wolf, sun and weasel. Weasel could change his coat to his surroundings so he could easily hide and then catch his prey.

Coyote is a most powerful spirit. He has done many things that kept me laughing and pondering as a child. Coyote and wolf formed people after a great flood. The waters covered land and they dove down deep into the bottom of the waters and brought mud to the edge of the waters. Then they threw dirt back into the waters, making people from the new formations. Later, coyote and a huge monster swallowed all animals and people creating a whirlpool. Coyote severed the monster's heart, creating a hole that eventually dispersed the people all over Turtle Island. In another story, a small boy stole fire from Thunderbeings in the sky, letting people become human. Elders told us that New'e can still find the subterranean passages leading to the lower worlds which are left from the primeval deluge.

Our families stayed in small groups, keeping mostly to ourselves. We always had a headman; when I was small it was my father's father. This man gave us our clan identity. He had great Puha for hunting and for making horn bows and chert arrows.

We walked in the desert, staying in any place a few nights, or sometimes longer. At designated times as told by the stars, we traveled to meeting places with other bands for dancing, hunting, or praying. We sometimes had great round-ups for long-eared rabbits whose fur was soft and useful and whose meat was treasured.

I do not know of any person left but me that I knew from those days and this is a sad thing. It was foretold that I would live long and do a great service for my people and so I should be protected. I do not yet know what this service is so maybe my time here is not yet completed. (*Note from Sugar: Grandfather has done many great things. He has protected many feet with his moccasins, has two children that lived to be parents who gave him many grandchildren. I think one of his great services will be these stories.*)

I am the least likely of our people to have lived the longest. I was born with a broken and twisted foot. For a people that walk, this was a sure torment. Upon my birth, it was told by our Puhagan {*medicine man*} that I should live. I would be a mild person who would make useful things for our people and be a good caretaker for the dogs. I should have been left to die as a young one but I was born in a fat time when my mother was strong and had come from far away and did not want to let me go. I was not a bother and always accorded myself around others as one who was given a gift to be allowed to live.

Because of my foot, I was taught to live in a quiet way, finding peaceful time with the stars and flowers, working with women and old ones, and watching and considering the many things I have seen. I have wandered in this way into the life of an old man when many others have gone to other worlds. As always, I walk behind, as a slow walker. I know this to be my fate and I still follow behind the others, watching, listening and now telling.

This world has moved faster than our people have ever experienced. I believe that in my life, I have seen New'e walk through as much change as all New'e saw since we crawled from the Third World into this Fourth.

We stayed with our family and extended family as a self-comprising group. We were never anything but a member of such a group. Two or three such groups would stay together and designate a headman. Two or three such bands would meet at designated times and places with their lodges and share, dance, tell stories. Then as life, nature and the weathers dictated, we would again go different ways. News would spread in these gatherings and through messages and words and tokens passed hand to hand. We could speak in signs easily and many would know what next to do and where to go by simple gestures many others would never see.

Once or twice each year, all New'e in traveling distances would meet for trade and friendship and hunting and talk of enemies and discussions of the sky movements, births, deaths, and very much laughter and dance and hunting and feasting. Many marriages were made and ended at these meetings, new children started, and stories told and retold. Our people had a very happy way. We understood new things at these gatherings in the contexts of the ceremonies performed, rites of passages made, and spiritual messages imparted by the elders and Puhagan.

Those were good years. Shoshones loved to joke and laugh and sing and tell stories. It was a very good time in a beautiful and peaceful place.

All New'e people spoke the Shoshone language, or something similar. But we could understand even strangers through hand signs that all Indians knew. Today, I still talk in hand signs. These are silent and are often missed by whites and young Indians that do not know of this language. For those of us who do know it, a small movement of the hands, or head or lips can tell a whole story, and keeps our secrets when we wish. Many people think we are stupid because we do not talk. But we are communicating, and they are the ones that are stupid.

That is all.

Story #5 HISTORY OF NEW'E LANDS

(Note from Sugar: I am always surprised by the depth and wisdom of the ancient stories. This one tells of the ancient history of our lands.)

All lands and places, change and grow over long times. I am privileged to see only part of my home and part of the very long life of these places, but I grew to understand the story of the places as they were young. Our people have lived long through this, in this, the Fourth World.

I learned from our Puhagan many stories about my homelands. This is what they told. When New'e first came here from the Third World, crawling from a reed through a hole in that sky, with many other animal beings to this place, the Salt Lake was a much larger water and was an ocean. *{This ocean covered most of Nevada, Utah, Wyoming, and Western Colorado.}* The lands to the east and southeast of the ocean were much wetter and had large herds of buffalo, elk, deer and other creatures like bear, cats, wolverines, foxes, rabbits, and all manner of ground rodents and insects. Buffalo were hunted by our most southerly cousins the Comanches and other relatives like the Hopi, and buffalo migrated far north into lands of the Cree and of course into the lands of our enemies the Crow, Peigan, Arapaho, and Lakota, Dakota and Nakota. Fish were plentiful and the salty lake ocean was less salty. But the ocean slowly shrank and became saltier.

After the shrinking of the Salt Lake ocean, but long before even the horse came, there was a period of great cold for many years. This cold changed the plants in the great basin and this changed the migration patterns of the animals. Animal herds moved into areas left by the shrinking ocean in the east and north. At the time of the changes in these migrations, the lands to the west of the Salt Lake became drier, until they became the desert lands they now are, with only hidden areas of green water places. However, even in my small life, I have seen changes to that desert, with many springs, marshes and creeks that previously sustained our wandering people drying up and disappearing. I know that these changes are due to the white men's numerous sheep, their killing of the beavers, and the slow and stupid cattle.

Our people have always adjusted to these kinds of changes to the Earth. We are a flexible and practical people. Our strength is in our many types of knowledge, and in our teachings; which tell us change is part of nature and is to be seen and respected but will not damage us if we adapt.

That is all.

Story #6 THE CREE MAN

After we left the Timbisha people we went to live with the Goshute people in the deserts around what is now known as Western Utah. The Goshute were my father's mother's people. It was when I still had that name that is now lost to memory.

At this time, my father became very ill. His illness came in the summer time when the people moved into and traveled over the mountains hunting for buffalo and seeking out friends among other family bands. I don't know if my father was injured in a hunt or whether he ate a bad spirit but word traveled about that all remedies had been tried and he would die. His old friends and family members came to sing a death song. A Cree man traveled with some of these people. He had long knowledge of healing herbs and knew songs our people did not know, or forgot. He came along because he was told of my father's strength, humor, good sense and importance, and probably because some of the people asked for his gifts in the usual ways.

When he saw my father he spoke to the Headman and to my mother in hand signs. They asked him to stay with us and heal my father. He went out and gathered herbs with which he made a tea and other herbs with which he made a paste. He first put the paste on my father and sang a song strange to our people. He then burned some paste in the fire making a smoke that was very bitter to breathe. When my father breathed the smoke he awoke. The Cree man gave my father tea to drink. The whole clan began to drum and to pray. After a day of drinking much of the tea, my father had to move out of the tipi lodge and made much water, some of it with blood. He continued to drink only tea for four days and after making much water, he was better. The Cree man had a strong laugh and my parents heard it many times as my father was healing. This was interesting to us because our laughter in those days was quiet and cautious, even when joyful.

When my father was fully well, the men went hunting together in the mountains north and east of the Salt Lake and were very successful creating much work for the women. The Cree man was given the hides and some of the best meat from that hunt to take away with him. He told his friends he would make new special moccasins from the moose hide he took away.

I asked my mother the story of the Cree man many times as a young boy whose name I do not remember. I very much admired the Cree man. I sang to my mother childish songs that may have been the strange song he sang. One example song was:

I put this paste on his face, hey ah
Stinky smoke worse than thunder pants, hey ah
Drink tea makes pee, hey ah
Hey ah, hey ah,
And on like that...

My parents laughed in that quiet way of our people of those days, with their hand over their mouths and the very little sound escaping. They told me that while the Cree man had some New'e words, we did not have his Cree language. Certainly, they said, the medicine that was in the songs was probably not about bodily functions, even though those are central thoughts to a little boy.

That is all.

Story #7 TRAVELING

Some Goshute New'e would go in the summers to the north and east, sometimes to hunt buffalo and sometimes to trade. One time, I traveled with them as far as to what is now known as Wind River; this Warm

Valley in the Wind River mountains where I now live all times of the year in a wooden house on a Reservation. How strange it is to me to recall how I thought of this place as a boy! It was only one of the places we knew. How could I know then that it would become the only place I am to ever know again?

My favorite place to walk with these Goshute New'e was to a beautiful valley near the Bear Lake filled with fresh waters, and hot springs for refreshing the tired bodies, which was north and east of the Salt Lake.

In the winter we moved to the desert and which had hidden marshlands made by the beavers living there. When I was a child, these lands were abundant with nutritious grasshoppers, seeds and roots before the Taibo's *{white man's}* cows and sheep ate up all the plants. The buffalo and other game also followed a complimentary cycle and we were not often hungry. Our lands were open and had many colors, both in the sky and on the lands, and below the blessed pools of water. The smells I still remember: grasses after a rain shower, hot breezes carrying scents of a buffalo herd, nettle bushes in early spring, the breath of a new puppy.

I know now that we were sometimes thought of as poor Goshute because we did not have horses. We moved much more slowly than other bands because we walked everywhere. Horses did not know how to drink from the roots of plants in the desert as we did and were more trouble for us during those winters. We walked often in order not to deplete any area with our needs to gather enough for our whole band. We could make a grass and bark shelter very quickly.

I remember now the beauty of those places, but at the time it did not interest me, as I thought it would always be so. The Earth had many colors and those colors changed in the warm morning dawn, and in noontime napping, and in the blues of starlight. The air was cool to breathe and sip, even when the days were hot. The quiet was filled with small noises of insects, wind sounds, bird talk, water moving. We knew very well these small sounds and from them we could read many messages about the coming of others, the presence of game, the likelihood of weather, and all those things that are of utmost importance. The sounds always told of these things before they came. The sky at day and night also told many stories; through stars, clouds, moon passages, and the ever present Tam Apo *{sun}* which either shone upon us or reflected its warmth from the ground in the darkness. The waters were alive and cool and the basis of our desert life.

Remember! Placing your finger in any of the Earth's waters allows you to touch all places on the Earth. For all these waters are connected and are one large being. Water is sacred and the basis of all life. When walking far across dry lands one learns the power of water places.

In the spring we would sometimes trade for a few horses for hunting but except for that, our dogs pulled or carried the possessions we did not carry. We traveled to many places by walking. I learned young that if you just keep walking, the landscape will change, so as long as you can walk you can find a new place with always better or different food or water or sights to see and people to know.

Our people would spread out with faster ones in front and others coming along as we walked together. Even the dogs had their own progression. The older among us were last; even though they were not expected to carry or pull burdens. The youngest were watched by the oldest. The old ones encouraged the young ones along.

The Creator gave me a foot that did not face forward, but was shrunken and twisted. My mother was glad that I was not left behind or drowned as a baby. But this foot meant that I was late to begin walking well enough to stay with even the old ones. My legs and knees were of an unhealthy shape and they jerked and buckled as I went about. I had a special dog and travois long after my friends and cousins were running. As I grew larger, I walked even though I often used great effort even to stay after the old ones. It seemed setting my foot forward and pulling my weight along was much work for my legs when my cousins gracefully ran or even danced with the men while carrying their share. I was determined, however, and could go for long stretches, which I often had to do to catch up after the others had reached camp.

Sometimes my dog would come back for me and allow me to rest as he pulled me on the travois. He was very strong.

Old ones usually walked with me. They sang old songs and told old stories. They also gathered herbs and foods that I could carry in my grass woven basket on my back. So as I came slowly in the back of the crowd, I learned many things that I did not realize others did not know. Sometimes I became afraid and frustrated because others were very far ahead and I had to continue in much pain and with much thirst to catch up to them.

We moved about for at least one half of each day. We rarely stayed in the same place for more than a few nights in a row. The New'e know the desert and ranges of mountains and washes and berry patches and best places for roots and even hot springs for days of rest and soaking. And of course we knew the gathering places and hunting areas and places to avoid that are frequented by dangerous Arapahos, Crows and Utes.

In the summer, and again at the time of the pine nut harvest in the fall, a favorite place which had news of good hunting or good trees would be designated for meeting and trading. Distant groups would come together. As family groups met decisions would be made about who would travel together the next year. These decisions were generally natural consequences of the last year's injuries or the aging of weak ones, the births of new ones and disputes that fermented among some over the winter. They were also consequences of the coupling or separating of men and women at gatherings and of course the success of hunting and weather conditions of the world. The better the wealth of places on the mother world the more people might go there to winter.

We went about with perhaps thirty people and twenty dogs. They included my parents and my older sisters and the dogs that my father chose each summer for their loyalty and strength. My special dog, known as Young Boy, stayed with us and was not traded because he pulled me faithfully after most boys were walking.

I remember there were five Elders, two of whom were my father's parents and three of whom were her uncles and an aunt. I knew them all as Grandparents. One grandfather was much older than the others and walked crooked with a stick but he walked quickly and often stayed up with the women and dogs who were pulling our lodges and youngest ones. In front were about eight men in their prime, about ten other children straggled back and forth among the groups. I walked slowly with the old ones, or was pulled by Young Boy.

That is all.

Story #8 SLOW WALKER

In my fifth summer our family band gathered at a good place by a shallow cold river with many fish to catch and roots to dig. Many other New'e from far away were there. I saw horses, which was not common among our desert people in those times. The many men in their prime and boys being taught to hunt were seeking buffalo within a day's travel in many directions.

Maybe two hundred others stayed in the camp but most were prepared to move as needed to successful hunts for butchering and caring for the meat and hides and bones and internal organs and tendons and brains and horns, all of which we celebrated. While we waited for news of a hunt, boys of my age enjoyed stories from distant aunties and games with cousins and new friends. Most young boys' favorite games were the many kinds of races. I avoided them and played in water games or with sticks or dogs. I watched the horses from a distance, being unfamiliar with the large frisky beasts.

Two particular boys a few years older than me were my friends that summer. These boys of whom I am speaking were one-spirit twins. Here is their story. Their mothers were pregnant at the same time. The two fathers were like brothers and both good horsemen. One of the fathers was riding a horse that was spooked by a rattlesnake then fell hard into a ravine taking the father along and badly breaking his leg. The father died a slow and painful death. His friend promised to take his wife and unborn child which made the dying man sad as well as burdened with pain. After the man died, his wife soon delivered her child, a boy.

Soon, the other pregnant wife began to have much trouble then she also pushed out her baby. She was bleeding much and then also died. Her little son lived. The grieving man and woman moved together and raised the two boys as their sons. By the time the two boys were two summers it was clear that they shared only one spirit and were strange in their thinking. In other circumstances, they would not have been allowed to live. The one whose mother had died was awkward of body and mind and the other imitated or chose to be like him. People said that their dying parents, or one of them, took one of their spirits with them but since the boys loved each other even before their births they agreed to live sharing one spirit.

The one-spirit twins were inseparable and even knew a special spirit language which they sometimes spoke to each other. The people honored and revered them, but I liked them very much because like me, they were very slow runners. Because they were not strong, and I was not strong, they came to be my friends.

One day, as the men and some women were returning to camp after a special hunt, a racing game was arranged for all children. I did not expect to play but at the gathering the one-spirit twins insisted that I run with them. I did not want to do this but other children jeered that I would not play. With my mother's encouragement, and with tears of frustration, I joined the race. My humiliation was full as I struggled after all the boys and most of the girls; behind even the one-spirit twins.

The men from the hunt arrived just then and I heard a loud and unusual laugh from the men. Was this stranger laughing at me? In shame I went as fast as I could to the river and went across swimming and falling. I ran away as fast as I could with my faithful dog Young Boy. I turned to see my father and the laughing man and my mother greeting each other. Could this be the mythical Cree? I began to cry in horror that my hero had seen my disgrace and laughed. I knew then I could never return to the people.

In the confusion of the returning hunters and visitors and preparation and tending of the buffalo meat and horses it was a day before the summer village realized I was not with any of the relatives or friends. I traveled all day and all night and fell asleep under a tree with Young Boy around me.

During the next morning I awoke to my father's loving face gathering me and placing me in front of him on the back of his borrowed horse. It was the horse of the Cree stranger and I sobbed that the Cree had laughed at my loosing a race even to the one-spirit twins.

"No, son, the Cree laughs only when he is happy and he was happy to see your mother and to be welcomed back to our people. The Cree is our friend and would not dishonor you or our family."

As we returned, I rode a horse for the first time. It was a big Cree horse and I was very proud. I was so relieved and thrilled to speed over the grass that my eyes were sparkling when I was delivered to my mother and a large buffalo stew bowl. Later that night the Cree came to our lodge. He was an honored guest since he had saved my father and had returned with his good horse to help in the hunt. I was content to sit behind my mother and peek out at him and notice his odd scent and strange clothes. His moccasins were very sturdy and thick and of an unknown design with unusual stitching and lovely quillwork. With a start I remembered the moose hide he took away with him before I was born, and I could not stop staring at those beautiful moccasins and very large feet.

With a shock I heard him call me out and beckon me from behind my mother. I then spent some of the most magical moments of my life. "Little One," he said to me, "I have a gift for you. I have brought you a new name. Because I saved your father's life when you were waiting to be born, you are a son to me and I am a second father to you. I have a right to your life but I choose only to give you a name that will make you proud. I wanted to meet you and know of you before I decided on a name. Now I have done this and I have a fine name. Your father told me that you left your people over shame that you are not as able to run as the others. But this is not a shame, this is something of which to be proud." I was staring at him, not knowing what to do except feel honored. He went on, "Your name shall be Ubidaa' Boyokami'a which means 'Slow Walker' so that all may know you walk behind them from where you can see all the people, and know their steps and their ways. You will warn them of threats from behind and you will gather what is dropped and not seen. Your place is a proud place from which you can learn many things and provide valuable services to your family."

I carried my name with pride. Even as I grew older and stronger and better able to run, I walked slowly and stayed with the elder ones and tended to them and to the dogs, as they had tended to me.

That is all.

Story #9 CAMEAHWAIT AND SAKAJEWEA

This story was told to me by my mother. It is the story of how her uncle found his lost sister, Sakajewea in a strange and remarkable way. Her uncle was the Headman Tootie Coon, which translates to "Fires Black Gun". He was also known as Cameahwait. It is also Sakajewea's story among the first white people known in the New'e world.

When Sakajewea was a child, she was lost from Cameahwait and his band. Absorke people {now sometimes called Crow people} raided their camp. Sakajewea was captured. Her family saw her held by a warrior on a galloping Absorke horse running north. They did not think they would ever see her again.

After being taken, she lived for a while with the Absorke people and learned their words. She was owned by the warrior who took her, but they treated her well. She grew older and moved with them to trade at the meeting place of the Mandan in the north along what is now known as the Missouri River, and known to the Lakota as Mni Sose.

There, she met many other Indian peoples who had traded with white men far downriver. She saw the marvels of muskets and metal knives and even a cooking stove, which was a heavy metal box with a fire burning inside. The Mandan stayed in large round lodges of wood covered with hide but shaped like many mounds of Earth. Their winter village was well established along the river and they were rich in horses, buffalo and trade goods of many kinds.

Some of the traders from far away spoke in a language called "French". They had red hair and yellow hair, and some had eyes the color of the sky. They were hairy on their faces. Some were hairy all over their bodies which was horrible to Sakajewea, as our people were not so.

One hairy blue-eyed man was looking for a wife and gambled with the Absorkes to win one. He won Cameahwait's sister, along with some hides and a knife. The man was kind and lived happily among the Mandan. He trapped for hides and traded them so he was wealthy with many fine possessions. She was afraid of him due to his hairy chest and back, but she grew to know him otherwise. His words were strange, and he taught them to his new wife over the seasons they were together.

During one autumn time at the Mni Sose, many boats of strange people came up the river. There were thirty strong men of these strange people. One was a man entirely black with hair like a buffalo, and they traveled with one large clumsy dog who looked like a bear. The men's faces were also hairy and they smelled very bad and carried many strange things including many muskets and ammunition. They were not trusted and after some disturbance with the Mandan, they moved upstream from the Mandan village and erected a large log structure that they called a "fort". They were visited by many of the chiefs, and soon Sakajewea's husband went to see them as he could talk in some of their language.

The men acted in a coordinated way at all times. Soon, the sister's husband agreed to speak for them in their strange words and to act as a guide to go to the western ocean when springtime came. Sakajewea's husband had seen the wonder of their stoves and tools and their odd methods of organization. He recognized great potential for himself. This is typical white man thinking.

After the winter spent along the banks of Mni Sose, the ice on the river broke and the water began to flow and the party began a journey together, including Sakajewea and her husband. The two leaders, one with red hair and one stern and serious at all times, were strict but fair. Sakajewea was the only woman and she was large with her first coming child.

The party moved west and north up the Mini Sose in wooden built boats and on foot, carrying all manner of heavy loads. The white men suffered greatly with cactus in their feet and cuts from sharp rocks. Even the dog limped and cried out and whined and plucked with his teeth at his paws each night. After only a few weeks of travel Sakajewea had her baby. It was of great interest to the leading white men that she used a rattlesnake rattle medicine to help with her pains. She was young and strong and ready to move the next day as is the Shoshone woman's way.

Along the way, she gathered many roots and edible plants, which the white men walked over as if they did not see. They added these foods to the vast amount of meat eaten by the men. The men were curious about all things and asked many questions about the land and the plants and animals. They frequently stopped to mark down little scratches, which they treasured and carried away with them. They stopped to draw depictions of plants, birds and creatures. These drawings were amazing to the sister. They drew lines representing creeks and rivers they crossed, asking many questions of the husband about where the creeks and rivers originated and where they flowed. Sakajewea's husband would ask Sakajewea and she would tell the answers, which the husband told to the other men. They spent time each night looking into a small tube with their heads facing the sky, as if their eyes were drinking from the tube. Then they made more scratches.

Cameahwait was hunting with a small party of New'e men when he came upon these strangers. From a distance, he saw they had large strange packs and the huge dog appeared to be a bear walking among them. The presence of the woman and child showed they were not a war party. Cameahwait watched and determined they were not our enemies but a new sort of people. They had no horses and moved slowly so he was not concerned.

When the groups came together, there was happiness and shouting and hugging as Cameahwait discovered his lost sister. This happiness was contagious and the hugging and excitement swelled among the groups, as often happens when people are without new company for a long time.

A pipe was brought out and our people removed our moccasins during the smoke to show the white men that we would not wear our shoes while their feet were so battered from walking such distances through the sharp rocks and cactus. They thought the men must be very soft and harmless for such small things to injure them. These weak men told that our people had a new Great White Father and we could expect to deal with him in the future. They gave gifts of bright coins with the picture of the Great White Father reflected on the coin. This was very impressive to our men. It seemed like nonsense to them however about the existence of such a father, especially when the men were so easily weakened; but their manner in the telling gave them pause to consider. Their gifts and trade items were good so we agreed to trade further with them.

From their packs they brought out foods and beautiful items and a mirror that gave Cameahwait a start to see himself as if in water. Our men traded them some good horses. Sakajewea asked for her whereabouts to be told to her mother and father. She remembered them crying and screaming as she was carried away as a young girl. She gave the gift of a pierced white shell to be passed to her mother for wearing on a cord around her neck. Sacajewea then had a fine fat baby boy and was a young mother herself.

These men then went on over the mountains and then to the sea. Our old ones heard they returned the next year, passing back through with different horses, and taking boats back to the east. We forgot about these men, as they did not return.

That is all.

{Note from Sugar: I was taught this story in the Indian School, but the books brought by the teachers told about the military leaders, named Lewis and Clark. There was a short mention of Sakajewea and her husband, and a picture of a woman but she did not look or dress at all like a Shoshone.}

Story #10 MOUNTAIN MEN

After those first white men came, more and more solitary hairy men began appearing at our trading meetings and began marrying our women and moving among us, taking on our ways. These men were very interested in furs, which they could trade for and trap. When I was about ten summers, one lived among us for a while. He started a half-breed family that was accepted by our people.

The "mountain men" came and married New'e women before the soldiers came. After the soldiers began to come to our lands, the mountain men's half-breed people often went to stay in the white men forts. They hunted and trapped and traded, some becoming lazy with drinking liquor. They learned our hand signs and could talk among all Indians. They often brought us valuable information learned from other Indian tribes.

Mountain men gave New'es a new idea in trading. This new idea was similar to our old meetings, but lost many New'e parts of the old meetings, so it was not good. These were called "rond-a-voos". The meeting places were along rivers so our goods could be moved quickly out and never be seen again. Strange new things like glass beads, items the color of the sky, metal goods, guns, ammunition, coffee, sugar and woolens could come in and find places in our new ways. Other New'e traded for these things with beaver pelts and buffalo goods. The rond-a-voos also became for gambling and drinking and talking, with competition among traders. There was trickery, which sometimes lead to fighting, which was not our old way of solving tricks.

Soon too, came other Indian men we had never known of, with their own languages and ways. They stayed in the forts with the white men and seemed not to know how to live as we did without the white men to give them food and shelter. These men were Iroquois, Seminole, Creeks and

French. Some of them married our women and took on our New'e ways. We were proud that they mostly assimilated into us, as they should. Those people's children and grandchildren were now considered Shoshone. I see those people's grandchildren now. Most of these young ones do not know, as I do, that their grandfathers came from far away and were of another people.

I did not go to these meetings, but I heard of them. New'e still separately held our traditional meetings. These meetings were better than the trading rond-a-voos. Our traditional meetings were for all of the purposes that make a good life: ceremonies, prayers, medicine, socializing, loving, songs, feasting, laughing, games, showing new children, displaying skills, and greeting our lost ones. As an old man I most surely miss these traditional meetings feeling strong and important as one happy community after long winters spent with our smaller band.

Now I do not know if these meetings will ever happen again which makes me very sad. I now see that the rond-a-voos were the first times when glory of one person was seen over the success of the community. This made us turn to trading things over telling stories.

Life for me, though, remained the same as it was for my grandparents for many years because we stayed away. We did not have those things most wanted by white men. Our family followed the known paths, walking to our favorite places long after other families changed with all the new peoples. As I grew, mostly oblivious to these changes in the world, the old ones told me learning stories and we loved very much. We were not hungry or cold very often and beauty surrounded us. We gathered in summer and met other bands along the way. Flowers sprouted in late winter, then flourished as plants, which then went to seeds, then blew away in the wind.

That is all.

Story #11 BEAVER

One winter we discovered that almost all the beaver marshes we traveled to for cattails and plants had no beavers left in them. The dams were still there, but they were quiet and were being slowly pushed away by the waters. Our Bannock cousins told of a man called Ogden, who came with a party of men speaking a new language who had been traveling along the great rivers to our north and west taking beaver furs. They had strong steel traps that tore away the feet of the beavers and made them easy to kill and skin and carry off. Some children had also died after they stepped on these terrible traps and their wounds became swollen and rotten.

We were colder that winter as we took no beaver furs for ourselves, in hope that a few beaver would continue to build their stick homes across streams and washes to water the sacred plants that had grown in those places. We grieved for the little cousins to our wolf God. They seemed to be almost wholly taken. Many found a reason to fear in this event. The winter stories and medicine talks had long discussions about the meanings of the disappeared beavers.

We heard many stories of these new white men that were present now in our lands. When my mother was young, there was a great light in the sky that foretold that these strangers would continue to mix in our lands, and would cause many problems for us. Some said that our peoples were to be gone like the beavers. But I felt safe in our desert home, though, as the strangers had not yet come among our family, and I had never seen one of these men. A child is secure and happy as protected by his parents.

That is all.

{Note from Sugar: Many of the animals from the old days, such as buffalo are unknown to us now. One of the white ladies who is married to a soldier at the fort has a hat that it is said is made out of beaver fur. I would like to touch this hat to see what it is like, but I do not think that would be welcomed. I hope that someday the beavers and the buffalo will return.}

Story #12 SUNDANCE

There have been many great sicknesses among our people. These new and horrible sicknesses began in my grandparent's time. Many of us carry marks from having fought and won the battle with the spotted sickness. The old ones said this sickness was another warning of the changes to come, and many talked of rejecting the new ways and going deeper into our old ways. Songs and dances were sung to reinforce these ideas.

Coyotes became suspect as ones with knowledge of these events, and power to influence some of these happenings. It was Coyote who carried our people in a basket, but since he was curious and unwise, he frequently opened the basket and allowed our peoples to fall out along the way. This is why we have many small bands that are scattered across the lands and not one large tribe of New'e. I pledged to be wise and follow the teachings of the old ones to assure that life would always be as when I was a child.

The oldest grandfather was especially concerned over these changes. When my mother was a young girl, this grandfather had gone on a special journey to spend seasons with a Puhagan named Ottamagwaya. He had great Puha, or medicine strength, and a large band of hunters and people.

Ottamagwaya was a Comanche Buffalo Eater who was given an important new ritual in a vision. This ceremony could reveal the hidden future. It was called a Sundance, in honor of Tam Apo, the Spirit of the Sun. If done according to the vision, this Sundance would ensure our existence and would stop the terrible diseases that were killing so many people and making life painful and horrible. It became that the Sundance ceremonies were held on a regular basis in early summer before the people split into bands to travel. This was so because the ceremony emphasized our togetherness and our value as one great tribe even though we disbanded regularly.

The oldest grandfather was the first person in our band that learned the songs and ways of the Sundance. He brought the ceremony to us and to other bands. The ceremony lasted many days and was sacred for those taking part and those in helping roles. Even women who did not perform the dance had places in the ceremony for preparing special foods and herbs. I do not tell of the ceremonies here, even though I now know them well from many years of being a dancer. These are ways that must be earned.

The Sundance helped us to understand the changes taking place. Later, soldiers prohibited this dance, with a punishment of death. They are rightly afraid of the power of this dance! The threatened punishment did not end the Sundance, but it is not held as often as the stars say it should be held because of the fear the soldiers have given us over our beliefs.

As a boy I recall the Sundance gatherings as especially exciting. While I could not go as a child to the dance, there were many peripheral warrior dances and womens' dances. There was also much cooking of special treats for little boys, gambling games to watch, and horse-trading. Many people would come from both plains and basin and rivers. Our friends would arrive and games and stories would begin. Dogs unfamiliar with each other would make quick fights for the rights to scraps of food. Dried fish and berries from far places were mixed into stews. Old people would sit together and talk late around fires. Beautiful beaded and otherwise decorated moccasins and other garments that had taken all winter to craft were shown off and given as special gifts to seal special relationships. The dancers would emerge after the dance as honored men, though they needed to recover for many days as their bodies had been through much trial.

Ottamagwaya was known to me as a great man. When I was a tall boy, the great spotted sickness came upon many of our people {1837}. It took Ottamagwaya and all of his band. With horror their silent camp was discovered. Packs of wild dogs had found them first. The people had perished as a group and only vultures and horses and dogs had been witness. I heard that their camp and all possessions were burned to stop the spotted sickness, with much crying and wailing by those selected for the terrible task. The spotted sickness was the first horrible thing in my life. Before that I did not know real unhappiness.

After that, many other Indian people joined in the Sundance. The power of the truths was proven as we found there were similar visions and practices that began in other peoples far away. The dance linked our basin people more strongly with knowings of the plains peoples. Later, another dance was called the Father Dance and was a plea to the Spirits to keep away the smallpox. It did not always come to pass in that way.

Eventually, this disaster struck my family. I was a boy only beginning my passage into manhood. *{One of the worst outbreaks of smallpox was in 1838.}*

This was a year later than the sickness that killed Ottamagwaya. Among us, it first appeared on and killed one old man who came back from a trading visit. Soon many more people suffered with terrible sores and itching and fevers and discomfort and breathing that stopped from the inside. I watched as both my mother and father grew these spots and writhed on the ground, tearing at their skin, and begging for water they could not drink, and churning in their sweat. I helped them as much as I could and ran among the other sick people carrying water, and dragging my dead friends to the side of our camp where I cursed the dogs that slinked around them. I piled rocks on their bodies to keep away the birds and rodents. As I was gone on these terrible outings my father died in our lodge.

My mother did not know of his death as she ranted and tossed on the floor next to his body. I applied mud to her sores to stop her from scrapping them with her nails but it did not stop her and she became covered in bloody yellow muddy filth. I went to one man who had recovered from his sores and asked his help with my father. He was slow and still ill, but he helped me pull his buffalo robe around him and drag him to the place of all the dead, where I sang a death song for him and covered him with many large rocks. I was feeling very strange and did not complete my task. At a later time, I awoke to the terrible smell of burning flesh and the cleansing smell of burning sage and I knew the disease had begun to run its course as the remaining people were cleansing our camp and performing many ceremonies.

I had a mild case, but was ill for many days. Many of us have marks from this time, showing where the spots had been on their hands and faces for all to see. Everyone lost many friends and family. Over half of our people were gone. Everyone cut their hair and we stumbled about tragically for a time with our remaining band after abandoning that place and those dwellings. Only a few did not have any body signs of the sickness. We later learned this horror was also experienced by many bands. We lived in much fear that it would return, which it did at odd times. We saw this terrible sickness as a sign of more horrors to come. We did not fully recover or begin to laugh or sing again for many months.

That is all.

Story #13 COOKING POT

We made many trades with other people as part of life. For example, my father once brought back from a "rond-a-voo" not only a new steel knife, but also a very heavy cooking pot with a perfectly fitting lid. This pot was wonderful for our stews and for a baked seed mush called bannock. It was so beautiful and offered so many ways of preparing foods that we almost did not mind carrying it on our walking days. We developed a new pattern of eating so that the pot would be cool enough to pack and carry in a basket on someone's back by the time we were to set off. If the pot was too hot, we could not carry it without burning a basket and twice we waited to join our family so the pot could come along. Eventually the pot was too much trouble and we left it buried near one of our favorite places, a pillar of rock in a beautiful valley. We found it again the next year and then for many years we would make a special trip to that place, and gather selected foods along the way for cooking in the pot. It was a large pot and very handy. We had many enjoyable discussions about what we would cook in the pot, especially when we had hungry times. Food always seemed extra good from that black kettle. If given the chance I know I could walk now to that place and find that pot! I would especially enjoy a prairie dog stew right now.

During these times, when black kettles and steel knives and muskets began to be known among us, the old ones sent wise strong men on what today would be called a diplomatic mission to the white trading places. When I was a small child I remember a New'e named Namaya and called Little Chief by the white men visited Santa Fe, which was a famed trading place in the south. He was a brother to Iron Wristband, a famous headman. He returned with success and many beautiful turquoises to trade. We did not have any troubles with white men for some time after this trip. My mother obtained one of the turquoise pieces that she sewed into a headband she wore with pride.

That is all.

{Note from Sugar: Grandfather has given me this headband. I wear it on special days only. I hope someday to give it to my granddaughter, if the spirits send one to me. It is not a large stone, but it is veined with black marks and has shades of both green and sky blue. It is precious as it was touched by the hands of all these famous Shoshones, my ancestors.}

Story #14 MOCASSINS

As I grew, I began to learn the making and repairing of moccasins. This was a good job for a boy with a bad foot, though it was usually the job of a woman. I was looked down upon by some of our people. I reminded them of the Cree's beautiful moccasins. I thought of these moccasins and copied from my memory the way his may have been made. I also spent a great deal of time walking with one Grandmother who told me secrets of the best moccasins and showed me her craft as we rested. I made the decision to allow myself this oddity of taking on this womanly craft. It was foretold when I was born.

I sensed it would serve me in my time and I truly enjoyed this sitting work after long times of sometimes difficult uphill walking. The upper parts and soles of our moccasins were made of single piece of buckskin with a side seam. A hunter's moccasins were best made of badger skin, which was tougher and lasted longer, but was also more difficult to sew and to obtain. Many of our people walked without shoes, but in cold times and while crossing lands with many sharp rocks, or when hunting we wore shoes of animal hide sometimes reinforced with bark.

I learned to watch the footprints of those walking before me for the stories they would tell. I knew each footprint, especially when they wore the shoes I had watched being made, or when the shoes had come from my own hand. I always made very good moccasins for my mother and older sisters. I marked each with secret stitches that would allow me to watch their tracks as they went in front of me. My sisters thought I was magical for knowing their mischief even though I was miles away from what they were doing. This was a private joke I shared with the old grandmother who also used this trick to gain valuable information about the goings on of our people. I never told this secret to anyone.

Each moccasin was different and carried a pattern of stitching along the edges and seams. I knew who was in front, who behind, who was off gathering, who carried burdens, who was hurt or limping, who walked together for times, and who needed solitude. Drops of blood left with a hunter's track indicated a success. Many steps toward small streams showed a good berry patch or roots where many had dug. Sorting of seeds from plants left plant stems beside the trail. I always noted a stranger's passing, be it a two or four-legged creature.

That is all.

{Note from Sugar: Today very few people know how to track, as does Grandfather. Because we sit in one place, and there is very little game to hunt, we have less need for this traditional skill.}

Story #15 SIGNS OF WHITE PEOPLE

{Note from Sugar: How frightening and threatening it must have seemed to the New'e to see more and more strangers come among them. The white strangers clearly were people, but were so very different from Shoshones. The Indian people must have had many conversations about how odd these people were and about their strange habits. Now I suppose we have adopted many of these habits and don't find them at all unusual.}

The signs on the Earth of the white people were at first very strange. The ruts of wheels behind horses wearing iron clamps, accompanied by no human footprints; then footprints with deep, square heel prints. We had nothing that square and did not understand the iron clamped shoes of the horses. There were camps in odd unlikely places. The droppings of the strange animals that followed the wagons were of curiosity to us. We avoided these people. I learned much about them when we crossed over their tracks.

There began a large migration of the singers, called Saints *{also called Mormons}*. They offered songs in one voice in their travels. We did not know what these songs offered to the land, as the land surely did not know their language. Then two years later very large groups of miners hurried through our lands at all times of the year on a straight path they created and did not generally stray from. They made boat crossings of the rivers where they had established trading posts on these trails. As I grew, my parents and the old ones with us said that it was best to stay away from these strangers. I did not have any wish to do otherwise.

Not all our people were standoffish to these white hairy men and their sun burned women who were dirty and smelled terrible since they did not clean themselves. As time went on, many had regular trading meetings at the settlements that grew up and at rond-a-voos. They learned to talk to those people and more about their ways.

They told how they would play the Saints and mixed breed fur traders and miners off against each other for fun and to see the strangeness of their ways. They told many rumors of what these white people would do and why. We laughed very hard at the stories we heard of the ways of these people. They built small square houses in which to shit. They drank crazy water and vomited their dinner. Women wore bulky long garments that must be hard to walk in; and very hot in the summers. They pushed wheeled carts in front of them across very bumpy terrain when pulling a travois was so much easier. They toiled long days to make plants grow in straight rows. Their horses and big bulls pulled scrapers across the ground. Their songs were sung in unison by men with women and children with everyone knowing many strange words and starting and stopping all at once as if of one mind. They seemed to retire to their beds at very early times and awake on a schedule. They stared very long at books, very thin animal skins bound in a square with small scratchings. Sometimes they chanted while doing this. They seemed to do the biddings of a Deity named "Saa ve your". They seemed to have many other names all for the same Deity. They had a curved box on which they scratched a long stick which made very merry and interesting melodies to which they would march with the same footsteps, forward and backwards. This looked very enjoyable.

We were told that some of these people would be friends to Shoshones and others, and some seemed very dangerous. One could often not tell, as it was said they would grimace with stern faces all the time.

I stayed far away in our desert place with my mother and father and a changing array of my sisters and cousins and old ones. While we made up tales of these strangers and pretended to shit in small square boxes, we went without too much desire to know further of the troublesome ways and fighting among these new people. As I grew older, I watched their tracks and leavings with more interest, since they seemed to be more of a force around us, and as I awoke from the comfortable cloud of my childhood.

I learned there were different kinds of the white people. The Saints were whole families, part of a great clan that wished to do frequent spiritual gatherings of group singing and what our people knew of as "reed-ing". These participated in constant group industry of scraping the soil into large regular plots and causing water to feed the seeds they planted. They made buildings, many of them appeared very fine and interesting. They made roads that intersected at square corners, when going in more direct routes seemed only logical. We did not understand their urgency to make these changes in such a hurried manner. We sensed there was a plan to their constant effort that was unknowable to us. In the beginning, we shook our heads and moved elsewhere, like moving away from a colony of ants staking out a place to make their hills.

The other type of white person that we recognized was the kind moving through our lands quickly with a clear urgency to their movements. These were mostly men just going past looking for gold, the yellow rocks one could sometimes find. They stayed to the trails that were made by those that came before. These later became full roads. Except for occasional examples, these peoples hurried past us on their way to other places. These men seemed harsh and violent, even to each other. They were direct trouble, while the Saints seemed a more indirect but worse threat because of their permanence.

When I was about seven years old, one expedition of miners killed six of our people, though not of our family. We were more careful to avoid them after that, and except for the goods some of our people traded, and the many and frightening stories we heard at seasonal gatherings, I continued to live as our people had for all time past.

That is all.

Story #16 SIGNS IN THE NIGHT SKY

{Note from Sugar: Grandfather says he does not know the secrets of the skies; that in his time there were many people who watched the night skies and marked down the sky movements with rocks. Or some knew what to expect from certain sky signs because they saw the patterns of the skies and remembered them with songs and prayers that told their stories. These people are now gone. I think that while many of the details of these matters are lost to us, some old ones can look at the stone circles and they remember more about what they tell of the skies than a stranger to these matters can know.

Because the patterns were expected, when unexpected sky messages came, they were given great credibility, like the comets that came in 1843, 1858 and 1861. We know now that they called the buffalo to the spirit world. They foretold the plowing of the wild places, and the new presence of cows and white men. They also told of the massacres of Shoshones at Bear River and the Cheyennes and Arapahos at Sand Creek. They told of reservations and hardship for Indians.}

When I was a young man, strong and energetic, but not yet ready to marry, another sign came to us. My mother had not recovered fully from the spotted sickness or from losing my father and her mother and two of my sisters, even though this happened a number of years before. She took part in the ceremony called the Cry by refusing to wash every day as she always had. Usually this ceremony ended after one year with a formal washing by the all the relatives participating in the Cry.

Mother refused the washing. We were generally a very clean people, always washing even in cold running water, or if there was no such water, then with clean sand, which we wiped off with specially made and readied skins. My mother had the notion that the dirt and caked mud she awoke to after my father had died was connected to him, and she believed that if she fully washed the dirt that naturally clung at the end of each day to all beings, she would die, or perhaps create problems for my father in his life beyond.

When this sign came it was to my mother's understanding that word had come from my father that she should begin to wash fully again every day, and to take another husband, which she did. This sign was a bright streak in the night sky. It was like a torch running across, moving slightly each night until it disappeared without warning. My mother saw things in the torch I did not see. We were all unsettled by its appearance.

We knew of these night-time sky signs since time immemorial, of course. They were part of the legends of the stars that our people knew well and charted and expected. But these traveling torches appeared without warning or without being part of the patterns we knew so they were subjects of much discussion, sometimes bringing good and sometimes warnings, as interpreted by medicine men, who usually independently came to the same conclusion, and who were always most certainly proved right.

The next such light was to appear as I was trying to win the beautiful girl who would become my first wife, Strong Branches. We took this new light streaking through the black night amid our individual star companions as a very good sign, and indeed it was. Then three years later another such light appeared in another set of the night-time stars. This appearance seemed to foretell evil. This one had six tails and started in mid-summer and lasted through the last of the berries. On a few days, the sky had a yellow, sparkly, glare-like look which we even saw during the day. The sun's light was feeble while in the spell of this evil warning in the Northwest.

Our Puhagan had different ideas of whether this meant we should flee to this direction, or whether the evil would come from this direction, or what other messages we were unable to clearly understand. This light eventually flew away, but not before its tails grew longer and longer. Two more times in my life these visions have been seen by our people and after the six tailed light and the horrors that followed, they frightened me greatly.

That is all.

Story #17 HUNT

Around the times of my father's sickness, my legs and knees began to grow straighter and stronger. My mother said my frame grew as tall as my father had been, but my body did not yet have the strength of a man. Because I had always insisted on doing my share of the work of those in our band, even though it took me longer, I was perhaps stronger in other ways than some other boys. These traits served me as a hunter as I was still and quiet and patient for many hours waiting for rabbits or deer. They served me as a moccasin maker since I was observant, quiet and skillful. They served me as a helper to the grandparents I had come so to love as a child spending so much time among them because I listened and considered their needs and thought ahead to those things that would make their way easier. I was becoming a man and the changes in my body served to greatly improve my ability to walk and to win contests of arrows, and other games of skill. I would never win running races, but it was no longer important to me.

I began to hunt around this time. My father was gone and my mother was in extended grieving, but many others saw to my education. I practiced for many hours each day with a rock hurling tool and with my bow and arrows. I learned to make arrows, and traded for a very good bow by making moccasins for a headman. As a necessity as the oldest boy in my family of now just girls, I began by providing rabbits and ground squirrels for our meals.

During the spring as we moved toward Bear Lake, I killed my first large animal, a young male moose. This was on the day that I received my first full sized bow. I was very lucky with this kill! Deer were generally a boy's first large hunt, but I was standing quietly admiring my brand new bow and wondering if I could join a hunt with some of the men the next day when a perfect young moose walked right into my line of sight. I had not yet even practiced with this bow, but only with a much smaller and more childlike bow.

I could not have imagined I would have as my first real hunt a moose, but the Creator sent it to me, so I touched my pounding heart in thanks to the Spirits and crept toward the place it was calmly munching marsh greens. The moose did not see me and I was very quite with the wind my perfect assistant blowing away from the moose so that he did not smell me there. I thought the moose must surely hear my heart, but it did not. As I put an arrow I had made for the first time into the strong and smoothly arch-ing bow, everything seemed perfectly in line and time stood still in a way I even now recall. I believe this was the presence of a spirit. I let the arrow fly, which pierced the moose deeply right into its heart. The moose jerked and buckled and twisted toward the arrow. It began to enter the water, which I did not mind, since it would be easier to pull it dead from the water as it floated, rather than to drag it up hill if it ran downhill and died at the bottom, away from our camp. I shot another arrow perfectly and directly into its neck as it entered the water, and it went down, dying quickly.

I stood still and shocked for a minute as the water swirled. Then within me arose a shrill cry. I began to whoop and yelled and blubbered without sense. This brought many of the other boys running toward my cries. I waded into the cold water where the moose thrashed its last and as soon as it was very still, I swam to it, and touched its leg, at the end of which was a sharp hoof. The leg did not respond to my touch. It was still warm, and smelled very musky with its strong scent and also now with the smell of blood that was spreading pink on the water. I grabbed the moose and swam slowly pulling it toward the place of our camp, some distance up the shore at the edge of the water. The other boys saw me and began a general whoop-ing which brought many others to the water's edge to help me with the job of landing it and beginning the ceremonies of my first kill and the ceremonies of butchering the moose and saving its many gifts.

My body shook for a whole day after this event, as the excitement was so unexpected and wonderful. Many commented that as the slowest one among us I was the first of my friends to make such a kill. New rever-ence was given to me, and I was never so proud as we shared the tender and delicious meat, and as I was able to present so many gifts of wealth to my mother for the use of our family. I gave a large part of the skin to the grandmother that taught me to make moccasins, and much of the bones to the maker of the lucky bow so that he could use them for tools and for trade. To have the ability to make these gifts made me very happy. My father would have been very happy to see this success and to know that I would not be seen as a crippled boy any more.

I was invited to sit with the men as they talked of hunting and planned where to go to assure a likely success when meat was needed. Most of our food was gathered from the ground or available from the plants and insects we lived among, but fresh meat was a good treat and dried meat or fish was always good to have when we knew a lean time was coming.

That is all.

Story #18 THE LESSON QUEST

I had many good friends, both boys and girls. We spent much of our time together. We had the one-spirit twins, who were sometimes with their home band, but more frequently with us as we grew older. There were also my three sisters, about seven other girls of various ages, most of whom were my relations, however distant, and a total of nine boys. The oldest of us was about 13 summers and the youngest was still almost a baby.

The four oldest boys, including me, began to make much mischief after the great sadness. It was maybe the grief and anger of losing so many loved ones, or it was maybe the nature of the young boy. We frightened people with our pranks, and hid away when we should be helping with our tasks. We threw rocks into the ponds and chased off the fish; we swam too far into dangerous waters; we captured and played with rattlesnakes, which was contrary to our legends for respecting these brothers. Eventually a grandmother decided that we were overdue for our first rights of manhood, since we were acting so badly and with such potential consequence.

One morning we boys were awakened by a frightening man we did not know with a painted face and traditional war implements. He whooped a loud song. The others in the camp moved around us normally and pretended not to hear. I knew they could secretly hear and see him because my youngest sister was very frightened and began to cry at his whooping and peeked out at him from behind my mother. This man gathered up my troublemaking friends and me. He was joined by other whooping painted Spirit-men. They pushed us along in front of them out of our camp. We walked without food or water for many miles. The first Spirit-man refused to let us talk but the spirit-men sang many songs we did not know followed by whoops and cries. The Spirit-man shook his war stick at us if we did not hurry along or if we looked back or if we tried to talk or go off the path he had chosen for us. My friends and I were frightened and did not know if we would be killed or ever allowed back to see our families. We wondered if this was to be our banishment punishment for the trouble we had been causing. My friend Iron Hair began to cry at one point and wet himself since we had not been allowed to stop to do these needed things. By the time we had reached our destination a number of hours later, we had all wet ourselves while walking which was a humiliation. Eventually we came to a bark house with a fire burning along side. No one else seemed to be there but the fire was strong and waiting for us.

The other Spirit-men left. The first Spirit-man kept us in this place for many days. We ate very little and heard many sacred stories that told us of the principles connecting our families, our landscapes, our practices, and our cultural values all called the Deniwape. We were painted, and drank teas with bitter tastes and sweet tastes. We were not allowed to speak and on the fourth night, we were awakened and run away from the camp. By then we knew we must trust this man, and listen carefully to his wisdom, and follow directions carefully. We knew we were to go alone for two nights to the different areas this man took us, and to return alone with one important gift, whether it was a token of the place we camped, a dream, or story, or something else that we would recognize. We were not to talk of this to any-one.

Once we got to a deep canyon, the man chased me and my friends away into the desert. One boy he pushed to the edge of a rock cliff and indi-cated he should stay there or in that area until the sun set on the third night. The one-spirit twins were sent together but tied with their backs together so they could not see each other. The next boy was me, and I was taken to a narrow box canyon with steep sides and very little sunshine possible in the day. I do not know where the other boys went.

I sat in the sand in this cool place and began to shiver. The night sounds were known to me but the eerie sense of being alone was not. I had spent all my life living under the sky, but never had I been alone for two nights. I could not sleep as my body seemed to hum with an inner irritation and my body twitched and jerked in my exhaustion and inability to sleep. As the night wore on I longed for the day. But as the day dawned, I was still cut off from the warmth of the sun and even from any direct light in that small and shadowy place.

For only one hour perhaps did the sunshine directly into my box dur-ing that day. I hated it when it finally came simply because I knew it would not last. This all made me feel very distant from my people. I began to wish for my sisters and the grandmother. I began to see how important this whole society was to me and how my mischief threatened me with harming those I loved. I ate the small pieces of dried meat wrapped in a skin for me and dug into the ground where I knew the water could be slowly drawn from deep against the plant roots in my little canyon. I slept.

When I woke it was the dark part of the night. There beside me was a large rattlesnake. He was not coiled, and he was silent. He came up toward me and flicked his tongue in my direction so I knew he knew I was there. The diamond patterns of gray and brown and black on his back shimmered into themselves as he moved. We sat like that for some time. I fell asleep again, and when I awoke, the snake had gone. I could see his marks in the sand where he had come to keep me company, then those he had left behind to go back into the desert. I felt stronger and began to look around my little canyon. The rock sides of the canyon glittered with layers of sparkly rock. There were dark layers and light layers, all swirling upward as the rock rose from the Earth. The layers made little ledges that a mischievous boy could climb up, but I had no desire to do this. As I looked to the other side of these cliffs, I began to see patterns. They were small handprints, half way up on one of the cliffs. There were also figures of men, and figures of deer or maybe dogs. There were other symbols of crossed sticks, and round figures that may have been the sun. I was deeply comforted by these signs of our people and the past peoples that had been here before me. I had a very strong knowledge that another boy would some day sit here in a time much later. That boy would look at these figures and feel the wonder I felt.

As the sun rose on the last morning, I made my way back to the bark lodge. I came upon Iron Hair, who had a deep cut in his arm, and blood splashed down his body. He was smiling, though and seemed excited about meeting me and he embraced me. We did not speak as was our instruction. When we arrived back, we were given some stew, and told to wait. When we all were back and seated, we listened to more important instruction from the man who was our leader. Now we were not afraid, and we felt strong and grown-up.

We were all given a final challenge. We were to know the pain of a knife so that we would know that we would feel but survive pain in our lives. Each of us in turn offered our arm, or our leg to be cut by the man. These small cuts were then filled with dark cool tar, which marked us forever. My cut is in the shape of a snake and I am proud of this mark.

We walked slowly home, and were very hungry and thirsty, as we had been given only very small amounts of food and water, and told to take from the Earth only what we needed. Upon our arrival, all the people came out to meet us with whoops and hugs. We could smell the stews cooking. First, though, we went to the fire of the oldest ones of our band, with the man who was our leader with us. We sat down and were offered the right to smoke with the old ones. This was a very proud time for me, as it showed that we were welcomed back as grown men, and we had left as boys. We ate with our mothers and sisters and cousins that night with a new attitude.

That is all.

Story #19 HORSE

My weak legs had grown stronger and no longer caused me pain. My foot would forever be twisted and deformed, but this became less important as I became a horseman. Here is how that happened.

With my mother's marriage into a clan of buffalo hunters, or Kutsinduka, I was given the option to go with her to areas north of the salty lake or to stay with the desert people. I knew that this decision was not meant to be permanent. If white men had not begun to rule our people, I would have had the chance to go with other groups all through my life, as I wished. Because it was best at that time, I choose to go live among the Kutsinduka people further to the northeast and to stay with my mother. Most of my sisters had their own children by this time. They stayed with the desert people. Saying goodbye to them and to their little children was sad for me, but I saw them again a few years later at a summer camp.

These new people had many horses, and I was given a fine brown mare by my mother's new husband, even though I knew nothing of horses. As this man probably intended, this made me very pleased by my mother's choice of a husband. This man was older than she, but this was common for all New'e marriages. Men commonly married after proving themselves as hunters, warriors, or through Spirit dreams, while girls normally married soon after they had their womanhood ceremony. Women could then bear as many children as were given to them. My mother's new husband had also lost his wife and three of his grown children in the spotted sickness, and one daughter to a drowning. He and my mother had each seen much sadness, but both gained a peace with each other. They began to regain a good sense of their worth and place in each other's presence. He later took another wife who became my mother's new sister with whom she often laughed and sang. Even though there had been many bad times, there was merriment in that new place.

I had to learn about horses as I had ridden on their backs and been around their heavy feet only one time, and I was nearly a man! The boys my age among my mother's new people had grown up as babies on horseback. They carried no fear of horses and could seemingly control them with their thoughts. I had loved the free and exciting feeling of riding upon the Cree's horse when I was still a baby, and remembered that ride with my father on the horse's back as a beautiful moment. I was in awe of horses and could not believe my luck in having one that was for me. My mother's new husband was very wise with this particular gift.

This horse was friendly, but also smart and quick. She loved to run. The first time I sat upon her after the other boys explained how best to approach her, and how to talk to her and how to establish bonds with her, she seemed to look back at me with her big black eye while she determined if I was worthy of her. The other boys instructed me how to run up and jump on her back. I ran as best as I could! I landed on her back, but I came very close to falling immediately off. She then "hurramphed"; then pitched up her head and walked a few paces to the edge of our camp seeming to let me straighten up. She then stretched forward and began a smooth and powerful glide with her hoofs making beautiful drumming sounds on the ground underneath us.

At first I was too thrilled to do anything but hang on with a stupid grin on my face as we raced around and through the large meadow above our camp. My legs began to feel tight at the knees but I did not want to stop. Eventually we were both finished with this thrilling experience and we began a more slow and experienced program of getting to know each other. I got off her and could not believe the pain in my legs. I stretched and managed to leap back on, even though the horse knew this was a clumsy thing for me at first. I will admit that more than one time I leapt too far or not far enough and ended up eating dirt and smarting from the laughs of the other boys. They could not imagine a boy such as me who did not know ponies.

At first my horse would walk near tree branches to see if I would allow her to brush me against them. When I warned her against doing so, she seemed accepting and even pleased that I exerted this role as the one who was the leader, as this obligation had been told to me by the other boys. I learned to read her movements: when she was ready to run, when something alarmed her, when she needed water, when she wished to go back to the camp, and her natural need to be near other horses and to assume her role as a member of that family. She learned my needs as well as anyone I have ever known. She knew when we must continue out from camp to hunt or meet a friend, when we were playing and exploring an area, when we were to race, and when we needed to be very quiet. The first spring and summer I spent with these people was as much as possible on the horse's back. By the fall I was almost as keen on the horse as the other boys were. I could not then imagine a life without a horse.

Inside my Spirit I thanked the Pueblo people, which we heard of from traders, who were the first to become familiar with horses. Then I thanked the Utes and Comanches who traded them from south to north and learned to train and breed them so that they became a part of the people. The horses understood Shoshones and we understood them, perhaps better than those people from which they came.

We heard that the white men used them for seasonal farming, making them perform difficult and boring tasks. These jobs did not make the spirits of the horses happy.

We Shoshones could use horses for hunting which gave us dominance in this area, and also for warfare. Warfare stories became a new passion for me, as perhaps it does for all immature boys. The horses loved the running and the ability to be among their own near water and good grass and in winter with bark or other nutritious food brought to them by people.

We saw ourselves as very good matches against the Piegan *{Now these people are mostly known by white men as Blackfeet.}* They were the common enemy of most tribes. They had horses a few years after the Comanches brought them north. The Blackfeet were more dangerous, because they had guns before we did, which they got from Crees and the Assiniboine who also had them through dealings with the northern fur traders. During some of the first known times of spotted sickness, when my father was young, the Blackfeet and Cree lost many of their people, so their hunting areas were scaled back. With our ally the Kootenai who were people with flat foreheads from their use of special cradleboards for their babies, we were able to expand our hunting grounds into what had previously been Blackfeet lands. This combination of riding horses for hunting with a prepared defense against these Blackfeet seeking to chase us from the rich lands to the north, required a new type of military organization. This organization was crafted over many years and involved knowledge of landscapes, spies, identified groups working together, discussions and secret planning of events.

These plans and pastimes could not have been more thrilling to a boy of my age. We knew that with our success in hunting we would also have success in war, which would earn us the rights of men.

That is all.

Story #20 I AM NOT A WARRIOR

I was challenged as a warrior only once. This was generally unusual for a man of my age but was also foretold at my birth. I had always determined to stay away far from any white people. Their ways were just too strange and dangerous to me. The making of moccasins was as important to me as tangling with the white men and their square houses was to other boys. This may have made me seem weak in some eyes, but it did not trouble me.

I did know well the rules of warfare with the Blackfeet and other tribes because the stories of our people's warring were told and re-told. I did love to listen in the late nights around the fires of the strategies of war to imagine past fights. This listening was stored within me for general knowledge. I knew it would not be needed for my own use since the Puhugen had said I would be a person always of small tasks and never of war.

I became involved in a fight with others only once. I was with an elk hunting party when a large camp of Absorkee people was spotted on a prairie where the wind blew the long grasses on gentle hillsides. *{The white men call Absorokees the Crow people}.* We did not realize that they knew of us before we knew of them, and as we crept on the ground to look over a hill at them, a clamor arose and we saw three of our horses being led away by two Crow warriors. My mare was not among them so I determined I must go after my friends' horses.

I was in the right place and cut in front of these Crows, followed closely by another man of our group. My horse was fast, and I caught up with the horse thieves, and swung my war hammer at the back of the fleeing Crows, which knocked one of the men off his horse. This caused him to drop the two lead ropes of our horses, and to lose his own horse. I grabbed these three horses and led them back to our men. One horse had been taken but one different horse retrieved.

We jumped on these horses and ran from that place as fast as we could, knowing that a very large group of people was just over the hill. I left my weapon on the ground with that Crow. I had bettered him as a warrior, but he had my fine hand-made war hammer. It was as white men say, "a tie", but we could each still tell this tale and brag of our success. Years later, I met this Crow man at Bridger's Fort. I knew him as he still carried my weapon, and we laughed as if we were good friends recalling that day. Each had certainly gone home with a good story and his pride intact.

This is my only experience of fighting against another man in a battle. I am a fortunate person to say this as I have seen the end result of other men killing in war.

That is all.

Story #21 TREATY

Among our people and other tribes, however, there was significant conflict with the white men. Because I now see this date is important, I will tell you that in 1851 the first treaty was made with the white men, although I was not part of this decision, so I did not feel bound by it. In later years, white men acted toward me as if I had agreed, and as if I had made many agreements that I did not make.

This treaty was to make agreement about the Shoshones allowing the white travelers to cross our lands undisturbed. The treaty set aside other territories that the white men would not go and which were to be reserved for the Cheyenne and Arapaho. I do not know if this was agreeable to those people.

The white men promised our people much in return for the permission to travel across our lands. I believe the white men thought the agreement was for more than we actually agreed that it would be. There is a big difference between "you may travel on these lands without fear of our harming your people" and "these lands are yours and no longer ours", as the white men now say it is. The white men also now act as if they promised us less than they did promise us for the agreement.

This is how this treaty came to be. Word was passed that during summer meetings some important white men, called Indian Agents would meet with us at Fort Laramie, which was a trading post. Jim Bridger, a trader along with a serious man named Brigham Young, who was the Governor of "Utah" and a "Superintendent" of Indians, had been coming among our people. One half-Flathead and half-Shoshone man who was a few years older than I was, Washakie, was familiar and friendly with Jim Bridger. This man Washakie knew English and Shoshone and had been Jim Bridger's friend in fighting with Blackfeet.

We were told there would be many gifts for us, so many assembled there. I was now with a band of people much more active in the affairs of the white men than my band from my childhood. For the first time, I was to attend a meeting with white men and maybe trade in a rond-a-voo or be given a gift such as a knife or a black cooking pot. In addition to Shoshones, there were Sioux, Cheyenne, Crows, Arapahoes, Arikaras, and many white men at this rond-a-voo. This was the largest gathering of people I had ever seen, and I was not comfortable among all these strange peoples. I saw the white men in beautiful uniforms with hair on their faces, only from far away. All our traditional enemies were there and while many men blustered and puffed, we stayed apart to avoid the dishonor of not finishing a confrontation.

I stayed in that place for many days waiting for the promised gifts and to see what would happen, but the grass began to be hard for our horses to find, wood was scarce for cooking fires, and when the opportunity arose, I left with many others to hunt. The arrival of the presents was delayed, or maybe they were a ruse, but I did not care as I decided I did not need these presents. Most of our headmen also left this place, including our Head Chief Gahnacumah. I was not at the meeting when the treaty was agreed upon. Again, I did not care because I had no plans to hinder the movements of white men.

Later, we heard it was announced that because the landscape was depleted, the meeting would move to Horse Creek at the St. Mary's stage station on the Sweetwater River, which is a tributary of the North Platt. We also heard the meeting began to be difficult when two days after the first white men spoke to the assembled Indians, Cheyennes killed two Shoshone people.

Washakie moved to this new place with the gathered white soldiers and Indians after Gahnacumah left to hunt. Washakie called in all the young men who had stayed and had previously been to war with him and told them he was going to stay with the white men in their ways and in their suggestions and others must make up their minds to stay in this manner or to go and fight at a later time.   After a few days of thinking, some said they would stay.   Most of these that stayed wanted peace. They selected Washakie their War Chief for the purposes of the meeting, but he was not to be confused with our head chiefs. Washakie wore red, the color of peace. He put his mark on this treaty with the white men. Washakie had agreed that white men could pass through our lands.

That is all.

Story #22 SAINTS

The next year after the treaty allowing white men to pass over our lands, other decisions of various Shoshone men decided my future. None of these men could speak for me, but it became that any commitment by an Indian was seen by the white men as binding all Indians of that tribe. This was done before most of us knew it was happening.

Shoshones were also now fighting with Utes over hunting territories. The traditional hunting rights were being disrupted by all the new people going about and hunting where they were not before. Washakie and four other Shoshone headmen agreed to a truce with some Ute leaders.

The Saints were the ones we had most often encountered in traditional Shoshone land. They were not violent like many other white men, however we still remained wary of them. The truce with the Utes was brokered by the Saint's serious man, Brigham Young. I heard that Young gave gifts of clothes, beef, flour, and ammunition, after which everyone at that meeting left very happy. This was not a treaty with the government, but the truce permitted Young's Saints to stay on lands around Bear River and Green River.

Washakie told the white men he did not object to the Saints making farms in the area. After Washakie agreed to this peace with the Utes, he and the other peace Indians moved far from the Bear River and Green River lands to an area around Fort Bridger. There was discontent among other Shoshones about Washakie's being part of the truce deal. Of course Washakie did not object to permitting those farms because he had decided to stay there no more! Other bands still wished to stay in these lands and the Saints were now acting as though they were free to move permanently on these traditional lands.

My own band of Shoshone as well as some Bannock and many Ute people were still traveling in those places! Many of our men and women were angry that Washakie did not protect these New'e groups before he took up and moved off with Bridger.

The Utes were not in any way bound by Washakie, however, and began warring with the whites. There were disputes over river crossing ferries, which the Saints tried to make. Jim Bridger and other traders were angry with the Saints and encouraged the Utes with words and guns with ammunition. We were generally affronted that these Saints in the new town called Salt Lake, in a place they named "Ute-Ah" thought they could agree to allow ferry crossings on lands that belonged only to us.

My family group did not like these issues and we determined to avoid these problems. We thought that these Saints would soon go away.

Our band, which included my mother one of my sisters and her family and about 25 others moved to the dry lands to the west of the Salt Lake. This was the area of my youth and I was very happy here, although it was difficult to find good water for our horses and the game was much harder to find. And even here in these dry lands, trails for carrying white men appeared, and farms began to divert what little water there was, and slow and stupid beef cattle continued to eat up the good grasses. My horse could not live in this place and I traded him to some Utes.

Washakie sent out messengers who encouraged all Shoshone people to stay peaceful. Other leaders disagreed with Washakie and those bands moved further north, many looking to Pocatello to lead them against these changes and to fight back against the white men.

The Saints liked Washakie and his band for his peacefulness. Some of these Saint men even wished to marry into Washakie's family. Washakie agreed to this but asked for some Saint women to become his wives in exchange for some of his daughters going to the Saints. I do not think this bargain was accepted and the Saint men did not marry Washakie's daughters. However, Washakie eventually accepted many of the other Saint ways. He liked the tools, clothing and food. The Book of Mormon was not then fully approved of by Washakie, but he was very polite about this, not wishing to make any trouble.

I hated these Saints and all their silly book sayings and their killing of the ways of Mother Earth with their farms. But I had to see that their farming seemed in some ways good as they made many new foods. Still it was very dangerous as it was changing our lands even in the most remote of places. Place after place was found without water or without traditional plants. Gone were places rich in roots and insects. Now they were farm crops with one kind of food, or cows that stomped out the many other kinds of plants and creatures that had lived there since the beginning of time.

Streams, springs and even whole rivers were diverted from the natural places where they flowed, to the square Mormon fields. Changing the places of the waters slowly changed the ways of the New'e.

My family tried peacefully to go away from these new hills of stinging ant people to places where we knew we could remain in peace and try to live in our traditional way. We went to these places only to find them manipulated into unnatural squares scrapped and planted and muddied by Saints and cowboys. We moved away from all these places to quite places where our songs were still loud and our dances expressed our oneness with our animal brothers and our Spirit Men helped us interpret our thinking and assisted our communion with our natural world. We knew our spirits could still be strong if we could find spaces that remained rich in all those Shoshone foods, hides, smells, prayers, tasks, games, and signs that we knew.

That is all.

Story #23 I TOOK A WIFE

A few years after this time I took a wife. Most New'e males did not take wives until they were fully able to care for a woman and their children. If men could care for more than one woman, he could have more women.

The ability to take a wife generally took at least ten summers after our first kills. No one wanted to take a wife when he was still a boy with a boy's ways. I was generally a very shy person who liked to stay near my family and the thought of a wife and further societal requirements secretly frightened me. Maybe it was my history with my broken foot, but I was always slower to do things than others and tended to keep to myself and among those I knew well.

At this time, I had participated in the summertime Sun Dance for four summers and was fully a man. This was about 15 summers after my voice changed. I do not now like to say the names of these lost ones for they are gone from me, but my wife was know as Strong Branches. She was the daughter of Sagwich, a great New'e Chief. She had a young boy when we married from a man who moved north with the more warlike people. This young boy was very clever and joyful and we laughed very much. I enjoyed Sagwich's family with whom I lived after we moved our lodging together. I was pleased to have little children around me again.

My wife was soon expecting our child. She delivered early and the baby girl was very small. I was determined that the girl would live and be strong. I ran up and down large hills so that this strength would fill her. My foot became stronger as did our baby. We named her "Bent Foot Healer" and she was a joyful baby who rode on her mother's back content to watch all things. She would hum and sing at odd times even before she could speak. We knew she heard songs when we did not. This was a great medicine.

{Bent Foot Healer was born about 1854. I remember this woman very well. She grew to marry a man called Arrow Shooter. The white men

later gave him the white name of Edward Homena. Bent Foot Healer had
many children for this man and he never took any other women. Most of her
children died young due to the difficult times on the reservation. When I first
met her in 1895, she was very old and fierce looking, though she was in her
early 40s at that time. She had many scars all over her face and body from
surviving smallpox. She also plucked her hair from the front of her head but
had very long thick black hair in the back that she wore in a long dangling
braid. She was a leader of her people in the quiet way that good women can
be.}

Soon after, Strong Branches became large again. Many people said
there was more than one child within her and when she gave birth she presented me with two boys. These boys looked just like each other, but they
had different temperaments from the beginning. One was very rosy and
peaceful, while the other needed more attention and grew to be one who
played tricks and even successfully joked on his lively sister and his clever
older half-brother. There were many happy times and teaching and caring
for these children became my most enjoyable past time. Strong Branches
was a sweet girl who quietly and generously gave all of us much laughter.

By the time my twins were at their very sweetest age, around seven
summers, competition for good water became more heated. The white
Mormon farmers and pioneers had taken over Cache Valley East of the Salt
Lake. Only about fifteen summers after the Saints arrived, their dirty and
stupid livestock had so overgrazed the native grasses and seeds that Indians began to starve. There were very few places to go in the old areas to
live.

The Mormon called Indians "Laminites" and said we were "Blood
cousins" from their long ago times. They said we forgot who we were and
did not know Mormon ways. We did not like Mormon ways. The Utes and
the Mormons also had been bickering with each other. California and Montana gold immigrants were following the Salt Lake road around the lake and
across the salt desert to Pilot Peak. Bear Hunter's band, a band of
Shoshone living to our north disapproved of the growing number of these
people and the disruption they caused to our hunting and lifestyles in general.

Bear Hunter and some of his men began to strike back. We heard of
other fights and killings and taking of cattle as the large place we had lived
forever became smaller and smaller. The Lakota were often told to be fighting the white men to the far north and east. They had first been moved from
their lands near the large forests and lakes to the east into Cheyenne and
Arapaho and Cree hunting grounds. New'e are a people of adapting, and
while the changes were large, we mostly made friendly when we could and
stayed away from fighting. Bad things were coming.

That is all.

Story #24 BAO OGOI (BEAR RIVER)

In the early winter of 1863, Strong Branches was pregnant with another child, and she wished to stay the winter with her mother and brothers who were with Bear Hunter's band. My mother and her husband's people were also traveling with Bear Hunter that year. Sagwich's whole band joined Bear Hunter's Band.

We were hungry then, with less small game and smaller stores of ground roots. Our band traveled with our horses and dogs to my wife's father Sagwich's camp where the Beaver Creek ran to the Bao Ogoi, or Bear River. This area was often abundant with fish and game. There was to be a Warm Dance. This was a social ceremony held to play winter games and to say prayers and dance to drive out the cold and bring back the warm weather.

When we arrived, food there, too, was scarce, but the lodging was warm and comfortable. To the north were small hills through which the creek flowed. The creek was only a trickle in the winter but it had cut a ravine about the length of five horses deep into the ground near the bottom of these hills. In this ravine, which was almost a mile long before it flowed into the Bao Ogoi, many willows grew. It was an ideal place to shelter the many lodges and horses. A ceiling of woven willows protected almost 500 horses and 700 people during the Warm Dance. Water was close and game could be hunted in the area, although hunting was not often successful due to the changing lands, the disappearing animal brothers and the many people in one place.

There was talk of rising tensions among many bands and the white men. The camp was made with a good defensive position in mind and extra stores of food were made. The camp had accepted some wheat and other supplies from the Mormon whites, who were friendly with Sagwich. The Mormons said they did not want these Indian people to starve and some seemed to pity us. I did not like seeing this Mormon food, but it sustained my wife and children so I said nothing. How bad of them to give us pity when they had taken our wildlife and plants from the land!

At the conclusion of the Warm Dance, some bands left this place to find better hunting. I was also determined to go to a place we call Echo Canyon to pray and consider the changing times in which we lived, and to seek guidance from Tam Apo about the loss of so many of our brother animals, and about the changes to the Earth that the white men were bringing. These accelerating changes were weighing heavy on my mind and brought me a creeping feeling and knowledge of frightening loss, which sometimes kept me sad and hiding like a burrow animal away from others. The prayers I intended were to refresh my spirit and grant me a new way of looking at these white men.

The little girl, Bent Foot Healer was about nine summers and was very active and liked special attention. I agreed to take her with me to pray. I would make a sweat lodge and she could tend my fire. Together, we rode the new horse I had traded for two pair of moccasins a day to the southwest of Bao Ogoi. There, my prayers were good, but my dreams were disturbed. I could feel the prayers giving me a different itchy and tense strength than I had before. This strength came along with a strange release, a detachment from what was happening.

Then on the last morning of my prayers Bent Foot Healer woke agitated. She was complaining and pacing around and wanted to go back to the camp. This was unusual for her quiet nature. Suddenly, a great white man's iron bell began to bang and clang in my head and heart and stomach. Bent Foot Healer also heard the deafening new metal sound. Bent Foot Healer began to cry. She put her hands over her ears and screamed.

The sound came rolling in the sky far away, like thunder. It seemed to come from the direction of our camp. The repeating, swinging movement of the iron bell and the giant crashing iron clacker knocked me off my feet and threw me about. The crash of the bell was so loud and horrible it blocked all other thought away and made my stomach wrench and left me unable to walk in dizziness. It covered the whole Earth and told of something terrible. From the first loud sound, I could no longer hear the same way. The sound was like a storm where the sky felt bad. Its echoes blocked all my previous perception of the quiet sounds that I was accustomed to listening for and changed my existence forever. Somehow I knew that the bell was saying that the old ways were forever gone. I knew then that the white man's sounds would forever muffle the old sounds such as birds, insects, wind, footfalls, breath, and the cadences and shushes of our language. I can say now that my ears and brain have rung forever since that day in Echo Canyon. I still wait with fear for this faint alarm to suddenly again be fully set in motion, and I wonder if some day the ringing will stop completely. The bell broke forever my belief in quiet. It foretold of chaos and cruelty. I did not know, then, how much that strange new strength and release from my prayers would be needed for the terrible, monstrous things that came next. For a long time I could not speak about, or even think clearly, of these things. The next days were times of only reaction.

I was panicking as I caught the horse. Bent Foot Healer and I broke camp quickly and rushed toward the camp. It was terribly cold, and the breath from my horse froze onto my moccasins. I wrapped Bent Foot Healer into my robe. As we rushed forward my own breath froze my hair straight out behind. I traveled in a panic all day through the valleys and then rough timber. When I got closer I dropped any concern for my mare and began driving her desperately toward the camp.

I was far off but I began to see an odd lack of camp smoke, and instead I saw burning smoke. My horse was very skittish and could smell something on the wind. The bell sound had become louder as I got closer.

Bent Foot Healer still held her ears and cried, moaning. My horse seemed to hear it too; she did not need urging to go on toward the camp. Soon we saw dogs and a few horses hiding panting in the woods. They jumped skittishly away in fright as we rushed by.

Soon I saw Broken Nose, an elder man that I knew. He was clutching a blanket to his clothes and carrying a young child away from the camp in the terrible cold. He shouted at me not to go there. Soldiers had killed everyone that morning and were still camped to the south of the ravine. He told me Sagwich was dead. His voice sounded so strange with the bell sound so loud. I gave my horse to Broken Nose. I told Bent Foot Healer she must go back to our prayer place with Broken Nose and not come to the camp until I came for her. I prayed Broken Nose could keep her safe. Bent Foot Healer screamed in her fear that I would abandon her but Broken Nose took her and the horse and I ran quickly toward the awful smoke and eerie quiet of the camp.

At the edge of the camp I came to the first dead person. He looked like a frozen heap. His black blood sat like a pond of dark shining ice on the surface of the ground. The noise from the bell was now continuous and would go in waves for hearing by all others for miles around. I was now inside the sound of these large events.

The huge ringing noise of this horror impacted me greatly. I felt that for years everyone in hearing distance would talk of the terrible sound each time they met. But the ominous horrible sound of that bell was not even heard by most people! It was not remarkable to them! I do not think white people knew any ringing at all! Later when I would be among them trying to get around the sound in my ears, they would live as if they heard nothing.

The dead one was a child of about fourteen summers that played with my oldest son. His arm was missing and his chest was blown open. Next there was a large patch of blood with a blond man's scalp and hair and many tracks. My own ax was lying beside the scalp. I could see by the tracks that soldiers, with their iron shoe horses had been there and had taken a dead one away.

At the site of my ax, my horror doubled because I knew that one of my family had done this – it was proof that they were part of this madness. Later, I became very proud that my little ones had defended themselves so strongly. I picked up the ax. None of my boys would have left the ax there unless something even more terrible was threatened. I was wild with fear for Strong Branches and boys. I was prepared to kill and die and do anything I was able to do if I could only hear beyond the bell. As I walked into the camp, I heard through the clanging the soldiers' bugling horn from the hills south of camp. It was nightfall. I had walked into a camp of the dead.

I know now that hundreds of soldiers from the California Volunteer Militia under General Patrick E. Connor, who were not the white men that we had come to know in our dealings around the trading posts, had come to kill Indians they saw as harming white people. In spite of the Fort Laramie Treaty which promised peace with New'e by our familiar soldiers, these other soldiers had carried the best guns and rode good horses and had attacked our camp soon after dawn. They had two large cannons, but they could not get them across the river, so they had done this massacre with their rifles, pistols and swords. Our people had managed to kill twenty-three of the soldiers. Almost 500 of our people were dead or dying. About 550 had been at camp that morning, since some New'e had left in the days after the Warm Dance.

A few others who were alive were in the camp, but most of the survivors had run into the woods and had not returned. One of Strong Branches' young brothers, Yeager Timbimboo, whose name meant "cottontail rabbit" was with his grandmother. They had lain among the dead pretending to be dead. He heard his grandmother being killed with a sword. A soldier had found him and had pointed the gun in his face. They looked at each other in the eyes. The soldier took the gun away. Then he came back and again pointed the gun in Rabbit's face. Rabbit again looked him in the eye, then maybe having some kindness in the horror, the soldier lowered his gun and walked away. I found Rabbit wandering in shock through at the edge of the camp where the bodies lay. When I asked about Strong Branches, our sons and my mother, this story of the soldier was all Rabbit could tell.

The soldiers had come from the southeast, then moved west along the river, and forded the river to the southwest of our camp, then had sat above the ravine and had first tried to shoot into the camp through the willows. This did not work, and our people crawled to the tops of the ravine, up the steps we had made and rested our guns in protection to shoot at the soldiers. Some people escaped to the east, until the soldiers moved to the north and then the east, surrounding the ravine, except where the river ran out of the ravine to the far south.

Within the ravine the remaining horses and dogs were in chaos. The horses that had become loose panicked and many broke free at the end of the ravine in the south into the large river. Those horses were caught by the army and taken away. Some people tried to run away through the top of the ravine in the north. These people were immediately shot by soldiers waiting there. Strong Branches' other brother and his favorite girl rode out this way on his horse. She was shot in the back but hung onto him so that he was not hurt by bullets fired into his back. She died a few miles away in the cold after his horse fell. He came back to camp soon after I did carrying her body and singing his grief.

We were mindful of making noise and quieted him. We searched inside the ravine, but none of our people were there, but the dead. My mother was there, a old woman shot in the back with a huge hole blown through her chest. She had hidden her prized turquoise inside her shirt. I found the one-spirit twins holding each other, both shot in the head. I covered them all with some tree branches so I could later come back to send them to the Spirit World in our way.

The ravine was smoking and stunk of burning flesh as the fires burned among the lodges and charred the bodies there. Inside the ravine, the New'e had been shot by the soldiers' pistols and big rifles after our ammunition ran low. The soldiers eventually found their ways into the ravine camp where they killed our people, bludgeoned our old ones, and stole our last food stores and any prized skins and beadworks.

Many women were ravaged by soldiers. How did those soldiers walk away from such a thing and what is in their hearts as they remember their own brutality? I could not imagine in this horror turning to a woman like this and doing these hateful things. One woman lay naked and sobbing and bleeding from between her legs even as her hands, which were spread out before her were turning white with frost.

We found one small girl, the daughter of Turning Woman, hiding unhurt at the edge of the ravine under some skins. I picked her up, but then returned her to that place so she would not see the terrible sights outside. I found a few other stunned and frozen people outside and moved them in near her to keep them all safer in the event the soldiers returned. A few did not want to go to the ravine, remembering the terror of being trapped there just a few hours ago by the soldiers.

The soldiers had many more bullets than our people, and many more guns. They had surrounded the ravine, and shot into the ravine until our people were out of bullets. Then the soldiers found ways to run down into the ravine and kill and scare the New'e into the open. They tried to light the willows on fire but due to the cold and snow, and the green wood, the fires did not at first burn well. But the people were slowly and then finally in a group pushed out of the ravine by the soldiers, where they were all shot as they ran from the shelter. Our people lay all about, dead. A large pile of our people showed where many had run from the ravine and been shot. The ground was red with frozen blood.

The river was ice, except in the center. Many bodies floated among the willows in broken icy patches. A few people came struggling up from the riverbed, their clothing, hair and hands and feet frozen from hiding in the reeds and willows in the water. One woman carried a frozen baby who she would not release from her arms. A dog ran by carrying a hand. I asked everyone I saw about my wife, my sons.

A boy, bleeding from a number of places, with a gash on his face, said my name. He said that Strong Branches and her oldest son were at the edge of the river. I found them there, dead. She was without a blanket or shirt, and her naked body looked so very cold. Our unborn child was a great quiet grey blue hill in her frozen belly. Her face was shot off and I could see into her frost filled head. Her son I could not look at, but seeing all of his blood frozen to the ground, I covered them with a robe I found nearby.

Then from the ravine crawled Sagwitch! He had been shot in the hand, and had fought the soldiers until the end. He survived three horses that day, all of which were killed, one saving his life by swimming across the river. He watched the end of the massacre among the willows, with two small children who had frozen in the night. He was in shock, and injured, but he remained a leader.

He told me that my twins, his grandsons, had seen their older brother shot. As a soldier caught my running wife and tore away her shirt, exposing her breasts to the cold, my twin boys had taken my ax and had planted it twice into the head of that soldier. Other soldiers came and killed Strong Branches as her sons watched. As they ran to the river, my little boys they were both shot in the back. Sagwitch said he saw them fall down the bank and into the water. He showed me where they went into the river, but it was now dark, and I could not see them. I asked Sagwitch if my boys were alive, and he said no. As the battle ended, he saw both of my boys float past him face down and still. Sagwitch was very proud of these children, his grandsons.

The small bleeding boy, Beshup, watched us and reached for my hand. In my grief, I gathered his little body to me and carried him to the ravine where a few people had put up some shelter and were huddled moaning and in shock. Some stayed in a huddle through the night, praying death prayers, expecting the soldiers to come back in the morning. Sagwitch and I and a few others located injured ones and dragged them to the ravine shelter. There was no food or fire for warmth. Some of these survivors froze to death that night from their wet clothes and hair. We found Sagwitch's wife, dead, but his infant daughter alive. He lovingly put her in a cradleboard, but as there was no woman to suckle her, she would die soon.

I encouraged Sagwitch to take one of the horses and leave. I knew the soldiers would want to kill him. He was in shock, but he helped as best he could with the medicine for the injured and prayers, then went away that night. That night I held Beshup and quietly sang the songs of death and prayer songs for strength.

At dawn the next morning, we heard the soldier's horns through the still ringing bells in our ears, but the soldiers did not come. We heard them break camp, and they rode away in straight groups to the south. They took our horses, and our small stores of food. We were alone with the dead.

As the sun rose higher, the birds descended. Then small predators circled the camp to peck upon the dead frozen New'e. Wolves appeared in the willows and dragged away a few bodies. Quickly, we began to bring our remaining New'e together for death rights. One small girl ran hysterically about trying to shoo away dogs and birds and forest creatures from the dead ones. The dead were frozen so hard, we often brought willows and dirt ground and frozen blood in flat circles with them when we were able to drag them to our terrible pile of frozen bodies. We found Chief Bear Hunter with many small torture wounds and a saber through his ears.

The small boy Beshup wanted to cling to me, but I pushed him to the edge of the water with some women there so I could do what I must do. I cared for Strong Branches, my unborn one, and our son. I looked for many hours among the dead in the river for my twins, but they had disappeared, taken away by the Spirit of the river. As the terrible day passed, other New'e came from the woods. Women crawled from under blankets and out of the willows in shame as the soldiers had taken them after the killing was over. The women who did not do this for the soldiers were killed. Their children were held by their feet and killed before them with the swords. These women were dead to themselves then and some lay down in their quiet way to allow the cold to take them. We buried our people as best we could in the frozen ground.

Some Mormon whites came. They walked around and looked at the horror with hands over their mouths. They expressed their sadness and said their prayers over our people. They had some food, and the boy Beshup strangely went to a Mormon man who treated him with kindness and gave him something to eat. The man asked if he could care for the boy, and I agreed. I do not know if that boy ever came back to his people. I hoped the man was a good man, but I know that some of the Mormons there that day were pleased by this horror. We later heard that many Mormons had cared for the soldiers after the massacre. I know only of the one instance of kindness and it was when the man took away the boy Beshup.

The next days the bell rang and rang in my ears. Some, like me did what was necessary through this noise. Others gave up and froze to death or fell into the river Spirit to be taken by water.

Some who survived crawled back from where they had run and formed a small band. When Broken Nose came to the ravine with Bent Foot Healer, I told him to go away with many of the children. It was not good for children to be in that place. Bad Spirits hovered over the ravine and no one slept. Songs were sung quietly by rote.

We pulled what we could together and crept away to make camp as far away as we could go from that horrible place. Others died. I found my daughter and without her sweet face, I would not have wanted to live. There was much pain as the people died from wounds that became infected. The bitterness in our stomachs did not allow eating, even if there had been anything to have. We burrowed away and became crazy with grief and anger and horror. We struggled this way through sharp and horrible months of winter.

That is all.

Story #25 AFTERMATH

The spring after the horrible winter, I remained very angry and would have joined in the battles that took place before all these papers, had I known of them. I had decided that I wanted to kill white men who had killed my family and my people. I had my horse, but no gun. I could have traded my horse for a gun, but in the times of heightened anxiety, it was not easy to find a place to do this.

I was lost during these days, without a place to go or direction for my frustration, anger and hatred. That iron bell was still loud behind my ears. Only Bent Foot Healer kept me living. We went into the woods where we stayed alone for many months to forget and to stop the ringing. During this time I cut toes off my damaged foot with my ax to punish myself for not saving my family and to grieve for them.

I did not want to live if I could not kill at least one soldier, and I formulated lengthy plans to attack a fort singlehandedly. I came across a young family of white people, probably Mormons, living in a dug out hillside near an earthen pillar where I had camped as a child. I did not have a gun, but I had my ax. I sent Bent Foot Healer to a safe place and hid in the woods near these people for two days deciding how I would kill them. I came to see that the woman was pregnant. I remembered my beautiful wife frozen in her blood in the snow and my child, cold and dead within her. I could not do such a thing to another woman, and this woman was not a soldier. I went away and gathered up my daughter.

My rage wore on. Then, I was visited by the Spirits from Echo Canyon. They told me to return there and pray. I did this, my foot healed, and slowly I put away my plans of revenge.

By the time the grasses turned brown, I became lonely for people. Bent Foot Healer had become serious and quiet. I dreamed of my family, both those dead and those alive. Sagwich came and found me. He told me of white men trying to make peace forever. He wanted to have a peace, and to do what the white men wanted.

He convinced me to come again to the people as they needed to all stand together and to remake ourselves with peace under the terms the white men gave us. I tried this and went to my sister's people and spent a number of angry and quiet months as a disgraceful burden to them, sleeping all day, kicking the dogs who I once loved, refusing to ride a horse, and not washing. Once or twice when white man's liquor was to be had, I drank as much as I could.

If the truth is to be known, if that liquor was available I would have drank it until I was dead. My sister may have seen this and she and her husband broke off with some other people and took me and Bent Foot Healer with them to the new reservation in the Owl Creek Mountains, in this place promised to us in the treaty, where we could forget about the new things happening around us and live like Shoshones again for a while. The temptations from liquor faded and we stayed in a place of our ancestors that had power and medicine that helped us in our healing.

Word spread that in late winter, a group of Goshutes lead by Chief White Horse, attacked the white man's overland mail stagecoach and there were small battles all summer and into the fall. New'e bands everywhere were stunned and grieving and speaking in Council about what best to do.

White men sent their chief to make the Treaty of Box Elder with the Northwestern New'e bands at one of our old hunting places, now called Brigham City, Utah that summer to end that fighting and to talk the New'e into small hunting areas.

Other New'e were now taking the free government annuities at a place they called Corinne, Utah. Other white chiefs came to seek treaties, as maybe the white men knew they were bad to kill us Indians as they had done at Bear River. That fall, their Governor James Nye and 12 principal men of Shoshone signed more papers at Ruby Valley near the place where my iron pot was buried in the ground.

Then in a bigger meeting of Indians and white men signed more papers at Fort Bridger. Those papers told us the new boundaries of the "Shoshone Reservation", which were to be "headquartered at a place called "Camp Brown". Many years later, the white men named this headquarters after Washakie, calling it "Fort Washakie". In that treaty white men reestablished their peace with us. The treaty set boundaries for Shoshone country. {This reservation was over 44 million acres in Wyoming, Colorado, Utah and Idaho.} Whites would be allowed to pass through but we would be protected from any bad men. Outside of Shoshone country, white settlers were to be allowed to stay, in what white men called a "homestead".

After all the horror then sadness then talk, we thought this was the end of our war with the white men. A war we knew we had lost. How badly it was lost, we did not yet know.

That is all.

Story #26 CONEFLOWER

At the time after the horror of Bao Ogai, another miracle took place, and a young girl, very beautiful, named Coneflower, began to sit with me. She was young and had no children so she began to mother Bent Foot Healer. My daughter began to love her like a mother. Coneflower brought me tea made from coneflower leaves and bade me make her moccasins. She helped me with her own sewing.

She had never experienced the bad part of white men. Her knowledge of whites was that they had provided her with three good sharp steel needles that were strong and sharp and could draw fibers through skins without first making holes in the skins. I saw that she was more willing to take on white man's good things. I knew deep in my body that this way of coping with our new world was coming. Being with Coneflower was like giving up and being born again at the same time.

I began to love her and she became my wife. Her tenderness taught me again to be a human. She talked of the meaning of my night dreams which were vivid and important. We knew that all was forever different and worse for our people and we did not want to leave our place in the Owl Creeks. She helped me to have hope. It was clear that certain aspects of life would go on.

We had our first child, a daughter, named Lupineflower, in the third winter after the Bear River Massacre. Lupineflower was born of sadness and she would later be lead away from me, but it has happened as it was meant. We named her Lupineflower because these flowers could heal a sick person.

From Lupineflower has come much happiness, as she became the mother of my granddaughter, Sugar, who has lived with me for many years and now writes this story for me today. In another year, Coneflower had a second daughter for me, whom we named Sageflower, but she was not strong and died.

Many Shoshones who had been at Bear River or had family there did not ever begin to live again. They became mean and did not wash. They did not teach their children. They left camp to sit at the white man's fort where they could trade anything for whiskey. Women sold their bodies and their dignity for trinkets.

People, even those who had not been at the massacre, were going crazy all around us with the knowledge of the horrible changes and their powerlessness to stop its happening.

Ceremonies were not held; Pipe Carriers forgot their medicine and put their bundles away. Gatherings were too much trouble; food was not gathered in time for winter. Many of our people became beggars, starving for Mormon flour and beef.

We heard that the Comanches, who were very strong and warlike, were being slaughtered and scalped by white men called Rangers. The white men were said to brag that no Comanches were to be left alive in Texas, the new name for part of the Comanche lands. I heard from a man who traveled about with the soldiers that before their defeat, a Comanche medicine man had put a curse on the white men. He said that all the lands that were once Comanche would, in less than a hundred years, be covered by a great drought. Great storms would pick up the land and carry it away. The grasses would die, and white people living there would choke to death.

A sense of hopelessness was upon us. If the fighting Comanches were to be lost, what worse thing would become of the quiet Shoshones who were more ready to take on new ways rather than fight for the old ones? If we stayed with these white ways, would we live through the poison they were making?

Many people forgot what it was to be New'e. They gave up. I can even say this happened in some ways to Sagwich. Later, in 1873 he became one of the Mormons, wearing a strange white cloth and humming their strange songs. He lived in a square wooden house and shit in a small wooden house. We became proud to be called a Church Elder. He remained my friend, but I could not visit him there.

I understood these people that stopped being New'e. They, too, had the bell in their heads. I understood they did not know how to be Shoshone anymore. The springs were drying, the tribes were fighting each other, wildlife moved from usual paths, and the buffalo were being killed as if the herd were one animal, by men with new guns.

We could not travel or meet in our usual places any longer. Some took opportunities to live a new kind of adventurous life among the soldiers as scouts, fighting alone among tribes they had never even heard of, traveling on floating boats to white places, and wearing white man clothes.

Many besides Sagwich turned to the religious ways of white men, since it was assumed their spirits must be strong to allow their people the many riches and useful goods and strange ideas. Some New'e became fighters, rallying around more warlike Chiefs like Pocatello. All tried the ways they could, most only to come back to the old Shoshones broken and lost; then to leave again for the whites when they became hungry or wanted whiskey.

We came to know that the white men were also involved in a great war with each other far away. It seemed the whole world was ugly, violent and turbulent. Injured soldiers, bad men running from their people, and even bad women, would come to our western places talking of President Lincoln and nigger slaves rising up, and of huge armies of white soldiers marching to kill each other at places called Bull Run and Chickamauga and Fredericksburg.

At the end of this war, we saw more and more and more of these people with tattered, bloodied, smelling woolen army clothes. The soldiers were very mean, as if possessed by bad spirits. We heard many stories of the horrors they brought with them from the hang-around-the-fort New'e. There were many new and dangerous people who came to our lands. These were far worse than the Mormons. They carried evil and war. They stunk of hatred. They carried ghosts of the dead and dying on their shoulders and in their pockets. Just seeing one of these could endanger a Shoshone spirit so many of us hid away in remote places where we could try to ignore their bad medicine.

Some of these bad soldiers found us in the Owl Creek Mountains and pointed their guns at us. The soldiers told us we must move to the white fort, among Washakie's people. We broke our traditional camp. We did not want their anger so pulled our lodges behind our dogs and horses to the white mans' town.

Once there, we lived among soldiers, half-breeds, other Indian men who were scouts for the soldiers, preachers who talked of "a new lord named jesus", mountain men and rough hunters bringing giant horrifying loads of buffalo skins, Mormons, whisky traders.

This was a dangerous time and we often meekly did as the soldiers told us to do, or we would be killed.

What bad place did they come from and why did they bring their bad ways to our lands? After Bear River I did not trust these people and stayed quiet so as to be left in peace in my new life with Coneflower, Bent Foot Healer, and Lupineflower. I pushed my anger away. For the sake of my new family I decided to live in peace as Washakie encouraged. I saw those who chose to fight die but accomplish nothing. I saw that killing for revenge or anger would not help my children.

In that winter and most winters after that, we stayed with a growing group of Shoshones now led by Washakie, who the white men thought was Chief of all Shoshones. Now we had a "reservation", but even here, Mormons and cowboys and miners were found behind every hill. The old places were all gone.

That is all.

Story #27 CROWHEART

{The "Battle of Crowheart Butte" happened in 1866. It was only a few years after the Treaty of Fort Bridger. The New'e were told by the army where they could go and hunt and live. However, there was much confusion. The army would explain boundaries to the Chiefs using metes and bounds and latitude and longitude. At that time, Indians did not appreciate boundaries at all, as the land was open to everyone, as long as they respected other tribes' ability to hunt. Of course, Indians had their own names and descriptions of places that were not considered by white men. Certainly the old Indians did not understand the white men's maps. This story shows how white men's ideas created disputes and troubles between Indians.}

Even though the white men were becoming a bigger presence around the reservation, we were still left most times to resolve our tensions in our old ways; like this story I will tell you of Crowheart.

This happened at the height of the time the soldiers from the American war were entering our lands. These soldiers brought with them many troubled war spirits from lands in the east, and these Spirits came also to our people and made us fight each other. At this time the white soldiers were so accustomed to fighting that they did not know how to live without this way. They came and made many forts within our hunting territories. The forts could have been for trade, but there were many soldiers who ominously fired their fancy guns and rode good horses and kept traders out except on trading days so they could build themselves up as fighters. I tell you it is strange to be a friendly person and have fighters move among you for an unknown reason. It was told our people saw them even fighting with their women and striking and hurting them in anger. This is not our way and would be a great shame for New'e. The soldiers were dirty and wild and seemed to want more than they could ever use, be it of buffalo or plants in great rows or trade goods or animal pelts or even women and whiskey. Their women seemed frightened or damaged and mean.

I told earlier of the Ft. Bridger treaty made in the white man's year of 1863 by the army and Washakie and other Indians to try to allow Shoshones to keep a true place of our own. But even on its first day the new treaty did not do this. In part of this treaty the Absaroka, or Crow Indians were ac-knowledged to have hunting rights down into what was traditional New'e lands. Washakie's bands hunted buffalo to the north across the Yellow-stone River one summer and went into these traditional Shoshone lands now shown to be for the Crow on white man's maps.

Camping on the way from this hunt, he heard of a large band of Crow, lead by Big Robber staying on these traditional Shoshone lands. Washakie sought to warn Big Robber away and sent a messenger to tell him to go away from these Shoshone hunting grounds. Big Robber did not listen and with a head full of big thoughts and white man's maps he instead killed Washakie's messenger.

Washakie's men, and a band of Bannocks who were camped fur-ther south along the Popo Agi River grew angry and went to Big Robber making a horrible battle lasting five days and five nights after this killing of the messenger. This battle left 50 of our warriors killed and over 100 Crows dead. Washakie decided to end the battle before all of both bands were dead and only children were left to care for themselves. Washakie also wanted these good lands back that white soldiers had, in their ignorance, partitioned to the Crow. These matters were Indian matters and should be decided in the Indian way.

So Washakie challenged Chief Big Robber to a man on man fight to the death. It was agreed that their fight would take place on horseback with lances and shields, well away from the rest of the people so that no others could interfere in the battle. The people from both tribes gathered to mourn their dead. I came with Coneflower as her brother was badly injured and died of puss and swelling around an arrow wound some days later. We watched from far away, looking toward the butte on the horizon, until only clouds of dust could be seen. After many hours, Washakie emerged from the distance: bloody and missing his ear, and very tired. His strong arms were streaked with sweat and dust and burned by the sun. His horse was said to be wounded in the neck and would die that day but faithfully finished this fight. Washakie had killed Big Robber by first wounding him with a lance to his right side, which caused him to fall from his horse. Then by giving him over 25 blows to his head, each after the other to make him fall. Big Robber did not fall for much time. Washakie was weary of this awful death, but it was required so he continued until Big Robber fell and did not again rise up.

Since Washakie came to know Big Robber as a courageous and strong man he did not scalp him. He paid an honor to him and instead cut out his heart and placed it on his lance. Washakie showed this heart to the assembled peoples. All agreed the lands were again Shoshone, including the bluff overlooking this battle, called now by the name "Crowheart".

This Indian fight made Washakie a revered man at a time when many New'e thought of him as a chief who only wished for personal presents from the white men. The New'e were frightened, angry, suspicious and divided about the soldiers and the Mormons and the government men that first took small nibbles out of our way of life then took large and horrible bites that left our way of life without all of its limbs, or all of its head or its usual way of reproducing.

Over the remaining years of his life, Washakie stayed there at the place recognized by the white men. Later the white men even changed the name of Fort Brown to Fort Washakie. For the next few years, most Shoshones continued to roam in out of the reservation, especially in summer. This was a time when we did not truly know if we could remain Shoshone or if we would do as the white man wanted. Eventually, the army stopped all Indians from leaving the reservation, unless special papers allowed a particular person the permission to go. We hate those papers.

That is all.

Story #28 PLAGUE OF INSECTS THAT WERE MEN

White men were like a plague of many insects. At first a few of them were interesting and unusual. Then more came and began to sting and itch, but we could cover ourselves in bear fat or move away. Then more came and the bear fat did not matter and there was no other place to go to avoid their bites. Then whole swarms came. The mere living of these ignorant creatures killed whatever thing they landed upon. I know of these insect problems. But real insects would destroy something, then they would die away and everything would heal back to what it was. These big white insects did not die or go away or allow the Earth to go back to what it was.

Their killing of our way was done in a sly way, like the altering of Mother Earth for their own purposes like farming, making permanent buildings and forts and then towns, and moving whole streams and rivers so that the fishes and beavers and wild game died from thirst. They also swarmed upon us and killed us in straight and not sly ways. They took our way of life by their numbers. We did not know how to stop any of these things.

In the early days our people would like to say that when white people come, you run away, you hide, you get away. They are going to get you! If an older troublemaking boy would want to frighten a child he would say, "It's getting dark, don't go out, the white people will take you away." We were terrified and all people responded to this terror in different ways. We were right to be afraid.

The most damaging effect of this swarm of white people was not the changes to the Earth or even the killing of our people with guns and rape, but was the stealing of our lands and forbidding us with a punishment of death of men, women and children from going to places we had relied upon for our seasonal way of life. At first this appeared to be something we understood from our constant battles with other Indian peoples; fighting or negotiating would happen that would identify who could hunt in what places. Then it became something else.

With the treaty made in the white man's 1863, in the summer after Bear River, New'e were told that to avoid other fighting and killing, and to promote peace, they must stay on a reservation. They divided up our former lands with boundaries for places of Colorado, Utah, Idaho and Wyoming. This was not believable to me because many of the places I had gone to as a child to the west of this reservation were places I was now not supposed to go. It simply was not imaginable.

But the "large reservation" did not last very long. White men became interested in the tar places and oil seeps and coal outcrops that Indians had used for keeping warm and for many other purposes. Men came to dig the coal. They said the tar and oil showed that other white man wealth was maybe under the ground. More farmers came too, digging water diversions and tearing trees from the ground.

Only five winters later, when the swarms of white people had grown more dense, the government came to Washakie and also to Pocatello, who had lost many of his fighters and was ready to stop the dying of his people, to say to us that they were taking more of our land. Pocatello would stay in a northern place for his people. Washakie must have convinced the army soldiers not to bring Pocatello to his home at Wind River, as they were never friends and this would cause problems for Washakie who was favored by the soldiers. We did not think this lessening of our land could be done, because all the lands were always Shoshone and never the white men's that they could "give to" us. So they said to this that we Shoshone would "cede" nineteen of the twenty-one bites of this land to them. They were stealing our home and leaving us one bite in the north for Pocatello and one bite in the south for Washakie, but there was nothing we could do.

They said that now, this final place in the north, Pocatello's one bite of Earth, which white men called the "district of country" was in the treaty for us to be "set aside for the absolute and undisturbed use and occupation of Shoshone Indians." No non-Shoshone person would be even able to pass over, settle upon or reside in this place. They gave Washakie and Pocatello and the other chiefs a paper to put their mark on, and the white men put their mark on this paper. But there were other marks on the paper too and we did not know what those marks said. I saw this paper. It was small and white but it was a very powerful medicine that made us no longer New'e, even though almost all of us then were old time Shoshones with traditional ways. While these areas were good hunting lands with many forests and some of our sacred places, we were nomadic people. This was prison for us. We were no longer to be free to leave, and we could no longer have our New'e life. So many continued to ignore this and to travel, but in much smaller groups, and for shorter times. Others stayed with Washakie and Pocatello.

This treaty had new laws for other Indians, too. The Arapahos, our long time enemies, lost the lands they had bargained for in the south, with the Cheyennes. They did not have strong a chief as we did. We did not think at the time that this was our problem, but it would come later to be very bad for us. Now my family is tied to these pitiful Arapahos.

Many sites sacred to me where I would go to pray were in these places where whites could now "homestead". I found though, that in those first years after this reservation was made, I could still go to most of these places if I was careful because these places were dry and far and few white men went there and then only to chase their big stupid cows. I could take my family and make a lodge here, but needed to go as if hiding.

Most New'e that were my relations did not move to the reservation, but chose to stay in these places, hiding like rodents in lonely existences for a time, then forgetting the silly wishes of white men and going back to our old ways until we were reminded in some way that this was dangerous. Many Indians were shot at, all were looked at and kicked like dirty dogs by white men. But this did not change our dances around the fires at night before hunts or travels. Our songs and drums and whoops were strong and loud and powerful. Our spirits were made strong through these important rites.

We could not travel easily to seasonal gatherings as in old, so we lost this part of our tradition. In later years, I chose to go with my family to the reservation because these people had become my family for many years and my wife and daughters still could live among all those they loved. We began to have summer and winter gatherings like old at those places approved by white men.

Washakie became very clever. Washakie tried many ideas. Many thought that learning more of white man's ways would help our children. Some saw that many of their ways were good and so we need to have our children understand how to live among the changes. In another such idea, Washakie promised that the New'e would become Mormon farmers. He negotiated for farmer-teachers and seeds and water-ways. Washakie talked to us of owning and herding cattle. This was not our way and many New'e laughed at Washakie. Some tried but this did not work out well.

That is all.

Story #29 CELESTIAL CHINAMEN

We were not a people that knew to stay in any one place, even if soldiers wished it. In the summers, we would sneak away from the reservation. We went to some of the old places and had hunts and gathered plants. We were now about ten people with many dogs and sometimes a horse or two. With Coneflower and our daughters, we had her brother and his wives and their children. Shoshone children always belonged to all of us and we did not make differences between those children of our own seed and our brothers'. To avoid the army, we often stayed in the very dry places east of the Salt Lake that I knew how to live in from my childhood.

There I began to dream of another kind of man. One day, in a larger camp, I heard of such men; with small backs, strange clothes, and bringing with them a long ribbon of iron from the west. These were not the white men. They came with white men, and were even more strange to us. They were slaves of the white men; driven by white men in a way that was maybe more frightening than our passive resistance to their dominance. We were perplexed that these men had agreed to this slavery and submitted to it willingly with horrible hardships.

These were very small dark men; almost the size of children, with slanted eyes. They brought strange medicine that disturbed my sleep and I could smell their strange cooking before I ever saw one of them or understood what they were bringing.   heard that some men meeting my dream description were moving in a large group, swinging shovels and axes and beating the ground. New'e called them "Celestials". I heard them coming to our lands from the west. This was backwards because most new men came from the place of the rising sun; not from the West. These men came with a sharp, metal hammering of iron; a drum-beat of unstopping sweat and strife, driving metal, which I could not understand from so far away. They shook the ground and made deep sharp pings in my head. It grew closer and closer. I believe I know the date these Celestials entered Shoshone lands, and the day I finally saw them and knew what all the noise was to be.

As I could hear these things in my dreams, and heard others tell of them, I went in search of these men. One evening I saw them on the horizon. A large camp of people were trailing behind them two perfect long metal ribbons with the ground scratched to dust where they had been. As they moved they seemed to generate these ribbons as an animal generates tracks. I watched them and saw these small Celestials being driven by white men on horses and making a horrible labor from sunup to after sun down. They had mules that were moving large square tree wood, strong heavy metal, and then spiking these pieces together to Mother Earth to form this new set of iron and wooded tracks that would never blow in the wind. On these tracks were large carts pulled by mules with whole camps moving behind. This was a new way to move a camp: to make tracks in front, and pull the camp behind. We New'e did not know the meaning of this track and talked many hours about what could be this purpose, since moving a camp could not take so much work and permanence.

Some young Shoshones said that a large smoking bear would come on these tracks and eat people and things and take them back away along these tracks. We did not see this as good and wondered why the small slanged eye peoples would wish to bring this large smoking bear.

One dark night, I was in my summer camp far away from the Wind River and back in our old traveling grounds near the salt lake. I was squatting and eating a meal of kamas {kamas are root vegetables similar to potatoes. They were the staple of many traditional diets} and pheasant that Coneflower had made when one of these small Celestial men was brought to us by one of our young men who had found him half dead in the desert. They gathered some of our most senior people who were camping close to us. The senior people included me since I was becoming an older person among our people. It was known that I had dreamed of these men.

This man was very sick, starved, and with many painful and bloody whip marks on his back. He was going to die and spoke with some white man's words that he wanted to die by Indians rather than die by white men, and his only wish was to have a taste of food before we killed him. I had no desire to kill him after seeing his bravery in death and knowing what I did from my many months of dreaming. The other men left him to me. Coneflower brought him to our lodge, and laid him in our tepee and gave him clean water and good strong kamas stew and the man slept. I watched his face go from lined and old and dirty with sweat and grief, to accepting of any fate that should come to him. Eventually his face became as soft as my daughter's in his exhausted sleep. I came to see that he was a very young man, perhaps twenty summers. I watched him sleep for many hours, then Coneflower cleaned him and woke him to drink, then we left him again to sleep. I smoked outside the tepee for two days waiting to see what the Celestial would say and do. Camping Indians moved closer to us as everyone wondered about this man and the bear tracks he was bringing across New'e land.

Finally he came out of the tipi to make water, and not knowing our way, stumbled around until a young girl in our camp showed him where to go, with giggles and nudges. He came back soon looking very frightened, certainly not knowing if we were now going to kill him or if we would feed him again. It was up to me to decide what to do with him, and the New'e knew I would not hurt him but would talk to him probably for a long time. He did not know this, however. Coneflower brought him to me. He was expecting his death with his head low and his eyes on the ground in a respectful way. I saw these things and bade him smoke. He did this, slowly, seeming to know what to do, but coughing at my tobacco. He spoke some white words, so we brought out a talker of English who would give his words to me. This is how I came to understand the clanging and banging of the iron ribbons that I had been hearing in my head for all this time.

He told me how his work was the rail road. This was a hard metal track pounded into the ground upon which a huge thing, which was not a bear, would go both forward and back. I could not understand what this "train" might be, but he indicated it was not alive, and at first confused in the translation, it seemed he was saying it was a thing that was dead. We wondered why white men would bring a large dead thing across the lands and go to such trouble to bring the Celestials here to make it possible. Then we came to understand that this train was made of the same iron as our kettle and would bring many things here from far away and take back many things to distant lands.

These Celestial men resembled some of our southern Shoshone, but still were quite different. They came from across the great sea in the west. Many celestial men from his place across the great sea left their mothers and fathers and came on a very large boat for many months to work on the rail road. Our celestial came with six brothers and two of them died on this boat from lack of food and water. He was very sad of this, and did not seem to understand how his hunt for this good thing in his future had gone so wrong. Then the living ones got here they began working as slaves for the white men putting the metal and wooden tracks all the way from the great sea to some place far into the East. Some white men did not want them doing this work because the white men could be paid more dollars if the Celestials did not do the work for fewer dollars. Those were the men that had almost killed him.

They worked from before sun until after stars without resting. They were given water and food but they missed their dead ones and wanted only to make "three hundred dollars" to go back home and marry their women. I questioned him many times about the "three hundred dollars", and why women would want this, and we looked at each other and both knew our words were not enough to make an understanding, but we both knew that we did not and would not ever know each other. This man tried to run away from the rail road after another of his brothers had died in the winter, and other men had caught him and whipped him and tied him to a tree. He escaped after many days and then was found by the men from our camp. He wished that we would kill him but I told him I would not do this as he was now familiar to my family and he should stay with us.

The name which he called himself was Yu-yuan and he said he came from a place called Shan-hi. We called him "Tiny Man from the across the Western Sea". He lived with us all summer and when we moved our camp to go east, he joined with some mountain men who were going west to California, near that sea. He wanted to go back toward the western sea, and start again to get his "three hundred dollars" so he could go eventually to find a woman back in his home. He also wanted to look for his other two brothers who were still working for the white men on the tracks. I told him to find a woman near the sea and stay on our side of the sea. I believe he may have done this but I did not ever see him again. He was the strangest friend I ever had but I am very proud to have his memory. I made for him a strong walking pair of moccasins which he wore with pride when he went away.

We listened with interest to the stories told by others of the tracks coming closer and closer to our home. Then we learned that another set of men, this time soldiers left from the white man's war and also some "I-rish" men were building a track from the east. They were also moving towards our lands to meet up with the tracks coming from the west.

We had jokes that these men were to bring dead things from both sides to fight here on New'e lands, and to eat and kill the Indians. These were uneasy jokes because we did not know if they were really to be jokes in the end. I wondered if the I-rish men knew that the Celestials were also building a track and whether we New'e should tell them that trains were coming on these tracks one day too.

Then we heard a story that the two sets of tracks were going to meet, each with its own train somewhere near the salt lake. I was very curious about this dead train, as we came to call it, and I took a horse on a journey with two of my friends to see one and to determine whether it would harm us. We went very far to the east, farther than I had ever gone in that direction. We hid away from all people until we came to the tracks. We could see them extending forever into the east. They were hard and frightening in their perfection. The wooden boards were so numerous you could not count them and they were firmly attached to the Earth, as if they had grown there by will of the Creator. But they were straight and perfect, and I saw them converging towards themselves in the distance; but never meeting where we could touch them. What medicine was this magic?

Then as we followed to the north of this track, going days to the east, we came to a settlement where the I-rish were working. Near this town, we felt a rumble and thought we may see a great buffalo herd. But this was different and we could see grey, not brown smoke coming from the East in equal puffs, like our signals, but moving closer.

First we heard it in the distance softly but insistent, then louder and louder. We could hear, "Huffahuffa, huffahuffa, huffahuffa, huffahuffa, huffahuffa ...." The "huff" sound was much like a buffalo's breath when listened to up close. But this was not a living "huff" because the sound was so perfectly spaced and building upon itself.

We went to the top of a small rise to see better and then we saw the train, extending behind the black puffing smoke through the grasses. It was not one large bear-like being, but a long snake with a black and red head. Its legs were round and made a constant drumming that grew so loud we could not imagine it. Huffahuffa, huffahuffa, huffahuffa, huffahuffa, huffahuffa ...

Then it passed and we saw two men sitting easily within the train, riding on it. Again the medicine of this wonder amazed us, and we saw cannons riding the train, and many houses in which people or other things may be coming. I then understood that this train was not a bear or a dead thing, but a road; much like the dirt road that brought their stage coaches and mail riders. This road was under the control and dominion of these white men and their trains could come among us many times bringing huge amounts of people and their things. The huffing train disappeared into the west, toward ancestral New'e lands.

I hated this in many ways. I was jealous of the mastery of such a powerful thing by the clever white men. But I was also impressed and awed at the same time by this idea. I secretly fell in love with trains. If I had been honest, I would have wanted to take a ride that first day on a train.

Yu-yuan's railroad changed our way forever. I was proud of our part in knowing the builders of these magical tracks. We knew the importance of the three hundred dollars and the difficulties these small Celestials made in doing this. We also saw this strange and amazing thing as absolutely thrilling but also terrifying since the quiet of our lands was always now to have these strange sounds and be marred with this destructive snake. The once quiet and the natural sounds of the Earth and its creatures were truly gone.

Many did not understand these things until the great bear-train finally came. Yu-yaun told us of trains but many New'e did not believe his words until it was time to see the first train come on these tracks that met from the west and from the east. My family and I wore our best clothes to see the day of the meeting of the tracks. In the spring-time of that year, 1869, many important white men came from all around to see the "golden spike", which was the last nail to be placed in the track. This spike was to be made of gold, the shining favorite possession of white men. I hoped to see Yu-yuan wearing my moccasins, at the golden spike, but I did not. Many other Celestials were there and I hoped Yu-yuan's two remaining brothers were there and would get their three hundred dollars so they could go to Shan-hi and marry their women.

I watched the proceedings from a distance with our whole family, but some Indians were at the front of the view. There were many speeches and tents with good smelling foods and ladies in bright amazing colors wearing beautiful bird tail feathers I had not ever seen before on their hair which was woven tall on their heads with little boxes of fine colors. We were near enough to see that the man to drive the last spike was not a Celestial, but was a big man in a dark suit. He was laughed at by us New'e and by many of the white men because he swung the big hammer but missed the spike all together. They brought in others to finish the job for him. Then two trains, polished and shining and huge nudged toward each other: HUFF... HUFF... HUFF...HUFF... so the men riding them could touch. The loudest blast of their whistles introduced us to an unforgettable and shocking call.

This unnatural discordant piercing scream accompanied by the rhythmic huffing thunder of the train moving became a far away cry that would break the sky from great distances all through the rest of my life until even today. It was much like the clanging bell from the time of the great death, which now is faded but still known to me. I sometimes wonder if this train's sound is heard by all or just heard by me and other Indians, as was that horrible bell on the frozen bad day at Bear Creek? I think this sound is heard by all.

It took a while for trains to be a frequent occurrence, at first when they would come, their cry would be heard far away and many Indians would get up from their moccasin making, cooking, weaving, or even leave their hunting to go to watch the trains pass. It was a horrible and fascinating thing.

Our children were young at this time. It comes to me now that they would never have known any time on this Earth before the trains and their cries and their magic. They did not know only the sounds of birds, wind, insects, storms, and New'e laughter and song. Their ears were always full of white man sounds that washed away the softer but more powerful whispers of the Spirits that were found on the air.

Lupineflower may have become a Mormon and changed her name to Helen in her later life for this reason. They may have made her forget she was a Shoshone. Is this why she went for the white man's God, because she did not hear our Spirits anymore? Every new thing brought by white men created for us many unexpected results.

That is all.

Story #30 CLEVER TRICKS

I see Washakie's talk of farming and reservations and Mormonism now as clever tricks and a wise thing because white men saw Washakie as an Indian who would try to take their advices and do as they said. I do not think he ever meant to do more than pretend to do these things. He was not a Chief in our way, he was a chief in the way that he tried to protect what New'e ways he could by being friendly and tricking the white men. He used the best of the New'e, and the best of the white ways and got on very well with us all, eventually he lived in a white man's house with his many wives and children and wore a white man's hat and sat in a chair to eat his food rather than squatting as I had known him to do as a young man and as the great chief of Crowheart when we did not know he would come to be this kind of a chief in between whites and Shoshones.

I was becoming an elder among my people, too, only because so many of our old ones were dying. The children that stayed with me and Coneflower at one time counted eight, as others died more frequently and the children were welcomed at our lodge. It is good to have many little ones with the camp to bring laughter and small smiles in all times. These children were carriers of Spirit and were many times stronger than our medicine men. I kept my wife and these children as far as I could from the changes and threats of white people and the other bad things I had known. It became more and more difficult to do this.

What once seemed like such a rich and varied New'e home, now dwindled to small areas where we could go to be safe and New'e. As a traveling people, we could no longer easily walk from one place to another stopping at good water places, warm bath places, berry spots or hunting areas. These places were covered with farms or had no water or were trampled and scoured by white man's cows and sheep. We were hungry and there were no longer good ways for us to remain outside of the changes around us. While I remained quiet, my wife Coneflower did not have this way and was cheerful and happy to talk with strangers. Lupineflower followed her mother in this.

More and more we stayed in the Wind River with Washakie's people. Washakie had carved away a place New'e could be away from the white men, for the most part. There, we camped in good hunting grounds, however we more often ate prairie dogs, pheasants, and caught fish and roots and berries, instead of finding buffalo. This food did not bother me as I lived most of my young life eating in this way. Many others were angry that many of our traditional buffalo hunts were against the army rules and that buffalo were more scarce when hunts were allowed.

That is all.

(Note from Sugar: I have known Washakie for many years as he has many occasions to visit at the agency with the government officials. I am sometimes called in to be an interpreter at these meetings, especially when other Indians come who do not have Washakie's gift of English. I see Washakie as a smart man with many clever tricks, just as Grandfather has said here. I also remember the story of Crowheart when I see Washakie in these white man meetings and I know that Washakie is more than what these white men see.)

Story #31 NOT KNOWING HOW TO BE SHOSHONE

The young ones, especially the boys growing up without long walks as I had, had fewer places to go to be New'e, so they began seeking horses and talking of killing soldiers. Some went in to the mountains to trap for hides. There were fewer hides to find. These young men did not have the knowledge of my fathers any more. These young men were not like we were: naturally quiet and respectful during the day, but showing their pas-sions in the night-time dances before hunts.

These boys were mostly very disappointed that they could not find animals in their hunts or in traps. So they sought whiskey and guns. They became rough and were scouting for the soldiers and trading in skins, and hunting for whiskey rather than hunting to provide life for their families. They sought money and coins. They began trading, in order to trade for other things, that they could trade for only to drink it all away in evil medicine whiskey.

I did not see this crazy circle as providing these men anything but dirt in their mouths. Medicine men were called in sometimes to cast out the Bad Spirits that made them do these things but we saw that they would all just become dizzy someday and die with a bullet or freeze away in the cold of a whiskey dream as strangers to their people. Every time one of these men did these things, or their women sold their bodies to have this whiskey, they took some of the New'e Spirit away with them and the rest of us be-came smaller and weaker.

Many of us old ones tried to teach these boys to be good New'e men with songs and drums but they only turned their faces and laughed at us. They were hurting inside with hunger and with a vast disappointment in where the New'e were going but they did not know what to do. I believe that they will someday wish they had listened to our knowledge. This wisdom may come too late for these boys.

That is all.

Story #32 GHOST DANCES

The buffalo were still to be found but not in the herds that covered all your sight as when I saw them as a child. It was common to see white people about but I still did not bother with them, except to have my wife trade for coffee and a new black kettle. Many people were hungry. Many people were lost. New'e were grieving for so many dead and for the animals and plants that were no more. To tell truth is to say that I too was afraid of the changes. I often became unhappy. When I was unhappy, my foot caused me great difficulty with its Bad Spirits of pain and trouble.

Puhugan began to interpret what had gone wrong. One of the Pai-ute Medicine Men, Wodziwob, known to the whites as "Fish Lake Joe" started the Ghost Dances. He was told in a dream that we New'e had failed in our ceremonies to honor the Spirits and that a new dance would bring back all our dead ones. He promised that this Ghost Dance would wipe the white men away and would return us to our known way of life. The Ghost

Dance was based on a very old traditional dance known as "Round Dance" in which the people stand in a circle facing inward and dance together.

Coneflower and I did not go to these dances. They made me sad that people could not see that the changes had come and would not go away. We kept to the old traditions: praying, drumming, singing and every-day constant communion with those Spirits that I could see all around us.

Many people were desperate. They followed these Ghost Dancers, and walked from far away as in the old days to be part of them. These dances even brought different peoples who never danced together before into one place in the hope that they would restore our old ways. These dances began to frenzy many of the Indian people. Night and day they danced. White people became afraid of the dances and soldiers tried to stop them. They said they would make laws that would not allow the dance to continue.

The dance spread to other Indian people. The Lakota practiced the dance. After their Sioux reservation was cut into five small pieces and the Lakota were told they must become farmers. The Lakota were starving after even the white farmers could not grow food on the buffalo lands. The people turned to the Ghost Dance.

The white men were afraid of the dance and called in many soldiers. They tried to keep the people apart so they could not dance. In that winter {1890} soldiers shot and killed Sitting Bull, the great Hunkpapa Medicine Man, because he did not stop the dance. A few weeks later, we heard soldiers with rapid-fire mounted guns killed a whole camp of Lakota, mostly women and children at a place called Wounded Knee.

The dance was not working and many people gave up that hope, too.

That is all.

Story #33 AGENCY

Washakie continued to trade with white men. He and the other chiefs had constant dealings with the "Agent" who was the government man in charge of gifts, and all other parts of what they called the "Agency". Soon after we moved our camp there white men from Fort Bridger came for an-other big meeting. They wished to move the Bannocks to the area of the Wind River that had been promised to the New'e through Washakie.

This land had become the heart of where Shoshones felt safe, be-cause Washakie kept peace for us there. We often camped there, but most Shoshone people never stayed in a permanent way at this place until all the buffalo were gone, in 1885.

Chief Tahgee from the Bannocks was there for the government meeting and argued that his people should not be moved to the Wind River Valley. He and his people wished to have the northern kamas fields which were common digging grounds among those salmon eating people with the wet lands around the salmon rivers. This place is now in the land of Idaho. The white government agreed to give the Bannocks those lands in the future, but because the Bannocks would not move to Wind River, they decided to take some Wind River lands for new white people moving into the area. We know now that they thought that New'e areas should be considered Bannock, too. If Bannocks were promised a different area, then the Shoshones should get less. There were now Agents at each of the reservations for each tribe of Indians, who were in charge of the white man's side of these bargains. Suddenly, we realized a new person that we did not know was able to control our lands.

Later it was decided that white men would give Washakie's people more farmer-teachers and we would be required to break up the Earth and plant seeds and tend crops. Some Indians did this for a time. This was the white idea, not the New'e idea. I have never seen these things come to be for longer than a season. Mormon men also seek to make us tend crops, but since few Shoshone wished to do this, they bring new white men to our lands. The few Shoshone "farms" that are tried look to be ruined, forgotten places.

In any event, a few years later white man's buildings began to be built out of lumber with glass windows on the "Agency" at Camp Brown, which is what they called the place where our agent stayed. Soldier men came there with the Agents and their Lakota and other Indian scouts, and they tried to govern the ways of the New'e staying in that place. This place that was to be Shoshone lands for Shoshone people became crowded with white people, traders, other Indians who followed the soldiers, and then their half-breed families who were neither Indian nor not-Indian. These lost people drank whiskey, had fights, and made much trouble in a place that they should not be.

About this time, the government paid some church people to start a religious Christian school here at the Shoshone Agency. They had morning prayers and hymn singing. Some Shoshones went to these places to get food, but many Shoshones at this time kept their children with them as they tried still to hunt buffalo in small groups.

We enjoyed watching the white people try many things to make us into white men, but we mostly remained Indians, which made them angry like children not getting their way. Some Agents were kind and gave us gifts, but these gifts made people lazy. They sometimes saved us with their strange foods when we were very hungry due to bad hunts or natural weather or changes to the land caused by the white men. The Agent promised to be there always, with rations they called annuities, and some Shoshone believed this and sat down to wait. But these gifts did not come and if they did they were sometimes rotten or not good for us to eat. With these promises not met, Shoshones did not make farms.

In small things and in our Spirit Ways, we remained ourselves, but in large ways we did not know who we were any more. One time a soldier came to our camp and brought us corn, which we liked. They told me I could grow this corn from the ground. Despite their guns, I did not tell them that this was woman's work. I did not answer them at all and they decided I was stupid and went away. They thought most of our people were stupid since this is how we all dealt with these types of suggestions. But we knew it was not us who were stupid. We continued as best we could with our seasonal traveling and meetings, coming to the reservation in times of need for the poor food that was there, or to camp with friends, and then leaving if we could.

That is all.

{Note from Sugar: The original 44 million acres was soon clarified to be 3 million acres. Then, in 1874, about a third of the 3 million acres set aside to Washakie's band in the 1868 Treaty was "purchased" from the Shoshones. In reality, the government was trying to convince the Shoshones to farm and promised them better farming assistance and seeds and other "valuable consideration". In "exchange" they took more land.}

Story #34 BAPTISM

{Note from Sugar: One successful Mormon mission to the Shoshone of Wind River happened in 1875. That was a time when Shoshone people were truly stepping out of the old times, and into the new times. The great buffalo herds were gone, the settlers were arriving and staying, and the last great chiefs surrendered to the United States Army. I think this was a very sad and bewildering time for the old Indians. They struggled to know what to do.}

This story happened at the time that Coneflower was to have another child. *{Note from Sugar: I do not know what became of the child Grandfather mentions. Grandfather would not answer my question, so he or she must have died or perhaps Grandmother had a miscarriage. Grandfather is a strong and wise man, and he is very loving of children. He still grieves and will barely speak of his many children that did not survive. In his old age, he has only one daughter left. Besides me, he now has one grandson and to grandaughters from his living daughter, my aunt Louise, who was known as Bent Foot Healer.}*

My daughter, Bent Foot Healer, had taken a man named Arrow Shooter as her husband. She was carrying her son within her. My daughter with Coneflower, Lupineflower, was eight summers, a time when her New'e childhood songs had been sung to her.

Mormon people came among us at this time with new ideas to make us come among their people. They gave the New'e cows, which we killed for meat. Later, the Mormons just brought us the beef since they seemed surprised that we did not keep the cows for milk or for making more cows. Shoshones did not keep such animals in our homes but hunted and killed them. These animals were too stupid to hunt. This was still also a strange food, but since many were hungry, this strange food was good and we killed it to eat right away. We were angry when Mormons brought us only meat. It was rumored that they cast away the skins, bones, sinews and organs, which we needed for tools, thread, clothing, and many other things. *{Note from Sugar: The Indians thought the white men were wasteful and the Mormons thought the Indians were wasteful.}*

Then they came about with speakers of our language and invited us to become like them. They told long and strange stories that our people appreciated. Many agreed to partake in the Mormon rites, and to see what may become of them. I thought perhaps these Mormons had some magic that they would share with us to help us live in this new world so I watched to see if they would transform the New'e in a good way. They called this "baptizing".

The man Arrow Shooter was taken with the Mormons ideas. My daughter, Bent Foot Healer and my wife Coneflower wished to take this baptizing. I gave them my blessing because I did not believe it would do anything harmful. They would have some gifts that the Mormons had promised. Coneflower and our two daughters and Arrow Shooter went to the Mormons but I stayed at our lodge to pray in our way. They came later to our lodge with white cloth garments which were useful to screen dirt from water. They also brought other beautiful checkered cloth that made me a very nice shirt.

At the meeting they were put into the water and told they had become Mormons. The women and Arrow Shooter had taken new names. I do not remember the name taken by Coneflower, because she did not use it. My daughters took the white names Helen and Louise. Arrow Shooter took the name Edward Homena. They used these names when it suited them. I think they only thought of themselves in their New'e language. I saw that some of these New'e who took on the Mormon ways became fools. I did not like it. A large group of almost 200 New'e moved to a place they called Corrinne to live like Mormons, singing songs together and planting farms.

We stayed away from others like this when we could so that it did not cross into our ideas. We had summer and winter lodges which we allowed us to avoid white people and sing and dance with our beautiful drums.

I had to watch to keep away the many strange New'e. They were sometimes drunk and dangerous and more than once I ran them away from my family.

That is all.

Story #35 QUANAH

Frequently, good friends and pleasant visitors came to our camp. They kept us informed on the goings on of the soldiers, the Mormons and the other Indian peoples. In this way, in the year of my daughters' new names, we heard that the great Comanche Chief, Quanah Parker, our New'e cousin, had surrendered to the army. He gave up his fight to go to a reservation, as we had also done years before after the murder of so many of our people at Bear River had broken our hearts. Quanah fought the white people longer than any other Indians.

As long as the Comanches were still fighting on their New'e ponies and living in the Comanche way, we felt that the ancient Spirits were still with us all. Hope still rang for us to go among other New'e peoples and maybe live this way too. That would be better than living among whites and their strange narrow ways. But now that Quanah had given up, there were no people left to protect our old way. The path to return to that time was gone.

I went away to speak to the Spirits after this happened. I did not know if maybe the Spirits were gone, since so many other New'e ways were gone. I waited for some time then decided I must make a quest to see if all the Spirit People had also surrendered. Perhaps they had gone away to a new spirit world. Did the spirits move with the buffalo and the beaver to another place far away? Could they still hear my voice? I could not hear their voices on the reservation.

That is all.

Story #36 HOW I RECEIVED MY NAME

The skies were vibrant blue but winter could come at any time when I went to the Owl Creek Mountains, north and west of Crow Heart Butte. This was a sacred place where men did not go to live but only went to pray. My horse took me part of the way but then I went on foot after coming to the sacred lands. I walked with only my pipe and offerings I had brought. As I walked I sang old songs taught to me by grandfathers for only very important quests. I walked for two days and nights, seeing many tracks but very few creatures.

The mountains were strangely silent. It began to snow in large light flakes. I had missed the signs of this snow, which was contrary to all my New'e knowledge. It was to be a big snow. I believed this to be a sign that our spirits had stopped talking to me or were gone. I was now to be alone in our sacred places without ancestors' wisdom or connection to the living Earth. I left like a forgotten one in a strange place. Perhaps I would die here and go to live at the place with the old Spirits, perhaps the sprits would send me back to my family.

I built a traditional shelter for places of snow, and since I was fasting, did not gather many foods. I prepared to die, singing songs to ready my spirit. I slept. I awoke to look out from my shelter to see clouds parting and showing a black sky with clear stars, too many to count but telling the usual story of early winter. It was very cold. Breathing hurt my throat and froze the inside of my nose.

There was no moon so it was very dark. I wished for the insights of our old star tellers from my childhood. They would know the stories of these stars and what they foretold to me. In them, I saw only my own death and a cold knowledge that maybe I would walk among those stars soon, or maybe be forgotten by the old Spirits. I would be eaten by wolves and worms when they found me.

I huddled back into my shelter and pulled my robe against me and slept again as I had no desire or hope to fight the fate which had come. When I next awoke, my shelter was a dark cave. I was buried alive by snow and it was warm and comfortable since the snow kept out any wind or sound or colder air from outside. I pushed the snow away from my shelter and stood up to see shafts of dazzling, sparkling light.

I had made my shelter under the arms of a great pine tree. It was very cold beyond my shelter. The steep snow walls had built up to the arms of the tree, about the height of my shoulders. The snow was dry and crispy and light so that when I pushed it away, it floated about only to resettle back where it had been. I ate some snow but it did not quench my thirst.

I thought that if I walked into the wall of snow it would be as if into dry water, but I would not float, only sink beneath the powder. I stepped out into the snow to test this. My foot fell away into a deep place and my head disappeared into the white. I sucked fluffy snow into my mouth and I pushed my weight back to scramble and struggle to the tree well. Gasping, I could see nothing on any side of me but a wall of white. Above I could see the strong arms of the tree and blue sky with beams of light shining on sparkling drifting snow flakes blown from the tree high above. I began to climb.

The great tree clawed at me as I broke through the smaller branches to move upwards and outwards on the larger branches. As I rose above the tops of the snow, a stunning beautiful world of blue and white and silver appeared. The Owl Mountains were all around me, silent and sparkling. Trees were robed in white. Large outcroppings of rocks were mere mounds of white with brown and grey shadows. The sun was early in the sky. There were no clouds. No breeze moved the trees. All was still but for my shaking of the tree as I moved upwards, snow dusting and drifting down to poof softly on the snowy floor of the forest.

I made a comfortable perch in the tree and looked about. I would go nowhere for some time. I believed I would likely starve, or freeze or suffocate in the snow. I tried to sing a death song, but no Spirits were there to help me and I could not do it. I sat in a daze surrounded by terrible beauty. This was not a bad place to die.

As I sat, the tree began to shift around me. It moved without the force of wind as if I were a baby in this tree's arms. I imagined the tree growing around my bones and taking my life to strengthen its own. This would be a good gift. I was at one with the tree. I began to hear the tree's voice. Ib-ib-ige. Ib-ib-ich. It was the first voice I had heard on this quest. I listened. Ib-ib-ich. The tree began to shake and move, and other trees began to whisper Shu-shu-ich. Ib-ib-ige. Soon a large chorus of trees were singing, with some in deep voice and others in high voice. Some in discord, some in harmony.

The wind began to join. It moved the trees and blew whisps of dry snow. Its sad notes were added to the trees' song. The wind notes were from far away and sounded of mountain tops and high clouds. Soon there were windy buffets against the snow covered cliffs. Inside it all I could hear the trees song. This song was for me, and perhaps for the New'e brothers who would come after me, and the New'e creatures that shared this forest.

I understood what the trees were saying. They would be here! They would stay strong and more trees would grow! Those around them may change the forest, but would never take all the trees. I was told to go back to my shelter and warm myself in my robe and sleep under the cave of snow.

I awoke again to darkness of the snow cave. I could hear water running in many small creeks. This time the snow walls were harder. I broke through to a cloudy morning that was warm and foggy. The winds had brought warm air and low clouds. Almost half of the snow was melted and many crystal clear paths of water flowed under the hard crusts of snow. I dug down to them and drank thirstily. I splashed my face and purified myself in these blessed waters. Many of the small branches from my tree, probably those I had broken off as I climbed, lay dry under the tree branches. I made a small fire and lit my pipe. I smoked with the tree. Ib-ib-ich. Ib-ib-ich. My heart was light and the trees rejoiced in the glory of the beauty around them.

The fogs rolled and separated for some time. Later, as the day grew even warmer, they cleared to allow a beautiful sun and a warm day. The snow disappeared as if magic within one afternoon. I began to walk away from the magical place to begin my life as a new kind of New'e, a Shoshone of the Indian Reservation at Wind River. Ib-ib-ige.

I saw this beautiful world in a way of hope, rather than in the way of grief for the first time in many years. I realized that the world was quiet and still and the loud ringing in my ears from the clanging white man's bell was gone. The tree Spirits had spoken to me in their language. They said that the New'e would always have troubles, but their ways could be retained if we continued to remember that we are New'e. It was a wisdom gift that was given to me, a man with the age to understand these things.

I wanted all the young people to know these things! I took a new name so that all would know the sacred message. I was honored to be named "Trees Told It" after I told of my time with the trees to our medicine council. The messages of the trees were good and brought comfort to many of our people.

During the next summer after the Sun Dance, Bent Foot Healer had her baby for Arrow Shooter. He was a son and he was strong and very loud in his needs. He quieted very quickly when he was wrapped in the cradleboard. He loved to ride in that cradleboard tied to his mother's horse as they went about. As he was older, she would hear him laughing in beautiful baby laughs as if he were being tickled every time there was a fast sprint by the horse.

One month after Bent Foot Healer's son was born, Coneflower and Bent Foot Healer went on their horses to show this grandchild off to far away relatives at the government town where so many of our people stayed. We called this grandchild Rides in Laughter. The white Mormons baptized him too because both his mother and father had been baptized. The Mormons called him Thomas.

As I am old and now telling this story, my grandson, who I have now agreed to call Thomas, is the father of his first daughter who he has named Betsy, a white name. He is a good man who now is a strong Shoshone and carries one of the four sacred medicine pipes of the New'e. He is a Sundancer leader. I think we have taught him well to be a good Shoshone in these changing times.

That is all.

Story #37 ARAPAHOS ARRIVE

{Note from Sugar: The Arapahos moved to Wind River in 1878. Despite treaties saying the Wind River Reservation would be a permanent and exclusive home to Shoshones, even today the government has not kept this promise. Shoshones do not really blame the Arapahos for this, as we know they had no other place to go. But resentment still exists. These people were our enemies, and now they act as though they have rights to this land.

They have set up their own council to make decisions about this land. Shoshones refuse to listen to these decisions. The federal government does listen to these decisions, so we are all in a difficult position.}

Washakie made a great mistake that turned many Shoshones from him. He allowed some Arapahos to stay temporarily with Shoshones. Later, more Arapahos were brought to our reservation by the Army. At this time I was already a tribal elder. I was 53 summers. Most Shoshones died long before reaching this age, so I felt at the end of my life. At this time, we had moved to the Agency because Arrow Shooter wanted his wife and children to be among his people. We went there to be with our grandchildren, so I was able to watch much of these goings-on.

The Arapahos had many problems with the army. One year after Bear River, a large camp of Arapaho and Cheyenne had been massacred by the U.S. Army at a place called Sand Creek. We were very angry and sad that these people had also to experience this terrible thing.

They continued to be our rivals, however. In 1869, the Arapaho chiefs came to Washakie and (Medicine Man, Sorrel Horse, Little wolf, Back Coal, and Friday) unsuccessfully tried to make peace with the New'e. They had always fought against our people and we did not trust them. So they stayed for a short time then left.

The trouble which permanently brought the Arapahos to Shoshone lands started in Lakota lands. The Lakota, or Sioux as white men call them, were north and east of the Arapahos, who lived in what is now Northeastern Colorado, Nebraska and the Dakotas. The sacred Black Hills were being taken over by white men who lived rough and dug gold rocks from the ground. The Lakota fought this, but so many white men were not possible to stop.

These white men were ugly and hard and even the other white people did not like their ways. Some white religious people came to evangelize these miners into a better way of life, but the Lakota saw even these church people as further taking of their sacred hills. So the Lakota attacked the mining camps and were successful for a while at driving everyone away. They killed two older white church-women with a traditional warning, by driving spirit sticks into them, spearing them to the ground.

In about 1873, many "gifts' for Indians were promised from Washington. The Arapahos, many of whom were survivors of the horrible massacre by white men at Sand Creek, were camped near Fort Caspar, but the army told them to go to Milk River (near the Canadian Border in what is now Montana) and join the Gros Ventres people. The Gros Ventres were related to the Arapaho and spoke a similar Algonquian language, but smallpox broke out there. So the Arapahos stayed near Fort Caspar and many came to Fort Washakie for government business and to seek the promised gifts. The Arapahos were fighters and caused much trouble when they came here. We did not like them coming to our lands and they probably did not like coming among us either.

By the next year, they moved further north, into a narrow valley near hot springs at the Big Horn and Owl Creek Mountains. The Owl Creeks Mountains were Shoshone land and the Arapahos were massing with Lakota, Cheyenne and other Indians that did not listen to the white ways. We could see this would lead to no good for the Shoshones.

Those Indians started raids on our people. Our people were causing no harm to the white people, so the army defended the Shoshone. They took soldiers under Captain Bates to run these bad Indians away to the north. Many young Shoshones who were seeking fights went with Captain Bates.

On a hot summer day the Shoshone and army soldiers attacked the Arapaho camp. Our warriors fought in the old way with loud whoops and cries which distressed the army who was trying to sneak upon the Arapahos. The army's way is not the Indian way to fight and to drive the enemy away. The army's way is a cold-blooded way to murder. So the stories we heard then were of many dead, some soldiers, some Shoshones but especially Arapahos.

With the large guns of the soldiers, the Arapahos did not have a likely chance but they fought bravely. We know that the battle was won because Bates brought back 350 Arapaho ponies and a very large heard of cows. These Arapaho, of Black Coal's band, would certainly starve the next winter. Winning that battle had some bad longer term consequences for the Shoshone. Strangely, we were free of the Arapaho as long as they had their own hunting and way to survive. By taking their survival, they became dependent on the army, who were closest to them at Wind River.

After the army found that Shoshones were good fighters, and after they trained our men to fight more like white soldiers, the army wanted Shoshones to fight with them in other battles among other Indians. Many elders talked against this, but young men with nothing to do did not like this talk and sought glory in war. So in 1876 many Shoshones joined Gen Crook's army against Sioux at Rosebud. Our men were led by Wisha, Nawkee and Luishaw, a French half breed.

At about the same time, the Lakota killed the army's General Custer at little Big Horn. He needed to be killed as he was a bad man. He wanted only to kill all Indians to take all that we have. In 1868, Custer had attacked the Arapaho camp of their Peace Chief, Black Kettle. Custer burned the whole village and all the stored foods, killed all the men and many women, and herded the other survivors away to starve. Later, other Arapaho Chiefs Stone Forehead and Keeper of Sacred Arrows made peace with Custer to stop this horror, but it did not, until he was dead in the ground.

The fights over the Black Hills were lost by the Indians. This meant that the Arapahos also lost their claims to the Black Hills. The army promised them subsistence gifts. They did not want to live among the Lakota and sought a Wyoming reservation. To show their good will to the army, they scouted against the remaining hostile Sioux and Cheyennes. Arapaho Chief

Sharp Nose gave the President of the United States a peace pipe and to-bacco in the white man's White House in Washington, DC. The government wished that they should go to Wyoming, but the army did not want to make another reservation.

In early winter, Black Coal had 170 lodges of people with no food and nowhere to go. They were camped with some Utes near a buffalo herd that could save them for the winter, but they had no ammunition. Washakie met informally with Black Coal. Black Coal asked to join us at Wind River. His people always wanted fine Shoshone hunting lands.

Washakie, Norkok, Wahwannabiddie, Moonbabe and Wesaw all agreed to terms of peace with Arapahos. I also agreed to this peace so that the Arapahos would not starve. They were to have temporary residence on Shoshone lands. They rested, then went away, but they had no real place to go until they finished treaty making with the white men.

In 1877, a man named Irwin who was previously our Camp Brown Agent came to us and said he talked for the President Hayes. He said they did not want to put the Arapahoes on our reservation but only to make certain peace with the tribes. Washakie agreed there would be peace.

In March 1878, the Army brought Black Coal and his band of Arapahos back to Wind River under military escort saying we had made peace with them. This caused all Shoshones to become very angry and gather for a council. Washakie and other leaders loudly insisted they be taken away. The government men sent papers and wire talk to their chiefs in the east telling them the Arapahoes must be taken somewhere else, and pointing out that our treaty with the government required that our lands were for Shoshones only. No response came from the east.

Many more pitiful Arapahos straggled in. Black Coal again asked for a council with the Shoshones. He explained that they and their horses were weary and without food and needed rest and food, which the government had promised. They were starving and many were injured or had terrible infections and diseases. Many children had spotted sickness and adults had itches. Washakie agreed they could stay but must leave when they were rested.

They stayed in three settlements outside of Fort Washakie led by Black Coal, Sharp Nose and Friday. After the horrors they had been through, the Arapaho were very cooperative with the agents. They did not leave these settlements. This was different from the Shoshone people under Washakie, whose people were still coming and going, hunting and riding even though the white soldiers were trying to stop this behavior.

The Arapahos were also different in tribal structure, with many layers of their society. They had slaves that had been captured in battle or stolen in other ways who were not part of the tribe but were servants only. Shoshones always made all members of the tribe the same rank, perhaps since we so often went from band to band as we traveled in the old days.

This type of Arapaho society appealed to some white ways. By mid-summer, many Arapahos; White Horse, Six Feathers, Washington, Buffalo

Wallows and Eagle Head to name a few, had joined a white police force, which Shoshones did not want to do. No Shoshone would tolerate being spied on or ordered about by an Arapaho. This caused many problems between the people. Eventually some of these men were killed. I saw that all Indians were less than the greater power of the white people.

With all the new Indians brought to our reservation, the government agents decided that they must do a count. On one day, all Shoshones were ordered to come to the fort with our families. We were told to stay in a long line, and come forward when the agent said it was our turn.

Then, we were asked to say our names. After we told our names, which many refused to do because it is not right to say your own name, or when the white men could not write down the New'e name in their language, they gave us white names. Some of the Episcopalians were there and wanted to make us have names that would inspire us to become Christians. I would not say my name to them, so they gave me the name Jim St. James. I do not use this name. Coneflower was not shy with these government men and told them her name and the name of our daughter. They wrote in their book the names of Coneflower and Lupineflower. They could not understand Bent Foot Healer or Rides in Laughter. They wrote down Bent Foot Healer as their Mormon name Louise Homena, and Rides in Laughter as Thomas Homena.

The Arapaho did not leave. Soon, they were treated as if they were Shoshones. They were invited to government councils and allowed two times to approve sales of Shoshone lands. Later, when New'e were assigned allotments, Arapaho also were assigned allotments. This was against our treaty and created much mistrust. We have complained to the Agent but he has done nothing and blames the important men in the east. We have been cheated.

That is all.

Story #38 LUPINEFLOWER LEAVES

Lupineflower did not keep her New'e name much longer. I remember with tears the day my daughter Lupineflower left the Shoshone people.

In the old days, Shoshones were accustomed to family members going and returning during the times of life and the seasons and the travels. We were all part of the Shoshone Nation and we traveled in groups of lodges or in camps. Sometimes there were many and some times there were few. Our children were safe as they stayed with one of these camps. We generally knew where they were traveling and how they were faring from talk at gathering and from other traveling friends. In addition to our own children, we accepted into our camps as no different those of more distantly related birth and even strangers that were adopted as ours.

Once the white men changed our ways, people began to hold on more tightly to their loved ones. It was from fear of these unknown ways and of the danger that could come to anyone at any time that families stayed more closely together. Coneflower, my woman, also began to follow the ways of the Saints and to tell of Mormon beliefs of the afterlife. She told of the importance of the Spirit acting in this life in certain ways. Some of the Mormon teachings were very much the same as some of our teachings. We both assumed we would be reunited with our loved ones and would go back to our old ways after death. I saw other of these teachings as nonsense superstition but Coneflower was much younger than me. She did not have all the old teachings. I attempted to tell her my stories but it was too late to turn her from these Mormon thoughts.

So when Lupineflower was sixteen summers Coneflower found a Mormon husband for her. This man had a white woman already and many white children, including strong sons. That Lupineflower would be his second wife did not concern me because some Shoshones also had many wives. This showed the man's wealth and ability to care for a large family. I could only hope this family of Saints would be like our common families, joyful and cooperative and strong.

My other side of my thinking told me that this Mormon man was like other white men and did not speak truths. He told Coneflower that we Shoshone are their family, but I say this is just talk. When I invite people to my family, they have all the privileges of my born sons. This man took Lupineflower away and I know we will never be welcome there. He would not eat at our fire.

In the end, I agreed that this was to be a good thing. The man seemed to have much food to eat. He had many horses. I wanted my daughter not to worry for the troubles that were becoming more difficult every day for New'e.

In the moons after Lupineflower left to go away with this man, Coneflower changed. She became very fearful of everything. I think she was worried about our daughter. Heaviness settled over her. She stayed often in her bed. We had no little children in our lodge and would likely not know Lupineflower's children.

I too, was saddened about Lupineflower's leaving us. It also put me in mind of the other family I had lost at Bear River, when my woman was the laughing and pretty daughter of Sagwich. I thought again of our clever and brave son that she brought to me. I thought of our twin boys who died killing soldiers, even though they were only children. I thought of the unborn one who was frozen forever inside his butchered mother. How I would like to see them again! How I wonder what great men they would be if they were now with the Shoshone people. I can see the Twins as warriors. I see their strong faces as men in their prime with brown smooth skin and long flowing hair and many feathers from bravery. The clever older one who would maybe be a great Chief. The little one, who was maybe a girl, who would have sons of her own. I should not have thought these thoughts, as they did not honor the dead but only brought me sadness. I believe that their spirits may come back to guide later Shoshone people in our times of difficulty. But this did not lift the cloud from the skies above me.

Coneflower did not have the old ways of family around the camps but had a new way of family that came from the Mormons and other white men that put those you bore ahead of the whole Shoshone people. It made mothers less able to see their children grow up and find new families. It made women worthless when their mother time was over.

Coneflower grieved and sat moaning in her skins all day. Only three moons after Lupineflower left us, Coneflower died one night. I had no warning. She was just cold and still the next day in her furs. Bent Foot Healer and Rides in Laughter shrieked and cried and rolled on the dirt. My heart was dragging upon the Earth for a long time.

That is all.

{Note from Sugar: It breaks my heart to hear this story of my mother and grandmother. How I wish I had known my grandmother! She could have told me so many things I should know as a New'e woman. She sounds like such a lively and friendly person. How her happy heart would be welcome here now. I would care for her as I care for Grandfather. As Grandfather says, this way of thinking does not honor her, and only makes me sad.

It is my strong belief that my mother would have been happier staying as a New'e. I have been thinking that all Indian people now must choose how they walk at different times. We must sometimes act as white people, and then other times act as Indians. This is exhausting work. I see many of our people give up the Indian ways because it is now easier to act white. New'e are loosing their songs and their words.

Young ones are born without full knowledge of the old ways and sometimes they are punished when they act in the old ways. In school, children's hair is cut and they are made to wear white clothes. They are not allowed to speak New'e. Most important, they must sing the songs of white religions, and take on those beliefs. If they carry their medicine bundles they are punished. Men are told to farm. Women are told to have their babies in hospitals.

White people want us to be white, but they also hate us. They laugh at us. They will not give strong men jobs. They say we are stupid. They say we are dirty. They say we are drunks. We are not allowed even to vote because they say we are not citizens of the United States. White people treat us worse than dogs or mules.

Sometimes I wonder about my brother, George who went back to live with the Mormons in Cache Valley. Does he know he is New'e? He will

*surely grow up with nothing from his mother's people. I see that he may
have a very empty life, doing nothing but work.}*

Story #39 THE LAST BUFFALO

*{Note from Sugar: I have never seen my Grandfather as he was
during the telling of this buffalo story. He carries himself always as optimistic, dignified and calm. Grandfather keeps a smile on his lined and creased
brown face and twinkle in his dark eyes letting you know he will always be
ready to hear a good joke. But some Bad Spirit moved into him when he
talked now. He became both old and also childlike. He wept frequently. It
alarmed me to see tears moving down his face and dripping off his chin. His
voice became low and quiet. He paused often with a distant gaze. He
curled forward as his straight strong back turned soft, his chin almost touching his chest. Where I have ended this story he simply stopped talking,
without any customary conclusion. Then he lay down and went to sleep. I
feared he would not wake, but though I checked him often, he continued to
breathe softly. He clutched his medicine bag through the night. The next
morning he woke as usual and after drinking his coffee and enjoying his fry
bread with sugar, his back was again straight and his gaze on things of this
world.}*

Only two years after Coneflower walked on, all the buffalo were
gone.

For a long time after the first treaties with white men, Shoshones
tried to continue to live in the old way. We often came to the Agency in the
winter to camp, but this was in large part because the climate of the place
Washakie had chosen is generally warmer, less windy and has soothing hot
springs that make winter more comfortable for the people.

Many white men of all kinds had already moved onto our lands: soldiers, farmers, adventurers moving away from the bad white man's war in
the east, men driving cattle, traders, preachers, Mormons, and of course
their women (good ones and bad ones) and many other half-breed Indians
and Indians of other tribes who followed the white soldiers. There were now
almost as many Arapahos as Shoshone, but they lived among themselves
to the east of the Agency.

We Shoshone mostly stayed to ourselves to the extent we could do
that. The white farms, especially off the reservation lands, were slowly taking over native plant areas. Roads and irrigation ditches and then even
telegraph poles and rail lines cut across open Shoshone lands. Many white
men's cows wandered and ate grasses for free on reservation lands. They
ruined native plants and waters, but the government would not stop these

cows. We were often hungry and tempted to kill these cows for their meat and other gifts, but Indians could be put in white jails for this.

On the mountains of our reservation there were still many wild places where we could hunt deer, antelope, elk, rabbits, birds, and where there were many fish. We also rode our ponies in small parties to other wild places off the reservation to hunt or find special foods when they were in season. We knew where and during what seasons to find many food plants and healing plants, and honey and pine nuts and many other useful gifts from the Mother Earth.

White men wanted us to be farmers. They wanted us to sell what was grown for money and then use that money to buy food. Money is BAAH. It is a bad trick. Many people made some effort to do these things but it did not make sense to us when the old way was so much better and less of a difficult toil.

As time went on from the days of the first treaty to the days of the last buffalo, we had fewer places to go to hunt and there were fewer animals. As our ability to live in our old way disappeared under the plows and guns of the white men, New'e tried more and more to become farmers, and sadly to become more like white men, just so our children and women did not become weak and sick and die from starvation and diseases that we used to be able to tolerate when we were strong.

We were always taught to take only those parts of any herds or flocks so that there would always be more for the next hunt. We were to leave some of the berries for seeds and for the birds.

White men did not have this wisdom. Terrible buffalo skin hunters who shot buffalo for money began to come to the prairies. We called them "skin hunters" because they did not take the buffalo, only his skin, and sometimes his tongue or hump. They killed whole herds in sickening destruction that left all the meat and bones while Indian people starved. Worse, they left the buffalo's spirit naked and rotting on the prairies.

The buffalo did not know what this was. They did not run away at the sound of the guns, but moved toward their fallen ones, pawing and snorting. When given an enemy, buffalo are honorable. They fight until the last, but this did not matter when the powerful repeating guns allowed the skin hunters to shoot them all where they stood, confused and doomed. The bulls would be on the outside of the herd for protection, with the young and the females inside. But this did not matter, as this was not a hunt; but a horror. They would come back from these horrors with their special buffalo guns with lines of wagons piled high with skins. They sold the skins for many white dollars, then went back to destroy more herds of buffalo. There was talk of killing these men, but this was against our treaty and so we did not.

These skin hunters, in only a few summers, erased all the great buffalo herds from the lands of all the Indians. For these summers, we tried to carry on with our autumn hunts. It was not fathomable to us that all the buffalo could be in danger.

We would have our medicine men speak to the buffalo to know where they would be, then, we would begin the drums and pray and dance the night before the hunt in the old way to assure success and to honor the buffalos' spirits. Our whole villages would go on the hunt. In those days it was a merry and joyous time to be Shoshone as every person had a job to do in this important event. We allowed our fierceness and courage to come out in our screams and preparations around the fires. We knew we would feast well and have all the essential natural products of the buffalo to work into useful lodge coverings, sinews for our bows, clothing, tools, utensils, ropes, and those other traditional things that came from our brother buffalo. After the hunts we had much work to do to prepare all the gifts for use through the winter. We feasted on the hearts, blood and livers, dried meat, cleaned and prepared bones and sinews, boiled hoofs and horns. Women prepared the skins.

In the old days we would be able to ride our fastest ponies for five long days from the beginning of the herd to the end, almost one hundred miles of buffalo standing all together. In the early days after the railroad tracks cut the large herds into two (one in the north above the rails and one in the south, below the rails), hunts would find many thousand buffalo roaming together. We would take perhaps a five hundred, to sustain our tribe of over 1000 people staying at Wind River.

In later years, the numbers slowly dwindled. We would see perhaps one thousand buffalo, and we would take three hundred, which was not enough to provide food and clothing for us. Then we would see only two hundred buffalo and we would take one hundred, which only kept us from starving and required that we take white food from the government. In the years we saw fewer buffalo, we would see more and more rotting carcasses of their dead brothers spread along the plains. During the last hunt I attended, you could never stand in one place on the prairie lands and not see many dead buffalo carcasses and skulls. But you could see no living buffalo. The prairies were full of flies, disease and smelled of putrid death.

In 1885, our Shoshone clans hunted for the last time. We killed seven buffalo. These were the only buffalo that were seen that year, and since that time I have never seen another buffalo.

White men promised us beef supplies to try to make up for our lack of buffalo. Some of the treaties required the soldiers to provide us beef, flour, corn, coffee, sugar and beans. Beef was of poor quality and the people did not, at first, like it. Soldiers did not give us whole cows for us to take and use for all their parts, but only gave us pieces of meat and left the rest to rot in Earth graves the white men dug to put the cow carcasses. We did not want to hunt these cows, but we could have used all of them! We had no leather, liver, hearts, intestines, or sinew or bone.

Then as Shoshone became more hungry, we began even to crave this smelling beef. We needed more than was given us to not grow weak and to die. The white men told us to grow crops for making money for buying food. Many Shoshone men and women did this thing as they are hard workers and do what they must to feed their people. But this was not the New'e way. Many people worked very hard and then the crops did not grow, or did not produce enough to have any worth.

Shoshone watched even their horses starve in winter. The horses knew they did not have buffalo to chase! Indians ate them if they knew they would not have grasses. This was a terrible wound to many New'es' pride that we would be that low.

In the years after the buffalo were gone we went through many dark times. Shoshone were turning to white ways of farming and becoming Mormon. Many younger Shoshone went to Bear River and had a great Mormon baptizing in that river where their people had been killed. I had terrible dreams of them coming from this river dripping in blood and eating of the flesh of the old ones. How could those Mormon people do this?

All the people were malnourished. One winter many people died of measles and many more were sick and miserable. Others died of the same disease that later killed Lupineflower. It caused horrible coughs and again took most of our old and young. *{In 1897, fifty-two people died of these diseases.}* Very few women had healthy babies, most died within a few days of birth. Two other winters, le grippe *{This was influenza in 1889 and 1890}* took away many of our people. Those that did not die were stinking and skinny and wretched. A few tried to care for all the sick but it was hopeless and many weeks we only ate after traditional funerals.

When Washakie died, only a small portion of our Shoshone people were left alive. *{This was 1900. There were 841 Shoshone left here, and 801 Arapahos.}* When our wives, children, and parents and husbands died it was almost as bad as loosing the buffalo.

Now, the white men say we can no longer hunt off of our reservation. This is not often done anyway because the game is gone and the white men's cattle and farms are everywhere.

The white men tell us to work or starve, but there is no work. Some young men who can dig irrigation ditches or drive wagons do this when they can be paid for it. If we live on the farms they "give to" us, it takes many people four days of travel to come to the agency to get their annuity percapita rations. These rations are critical, although they are only a few mouthfuls every day.

Some people, like Sugar, work for the Agency. Sugar works for 25 white man's dollars each month, while most Shoshone people at the Agency work for less than ten dollars each month. People do what they can and seek out prairie dogs, grasshoppers, seasonal fruits and berries and hunt for small game in the summers.

Some Indians believed the buffalo went away to a place planned by their spirits, and that the buffalo would come out again upon some special medicine. Some medicine men told stories about how we must again do the

Ghost Dance to bring them back and have the white men disappear. I did not believe these things, for I noticed that we no longer saw the skin hunters' wagons piled high with skins on the way to the trains. This meant that the white men could not find the buffalo either. I believe the white men killed the buffalo to kill the Spirit of the New'e.

{Note from Sugar: I have never seen a living buffalo.}

Story #40 WALK

I have decided that tomorrow I will walk into the mountains to pray at a stone circle that is sacred to our people. The stars tell me the time is right for this walk. I have been sitting like a worm in its burrow for a long time and the moons have come and gone so that now it is early summer and it is time to go from this place.

My grandson Rides in Laughter brought me some fine beaver skins to be made into moccasins or traded and it has put me in remembrance of those days when there was so much of everything. Maybe it is an old man's wishing for his early days but I do not think this is all. When I was small, there were many beaver in the streams. Even in the very dry places west of the Great Salt Lake they could be found in certain places in abundance. It has been a long time since I have seen a beaver swimming and slapping his tail in warning.

This nonsense about cutting up the Mother Earth for "land" could not have been imagined by my father who did not see the ground as if it were in pieces. The ground upon which he walked and hunted and which gave him an abundance of food and all other things for life. He saw it all as one being whose arm could not be removed for one purpose. One whose leg should not be used for another. We old ones know that taking an arm will change the whole. This is what the farms have done. The buffalo used to walk everywhere they wanted. When it was time some would be taken for food and tepee and clothing and tools. They ate the grasses and gave their breath to the air.

When the white men came we thought that there would be fewer buffalo but we did not know that there would be no buffalo any more. This is what cutting up the Earth has done. It has made us sit like worms in these white man towns and slowly see our hunting and traveling grounds cut away for white man's purposes. We are left now with this town that smells of cattle and waste from so many people who come here and have no other place to go. I feel I must go to someplace that has the smells of my earlier years. I wish to see elk, a beaver lodge and maybe a buffalo. I will hunt. I will take early shoots of plants and young roots if I can find them to eat.

Sugar does not like this idea of my walk. She goes every morning to sit with the Superintendent's people on this reservation to turn the Shoshone words into English words. This is one reason we have been given this square house in which to live, because my granddaughter has become a very important person with her words and writing she learned when she was a Mormon.

Now she requests that I tell these stories. I think it is because she looks at me and sees what is past and she looks at the white people and sees what is future and she stands on the blade of that knife and wishes to fall into what was rather than go as she must into the future. My words also help her to know the Shoshone again. So many young ones do and say what they do because their knowledge is gone. These new people, the whites, the young Indians, the half-breeds, the other tribes never knew Shoshone ways. The Arapahos' old ones are all dead now, so the ones that are left do not even know their Arapaho ways.

Knowing old Shoshone ways makes my granddaughter understand and makes her proud but it also makes her sad. My heart was broken long ago. I am still maybe in a numb place with a veil over my eyes with the speed of what has been swept away. This is maybe the reason that I must walk away into the past for a while. I can see clearly away from this veil.

Two shocking things happened yesterday. As the sun became warm in the middle of the morning I was outside squatting on the ground wrapped in my striped blanked to enjoy my coffee and watch the grasses blow. A white lady from the government came to see me. She was the wife of a soldier of high rank who has come here to watch us Indians to see we are peaceful and kill us if we are not. She scurries about the reservation town now and calls this place her "home" and seeks to make it into wherever she came from with fine cloths and delicate cups and shoes with buttons that are black and shiny.

She came strongly up to me with another young Shoshone man who did her talking for me in my language. She stood over me with her hands on her waist and said she came to talk to me about my walking. She said she heard from my daughter of my walk and that I should not go on this walk because it was not safe for me to be out walking when it was still cold in the mountains and there were no soldiers to protect me. She said I was old and should stay comfortable in my house and she could arrange for gifts if I needed anything.

I did not know what to say to this so I said nothing. I think she believes I am stupid but inside I am laughing because she does not know that I have walked in all seasons from the far away lands of the fish eaters in the far north and west to the California deserts in the far south to the lands of the Absorkee and Piegan in the high north. I have done so as a part of these lands! There is no harm to me by doing these things. I would be offended by this white woman's visit if I did not pity her with her strange thoughts and fears. She is a crazy person in my thinking.

As I sit thinking about this it occurs to me that she feels that people are bigger than nature. Because white people believe this, they are separate from nature. Maybe they think that we Shoshones long ago fell to a lower level, that of nature. We Shoshones know that nature, and all its life, is on the same level of human beings, that we are part of nature and Mother Earth so we have nothing to fear. The living things of the Earth have human characteristics, and humans have theirs. These thoughts made me more determined to go on my walk even if I am feeling the pain badly in my old bent foot.

The other thing that came about is that as this lady was finishing her talk to me, a magic wagon came to take her away. Sugar said it is a "motor car". It is a wheeled wagon that moves without being pulled or pushed. It is black and metal but very dusty so it has come from far away. What medicine these white people have to make such a thing! My people have very strong medicine and can make many things and know many things about the stars and the weather and the grasses and the animals that these people do not even dream. But it frightens me deeply that I have not ever dreamed of their types of medicine wielded by these foreign people. I do not know how this can be part of nature at all.

Today I will not carry these thoughts and scars. I must go and smoke and think on the beautiful things of my life and maybe I will die in the mountains so that the great losses do not any longer disturb me. I will no longer be perturbed by these new and strange ways.

That is all.

{Note from Sugar: Grandfather died on his walk in the Owl Creek Mountains in 1910. He had camped near a lake and eaten a meal of fish and onion roots and had smoked his pipe. He died sitting against a boulder looking out at his campfire and the beauty of nature. He was wearing his rabbit skin shirt, his best moccasins and his favorite striped blanket. We suspected he was leaving us to make his way to the Spirit World, so a few days after he left, the whole family, and many other New'e walked together in the direction he went. We followed his tracks on the ground where the snow had melted. We buried him in the traditional way in that sacred place. His Spirit is now with his wives, his elders and his dead children and they are, perhaps, hunting buffalo.}

Second Generation Lupineflower

(Lupineflower Born1869)

Prologue From "Introduction to the Book of Mormon"

*"The Book of Mormon is a volume of holy scripture compara-
ble to the Bible. It is a record of God's dealings with ancient
inhabitants of the Americas and contains the fullness of the everlasting gospel.*

*The book was written by many ancient prophets by the spirit of
prophecy and revelation. Their words, written on gold plates, were
quoted and abridged by a prophet-historian named Mormon. The
record gives an account of two great civilizations. One came from
Jerusalem in 600 B.C. and afterward separated into two nations,
known as the Nephites and the Lamanites. The other came much
earlier when the Lord confounded the tongues at the Tower of Ba-
bel. This group is known as the Jaredites. After thousands of years,
all were destroyed except the Lamanites, and they are among the
ancestors of the American Indians..."*

Book of Mormon, Enos 1:20

*"And I bear record that the people of Nephi did seek diligently
to restore the Lamanites unto the true faith in God. But our labors
were vain; their hatred was fixed, and they were led by their evil nature that they became wild, and ferocious, and a blood-thirsty
people, full of Idolatry and filthiness; feeding upon beasts of prey;
dwelling in tents, and wandering about in the wilderness with a short
skin girdle about their loins and their heads shaven; and their skill
was in the bow, and in the cimeter, and the ax. And many of them
did eat nothing save it was raw meat; and they were continually
seeking to destroy us."*

Book of Mormon, 3 Nephi 2:14; 2:15; 2:16

*"And it came to pass that those Lamanites who had united
with the Nephites were numbered among the Nephites; And
their curse was taken from them, and their skin became white
like unto the Nephites; And their young men and their daughters became exceedingly fair, and they were numbered among*

the Nephites, and were called Nephites. ...."

Part 1. Slow Walker's Lodge

Lupineflower's father, a respected Shoshone elder, made the finest moccasins of any Indian, Shoshone or not. They were always made just for the particular person, with each of their individual feet in mind, and made to last that person's life, with reasonable repairs. Wherever they were camped, at Washakie's camp on the place designated for them by the white men a few days travel northwest of Fort Bridger, or out on hunts or at other favorite camps, Indians from all over would come to him with their very best animal skins and ask him to make moccasins. He would look carefully at their feet, and give the hand sign that he would do it. They would leave him a gift of tobacco and maybe something else like a button or a brace of prairie chickens.

Then he would put the skin with all the other skins and he would resume cutting and punching holes and sewing, as he did all days that they were staying in one place. He would have so many pairs of moccasins going at once, Lupineflower did not know how he knew one from the other. Then word would go out that the moccasins were done and the stranger would ride to meet them with his trade, sometimes a pony or a set of straight and strong arrows for a bow. Good moccasins were not undervalued. They covered the soles of the feet with strong protective bark sewed into the skins, then wrapped all around the top and sides of the foot and then they wound up the leg to the knee.

Sometimes Lupineflower's father Ubidaa' Boyokami'a or Slow Walker as he was known in those days, would trim the outer leg with furs or with fringes that would dance and bounce as the man walked or rode. Protecting and warming the feet was a life and death business in the harsh climate of what is now Wyoming, Idaho, and Utah. Lupineflower noticed Shoshones and other Indians everywhere they went wearing his moccasins.

Although she was very proud, her father seemed to take no notice of her or the other children of their lodges. Lupineflower could do as she pleased and there was always something pleasing to do. Her many mothers, Coneflower, Walks Away, Arrow in Cup, and Daisy did the hard work of making shelters from wood and skins, preparing meat brought in by men, finding roots and other foods, and finding and chopping wood for making the constant fires. The grandmother, Tender Ashes, instructed the children and could, with one look or slight hand-sign, stop any one of the children from a fast run. She was not always "tender" as her name implied, but she was greatly loved. Lupineflower did not know, or care, how Tender Ashes was related, but in the Shoshone way, her position as Grandmother, not her blood or parents, made her who she was among the others.

One evening Slow Walker gave Lupineflower the sign that she should come to him. She sat in front of him on the edge of his buffalo robe before the fire with her head dipped so as not to look at him in the face, as was respectful. He pulled from behind his back a little deerskin doll, with soft beaver fur for hair and a red calico wrap for a dress. It had two blue buttons for eyes. Lupineflower was thrilled to have this doll for her baby, or "ohmaa". She cradled it and cooed over it and carried it everywhere.

The doll was not a happy thing for everyone, however. Tender Ashes stomped up to Slow Walker and spoke to him in loud and firm tones that only a grandmother can use with a respected man. She told him he was calling up dangerous medicine by giving a child a blue-eyed doll. He told her to "go away old woman", he was only using blue buttons for which he had no other use. If she had dared, Tender Ashes would have burned the doll, but she did not dare.

Other children, though, did dare to try to take the doll away. Very few things were owned by anyone, as all useful items were shared: food, cooking pots, water skins. Goods were freely traded: horses, tools, clothing and even sometimes women and children. But the blue-eyed doll was Lupineflower's and no other child was allowed to hold it or pet it. Lupineflower would scratch and fight and yank out hair to keep the doll. She never went anywhere without it. Lupineflower's strong friend, Long Shadow was a few years older than Lupineflower. He thought she should keep the doll, and he let the children know he would tear the foot off of anyone who took the doll. So the children left the blue-eyed doll to Lupineflower. Eventually, the jealous ones decided that the doll was bad medicine and they did not want it anyway.

There were about forty children in all so there were endless games and races and places to explore. They loved playing on the edge of the stream, seeing all the shimmering pebbles and sometimes finding small insects, larvae or other good things to eat. They camped in winter at Washakie's camp, which was generally made a few miles away from the white man's fort. The children knew not to go near the white people, as they knew these people could be very bad and take them away or shoot them with big guns as had happened only a short time ago at Bear River.

In summer the Shoshones often went to a valley to the west where three rivers, including the Snake River joined. Mormon settlers had come there in the late 1870s and named it the Star Valley, perhaps because at first they starved there. But eventually, they settled many towns.

Coneflower, Lupineflower's mother, was friendly and curious and loved all people. She often went to the new white houses and farms in the Star Valley or on the reservation, where the white people were not supposed to be, but had settled anyway. Coneflower traded with white women for useful things. She said that those white people were not like the white people that had killed so many Shoshones. Sometimes she asked for gifts if she had nothing to trade and the people were hungry.

One time a white woman gave her many small cakes made with sugar after Coneflower showed the white woman how to make a poultice out of bark and roots for a white child that was sick with a cough. Coneflower was clever and knew how to be helpful but she also knew to ask for or take what she wanted from the white people, if needed.

White people did not understand this sharing as Shoshone did among their people. It was very confusing because the whites would proclaim friendliness, but then they would become angry when Shoshones acted as if this was so.

One summer evening, a big man among the white men came to the camp to talk to Slow Walker and said that Coneflower was a bad woman, a "thief". Slow Walker explained to them in Shoshone that she was a good woman and he offered them dog meat stew, which was all that the children were going to eat that day. The man said no to the stew, which made Lupineflower happy, and Slow Walker felt that payment had been offered so the matter was done.

Coneflower stayed away from that man's house during the rest of the stay in the valley. But they continued to enjoy white man's food, such as coffee and sugar, brought to them by Coneflower from her wanderings, and they also had meat more often than some others because of Slow Walker's trading for moccasins.

Lupineflower was content among her people and grew to be a strong girl, who could always be seen with her blue-eyed *ohmaa* in a baby sling on her back.

Part 2. Mrs. Weber

The Shoshones continued to travel with the seasons, but were more often encouraged by the Indian Agents to stay on the reservation, and by the many white farms that began to appear in their usual camping places. After the Arapahos came to stay on Shoshone lands in 1878, Slow Walker and his family attended many Councils about the Arapahos being brought there by the white soldiers.

During this stay, Coneflower resumed her friendship with the wife of the rancher who had once called her a bad woman. They had many cows and a big garden with many fine vegetables, including corn, which was one of Coneflower's favorite foods. They also plowed up the land with large oxen and grew many long and straight rows of wheat. Coneflower saw the fields and was very curious, especially regarding the garden. The white lady saw Coneflower squatting along their barn fence. The white lady knew her garden had some particularly large tomatoes that were soon to ripen, so she was *not* going to let Coneflower help herself to any of those prizes that were expected soon on her dinner serving plates.

Brigham Young's constant advice to the Latter Day Saints was, "It was much wiser to feed Indians than fight Indians." In most towns, the Mormons had established a community "Food Bin" to provide food to the Indians. Here there was no town. So the lady, Mrs. June Weber, motioned to Coneflower to come over to the edge of the garden. They had some acquaintance from other times when Coneflower would come up to the house and ask for flour or other food. Once, Coneflower had stuck her absolutely filthy finger in a new pound of butter, which of course Mrs. Weber then gave to her. Mrs. Weber's second oldest, her daughter Marie, had worked all day to churn about four pounds of butter and she was very annoyed. Mrs. Weber used it as an opportunity to teach God's commandment to bring the Indians back to Christ's word, as said in the Book of Mormon. Another time, Coneflower brought them a recently killed rabbit, which Mrs. Weber pointed out to Marie as proof of the wisdom of Mormon teaching.

Coneflower's recent absence was no surprise to Mrs. Weber, because the Indians traveled about for many months and then appeared back in the area and sometimes in her yard on their impossibly quiet ponies when you least expected them. All this was despite government efforts to settle them down. However, Mrs. Weber and her husband and seven children were quite thankful to be living among the friendly Snakes, under Chief Washakie, than to take the risks of being in Utah where the Utes and more dangerous tribes of Snake Indians under Pocatello and formerly Bear Hunter (who, she thought, was thankfully now dead at Bear River) could murder your whole family as soon as you closed your eyes at night.

The most dangerous thing the Webers, and their neighbors, worried about was whether their land claims would be honored, since technically all the lands that Brigham Young dedicated for Mormon settlement in 1878 were Shoshone lands. Here, their farm was actually on lands designated as Reservation. The Indians had complained, but still the government allowed them to stay.

After seeing the vast expanse of the Salt Lake Valley, the Mormons had abandoned their eastern policy of buying land from Indians. Instead, they declared ownership based on "divine donation" and "beneficial use". The Church told them not to worry about this and to continue to plant and build up the farm and if they needed to pay a small fee to the Indian agents to run their cattle, that could be arranged. The Webers wanted to keep peace with their Indian neighbors.

Coneflower smiled and stood straight and tall and came to Mrs. Weber. Coneflower's hands touched Mrs. Weber's up-swept blond hair and her blue cotton dress. Coneflower appreciated with her hands. Mrs. Weber stiffened. She was not accustomed to being touched so freely. But she smiled back and she and Coneflower renewed their acquaintance with a few fond words in the others' language.   "Hello" said Coneflower, and "penaho" said Mrs. Weber.

Through smiles and gestures, Mrs. Weber acknowledged little Rides in Laughter, who was traveling on Coneflower's pony in his cradleboard and Coneflower glanced shyly at the children silently clustered around the door of the cabin. Mrs. Weber noticed that although Coneflower appeared very dusty all over, her hair was neatly braided and she smelled clean and of smoke and leather and some other plant-like scent. The baby was fat and content and tightly bundled in his board. Coneflower thought that Mrs. Weber smelled sharply of sweat. A baby cried inside the cabin.

Coneflower indicated the corn. Mrs. Weber indicated it was not yet ripe, but offered some, if Coneflower would return later. Coneflower pulled a bundle from her horse blanket and opened it to show Mrs. Weber a brown powder. Mrs. Weber did not understand, but Coneflower indicated that it could be made into a tea in the event of stomach pain. She showed Mrs. Weber a low growing plant that was done flowering now, but whose flowers had been dried and ground to make the powder. Mrs. Weber was confounded that heathens who were so poor and undisciplined, casually knew so many secrets of the lands around them. She gratefully took a portion of the brown powder after Coneflower indicated the right amount for the heated water. Mr. Weber often had stomach trouble. Mrs. Weber gave Coneflower two squashes from her garden.

After Coneflower's visit, Mrs. Weber thought about her religious teachings and her place in improving Coneflower's, and her Indian family's lives. While Coneflower seemed quite nice, another time an old Indian woman had come to the cabin and walked right into the house. She picked up the whole bag of their sugar, two bars of soap and a knife and attempted to walk out. Mrs. Weber had stopped her, but then two young braves had arrived and rode about the yard whooping and careening loudly so that Mrs. Weber let her go. After that incident, she kept all her supplies out of sight during the fall and winter when Indians were about. The occurrence had reiterated to her, though, how important it was to civilize these people.

Some whites had questioned whether the Indians really were *people*, but Mrs. Weber knew, from the Book of Mormon, that they were actually a lost tribe of Israelites called Lamanites that had migrated to America hundreds of years ago. Jesus had actually come to America and had personally converted the Lamanites. But then after these Lamanites killed their relatives and rejected Christ's teachings, they were cursed with dark skin and a degraded existence. However, it was written that once they again accepted Christ, their skin would miraculously once again become "white and delightsome"! Heavenly beings had instructed Joseph Smith to bring them back to salvation.

God knows that Mrs. Weber felt that she had enough to do, but something nagged at her that perhaps, through Coneflower, she could be an instrument of God's work and could help earn her place into the Celestial Kingdom.

A few years before, the Indian Chief who had survived Bear River, Sagwitch, and his band of about 100 other Indians had been baptized in the Mormon Church in a stunning successful mission by Elder George Hill. They were now wonderful examples of Indians that attempted to farm and become civilized. Why, Sagwitch and his wife had been Sealed in the Endowment House, and he was a true Mormon Elder! Even Mr. and Mrs. Weber were not yet Sealed, as they were so far away from a proper Temple. Sagwitch and his band were contributing to the building of the Logan Temple. It seemed ironic that someday she and her family could be Sealed into eternity together in a Temple built in part by Indians! Mrs. Weber wondered if those Indians had turned white yet, but perhaps it was a process.

Part 3. Testimony

Coneflower rode away, considering when to return for the corn. She would go back when the moon was new, which was a good time to gather seed plants. She would bring more of her children so that there would be arms to carry and so the white lady to see that her family, too, had many healthy children. She urged her horse to a rocky hillside that was not planted with white men's plants, there she could find the flowers, blooming in late summer, for which she was named. They were close to the ground, with shoots of brown centers surrounded by bright yellow petals. She wanted to pick many of the leaves from those flowers to have for a satisfying and pain relieving tea around the fire that night. The white people called the flower Echinacea.

Coneflower thought of a dream she had. It showed her daughter, Lupineflower, going to a new place, with lovely blue flowers. Blue flowers, or really anything blue except the sky or water, were rare, therefore, held in great value. Lupineflowers were usually purple, but sometimes could be found in a blue color. They too, were healing flowers, as they could cause a person to expel intestinal worms, such as tapeworms, hookworms, or pinworms that kept one from gaining weight.

Shoshones gave great credibility to their dreams and visions, which often helped interpret their beliefs. Coneflower felt that Lupineflower was to be offered and would obtain something rare. Coneflower wondered what it would be?

In the fall of that year, after Coneflower had visited Mrs. Weber again and received a nice sack of ripe corn in exchange for more of the brown powder tea, which was very useful for Mr. Weber's stomach pains, Mrs. Weber heard of a missionary, Amos Wright, who was to visit the area. Mr. Wright was known to speak the Shoshone language, and to be very friendly with the Indians. While it was generally forbidden for Mormon missionaries to seek to convert the Shoshones (who's souls had been promised to the Episcopalians by the government), the Mormons knew that this was not the will of God. Brother Wright was already acquainted with Chief Washakie, and it was rumored that at a meeting of the Indians Mr. Wright would give his Mormon testimony in the Indians' language. He asked for some local people to attend and to sing some hymns for the Indians. Mrs. Weber spoke to her husband about this and felt a strong calling to attend this meeting. So with Mr. Weber's blessing, she joined the ten singers that would go by oxen-wagon to meet with the Indians. They went the long way there, to avoid being seen by government agents.

Mrs. Weber had never been to the Indian camp. She was surprised by the hundreds of teepees with all their openings facing the same way, and the obvious organization and quiet productivity of the place. It smelled of wood smoke and strange cooking. While there were no gardens, each lodge showed industry, with drying meat racks, groups of women or young people working hides, or working with tools. The Mormons stared, but the Indians seemed to ignore them. The Mormons did not understand why the Indians would not meet their eyes in some welcome. Mrs. Weber squirmed and her heart beat faster. What if this had been a trick and they were to be horribly murdered!

It was already towards evening. There was a fine crisp feeling to the air. A large stack of wood had been piled in a central place, and as the wagon pulled up, a woman struck a flint and lit the interior flashing. Slowly, the wood caught and after some smoke, the fire began to engulf the pile.

As they were dismounting the wagon, an Indian drum started nearby with a loud, rhythmic, slow beat. It boomed into the hearts of the Mormons, who were made even more uncomfortable. Mrs. Weber could not help feel the excitement and power of the drum, however, a part of her wanted to scurry back into the wagon as quickly as possible.

Brother Wright, however, seemed familiar with this signal, and stepped forward to greet a skinny old man with long dank hair who was wearing a wide brimmed hat, a cotton shirt, baggy pants, and tall moccasins. They hugged each other then sat down to smoke while the rest of the Mormon Elders stood behind, as close to the wagon as possible, in a nervous formation. An Indian started to cry out to the beat of the drum with his high pitched screaming song. It was very disconcerting. Her comfort from the organized manner of the camp fled in hearing the base savagery of the screaming song and the steady drum.

Indians started to appear from all directions. As soon as the Indian song was done, and the drum abruptly stopped, the place felt very quiet. The Mormons, who had parked a little too close to what was a cold pile of wood were now feeling the rising heat. Then Indian women filed up to the strangers with happy smiles and offered baskets of cooked meats and other lumps of food that were unfamiliar to the Mormons. Mrs. Weber spied Coneflower with a frightening looking older woman whose face was pocked with fever scars and whose forehead was completely bald, a pretty young girl, and a number of other children, including the fat baby in the cradle-board. Coneflower smiled and approached with her brood. The Indians touched and petted the Mormons who stood as if in shock. Mrs. Weber was so pleased to see a friendly face that she spoke warmly to Coneflower, which put many of the other Mormons at ease.

The old man, who must have been Chief Washakie, called out to the Indian people, who respectfully sat around the perimeter of the fire. Men were closest to Washakie, with women and children near the back. Brother Wright then stood next to the Chief and began to speak in the Indian language. He very soon indicated the singers, and said it was time for them to begin.

The choir, a little too close to the fire, had begun to sweat. They did not dare move, though, with the importance of the occasion. A few songs had been prepared, to be sung in harmony, with words that the Mormons thought would be appreciated by the Indians. They began with "High on the Mountain Top". Mr. Wright translated by giving the Indian sign language for the words.

> High on the mountain top,
> A banner is unfurled.
> Ye nations, now look up; It waves to all the world.
> In Deseret's sweet, peaceful land,
> On Zion's mount behold it stand!
> For God remembers still
> His promise made of old,
> That he on Zion's hill Truth's standard would unfold!
> Her light should there attract the gaze
> Of all the world in latter days.
>
> His house shall there be reared,
> His glory to display,
> And people shall be heard
> In distant lands to say:
> We'll now go up and serve the Lord,
> Obey his truth, and learn his word.
>
> For there we shall be taught
> The law that will go forth,
> With truth and wisdom fraught,
> To govern all the Earth.
> Forever there his ways we'll tread,
> And save ourselves with all our dead.

When they finished, a murmur went through the Indians. They seemed to appreciate this gentle singing of harmonious tones after the screeching of the Indian song.   Wright then continued his testimony for some time, with the Indians listening with what appeared to be interest.

The choir continued sweating and squirming. Mrs. Weber was fascinated by the Indian language, which seemed to be very complex. She also noticed that although there must have been well over a hundred young children, not one of them made a peep or acted with any disruption, as children generally do. After Elder Wright was finished, he asked that the choir sing again. They had prepared a favorite, "Come, Come Ye Saints":

Come, come, ye Saints, no toil nor labor fear;
But with joy wend your way.
Though hard to you this journey may appear,
Grace shall be as your day.
'Tis better far for us to strive, our useless cares from us to drive;
Do this, and joy your hearts will swell--
All is well! All is well!

Why should we mourn or think our lot is hard?
'Tis not so; all is right.
Why should we think to earn a great reward
If we now shun the fight?
Gird up your loins; fresh courage take.
Our God will never us forsake;
And soon we'll have this tale to tell--
All is well! All is well!

We'll find the place which God for us prepared,
Far away in the West,
Where none shall come to hurt or make afraid;
There the Saints will be blessed.
We'll make the air with music ring,
Shout praises to our God and King;
Above the rest these words we'll tell--
All is well! All is well!

And should we die before our journey's through,
Happy day! All is well!
We then are free from toil and sorrow, too;
With the just we shall dwell!
But if our lives are spared again; to see the Saints their rest obtain,
Oh, how we'll make this chorus swell--
All is well! All is well!

Elder Wright then turned to the Chief and talked to him, to ask him if he would be baptized. Washakie seemed to not hear, but sat silent, lighting another pipe. He was quiet for some time, while Elder Wright waited patiently. The choir each folded their hands and began to pray silently, that they may witness a miracle. When Washakie spoke, it seemed to please Elder Wright, and he asked for one more song. So the choir finished with "The Holy Ghost", in hopes that the inspiration, and movement away from the now raging bonfire, would be near.

> When Christ was on the Earth, He promised he would send
> The Holy Ghost to comfort us, Our true, eternal friend.
> The Holy Spirit whispers
> With a still small voice.
> He testifies of God and Christ,
> And makes our hearts rejoice.
>
> And when we are confirmed
> By sacred priesthood pow'r,
> The Holy Ghost is giv'n to us
> To guide us ev'ry hour.
> Oh, may I always listen
> To that still small voice.
> And with his light I'll do what's right
> Each time I make a choice.

The Indians whooped and called after the song was done. The choir was pleased as this seemed to be a great compliment. Finally, Elder Wright indicated the choir should get back into the wagon. They gladly did so, with many different kinds of relief. First, they were thrilled that they could simply move away from that enormous fire, the likes of which they were not accustomed. Second, they were very pleased that the Chief seemed to be considering a baptism. Lastly, they were all privately very thankful that they had not been tomahawked and eaten by the savages. The Indians sat quietly as the Mormons left the moonlit camp.

Washakie had been moved by the stories of his friend Amos. Since the death of his son, Wanapitz, Washakie wondered if the Ne'we Gods were still strong. Perhaps this other God was truly a better God, as Amos said. Washakie had been thinking hard about the future of his people now that the great herds of buffalo were almost gone. They had seen only small herds of buffalo in recent years. This was a very dangerous and alarming development that foretold great changes. Maybe new Spirits were needed to understand this new world.

Washakie knew that many other Ne'we appreciated what the Mormons said. No other white man's belief stories included Indians in the olden times. And it could certainly be true that Jesus could have come among earlier generations of the Ne'we people. Certainly the part of the story about Indian people fighting with their ancient cousins was true. And Mormons and Indians had other similar beliefs: that it was natural for a man to have more than one wife, if he had the means to do it; and that after death, we would all be reunited with the ones who had gone before us. Most importantly, Mormons told their stories in the Indian language, and not only in the white language.

Washakie also knew that alliances with white men were good, and the Mormons appeared to take care of their own. So at the end of the meeting, Washakie had signed to Amos that his Mormons could all go to a particular place near hot springs on the Wind River, on the next full moon. Washakie may, or may not be there to be baptized. Washakie would seek council with his men, and his spirit, and decide.

So, on September 25, 1880, Wright and a contingent of Mormons went to the river. There, they found Washakie and perhaps two hundred other Shoshones, including Coneflower, Lupineflower, Bent Foot Healer, and all of their children waiting for them. They were baptized that day, and a month later, another group of 100 Shoshones again were baptized. Mrs. Weber was thrilled. The Episcopalians complained to the government, but there seemed little the soldiers could do in matters of faith.

All the Shoshones disappeared from their camp soon after. Mrs. Weber did not see Coneflower for a few years, but when she did, they were reunited as friends, and sisters. Coneflower had not appeared to change at all, or to take on any attribute of the Mormon faith, but Mrs. Weber supposed that perhaps Coneflower was already too ingrained in the Indian ways, and perhaps it would be her children who would truly be part of the Mormon Church. She was thankful that Coneflower, and her family, would see the Celestial Kingdom.

Part 4. Hungry Times

The years after their baptisms were hungry and confusing times for the family of Slow Walker. The wide-open spaces of their great Shoshone lands were gone. They could not travel a day in any direction without finding farms that ate up the useful plants or cattle that ruined the watersheds and displaced the wildlife. There were sharp metal animal traps which snapped the small ankles of children going to bring water from the riverbeds. These horrible maiming traps crippled many who did not see them hidden under leaves and branches.

And always, there were white people with better guns and more bullets standing guard over the traditional places New'e had gone since coming from the third world.

All these things made New'e unwelcome and endangered in their own homelands. Where meat was before plenty, it was now a luxury. Hunger times were frequent. When they had food to eat, it was not the food they were used to or the food they wanted, but maybe only handfuls of berries in the summer, or one rabbit to share with six or eight people. People were sick because they could not find the natural foods to balance their spirits. Suffering with pox and pain and grief over the deaths of so many. Winters were horrible with coughing, and sores, and weakness. Many old ones went away early to die, or were left when sick, so that others could eat. There was initial relief in that, but more gradually the old ones were missed greatly when their wisdom was needed. The few old ones that remained were loved greatly. Young ones were often left to die at birth if they did not seem strong or if they were born in fall, when surely the mother's milk would not last through winter. This heartbreak was made worse by the overwhelming feeling that their way of life was ending. These clouds loomed over their spirits.

Lupineflower became a woman in this time. She put her blue-eyed doll away. Her people were sometimes luckier than others of Washakie's band. They had trade goods for Slow Walker's moccasins, and Coneflower and Tender Ashes organized the family well for food gathering, trading, hunting, wood cutting, and medicine. They had many horses, and Slow Walker's quiet wisdom. They traveled to winter, spring and summer camps, then prepared to do it all again. As in old times, they formed into smaller groups to use the widespread resources in a good way. They came together with the greater New'e people for hunts and games and celebrations as in the old days, but these were very often distracted by murmurs late into the nights of the old men and strong women in council, pondering and arguing over the best ways to act and places to go to keep alive their way of life.

Part 5. Elder Smith

When Lupineflower was sixteen summers, the family came to their camp near the Mormons where they had been baptized. Lupineflower knew that the washing in the river had been somehow significant. Many of the Ne'we did not attend the washing, but those that did knew they were bound to those Mormon people in a new way. Perhaps they would learn to sing as those people had sung? Perhaps they would be given extra food rations? But nothing changed. The baptism did not matter; as those Mormon people were simply not in their lives to bother about.

One summer day, word went through the camp that Washakie would again host the Mormon Elders. Those that had been baptized were anxious to attend the meeting as they expected presents. Others were curious to see the strangers and be part of the novelty, and still others, like Slow Walker, kept away from this mischief.

Again, the meeting took place after sundown and a fire was lit and drums called the people to the fire. When they arrived, a table had been set up by the Mormons. Presents had already been given to Washakie, for all to share. Lupineflower was disappointed as it looked as if only a few white Mormon men had come and there were no singers.

The meeting was a disappointment for almost everyone. The Ne'we that were not baptized were asked to leave, which angered many. Some of the baptized even left. Then the meeting consisted of the white men talking, and they did not have good Shoshone language skills. Most Indians drifted away once it was clear there would be no further gifts. One of the white men was very dark haired, clean-shaven, smiling, and strong looking. The most striking thing was his icy clear blue eyes. He smiled at Lupineflower when it was his turn to talk. She wondered if he was an Indian, but with those eyes, he was likely not. Nor did he appear to know the hand signs or be familiar with the niceties of Indian culture. His voice was loud and booming. Lupineflower stayed after many of the others left but then she too moved away when the words were of no further interest.

Soon after, Lupineflower and Coneflower were out with their baskets seeking food: roots, grasshoppers and other edible insects, plants, and berries. They came near to Mrs. Weber's house and decided to see what ripe vegetables may be in her garden. When they drew close, they saw many horses, some being very fine. They watched from a distance and saw quite a lot of activity with many children and teenaged boys about the house, including quite a few they did not know. Mrs. Weber's oldest daughter, Anna, spied the two Indians and stopped and pointed. "Look! The squaws!"

At that time, the blue eyed, dark haired man came out of the house with Mr. Weber. They all looked to see Coneflower and Lupineflower, who hesitated, not wanting to step in to the lively scene. Mrs. Weber then came out and called to Coneflower. She came forward and held out her hand, so Coneflower and Lupineflower went forth and greeted Mrs. Weber. The men appeared to be talking about them, and all the children were staring. Mrs. Weber shooed the children away to work in the barn, but led the Indian women to the men, and for the first time, they spoke to each other. Coneflower knew a few words of English. They knew who Mr. Weber was from seeing him at a distance in the past, but Elder Smith, the blue eyed, dark haired man, was introduced to them. He appeared very pleased that both Lupineflower and Coneflower had been baptized, and they were invited in to the house.

Lupineflower was very impressed with Elder Smith. Not only did he have those piercing eyes, but a strong appearance. He also spoke with great authority and was the owner of the many fine horses out in the corals. It was explained that Elder Smith was from Utah, in the west, and was traveling through after selling many cows and trading horses. These horses were part of a bigger herd. He would be going home soon, to Utah. Elder

Smith had a wife. Four of the boys outside were his sons. He was looking for someone to help him with his sons, and had asked Mr. Weber if Anna, the Weber's eldest daughter may be willing to ride with him back to Utah, and become his second wife so that she could do this. Anna, however, was not yet ready to leave her parents, so it was decided that Elder Smith would return in two years and would marry Anna then. This seemed a good compromise as Anna would be promised to a wealthy and prominent man, and her mother could keep her safe at home for a few more years.

Lupineflower and Coneflower listened politely, even though they did not fully understand and were confused by the strange marriage customs.

Mrs. Weber then described to Elder Smith Coneflower's knowledge of healing plants. Elder Smith was very interested and told Coneflower he would like her to tell him many things about plants, as biology had been a fascination of his since he was a boy and he wished to know more of the native plants, in the event maybe some of them could be cultivated as cash crops, or sold as medicines. Coneflower was, for once shy with this attention. Generally, she felt totally in control, but this sitting around a white family's table and having conversation in a language she did not fully understand was unnerving. Lupineflower appeared to understand, however, and began to show the Webers and Elder Smith some of the plants they had gathered and were carrying in their baskets. In the few words they had in common and in signs, they talked of the plants.

Elder Smith sat considering Lupineflower. She was certainly beautiful, if maybe a little malnourished. It would be hard to know if she was a virgin, as she was after all, in his thinking, a savage who lived among savage ways. She did appear very knowledgeable however, and she was, after all, a baptized Mormon. Elder Smith had been curious about the Shoshones, and in particular he hoped to learn more of their ways and apply them so they could be beneficial to the Mormons. An exciting plan snapped into place in his mind. He had been very successful at his ranch and was ready for another wife, but there were not many available women in his remote part of Utah. He had hoped to return with Anna but that did not work out. What of an Indian bride?

On impulse, he told Coneflower and Lupineflower that he wanted to give them a present. They went outside, and there, Elder Smith brought forth a tan colored colt. Its mare had gone lame and was put down and the colt was just past weaning, not broken and was proving to be disruptive with the rest of the horses. Lupineflower did not believe the colt was for them but then smiled at the generous present. She studied this man shyly, but with even greater interest than before.

Coneflower was at the same time happy and concerned. What did this gift mean? They were given a bit of rope with which they haltered the colt, and the two women began to lead him away. After they were almost across the yard, Elder Smith called out: could he come to the Indian camp and see them again? Coneflower did not know what to answer, so they did not answer, but turned and quickly went away.

When they returned to the camp with the colt, Slow Walker was not pleased. He did not like to mix with white man's business, and the colt could have no good result. They did not need this horse. He told Coneflower that on the next day, she must take the colt back to the Webers. Or perhaps they should butcher the colt as they had no meat and the women's gathering had not brought enough roots or other plants to feed the family. Coneflower sighed, and went about making a stew out of some dried fish and the plants they had brought from their day of foraging. The colt was put out with the other horses to wait for tomorrow.

Returning the colt did not happen, however, because that night Elder Smith came to Slow Walker's lodge with Amos Wright and Washakie. It was explained that Elder Smith was a prominent man who had many cows and horses and he needed a wife to return with him to Utah. He wanted to pay a bride price for Lupineflower.

Lupineflower sat behind her father listening quietly, in shock. She was excited by the idea of the many horses and the strength of these Mormon people who had so many good things to eat, and seemed very happy in their strange lives. She was also very interested in the handsome Elder Smith, even though he was not Indian. Even now, he had a growth of dark stubble on his face that Indian men did not have. What would it be like to touch that? She was terrified, however of this idea. She had not considered leaving her family although she knew a time was likely coming that this would be expected. There were fewer and fewer Indian men who were able to take wives, however. The Shoshones were poor and no man wanted to take a wife and make babies that would die for lack of food.

Lupineflower, Coneflower and Slow Walker all seemed to wake at the same time to the real possibility of a marriage with Elder Smith. Washakie seemed to like the idea of a further binding with the Mormon people. It gave his people one other way to assure friends among that dangerous society.

Slow Walker was very frightened but sat stone-faced. He thought of the butchering of his first family by white men. He once again felt powerless at white men ripping away at his family and his comfort.

Elder Smith brought five silver dollars out of his pocket. This money was a great wealth in the Shoshone camp. Very rarely did money serve any purpose to the Shoshones but it was known to be of high value for buying things. It was certainly not, however, a customary wedding trade. Everyone in the lodge became very quiet. The appearance of the dollars brought the bitter smell of insult into the room. The silence lingered. Elder Smith sensed his mistake and slowly moved the dollars back into his pocket. Amos Wright then began to speak fast, trying to explain away the graceless act. He suggested instead that Elder Smith bring five head of cattle to Slow Walker and his lodge. These cows would help the family begin a herd, and would allow them to settle down and become farmers. Why, Lupineflower could learn all about farming and could teach her brother and sister some day... His words trailed off as he sensed the ludicrous nature of what he was saying, even if turning the Shoshones to good farmers was the common thought among whites.

Slow Walker had enough. He asked that all leave his lodge.

Part 6. The Decision

After the visitors had mounted their horses and ridden away, Slow Walker reached for his pipe and began to smoke. Lupineflower and Coneflower huddled in the back, overwhelmed by the events of the day. Lupineflower reached into her furs and pulled out the blue-eyed doll from long ago which she still cuddled when she was frightened or sad. The blue eyes looked up to her with their blank stare.

Coneflower barked at Slow Walker, something that Lupineflower had never seen. "That doll! You cursed her with that doll and its blue eyes! She will be taken by the blue-eyed people and we will never see her again! Her sons will grow to be white men and will call us thieves and dirty! Our daughter is lost to us now forever!" Coneflower started to cry, then to wail, then to keen.

Slow Walker smoked quietly. After Coneflower had quieted to a moaning, he gave a deep sigh. He turned and pulled Lupineflower to him and held her close. "My daughter, I see that you should go with this man. He will have much for you to eat, and your children will learn both Indian ways and white man's ways. If ever this man is not good to you, you will come back to the people. Do you agree to go?"

Lupineflower listened to her mother moaning. She thought of the many horses and the strong voice and the blue eyes. The eyes were not kind or laughing, but they were ... interesting and foreign and dangerously enticing. Perhaps given her youth, Lupineflower felt that this decision could not have such great consequence, as she could always come back to her family if she wanted. Marrying this man would be an adventure! So she smiled, and said, yes, she would go. Knowing her mother disapproved, she gave her mother the blue-eyed doll as a comfort. Coneflower threw it into the fire and cried more loudly as it caught the flames and burned; giving off a musty, bad smelling smoke.

The next morning, Lupineflower woke as usual, her stomach slightly sick. She tried to believe that the day and night before had not happened. Coneflower stayed in her furs, and Slow Walker got up as usual and worked on a pair of warm moccasins. Then, at mid-morning, a large group of horses was seen coming in the distance. There were two large wagons, with perhaps six people. One was Elder Smith, his four sons, and Amos

Wright. There were perhaps one hundred good horses and twenty cows. The entourage stopped outside the Indian camp, but Elder Smith and Amos Wright got off their wagon and came toward Slow Walker's lodge. Tender Ashes, having heard of the bargain, had yanked Lupineflower to the creek upon seeing the approach of the white men, and had held her there and told her to scrub and then to make herself beautiful with the red clay of the waters' edge for her new husband. Lupineflower did as she was told, and covered her arms and legs and neck and face with the fine red clay. Tender Ashes put red into the part of her hair, and knotted her shaggy trusses into two long braids that she tied off with strips of deer hide decorated with beads. Coneflower had not come out of the lodge. When Lupineflower was ready, she sat before her father, who spoke to her quietly with a Shoshone blessing song. Then, without further ceremony, she walked to Elder Smith and sat before him.

The Elder, not knowing what to do, looked at Amos Wright. Why was she covered in mud? He asked. Elder Wright said that he guessed the Indians had decided she was going to be his new wife. Elder Smith wished to tell her to bathe, but knew this was not the right thing to say. Instead, they decided to complete the practical part of the transaction.

The white men walked back to the wagons to separate out the promised cows. Lupineflower followed. She climbed into the back of the first wagon without words and waited patiently. The older boy and the young boy in the second wagon and the other two older boys on horseback snickered and pointed, and one of them said something in English about the "squaw". Lupineflower heard the words "dirty" and "scrawny" and "muddy". They were laughing and guffawing as teenage boys do. The Elders shushed them with a threat, and then the men broke away the bride-price cows, which were herded away by Slow Walker and two other young Shoshone boys. The white men and boys then stood about awkwardly, expecting some kind of goodbye, or a celebratory send-off.

When Slow Walker did not return and the camp continued its morning routine without further notice of the white men, they finally looked at each other, then at Lupineflower sitting quietly and alone in the back of the wagon with the supplies. Elder Smith approached her. Did she need anything to be loaded? Did she want to sit with him in the front of the wagon? Lupineflower understood part of what he said, but looked away shyly and did not answer. Elder Smith pushed away the question of whether he was making a mistake bringing this strange woman to his home. Well, he thought, it is done. She will have to be broken of her strange ways and taught to speak English completely so that she can contribute her Indian knowledge to the family. Elder Smith walked away and decided perhaps it was more proper after all for her to sit in the back until they were married. He walked to the front of the wagon, checked the hitch, and climbed up.

Amos Wright mounted his horse and rode up to Lupineflower. He said to her in Shoshone that she would be soon in her new home a week's ride away and that when they arrived, they would have a wedding ceremony and she would be welcomed into her new home and be part of a prosperous Mormon family. These were the last words of Shoshone, not spoken by herself, Lupineflower would hear for many years.

Lupineflower nodded and sat patiently. She thought how nice it would be to ride in a wagon, as she had never done so before, and this would be her first experience of her new life as a Mormon.

The wagons pulled away. The boys on horseback moved to round up the rest of the cows and horses and began to move them down the road. Lupineflower saw Tender Ashes going back into her lodge. No one else remained about to see her leave. The wagons moved off, followed by the horses and cows.

Part 7. To Utah

For the first hour, being a Mormon and riding a wagon was almost bearable. The wagon lurched and banged over the rutted trail. The boards were hard and did not feel good on her bottom or when her back or head hit the edge of the wagon bed after the wooden wheels fell into a particularly deep hole. Lupineflower could not gain a place to hold on to or a comfortable position. She was at the mercy of the white man's wheeled monstrosity.

After the second hour, Lupineflower had enough. She stood and jumped from the wagon. The boys driving the second team called out to their father that the squaw had fallen. But she disappeared into the dust, and as the group stopped the wagons to determine what had happened, they looked around and could not see her. Elder Smith wondered if she was trampled, or worse, if he had been tricked! Did she run back to her people, effectively stealing his cattle?

The men called to themselves, but within minutes, one of the boys driving the horses in the rear shouted, "Pa! The Squaw is back here with the mustangs!" Then, before they could even see her among the horses, she bolted to the front wagon, bareback and astride a feisty little roan mare, which to the men's knowledge had not been broken. The horse danced and shied and bucked lightly, but she held him with her naked thighs, and a handful of mane, and cantered ahead of the party down the trail. She turned the horse and cantered back, looking at the stunned men. Then she looked away. Maybe to prove her mastery, she drove the nervous horse in a circle, all the while talking to the mare in Indian words. She looked back, then turned on down the road, her black braided hair swaying and bouncing, her feet comfortably gripping the horse.

The boys were speechless. Elder Smith was speechless. It was shocking enough that she would ride astride a horse, instead of sidesaddle.

It was amazing that a woman would be unafraid of the mustangs while they were in their herd mentality. But it was unbelievable that she could choose and catch a horse, mount it while they were moving and tame it so quickly or easily. Worst of all, she could ride more skillfully and gracefully bareback than they ever could have with a saddle.

Elder Smith could not wrap his mind around what he had seen. Adding to his confusion, he was fully sexually aroused by the small, nimble, sprite with the naked legs and arms. This...woman...was to be his wife! The thought of her as a woman made him groan. He could not wait to touch her and put himself inside her young sex. On another level of his mind, he was beginning to understand that bringing her to the ranch as his wife would be terribly disruptive to his household.

How would Susan, his current wife feel about – what was her name? He could not pronounce the name he had been told, and truthfully, he could not now even remember it. Oh yes, Mrs. Weber said "Helen" was her Christian name. So many things to think of! Every time he thought of another problem with what he had done, he thought of her young naked body below his, and he did not care what must be done. He would make this work, no matter what.

His sons, two of whom were older than Lupineflower, were thinking that she was quite a fine young girl and so very different from any white woman they knew. They were all puzzled, wondering if she were to be a servant in their home, or perhaps they were delivering her to another group of her people.

Lupineflower was having a wonderful time. After the uncertainty of the day and night before, she was now on the trail and on a good horse, a comfortable place for any Shoshone, even if she were traveling with strangers. Lupineflower was surprised at how slowly the men moved. Certainly the horses could move faster, but perhaps the wagons could only go at that rate. She rode ahead and scouted out roots and other fine things to eat when they stopped. By late afternoon, she had snared a prairie dove and gathered quite a nice bunch of thistles and other greens. She filled her water bag at a cold creek. As she saw the wagons pull into a formation behind a hillock to keep out the prairie winds, she rode up and threw down her contribution to dinner, and proceeded to build a small shelter on the edge of the wagons with willows and skins and to make a fire to cook.

As Elder Smith and his sons set up camp, they all watched her cautiously, wondering what she might do next and wondering what arrangements she might want from the men for her needs. Elder Smith had perhaps not explained the situation fully to his sons, and they looked fretfully at each other and at the Indian girl. He realized that they needed to be told of his plan.

"Boys!" He said, "Come here and let us pray and thank God for our new friend — eh, Helen — ."

The youngest boy, Alvarnus, said squinting into the late afternoon sun, "Pa, Who's Helen?"

Thom, the oldest glanced at the Indian girl, and elbowed his brother. The second son, Orson, asked, "Who is she Pa, and why is she coming with us?"

Elder Smith motioned for the boys to attend him and said loudly, "Let us Pray! Merciful God, you have delivered us here today safely on our way back to our home, and we pray that tonight you will grant us a quiet and peaceful night free of storms and danger. We thank you for our successful buying trip allowing us to bring with us these fine horses and cattle, that they may help us in creating a good life to better serve you!" Elder Smith went on, his voice a bit shaken, despite himself, "We also thank you for — eh, Helen, who will become an important part of our family and these boys new m-mother."

With that word "mother" the boys' bowed heads all shot up. Mother! How could that be possible? They knew that their father was to soon take a second wife, and even Thom was soon to be married, but they expected perhaps a widowed pioneer woman, or a schoolteacher brought in from the east... *not* a *Squaw*! And certainly not someone who was still a child, and so wild and unclean and just purchased right from the reservation for six cows!

But Elder Smith rallied and raised his voice, still in prayer, "Dear God, you know that we serve you by saving the souls of these heathen people, and that you have blessed this, eh —woman, with her previous baptism by our Bishop Wright, and that this woman will be brought more fully to your ways if she is brought into a loving home and that this eh — woman will bring to us her knowledge of plants that we may use what she knows for the benefit of all the Saints, and —" With this Elder Smith raised his head and looked directly at each of his sons in turn, "We pray that *All* will treat this eh — woman with love and respect and welcome her as our sister. AMEN!" The boys were too stunned to answer with their usual, "Amen", so Elder Smith turned toward the newly christened "Helen's" camp and made his way away from his sons.

Lupineflower had found a flat stone and then dug a pit in which she was preparing to roast the dove with the gathered roots and greens. The stones for the pit were heating in the fire. She had gutted and plucked the bird. The greens had been rinsed and the roots wiped clean. She heard Elder Smith approach and kept about her work, as she was accustomed. Elder Smith stood before her, removing his hat. His face was smeared with sweat and dust. He looked down at the red dirt in Lupineflower's parted hair. She wordlessly indicated the dove. Elder Smith again marveled at her industriousness. How had she managed to hunt that dove without a gun? "Awh," he said, "Thom will be cooking up some dinner in the chow wagon, you best be joining us. It'll just be some pork and beans, and biscuits left over from Mrs. Weber, but they are good." Lupineflower looked up and softly said one of the few words she knew how to say in English, "Good". Elder Smith stood awkwardly in his hesitation, then nodded his head and turned back to finish setting up camp. To his dismay, he was again fully sexually aroused. Well, he thought, best to know that'll not be a trial.

Within a few hours the sun was setting and the animals had been watered and the lead mares hobbled. The cows stood stupidly munching grass. It was a fine evening without mosquitoes for once, and a soft rosy tint to the sky. The boys were all preoccupied with their thoughts as they went about the necessary evening chores.

Thom lit a fire and put a large chunk of ham purchased from Mrs. Weber into the big black traveling dutch-oven with some water and the cooked beans and put them to simmer over the fire with salt and pepper and cloves. Thom and the other men liked their dinner hearty after a day on the trail. Soon the smell of cooking ham drew in the boys. Elder Smith wanted to avert any inappropriate conversation, so he joined them immediately. To his surprise, Lupineflower also walked up to the group. She carried a brace of leaves upon which sat a beautifully roasted dove. Around it were strange looking roots and what looked like cooked grasses. She sat on the ground and placed the dove at his feet.

"I ain't eatin' no Indian food!" said Wilford, the third son.

"Well then, all the more for me!" countered Elder Smith with an authoritative glare, stopping all other negative comments.

Everyone but Wilford, out of pride, tried some of the dove and the roots, and all were surprised they were quite good, though it needed salt. They ate quietly, sharing a plate with Lupineflower, who sat on the ground and ate with her hands. This caused looks all around the boys, looks which Elder Smith stonily ignored. Any white woman would have sat on the edge of the wagon, or fashioned a stool and of course, used a fork and knife.

Lupineflower had not eaten pork before. She liked it very much with the beans and ate all she was offered. The biscuits sliced with butter and dipped in honey were her favorite, however. How did these white people make these? She could have eaten ten. After the meal was over, she wordlessly retreated to her shelter. She was up at dawn with the men and they quickly got onto the trail. She continued to select the roan mare and leapt up onto her back each morning without benefit of even a saddle or bridle. She disappeared most days but reappeared in the evenings, sometimes with additions to the meal, and sometimes, without.

They had good weather and no emergencies for the rest of the trip and fell into this routine until the last night before they were to arrive at Pillar Cache Ranch, Elder Smith's Utah home. It was named for a tall stone pillar in what was now called Cache Valley. It was a place where signs showed Indians had camped for hundreds of years, and more recently the mountain men had made caches of furs hidden in the dry rocks around the pillar. Elder Smith had himself claimed this land around the pillar and then broken ground and began to use its fertile soil and moderate climate for fields and orchards and livestock. In the building of the family house, they had even found a cast-iron pot with a tight fitting lid, left buried by some earlier visitor to the place of the stone pillar.

In the thirty odd years since the first Mormon pioneers had pulled their handcarts or walked from the east, the Cache Valley, a prized part of the New'e peoples' lands, and not far from the terrible site of the Bear River "tragedy" (as some soft hearted Mormons called it) had been made into a thriving and specialized community of Later Day Saints. The saints had even constructed a railroad through the valley with volunteer labor to spur off the transcontinental line. The new Temple at Logan was a half-day's ride away and was under construction. It would be dedicated the next year.

Elder Smith had become more and more nervous about his return to the Pillar Cache Ranch with Helen. Since the first night, the boys had been entirely silent to him about her presence, but he knew there would be more questions to come. The boys were not to be his greatest challenge. He expected the challenge was to be his wife. What the boys said among themselves was a secondary matter he would deal with later. He told himself he was the man of his household and all knew to obey him. He was, after all prepared for an adjustment period related to bringing in a new wife. He knew the boys were waiting to see what was to happen.

When Elder Smith tried to think of a plan, however, his mind went numb and he could only think of the woman's naked thighs around the back of the roan mare. By the last evening on the trail, he had begun to feel secret flashes of panic.

Certainly, he had discussed with Susan, his sealed wife and mother of his seven children, that he was to marry again. Both he and Susan were in their early forties and she had many problems with her last two pregnancies. She had lost two babies, the latest a pregnancy only a few months ago. He did not want to put her in danger of more pregnancies at her age. On the other hand, his need for a woman had not diminished, and he knew that his lust, correctly directed in a sanctified marriage, served God. He was one of the few men in his valley with one wife. Brother Chancy Wilson had four wives and seventeen children. The wives and children certainly helped with the everlasting workload of a pioneer ranch. Susan had agreed that another wife was the right thing to do. She told him she was looking forward to a woman she could call "sister" who would be ever at her side to assist her in the immense task of running of the house. He knew she had other feelings that lurked beneath this agreement, but he knew other men were able to manage their women and the church and its supportive doctrine was a great help.

What had he done, though, to bring an illiterate savage in the place of a good Mormon woman? Susan was expecting a homely, bonneted, chaste, humble housemaid. She, and probably the neighbors and church elders, would be shocked by this feisty, dark, unkempt, mud covered child. She would not even be worthy to enter the temple as she certainly had not taken the Code of Health which required one to swear off alcohol and other unclean habits. How would they know if she was Morally Clean under the church doctrines? She did not appear to speak more than a few words of

English. She would have no idea how to behave in polite company, not to mention know fine Mormon ways.

But it was too late. He briefly wondered if he could not say she was to be a servant, but alas, as he had announced his intention to the boys. No. He must marry her. His mind had been poisoned by delicious lust.

How on Earth would they tame her? Would she go to school with the children? Good God, she was probably younger than Thom and Orson, and maybe the same age as his daughter Clarissa. They would have to clean her and cut her hair and dress her and teach her to behave. She must be made to look the part of a good Mormon wife, not a wild animal. She would have to be kept at home to avoid embarrassment upon the family in the close-knit, righteous minded community. Certainly much of this transformation burden would fall to Susan. Would she ever forgive him?

The more he pondered these concerns, the more complicated it became. But panic would not be useful. As he drove the team he tried to grip onto his thoughts and feelings. After prayer, he decided to put on a stern face and explain his decision to his sons. It was the Christian thing to do to bring this Indian in to his family. Didn't the Webers and Amos Wright support the marriage? They would all face this as Christians. Overarching, however, was his knowledge that he would enjoy her perfect flesh as if the act of love was entirely new.

So on the last night, when they were camped in the mountains before entering the Cache Valley, he called the traveling party together. Then he went to Helen's small shelter, and indicated she was to come to the fire. Thom was poking potatoes around in the coals and turning a large amount of sizzling rabbit meat, which Helen had brought them, in a cast-iron pan.

"Listen to me, all of you!" he said.

Thom looked up but kept his squat before the fire. The rabbit meat smelled good and they were all hungry.

"Helen!" He looked at Lupineflower, who looked back at him quizzically.

"You are Helen!" He placed his hand over her hand and pulled her into the circle. "Helen! Helen!" He said, indicating her.

"Aelen" she repeated.

"Yes!" he said.

Lupineflower thought that this was the white Mormon marriage ceremony, and that Aelen meant "wife". She pointed at Elder Smith, and said "Husband?"

"Yes!" he said.

Orson sneered. Wilford started to walk away, but Elder Smith wished to make his point.

"Wait boys! Don't you know that it is our *obligation* to convert this woman and teach her to be of our faith? We know that the teachings of Brigham Young, told us that there is a curse on these aborigines who roam the plains. They are wild, but they were from the House of Israel! They once had the holy Gospel delivered to them, they had oracles of truth and

Jesus himself came and administered to them after his resurrection. In those early days they received and delighted in the Gospel until the fourth generation when they turned away and became so wicked that God cursed them with their dark skin and their benighted and loathsome condition.

It is Christian to bring these Lamanite people, through this one brown Indian sister, to our faith? Does not the Book of Mormon tell us that the Lamanite people will "blossom like a rose" when they become again one of the faithful? Through us they can go to the Celestial Kingdom! It is our duty to do what we can. And you know that your mother and I have decided that it is right and proper that I take another wife. Is it not Christian that I should take a wife that needs salvation and through our family we can save her from the Jesus' condemned brother, the Devil and from eternal damnation?"

The boys appeared unconvinced. Thom continued to poke at the rabbit, but as the oldest, and the most mature of the boys, he finally stood and offered,

"Yes, father, if that is your wish, we will be good Christians and we will do our best to love her. Maybe not now as our mother, but maybe someday..."

Wilford stared hard at his brother. He was not convinced. He was his mother's favorite and he felt very protective of her just then. He kicked dirt toward Thom.

"Stop now! I will have no further disrespect of my decision from any of you. There will be discipline if I hear of any further!" Said the stern father.

Lupineflower appreciated her new husband's authority and speech making. This was much prized in her culture. She had been confused these past nights that the Elder had not come to her shelter to act as her husband, perhaps he had been waiting for this ceremony and tonight he would come to her?

But later that night she waited and still, he did not come. She did not know what to think of this strange husband behavior. She wondered if what she knew of the sex act would apply to this man. Perhaps he did not take his manhood and push it in and out of her womanhood to make a baby, as she had seen many times with men and women of the Shoshone camps. Would he do something to her that she did not know of? Did he have the same manhood parts as Shoshones? She wanted very much to find out.

Part 8. Pillar Cache Ranch

The next day as they broke camp there was a sense of excitement and urgency among the men and the animals. Lupineflower sensed that they were close to their destination. She would meet her new family today! She again sat in the back of the wagon to ride. Elder Smith was terribly relieved that he did not need to try to explain why she could not ride the mare into the valley. Much to the annoyance of the boys, Elder Smith had gone out of his way to avoid the other communities and ranches in the valley so that the wards would not be buzzing with the news of his new Indian wife before Susan herself knew.

Finally, in early afternoon, they turned down the rutted path that led to the Smith property, Pillar Cache Ranch. The ranch was three miles outside of Clarkston, Utah, a secluded town that had been founded by Mormon pioneers in 1869. In town lived one of the three witnesses to the divinity of The Book of Mormon. The town was about twenty miles, a good day's ride, from Logan. Clarkston, however, had many of the essentials to a comfortable life, including the Rock Meetinghouse built in 1877, a post office, a cooperative store, a schoolhouse made of local stone, a tithing granary, a woolen mill to improve the profits from the annual shearing of sheep, and a very long bridge to cross the Bear River. The railroad between Ogden and Soda Springs was near enough to move goods into and out of the area. There were cold springs and streams, and climate and soils perfect for dryland farming.

The Pillar Cache Ranch was far enough from town, and the work there plentiful enough to make it difficult to go often to town, except for Sunday meetings and some school during seasons when farm work did not keep the children home and travel was possible through winter weather.

When they started down the road to the ranch, Elder Smith's daughters Clarissa, who was 16, and Amy who was 9, and his youngest, little Phineous, who was 2, were outside working in the garden. They came running to meet the outfit, yelling, "Papa! Papa!" Susan, who had seen the dust of their approach was also waiting on the porch, shelling garden peas. She rose when they got close. The four older boys directly drove the animals and wagons to the barn, attempting to stay out of the private meeting their father had coming with their mother.

Sensing something out of the ordinary, Susan walked down the path and said "Brother Elmer, was your trip a good one? Is everyone well?"

"Oh yes, wife! Exceedingly well!" He puffed.

"I see you have brought many fine horses, husband!"

"Yes, wife, and I have something else we must discuss right away. Girls! Please take Phineous to the house!"

But it was too late. Lupineflower had jumped down from the wagon and walked barefooted around to the side where the girls were standing with Phineous. "Mama!" said Amy, "There is an Indian girl!"

Susan drew in her breath. She had expected her husband could return with a woman who she could determine may be his second wife. Of course she knew she had the power to reject any woman he could bring home. But this, she did not expect. Perhaps this Indian child was intended for something else? Were they to adopt her?

But no, the minute she saw her husband's face looking at the Indian, frozen in a moment of terror, she knew. The girl was young, but clearly a woman with healthy sized breasts under her tunic and strong long brown legs indiscreetly exposed below her dress.

In the stunned silence that followed Amy's announcement, she clearly knew that she had no power to disapprove of this second wife. It was certainly done. Her husband was terrified, but his mind was beyond changing. Unlike other women, Susan knew without explanation, that this Indian girl could not be sent back, nor would any decent Mormon home take her in if they rejected her. So, in the course of five quick seconds she saw her life change, and she realized she was no longer to be the main object of her husband's affection.

She was old and had just been replaced by a pubescent savage. How the faithful would talk! How could he have done this to her? She looked at her husband. In her face he saw it all, including her revulsion.

In one quick second he decided not to care.

He went to Helen and took her by the hand and led her to Susan. He surprised himself by saying aloud.

"This is Helen. We will be married as soon as we can travel to Logan."

Susan stared ahead for a moment, involuntarily smashing to mush a pea pod she held between her fingers.

"Certainly you will not be able to marry her at the Temple!"

But this was the least of her concerns. She slowly turned her eyes to look at her husband, then down to the girl. Lupineflower looked to the ground, in what to her was respect, but to Susan was weakness. Susan looked at her own hand, green with pea pulp, then threw down the pea pod and began to laugh. Then she stopped, composing herself. She said,

"Girls, introduce yourself and take Helen to be washed. She is filthy."

Then she walked to stand before Helen.

"Helen, I am Susan, your sister-wife. Welcome to our home."

Then Susan turned and walked into the house, closing the door behind her firmly.

Clarissa, who never seemed surprised by anything, took charge of Lupineflower. While the same age, Clarissa showed deference to her new mother as she politely offered to show Lupineflower to the pump and outdoor washbasins used after farm work. Lupineflower followed her without comment. Elder Smith did not know if anyone realized that Helen did not know English. Her quiet disposition was working to his advantage so far. He thanked God she was meek.

Lupineflower noticed with interest the large barn, the many cows and horses, the smell of pigs and sheep, the neat rows of garden vegetables, the plump children, the large white painted house with glass windows. There were bright flowers planted at the entrance to the door. For what seemed like miles, straight lines of planted crops went to the edge of the valley. The smell of roasting turkey came from the house. The many people about seemed healthy and content. There was an industry about the place that was different than the industry of a Shoshone camp.

Elder Smith led the team and wagon to the barn. The introductions had gone better than he thought it would! Now, in his barnyard, he was back on solid ground and jubilant! He could simply take care of the livestock. They had to feed, water, corral, then later brand break and sell the horses. There were the cattle herds to round up and feed in winter. There were the crops to be harvested soon. The hired shepherds would bring down the sheep in fall and there would be the shearing and the sorting and the binding of wool. Then the trading and banking. They had two community barn raisings coming up.

He knew that he could avoid going into the house until the wedding, except to eat dinner and sleep, for months, if necessary.

Part 9. Smith House

Clarissa, with Amy and Phineous trailing behind, led Helen to the pump behind the house. Lupineflower needed to urinate, so she stepped away from the pump a few paces and began to pull up her buckskin dress.

"No! No! No!" Clarissa said with horror.

Phineaus laughed loudly. "Amy, take him in the house right now!"

"But no, Clair! I want to see the Indian!"

"Do as I say!" They reluctantly left, but Clarissa could see them looking out the kitchen window, watching every move of their new Indian mother.

Clarissa pointed at Helen then at the three skinny outhouses at the edge of the yard. Lupineflower knew white people used these, but she had never done so. It seemed odd that they would go inside a structure for this. Lupineflower hesitated until Clarissa pulled on her tunic and walked her up to them and opened the door of the closest tiny structure. A hot contained smell of human waste came forth. Lupineflower almost wished she did not need to go in, but since she did need to go in and squatting on the ground did not appear acceptable, she went in. The door slammed behind her and she attempted to hold her breath. There was a crude hole in a shelf and it appeared that the waste was put into the hole. Lupineflower was very glad the small structure was not filled with a large pile of human waste. She rather liked sitting on the shelf and going into the hole rather than squatting.

When Helen came out, Clarissa covered her growing realization of the appalling situation by sizing up Helen. She touched the beadwork on the arm of her tunic.

"This is beautiful."

"Yes," said Lupineflower. "Beautiful" she said, touching Clarissa's pinafore.

Clarissa was surprised. It was a garden smock, and a poor old one at that.

"Thank you," she said.

"Thank you," repeated Lupineflower.

Clarissa thought Helen seemed very nice, but very dirty. Clarissa filled the washbowl from the pump. Lupineflower cupped water and took a long drink.

"No!" said Clarissa again.

She did not want Helen to drink from the washbowl.

Lupineflower realized that everything she did was creating a "no" response.

Clarissa pushed Amy who had come back outside.

"Run to the house and get her a drinking cup!"

Lupineflower stood at the washbowl feeling frustrated and confused. It was clear something was wanted of her, but she did not know what and she was quite thirsty. Clarissa indicated no to drinking and yes to washing. In some of her few English words Lupineflower responded with "water-well."

"No! Water pump and wash-bowl!" replied Clarissa, who now realized that this new mother would need be taught to speak English. "This was a job for Clarissa if ever there was one!" Thought Clarissa to herself, 'why I can teach her everything!' A feeling of excitement and power overtook Clarissa. Amy returned with a tin cup and handed it shyly to Helen. Clarissa pumped cold water into the cup.

Lupineflower took it and drank two more cups full. "Thank you" she said to Amy. Amy curtseyed. Lupineflower curtseyed back awkwardly.

Lupineflower remembered the water well at Fort Brown that the white people seemed to constantly use. The Shoshones did not know why this was important, since there were many clear and clean creeks and rivers nearby.

Clarissa said, "Would you like to wash-up?" She picked up the soap and mimicked washing. She handed the soap to Helen. Lupineflower smelled it. It was harsh and medicinal and she made a face. Clarissa realized she should take on this project completely, so she took the soap, made a nice foam and began to scrub Helen's hands. She washed and scrubbed and soaked and then rinsed. Lupineflower was used to a daily washing in the nearest creek or river, but she did not use soap, nor did she scrub quite so hard and thoroughly. When Clarissa was done, she began on Helen's face, using one of the folded rags left at the washbasin for that purpose. Lupineflower did not like this, but determined to accept those things that were needed for her new life with these people. Clarissa bade Helen bend down, and attempted to wash the red clay from her part.

Lupineflower jerked up. It was her turn to say "No!" Clarissa realized this must be of importance to Helen and stopped. Lupineflower smiled her thanks. They were bonding in their roles and Lupineflower was glad that Clarissa had not pushed her to remove her red hair part.

"Well that will do for now!" said Clarissa as she reached for another clean cloth to dry Helen's hands and face.

Lupineflower liked this girl. She began to trust her and see her as a friend. Lupineflower vowed to do as this girl showed her.

The rest of the afternoon and evening was a blur to Lupineflower. She was ushered into the big white house, which smelled wonderfully of roasting turkey. They had come through a door on the side of the house (which Lupineflower noticed faced to the west, not to the east, as doors to dwellings always should). She was shown around. First there was a large main room with a kitchen, polished pine communal table with bench seating, and fireplace. The pine walls had been whitewashed and were of a different kind of wood than the outside of the house, indicating that there was an inner and an outer wall. Lupineflower had not seen this before. She touched the walls carefully to see if they would peel off on her fingers. They did not. Clarissa watched in amazement that someone would not understand walls. Had this Indian never been in a house?

In the cooking area there was a long shelf with many pieces of delicate china dishes and then other shelves displaying more sturdy tin cups and plates and at least four iron pots of different sizes. An iron wood-stove held the place of prominence near a counter with a large sink with its own water pump. There were knives, tools and on other shelves, many tins of food. A curtain hung in front of a cubby behind which Lupineflower glimpsed many-colored jars of all kinds of good things to eat. There was a stack of newspapers and a shelf of perhaps five books. The whole placed smelled homey; of bacon grease, smoke, newsprint, and the delicious damp warmth of the turkey. The windows were open, letting a small breeze move the warm air. Lupineflower breathed deep in anticipation of the earthy meat cooking there.

On the other side of the large room there were four comfortable looking chairs made of bent willow, their seating areas covered with sturdy over-stuffed cloth pillows. The chairs made a small parlor area near the fire. These four chairs sat upon a braided oval shaped rug. On the wall there were a number of framed cross-stitched samplers with white squiggles among the little floss pictures of houses, suns, and flowers. An open door lead out to the small porch at the front of the house, which held two rocking chairs. It had a second screen door that let the nice cool air into the house. Lupineflower had seen rocking chairs and wanted very much to try it on. She obediently followed Clarissa, however.

Off the main room were four large doors with ironwork hinges and bolts. One of the doors was closed. Clarissa's running monologue indicated "Mama" so Lupineflower assumed that Susan, the other wife, was behind the door in whatever other dwelling was there. She showed Lupineflower the second door beyond which was a small room with a braided rug and two bunk beds covered with hand made quilts. There were pegs on one wall with a number of gingham cotton dresses, and on another wall homespun clothes. It was neat and sunny with the afternoon sun through the white cotton curtains. Clarissa indicated with pride her place to sleep and then pointed out the sampler on the wall with more symbols and pretty flowers depicted.

The next room smelled of boy and had three bunk beds that could sleep six boys. It was less neat but still cozy with quilts on each made up bed. There were pillows that Lupineflower wanted to touch as they looked so soft. Then Clarissa took Helen to the last door. The door was newer and appeared to be recently made and installed. It still smelled of fresh-cut pine. She opened the door and inside was a larger bedstead with mattress, some empty pegs and shelves on the wall. There was a book on a table next to the bed. There was no linen or soft pillows. Lupineflower did not understand that this was to be the room for the new wife and the new wife was to have brought her own linen and a trousseau of clothing.

Lupineflower liked the house but began to have the strange feeling of permanence and more ominously, entrapment. She realized these people stayed here in this house and did not travel with the seasons. The smell of turkey pushed away Lupineflower's idea of going anywhere else just then.

Even with the advent of such a novelty as a new Indian mother arriving at their home, a certain routine was in place at the house and very little extra attention was available for Helen. Clarissa sat Helen down in a chair in front of the fireplace and handed her a large bag of fresh corn. She indicated that Helen should husk the corn. Lupineflower assumed it was not for her to eat, so she began to husk the corn, making three neat piles of corn and husks and corn silk.

Soon, the boys could be heard outside washing and roughhousing. A high energy seemed to fill the homestead as the family came together and tried not to discuss the certainly shocking new development that was Helen. Susan's door opened and she bustled out as if nothing new had occurred. She took charge of her kitchen and children and completely ignored Helen. Helen sat uncomfortably in the chair, wishing she could move to the floor, watching and waiting until someone, anyone gave her another direction.

Susan asked Clarissa to join her in her (and what used to be Elder Smith's) bedroom. Once there, Clarissa, who did not often enter this adult space, looked at her mother, sensing her hurt. She hugged her. "It will be alright, Mother. I will look after Helen."

Susan sighed and was much comforted by her daughter. "Every condition produces some comfort," she quoted the well worn Mormon saying, "I dare say that we must look for the blessing here. Daughter, I made you a new dress for your birthday but it appears Helen has nothing to wear and we can't have her nakedness showing in our home. If you will, we will give her your dress and I will make you another one." Susan brought out from her closet a light blue cotton dress with dark blue flowers. It had long sleeves, a button-up prim collar with four white buttons, and fell to just below the ankles, as was appropriate for a young woman.

"Oh Mama, it is lovely! But yes, let's make another for me and I will give this to Helen."

Clarissa came out of the room with the folded dress. Helen noticed it immediately. Blue was a prized color by her people because it was not an easy color to make from any dyes, but was the color of the sky and some still waters. It was also the color of the some of the flowers for which she was named. Lupines were blooming at this time of the year and she had seen many along their way. She loved the fragrant and fragile blooms of the flower, but part of their magic was that they could not be made but by nature.

"Helen, come here!" said Clarissa, walking into the empty second wife's bedroom. Lupineflower followed. After Clarissa closed the door behind them, she unfurled the dress. Lupineflower gasped. She had never seen such a long sea of flowered cloth made into a woman's garment. The flowers did not look like Lupines, but they were the same color. If it was for her, this was the most wonderful of dresses. Clarissa indicated that she should put it on, so Lupineflower quickly threw off her tunic. Clarissa was shocked that she was totally naked beneath, no underwear of any kind. Her skin all over was very brown. Clarissa imagined that she must be about her same age, but her breasts were well developed and had large dark brown nipples. Her body was creased with dirt from her days on the road, and she had the strong but usual scent of perspiration. Clarissa deemed to deal with that tomorrow. There was only so much to be done at one time. Helen put on the dress. It was rather too blousy around the waist and across the shoulders, and the sleeves needed to be rolled up, but it would do.

Lupineflower felt transformed. She decided she would think of herself as "Helen" when she felt Mormon, and "Lupineflower" when she felt New'e. The material smelled so nice and fresh, and for once Helen felt she had become the flower of her New'e name. The skirt was long and swirled around her legs. Clarissa laughed and opened a box of pins and brought out a needle and blue thread and had Helen stand still while she pinned along the bottom so it would be just the right length. The pins scratched at Helen's ankles but she did not care. This was wonderful!

After a quick baste of the hem, Clarissa looked at the finished product. Helen's hair was a mess. Dirty, unbrushed, and full of knots. Again, she vowed to deal with it tomorrow. Clarissa smiled.

Helen, not knowing what else to say, said, "Aelen. Good. Thank you."

"Why aren't you adorable!" said Clarissa.

This woman is no savage, she said to herself. She opened the door and bade Helen step out of the room. The busy kitchen came to a stop as everyone looked, then went back to what they were doing in a new silence. Helen smiled shyly, with her hand in front of her mouth and her eyes down. Amy asked her a question, but Helen, not understanding, did not answer.

The women in the room glanced at each other. They now understood that Helen did not speak much English.

Helen was sure now that this must be the white man's wedding activity and her husband would come to her tonight. Everything was becoming too much for Helen to process. Even Clarissa's box of pins was amazing to her. Her stomach began to be queasy. She went back to her chair by the fireplace and sat alone, watching the family and feeling entirely confused and alone in her beautiful but slightly uncomfortable dress.

Clarissa was standing over the stove stirring something in a large pot and running back and forth in the kitchen using a number of strange tools and preparations.

Susan was placing dishes on the table in a clear pattern. Amy was washing dishes in a big tub. She could hear the boys outside. Someone was chopping wood, which to Lupineflower was woman's work.

The little boy, Phineous, toddled up to Helen, his fingers in his mouth. Helen sat on the floor and took the little one onto her lap, grateful for something familiar. She held him and told him a story, quietly. It felt good to speak Shoshone. He looked at her with his blue eyes and listened to the cadence of her voice. She wondered if soon she would have a child like this, with blue eyes, of her own.

By and by, Susan who was utterly ignoring Helen, went to the porch and rang a bell. "*Ding-clang! Ding-clang! Ding-clang!*" Within a few minutes the whole golden turkey, cut into many slices, a number of large steaming dishes and a pile of fresh baked rolls were on the table. The boys poured through the door, wiping their hands and faces free of water from washing. They each took a seat at the table, admiring the food and glancing Helen's way. Elder Smith was the last one in. He noticed right away that Helen was sitting on the floor, apart from the others, Phineous content in her arms. Clarissa again saved them from the uncertain next steps. She went to Helen and lifted Phineous, and indicated she should come to the table, pointing to a place to the left of Elder Smith who was seating himself at the head of the table.

Lupineflower had never sat at a dinner table with other people; she had rarely sat in any chair. She had never been around this many white people. Her Shoshone family had three mismatched metal spoons that were kept wrapped in a skin with two "trade knives" and one sharp stone knife used for butchering. She certainly had not used a fork or even seen so many dishes or utensils in one place. She meekly sat, head down. She was terrified.

Elder Smith began a prayer. He spoke for some time, with the family sitting quietly with heads bowed. Lupineflower knew some of the prayer was about her, as she heard her name and several times the words "Indian" and "Laminites" and "God" and "Jesus" which she generally knew. She suspected it was the same talk he had made to his boys when they were traveling.

Finally he was done. All the family members said some words in unison which Lupineflower did not understand. Elder Smith then began to dish up a large plate of food. He passed the dish to Susan, who sat at his right, who also dished up, then passed the dish to Helen without even looking her way. Helen did not know what to do, so Clarissa, seated at her side, took the bowl and began to put a huge amount of each of the different types food in separate piles on Helen's plate.

It was uncommon for Shoshones to have more than one type of food to eat at any particular meal; they generally cooked everything they had together in a stew-pot or buried and baked or roasted over a fire. Here, there must have been five separate foods plus yeast rolls and butter and jam and salt and black pepper in shakers. Lupineflower was amazed at the feast.

She happily saw Thom pick up his turkey leg and bit into it. She picked up her slice of turkey and was immediately nudged by Clarissa who indicated the fork. She guessed that only boys were allowed to eat with their hands. She picked up the fork with a fist and was shown by Clarissa a delicate way to hold it. She tried, but eating the good food with that funny and difficult way made eating very slow for her.

But my! The food was so strange and wonderful and satisfying. Lupineflower could taste apple in the smooth mush next to what were potatoes with a mixture of cheese and something else creamy. The green beans were buttered and good. The pepper sprinkled on her turkey by Clarissa tickled her nose but was very pleasing. Again, the roll with the butter and strawberry jam were her favorites.

After the dinner, Clarissa and Amy began clearing everyone's plates, while Susan went to an icebox and brought forth another large bowl. Each person took a serving spoon of the golden shining stuff. Clarissa said "butterscotch pudding" to her, and demonstrated taking a small amount with her spoon. It was unlike anything Lupineflower had ever eaten. It was cool, sweet, creamy and flavored like candy. Lupineflower would remember these new words!

When everyone was done and another prayer was said, the women cleaned up and the men sat in front of the fire which was lit after the high valley air became cool in the evening sunset. Elder Smith lifted one of the books from the shelf and gave it to Thom, who was reading. Since it was clear Helen was exhausted, Clarissa placed her in one of the rockers, which was brought in from the porch to sit behind the men. Lupineflower soon had the hang of rocking the chair and put her head back and listened to Thom's voice. Helen was curious about the reading but after her long and eventful day she gave up being curious and dozed.

When she was awakened by Clarissa, she wondered if her husband was ready to come for her. She was shown into the room where she had dressed. She saw her tunic on the peg on the wall and the bed had been made up with a sheet, woolen pillow and patchwork quilt. She took off her new dress and lay naked on the bed. It was very soft. Soon she was asleep and heard nothing until the roosters began to crow and carry on with the first light. She began to worry that her husband did not want her and that she would be sent away in shame. While she would be happy to go home to her people, she knew it would be an embarrassment if she were sent back. She decided to try very hard to learn the ways of this new family.

Part 10. Ranch Routine

In the next days, Helen was fit into the family's hard-working routine. Clarissa took charge, teaching Helen in the first hours of light to milk the cows that stood waiting at the barn fence. Helen was not at all afraid of the cows, but giggled at the idea of reaching under their low bellies and milking their teats. The benefit of the warm milk was easily understood, however. At first her hands ached and very little milk made it into her bucket. Slowly, however, she learned.

Then Clarissa taught Helen how to gather the eggs from under the chickens. Wilford was in charge of the chicken coops and turkey, duck and geese in their pens. But it was women's work to gather the eggs. Then Helen was shown how to cook the family's breakfast mush, and set aside some fresh cream to dip on top. Some days when they expected a heavy morning's work, she scrambled some eggs to go with the mush.

Helen also easily learned how to wash the many family dishes after each meal, and because this was a constant in the large home, it became an easy but dreaded chore Helen could be trusted to do. She stoked the fire with wood waiting in a pile then pumped the cold water into the water bucket. After the water was poured into the wood stove's water pot, she scrapped the few bits of leftover food into the hog slop bucket. When the water was warmed, it was poured into the wash bucket and Helen sprinkled powdered soap in the warm water, swishing it to incorporate the soap. She then worked the large pile from the dirty side of the wash pail to the clean. Then she carried the heavy dirty water to the garden for watering. Lastly, after the dry mountain air-dried the dishes, she stacked them neatly on the shelves. It was at first satisfying, but soon became monotonous when she realized this would be repeated many times through the day and would seemingly never end so long as there was a hungry family.

Between meals, which were cooked by Susan and Clarissa, she was taught to similarly prepare water for washing clothes, then boil, scrub, rinse, twist and hang the clothes with the ingenious clothing pins on the outdoor lines. While the family each had only a few sets of clothes, there were always very dirty and smelly men's work clothes, women's smocks, bed linens and now three women's rags or to boil and hang or lay out to dry in the sun. There were also the strange long-sleeved, long legged undergarments worn by Elder Smith, Susan, Thom and Orson to wash. Some of the nicer clothes were steamed and ironed by Clarissa using a metal object heated on the stove. Clothes were then neatly folded into perfect shapes and put on the bedroom shelves.

Lupineflower felt that if this routine did not alter itself at some point, her hands would likely be in wash water for a good part of the rest of her life. She preferred to sweep the floor and to churn the cream into butter. She also was, along with the others who came and went doing chores, expected to keep close eyes on Phineous, who was a calm and sweet child. Lupineflower found it hard to imagine that these people kept up such an un-ending schedule of industriousness.

The women stayed in the house preparing and preserving food, cleaning, washing, sewing and gardening. The exception was nine-year-old Amy, who was in charge of watering, weeding and watching for pests in the large vegetable garden and assisting with the harvest of the vegetables. She wore a large bonnet and gloves along with her long sleeved dress, smock and sturdy shoes to keep her from becoming dark. The gardening took her all day, but Lupineflower wished it were her duty as she missed being outside. She was unfamiliar however with growing and tending plants. The men were constantly outside, in the barn, or off in the fields or orchard or riding away on horseback. Lupineflower did not know what they were doing but she was used to Shoshone men being off hunting or taking their leisure.

Lupineflower generally did not speak, but was learning the language of a housewife. In addition to kitchen words, Clarissa had what she called the "word of the day" which they made Helen repeat. In the beginning these words were meant to teach her important Mormon concepts such as "eternal", "anointing", "Trinity", "Council", "Jubilee", and "Epistle". But after much confusion in explaining the out of context concepts, they began with easier words like the days of the week, colors, numbers, and units of measure.

Lupineflower was fascinated by the food. There was a hillside door outside with steps down to second a tight-fitting door behind which was a room with a lantern and matches. Clarissa explained that Elder Smith and Susan had once lived in this hillside when they first came to the valley.

Now, there were large barrels of apples, potatoes, hard squashes, onions, cabbages, and dried corn. There were a number of large sacks of flour and some smaller sacks of sugar. Wheels of cheese sat wrapped in cloth, some waiting to be sold in Logan. There were also many shelves that contained a few brightly colored jars of tomatoes, beans, strawberry jam, apple butter, and peaches. Clarissa informed Helen that the barrels and shelves were now almost empty from the winter of eating, but they would be filled again soon, as the garden was beginning to produce. This required that the women spend many days harvesting in the garden or picking wild fruits or berries, then washing, slicing, filling, seasoning, jarring and boiling the many jars of fresh vegetables for eating through the long winter. Then when the orchard began to produce, the fruit would be picked, then the peaches, apples, pears and apricots dried or canned or made into jellies and syrups. Some would be taken by wagon into town and sold for silver dollars.

At the back of the root cellar room was a third very thick door. Behind it was a chilly room with huge blocks of ice sitting on wood slats that had been cut from the pond in the late winter. Each day a smaller piece of ice was hacked from the blocks and brought up to sit in the kitchen ice-box for keeping drinking milk fresh.

This room also contained metal containers for milk waiting for the weekly cheese making morning.

Mealtime was wonderful with the many varieties of delicious and fresh foods, and meat at almost every meal. The meat was not often deer or rabbit as on the Reservation, but was usually pork, beef, chicken, mutton, or sausage. Lupineflower did not know where the sausages came from, but they were salty and good. Slowly, Lupineflower began to understand how to make most of the other dishes from the many natural foods she recognized. She watched and learned.

Part 11. Council House

After a number of days of the routine of washing dishes and bedding and clothing, Clarissa informed Helen that tomorrow would be "Sunday", a day of rest. Of course the women did not really rest, there were still cows to milk, food to cook and dishes to wash. Special foods were made ready for a later feast, and stored on the counter under napkins, or in the icebox. But after the breakfast mush was eaten, the routine changed and Clarissa told Helen to put on her blue dress as they were going to the Council House.

Elder Smith interrupted, however, saying Helen would stay home that day, and Clarissa would stay with her. This would be the case until the wedding was held. Clarissa suspected that though the whole valley by now knew of Helen, and everyone was undoubtedly whispering madly, no one in the family was yet ready to satisfy the curiosity of the busy tongues.

The community had always talked about the Bad Indians and Good Indians. Sagwich's band was known to be Good Indians. They were Mormon, but the whole band lived among themselves and were employed to help build the Logan Temple. Some Indians, especially in the past, had come around on occasion to beg for food at the farms and ranches. Other groups of Indians, mostly half-breeds, were employed as pickers when the orchards ripened and day labor was needed. Very few Indians, especially those with a history of living in the wild ways, lived with the Valley families, though. There were known stories of Bad Indians stealing white children, but that had not happened for about twenty years.

Truthfully, the Smith family thought Helen was not yet ready to be displayed in company. She still refused to allow anyone to wash or comb her hair, and her eyes, when she looked up, showed a particular anxiety, which in their minds was "wildness". Though they believed her to be a Mormon, she had not been to a Mormon meeting in many years, so what was the harm in missing a few more?

After the two wagons rattled off down the road, Clarissa and Lupineflower found themselves alone for the first time. They wandered out through the barns and along the creek and into the ripening hay, corn and alfalfa fields. They talked, in the way they could understand each other, and Clarissa finally helped Helen understand something of the wedding that was to come.

It would not be in the Temple, as Helen did not have the "Temple Recommend" needed to enter. Lupineflower did not care, as she did not know what the "Temple" was anyway. Perhaps, Clarissa said, as Helen learned more of their ways, she would be worthy to take the Code of Health (swearing off unclean foods or drink such as alcohol), be Morally Clean (did anyone know if she was a virgin?) and follow the Law of Tithing, which of course as a member of the upright family this was assured. No, the wedding would be a simple ring ceremony. Later, after she was worthy, they could go to the Temple in Logan for the Sealing Ordinance, in which she would be dressed by the Temple matrons in her Temple white dress with green aprons, learn the secret signs and tokens, and they would go through the veil at which time Elder Smith would whisper his real name to Helen, and tell her the name she was known by in Heaven. Then they would be bound to each other for "eternity". Maybe Helen would even hope for an Endowment with its washing and anointing after which she would be given the magic garment to always wear under her clothes.

Lupineflower did not understand all of this, but now knew why her husband had not come to her. It was such a relief to know that they were merely waiting for some ceremonial practices! Lupineflower indicated the part in her hair, and asked if she needed more red. Clarissa laughed and laughed, realizing Helen thought her hair was to do with her wedding. When everyone arrived home, they were pleased to see Helen with clean washed hair, trimmed, combed and done in a bun. But for her brown skin and funny way of saying words, she was becoming one of them.

With these successes, it was decided that the next Sunday would be the wedding day. For Helen, she was most happy to be leaving the milk barn and kitchen and washbasins. She marveled that these people stayed so long in one place.

The family had prepared a large picnic basket with a berry pie made by Clarissa, potatoes with cheese and cream, and two chickens that Susan had killed, dressed, cut and fried that morning. Helen had made the family's breakfast of mush with butter and cream, bacon and warmed leftover biscuits. Helen had washed all the dishes.

She happily wore her blue dress and a new bonnet and climbed into the wagon to go to the meeting with the others. Lupineflower had changed much in the two weeks since leaving her Shoshone family. Her clothes, hair, and language were dramatically different. She had a new family, too, whom she mostly liked, although she had yet to interact much with Elder Smith and the boys, who all ignored her.

The meeting was held in a square building called the Rock Council-house made for many people. It was near that place that served as a schoolhouse for the children in winter. The building was full of families, all neighbors in the Cache Valley. Men and women sat separately, and children were ushered out for their own meeting on benches under a shady tree on the side of the building. Without speaking to her, Susan took Helen's hand, as Clarissa went with the children. Susan donned a green apron. She held her head high as they both walked to the women's area wearing their good dresses and gingham sunbonnets. Lupineflower kept her head down, afraid of all the white women; perhaps fifteen in attendance, all of whom were wearing the apron. She could feel their eyes on her.

The service went on for a very long time. Early in the meeting she heard "Helen" and at first did not know if it referred to her or to wives in general, but then she saw the Bishop smiling and looking right at her. She blushed and kept her head low. There were a number of songs which made sitting on the hard benches bearable. After a while, she began to hum softly, mimicking the sounds of the singing. A strange woman sitting on the other side from Susan stared. Lupineflower watched the light and shadows made by the sun through the glass window move across the backs of the women. Occasionally someone would get up to go outside to the privy.

Then finally, the service ended. A commotion began and Susan rose, pulling Helen along. They went forth to the front, and Elder Smith met them. Susan sat down leaving Helen alone with Elder Smith. A brief blessing by the Bishop took place and Elder Smith took Helen's hand. His hand was sweaty and hers was cold. He turned and gave her a small silver band and indicated her left hand. He slid on the ring. Then he turned her to face the people. There were so many white people, Lupineflower thought she may faint. She saw that Clarissa and the Smith boys had entered and stood at the back. Clarissa smiled at her. Phineous loosed some loud baby noises. A few more words were said then everyone clapped politely.

The meeting broke and she stood quietly while Susan joined them again. The family was the first to proceed out of the building as another song was sung. Elder Smith greeted all the other men and women as they came outside. The men ignored her, but some of the women spoke to her; Lupineflower did not reply and looked down respectfully. The other women then became busy with the food. It was a lovely summer day and there was to be an outdoor picnic. Many baskets and platters of food were lined up on the tables. Elder Smith and Helen, being the important guests that day, along with two boys who were having birthdays, were the first to go through the line to dish up their food.

Lupineflower was reminded of her communal feasts at home, which were certainly different, but were also strangely the same with happy people working together. There, the food and service were different and the eldest ones went first and were given the honor of special food. Here, after the important guests, came the men, then the children, then the women. Here there were so many foods and many versions of chicken, potatoes and pies and cakes. Lupineflower wanted to eat only the cakes, but she followed Elder Smith's lead and took what he took. They sat at one of the tables and ate quickly. Then Elder Smith bade her get up and they went straight to the first wagon, climbed up alone, and rode off toward home. Many of the congregation clapped half-heartedly. The rest of the family would come home later in the second wagon.

While everyone acted as if following a script, they each harbored secret thoughts.

Elder Smith wanted only to finally taste Helen's sweet body which he had so many times imagined, would be deep brown outside and pink, sweet, firm and succulent inside. He imagined her legs moving apart for him. He spurred the horses to make the hour-long ride home more quickly.

Susan was enraged by being replaced by a mute child who so clearly would never be like a sister to her, as sister wives were to be. Susan felt abandoned and discarded and humiliated by her husband in front of the whole valley. She had the sinful thought of hacking at the Indian girl with her sharpest kitchen knife.

Thom worried of his own lustful thoughts about his fiancé, Harriet, and his shameful frequent touching of his own penis when he found himself alone in the barn. This was a breach of his vows of cleanliness. He worried his own wedding, a true proper Sealing Ordinance, which would take place next year, when the Temple at Logan was finished, would be cancelled if he could not receive the Temple Recommend.

Orson, who was eighteen, was thinking of a horse he was trying to break. It was stubborn and he wondered if he should try a new method of spending extra time working it on a lead rope.

Clarissa was so thrilled to have what she thought of as her "project", an Indian friend whom she could teach and mould, firmly within the family.

Wilford, who was thirteen, was disgusted by the squaw and vowed never to speak to her or acknowledge her presence. Earlier he had heard his friends snickering at her and calling her names. They had better not be laughing at his family.

Alvarnus, who was twelve, had told mean Joseph Browning that "Smith's Squaw" could ride a horse better than he ever could and they better think twice about saying anything about their family saving this savage from hell by bringing her to the Mormon way.

Amy, eight, wondered what had Phineous been into? She was wiping the dirt off of his face and clothes with a wet rag. He had something sticky on his hands, then he had rolled on the ground and smeared it all over himself.

The Mormon men had various thoughts, whether they too should save an Indian maiden, what difficulties Elmer Smith would find with Susan and the squaw, and how the times were changing.

The Mormon women were aghast. Poor Susan, to have to keep a savage in her home, and share her husband. They hoped the savage was safe and would not bring her bloodthirsty tribe to kill the family in the night. They were also curious. What was this woman to be like? Would they get to know her eventually, or would she stay a savage?

Lupineflower was still dizzy with the unending new experiences. She sat jostling on the wagon seat next to Elder Smith and missed her mother.

Part 12. Healing

During the hay cutting, Orson badly broke his leg and some of his ribs. He had been driving a team of two work horses pulling the new Twine Binder, a wooden machine that cut bunches of hay and twisted and knotted twine around each bundle. Alvarnus had been walking alongside throwing the bundles into the wagon, driven by Wilford. Wilford's team of horses had spooked, probably by a snake in the field, and began to career wildly toward Orson's team. Orson struggled to keep the two teams from crushing Alvarnus between them, and in doing so he wrenched his team to the other side and overturned the Twine Binder, breaking some of its parts, and bending the hitch. As Orson fell, he rolled under the machine, pinned his leg.

Alvarnus was unharmed so he and Wilford worked madly to get the team to pull the machine back upright. In doing so they heard Orson's leg snapping. Orson screamed and swore. Finally, they pulled him free and put him in the wagon on the cut hay for the bouncing ride back to the house. His skin had not been broken but the bone was jutting beneath the skin in a bad way.

By the time they arrived at the house, Orson was in shock. Wilford was sent running to the orchards to fetch Elder Smith. Susan and Clarissa attempted to make Orson comfortable on his bunk. Alvarnus was sent to the lumber pile for wood of a certain size. Amy was told to cut six cloths for wrapping the leg. Elder Smith arrived and soon screams came from the boy's bunkroom as they attempted to set the broken limb.

In all this commotion, Lupineflower, who now thought of herself most of the time as Helen, slipped outside and barefoot ran down the road where she remembered seeing a natural pain reliever. She frequently stayed home from Sunday meetings to cook but she always found a good part of the day to ride out in nature and be alone, something she treasured in the busy house. Along the way she looked for leaves which she knew would help Orson to sleep, and while it was too late for the flowers, the roots of another plant that could be used to draw out poisons, should they build up in Orson's body.

When she returned, Orson was whimpering and Susan was sobbing. Attempting to set his leg had made the break worse, and the bone was now poking through the torn skin of his leg. The Smiths knew of at least three community members who had died of infections from accidents like this one. Helen quickly ground some of the plants and spread them on a cloth. She began a tea with others. As Susan and Elder Smith whispered on the porch and the other children were sent out to continue to work, Helen poured cool water on cloths, plastered the ground plants on the cloths and went to Orson. He allowed her to gently remove the bloody cloth to place the new cloth onto his wound. She then went to the tea and stirred in a powder from the pouch she had brought with her. Susan and Elder Smith came back inside. They had determined to send someone for the nearest doctor, a few hours ride away.

When they returned they saw Helen's poultice. Susan was disgusted. She began to remove it but Elder Smith held her back saying Helen knew Indian medicines. Helen came in with the tea and bade Orson drink it all. He began to relax. Reluctantly, Susan allowed it. Tears of helplessness streamed down her face. Helen put her hands on Orson's shoulders. She looked meaningfully at Elder Smith.

In the three months since their wedding, they had established a way of understanding and caring with each other. It was private and genuine. While Elmer did not speak often to Helen, he shyly brought her small gifts, pretty stones or candies. After dinner and upon awakening, he did not tire of her body and slept in her room every night. After their lovemaking he was tender with her if he was not asleep or up for his chores. She liked his attentions and especially, after the first few times, the sex act. Elder Smith knew how to tease her and keep her wanting his flesh inside her and his tongue on her nipples. Helen so wanted to have a blue-eyed baby.

Elder Smith saw the look and knew it was time to try again to set the leg. He firmly grasped Orson's foot and pulled slowly and deliberately. The leg slipped into its place. Orson gasped. Susan gasped. Elder Smith was sweating. Helen tied the poultice to the leg wound to hold the skin in place. Much of the bleeding had stopped but now started again. She spoke a few words in Shoshone and went for more tea. After the second cup of tea, they splinted the leg as Helen showed them so that the poultice could be changed. Orson slept. Helen went out to find more medicines.

As Orson's leg and ribs healed, he was moved to the parlor to a soft pallet. He often read to the women as they worked from the Book of Mormon or from the newspapers that were published a few times a week, and available on Sundays at the Rock Councilhouse. He read of happenings in Washington, local advertisements and letters from the community, and discourses from the Church President. He also did other odd jobs like whittling a new set of clothespins, and sharpening the knives. He looked at Helen with a new fondness.

Autumn was one of the busiest times at the ranch. I addition to the usual chores, everyone helped picking fruit in the orchard, and harvesting in the fields. Single men from every walk of life, all Mormon of course, were brought in and paid a wage for their work. There were numerous long days for the women canning and making jellies and pickles and syrups. On days in the fields they were out from early morning until after sundown. Amy carried a basket of food by horseback to the hungry workers. There was a sense of accomplishment from it all. Seeing the products of all the year's work with God's blessing of good growing weather.

Some days men from the Council House came to help with large jobs at the Pillar Cache Ranch and other days Smith family members went to help other families. Helen stayed home that first year, except for Councilhouse, feeling unsafe among the neighbors. Her reputation had grown, however, as a healer. More than one family asked Elder Smith for a powder or tea for their stomach trouble, or for pain. Helen found more time, usually in the late morning after the milking and breakfast dishes to gather herbs. Amy, the gardener, was interested and often went along to learn about the wild plants of the valley. Helen wished Coneflower were there, as she knew so much more! Amy looked at Helen with new respect. She never imagined that the weeds could be as important as her garden vegetables.

One day as they were putting up tomatoes, some Utes rode their horses up the road and came to the door. Helen, seeing them outside, hid in her sleeping room. She was irrationally embarrassed for the Utes to see her wearing her hair in a bun and an apron and Carissa's black white-woman's shoes. Susan gave them a small sack of flour and some squash and they rode off. After they left, Helen wished she had talked to them in hand signs just to see if there was news of her people that they may know. She might have told them to send word to her mother that she was pregnant.

Part 13. Winter of Sadness

The Smith family, except for Helen who stayed home with Orson and Phineous, had gone to Logan in the fall with their two wagons, and two wagons borrowed from the Heber family. They were loaded down. One wagon held straw packed barrels of fruit from the orchard, numerous perfectly aged cheeses, a large sack of dried apple slices, and a barrel of cucumber pickles. Two wagons were fully loaded with sacks of flour that had been milled from their wheat at the local mill. The last wagon was heaped with ears of seed corn. Harvest had been bountiful, and they expected a good trade for all their hard work.

After a long ride to town and two nights spent with Susan's sister, they returned with one wagon filled with lumber and various farm implements and a second wagon with all manner of goods for the house. There were two bolts of colored cotton cloth for nice dresses and shirts, two bolts of flannel for winter wear, sewing supplies and extras such as ribbons and buttons. There was also coffee, sugar, vinegar, baking powder, spices, tonics, soap and more glass "ball" jars and lids for canning. Elder Smith told Helen they had done very well and brought her a cameo on a small chain. Helen was very proud.

The winter was mild. They drove their wagons rather than the sleigh to Councilhouse. The night fires in the fireplace and stove kept the Smith ranch house fairly warm. Work continued, with the women sewing, and the men continuing to work with the animals and preparing for the next spring farming. Helen made an easy version of moccasins for each family member but hid them away until they were all finished. Her gifts were the hit of Christmas, except for the lemon peel candies, nuts and raisins.

The Community women began to treat Helen with more ease once she began to speak shyly to them in English and sing along with the celebration church music. She had a nice voice. They were fascinated and appreciative of her herbal remedies. They all, except perhaps Susan who could not help but be a little jealous, shared her happiness when she began to show in her pregnancy.

The Smith family was well respected, with a self-sustaining farm, strong and successful children, and a large tithe to the church. Their ten percent of the sale from their wool from the sheep, their horse and cattle trade and their farm sales went right to the Councilhouse and helped sustain the church mission, charity work, and all the locally needed improvements. All was going so well!

In late winter, Helen went into labor. She knew she was too early, as she thought the baby would come in spring. She had a fairly quick delivery, assisted by Clarissa and Susan. The baby, a boy, was born dead. Helen insisted in wrapping the little body in the Shoshone way, and they buried him next to three other small graves, Susan's children, on the other side of the house from the barn. After this death, Susan cried with Helen. It would have been her child, too. Susan missed having a wee baby around.

Everyone was terrified the next day after the burial when Helen was not in her bedroom. Her deerskin tunic and moccasins were missing as well as an elk skin wrap she had made after the boys had hunted in the fall. The night had been colder than usual and light snow was on the ground. There were no tracks so she must have been gone all night. The family gathered to talk about what to do. Thom determined that a mare was missing.

Clarissa and Elder Smith insisted they give her a day before searching. They felt she would not leave the family, and she knew how to live outdoors. They knew there were Shoshone rites but did not know what they were. Susan was frantic. So many times she had wished the girl would just disappear, but now, after months of her quiet helpfulness, hard work, her friendship with the children and now this dead little boy, she wanted her home safely right now! Amy cried and even Wilford looked distressed. Phineous asked over and over "Where Aelen?" They wondered how she could ride a horse so soon after giving birth. That night they heard an eerie howling coming from far away.

As the sun was setting that next night, Helen returned, riding the mare slowly down the road. Her face was smeared with ashes, and her arm was bleeding where she had apparently cut herself in three long gashes. Clarissa, Amy, Phineous and Alvarnus all ran to her and hugged her as she slid off the horse. Elder Smith carried her inside. She indicated she had been praying, and would not talk. She went to bed, with everyone's relief. Susan brought a cup of hot tea. Elder Smith lay down by her and held her close. As Thom was stabling the mare, he found the horse had been painted with ashes and mud around her eyes, and in patterns on her body. The mare looked at Thom with a knowing and honored expression.

A month later, Elder Smith came home from a church meeting feeling unwell. Soon he was shivering and sweating and vomiting. He had influenza. His coughing, when it started, was wet and rumbling and heard all over the house. Soon, Clarissa, Orson and Susan were sick. They all moved into the girl's room so the others could sleep. Helen brought them teas and cold cloths. Elder Smith finally stopped coughing but remained weak, laying on the pallet that Orson had used during his broken leg.

Thom worked very hard chopping wood in the cold, and he, too, began a fever. Just as Susan and Clarissa were getting well, Phineous became sick. Then, the next day, it was Amy and Wilford. Anyone who was well enough was needed to put on a coat and go out to tend the animals. Word came from the mailman that already four people in the community had died.

Phineous had it the worst. He slept fitfully, cried and threw up any fluid. On the third afternoon, his fever became very high and his eyes went glassy. He coughed pitifully. His little chest began to rattle, and that evening he stopped breathing, turned blue, then went waxen white as the life left him.

That night the house was quiet except for Helen making and serving soup, Susan sobbing, Elder Smith praying, and everyone, except Helen and Phineous, coughing.

The next winter, Helen again grew large with child. Right before Christmas, she delivered a healthy boy with blue eyes. Elder Smith proudly named him Roland, and Helen called him Happy, in her language. Then he too, died of influenza at the age of three months. This time, Orson painted ashes around the eyes of all the horses in the barn. Helen was so touched by this when she stole away at night to the barn, to take a horse, to ride to the mountain, to wail and say her prayers, after Happy was wrapped and put into the ground next to the five other small graves.

Part 14. Zion

One mid-afternoon the next summer, the family was uncustomarily seated at home before a blazing fire. A sudden chilly thunderstorm had blown in, interrupting work, and leaving everyone with a feeling of naughty work-escaping freedom. Elder Smith, sensing the family needed a bit of joy after the difficult and emotional months of mourning Phineas and Roland, surprised everyone by going to the kitchen himself and popping a large pot of popcorn, creating a party atmosphere.

Thom and his new wife, Harriet, saw the storm coming and joined the family. They had been married the month before at the new Temple in Logan and now had moved to a one-room house onto some newly cleared acreage on the edge of the Pillar Cache Ranch.

Helen felt Harriet was bossy. Harriet liked to be the center of attention and often asked Helen embarrassing questions about her life with the Indians. Helen would have been pleased to tell about this, but not in response to Harriet's insensitive intrusions.

To Helen's relief, Harriet ignored her for once and took charge of the family's discussion by asking Elder Smith to tell all about his childhood and how he came to be at Pillar Cache Ranch.

Helen was, for once, very interested in Harriet's question. She had never considered her husband as a child or imagined that he had been anywhere but on this ranch. But of course she knew her imaginings could not be true because this land was New'e land and no whites were here when Elder Smith was a child. Elder Smith told his story.

Well, let's see now. I was born in Liverpool England. My Da's family were all Blacksmiths and worked hard for 14 hours a day. He eventually married my Ma, and they had three children, first me, then my sister Loisa, then my brother, John. Da had some problems with his brothers and after my Ma's parents died and left our family a little money, Da decided to move to America. So when I was ten years old, the whole family took a ship and arrived in New Orleans in 1851. We were going to St. Louis, where my Da knew of someone from Liverpool, so we took a river steam ship up the Mississippi.

On the steamer, we met a Mormon missionary who gave his testimony to my Da and Ma. I remember him. His name was Elder James. He spoke so convincingly of Jesus Christ and the Latter

Day rewards that he made a great impression on us. He also told Da that Blacksmiths and forges were surely needed in Zion, and encouraged him to join up with a wagon train. He also mentioned the Cache Valley, a few days ride north of the Salt Lake and how Oregon pioneers said it was such a beautiful place with good timber in the bottom lands, lots of clean clear water, a nice climate and perfect for farming and wintering cattle. For some reason the Cache Valley always stuck in my mind.

Well, at first my Da did not want to go off with this stranger, so he listened politely but said he had plans in St. Louis. When we got there, we could not find his friend. Then my brother John died of a fever. Ma did not want to stay in a place that had killed her little son so she asked my Da to find Elder James. Da found him alright, and before you know it, we were baptized and all going to Zion in a wagon company.

We went about 100 miles a week; walking or riding in the wagon pulled by oxen. We had spent the rest of Ma's family money on a few horses, a cow, seed and supplies. After the long ship journeys I was so happy to be able to walk about and see the country. I remember we passed graves of other pioneers killed by Indians, and graves of Indians, which scared us plenty. I remember the amazing new plants that we didn't have in England and the wide spaces with no people whatsoever, and clean air with stars as bright as lanterns.

Mostly we kept to wagon roads and river bottoms. At night we kept men at watch but we never saw any hostiles. I slept on a quilt we brought all the way from Liverpool.

We ate a lot of crackers, potatoes, deer meat, and gravy made from grease and flour and water, or milk when we had it from the cows walking along with us.

We had all kinds of problems on the way. Storms, like today, dog fights, upset wagons, mud making the roads impassable, an accidental shooting where a man killed one of our best milk cows, and teams stampeding. And of course so many blisters on our feet from all that walking and even on our butts from bumping on the wagon seat, especially in the first few weeks.

Sometimes my Da would set up a temporary forge for repairs of the wagons and he became a real popular part of the wagon team.

It was hot and humid during the first part of the trip, then the air got nice and cool after we crossed the Continental Divide and the creeks we crossed flowed to the west rather than to the east. That was somewhere in Colorado, I think.

Sometimes we saw big herds of bison. I wished you kids could see those buffalos, but they're all gone now, to make room for cattle. The buffalo were huge in overall size, but with little rumps and tails, delicate feet, large strong chests and big mangy heads. There were so many of them you could not count them. And they left us lots of dung to burn for our fires. All day we gathered up bison dung, which we called "meadow muffins" to use at night for campfire fuel. We sang this one song about it.

> There's a pretty little girl in the outfit ahead,
> Whoa, Haw, Buck and Jerry Boy!
> I wish she were by my side instead .
> Whoa, Haw, Buck and Jerry Boy!
> Look at her now with a pout on her lips
> As daintily with her fingertips
> She picks for the fire some buffalo chips!
> Whoa, Haw, Buck and Jerry Boy.

Susan smiled and sang the last part along with Elder Smith. Harriet picked right up on that. She asked Susan if she had also come across in a wagon. Yes, she had.

I was born in Germany and came to America as a baby. We lived in Illinois and met up with the Mormons there. My father even knew some of the prophets! My family made it to the Promised Land and they now have a nice home in Salt Lake City. We arrived about a year before Elder Smith. We met at Council House and it was love at first sight. We got married when we were both eighteen.

We left right away for the Cache Valley, which was pretty remote and unpopulated, except by Indians coming through. We were lucky to have met some of the folks who had arrived before us and helped us know how to start this farm. I am so happy my husband had remembered what Elder James had said about this place. We had big plans to make this place our home.

There were many lonely times when we lived in the "soddy", you know, the room we now use as the root cellar, then when this house was just one room. We both missed our families in Salt Lake and only saw them every few years. Your father's parents are gone

now, but one of my sisters and her family are still there. They own a
dry goods store.

You know that since we arrived here, we have been adding on
to this place almost every year, whether it be a bigger barn, a new
bedroom, the icehouse, or more plowed ground. We want to make
this Valley ready for when Jesus Christ comes back to this Earth.

Helen thought that last bit was rather odd. If Jesus Christ had made
the Valley surely, would he not want it the way it was before the Mormons
came? But that was only one thing about these stories that made her think.
Aside from all the silly talk about Indians, (did they believe those things after
knowing her for so long?), she had never thought of her husband as being
born across the waters and coming so far to be here, and building this farm
up with his own hands and those of his sons and daughters.

She was faintly proud, but also felt very separate from these people
who had come on to New'e land and acted as if it were already theirs. An
anger rose up in her. She remained quiet, so as not to break the happy
mood of the party.

Part 14. Thanksgiving

Orson had spent six months helping on the farm of a neighbor who
had many daughters but only two sons. In return he learned the art of
smoking meat, and married their oldest daughter, Diantha. He returned
home to help with the spring planting. In two days, a cozy one-room house
was built near the orchard for him and Diantha. They ordered a stove and
other household items, and the hardware necessary to build a smoke
house. The smokehouse they built was about five feet square and only high
enough to step into. It had special insulation and firebox and racks for
hanging and holding cuts of meat.

By that fall, his craft was well established. The hams were delicious
and he began experimenting with deer, elk, mutton and even trout from the
Bear River. Diantha made wonderful sausages from scrap meat, or game.
Soon neighbors were bringing meat to be cured. They left a portion of their
meat in payment for Orson's services. He began selling all varieties of
smoked and cured meats to the families of the valley. He discussed with
the family how he had decided to open a meat shop in Salt Lake, after he
had saved some money for his venture.

Helen was fascinated by this process. It was not unlike the traditional way Shoshones cured meat, by cutting thin strips of meat and placing
them for days on racks over a smoky fire. Of course in the old days it was

buffalo that was cured. In Helen's life, though she had seen only one buffalo, which appeared across the plains one day all alone. The whole band went out to see it. It invoked such reverence, and grief, too standing there alone in the grass. The old ones told stories of the millions of bison that had roamed these lands just fifty years before.

In her life, they mostly cured venison and elk. She remembered as a girl staying awake for days and nights at a time guarding the racks of curing meat from hungry birds, wild critters and even the local dogs.

Here though they cured mostly pork. After butchering, cuts of pork were allowed to get very cold in the icehouse. Then, warm salt was rubbed into the meat so that it drained for a few days onto clean cloths. If it had not dried properly, more salt was rubbed in. Anywhere there were holes or depressions in the cut, such as around the bones, there was danger of spoilage, so potassium nitrate, or saltpeter, was rubbed on in those places. Once the meat rested in a cold place for a few weeks, it was hung in the smokehouse and exposed to fragrant smoke made from burning corncobs or sometimes various kinds of wood chips for a number of days. The meat was so delicious when sliced thin. These smoked meats did not rot and so could provide a delicious source of protein all winter long. It was beautiful to see the sausages and hams stored in Orsons's meat house.

Since 1863, when President Lincoln had proclaimed November 26 a national day of Thanksgiving, the family had been celebrating the day with wonderful savory and sweet foods. A pig was always butchered for the many menu items.

The morning started with "scrapple". The meat was taken from the head, heart and other lean scraps, which were boiled until the meat became tender. The fat, gristle and bones were removed from the pot then the meat was finely chopped. The fat was allowed to separate from the boiled water and it was added to the chopped meat which went back on the fire with salt and pepper. Once it boiled again, it was thickened with corn meal and stirred for some time. It was poured into a mould then left to harden. It was so delicious cut into slices and fried.

For the main meal, the women made many pies, including some from the preserved berries that they had spent so much time picking in the heat of summer. There were cinnamon apples and of course creamy potato dishes and many hot rolls with butter and preserves. They enjoyed some of the first fresh pork of the season.

The Thanksgiving of 1888 was very festive, as Thom and Harriet recently had their second son, and Helen and Elder Smith had a beautiful two-month old brown-eyed daughter they named Sarah. It was such fun to hear the coos of the two babies and to see them rosy with health. Orson and cheerful Diantha made the party complete. Helen truly felt a part of this lively and cohesive group.

The only sadness came in knowing that in a few months Clarissa, now nineteen, would leave them to become the first wife of a fine boy just returning from a Mormon mission to Austria, in Europe. She would move to

Salt Lake, his family's home. Fortunately, Orson would soon be there to look out for them, along with the boy's family, who was quite prominent. They would enjoy their trips there, too, to visit their loved ones. Helen now traveled easily and took part with the family of the many special Mormon meetings, and shopping trips to Clarkston. Helen was proud that the family was successful and wealthy by pioneer standards. Elder Smith was a good husband and a smart leader of the family.

Next summer, when traveling became easier, Anna Weber, from Wyoming Territory, was to join the family as planned (albeit a year late) to become Elder Smith's third wife. Helen was anxious for news of her family on the reservation, and thought that certainly Anna would bring some word. Secretly, she hoped to be able to go with the party to bring Anna.

Part 15. Anna

Instead, Anna arrived on the Utah and Northern Railway, which ran on schedules through the Cache Valley. She seemed very young to Helen, although they were the same age. She appeared to be a silly girl. Susan and Helen shared a glance when she got off the train wearing big yellow fabric flowers on her bonnet and giggling for no reason. Even Elder Smith did not seem to know what to say to her chatter and seemed anxious for the wagon ride to be over so he could retreat to the barn and fields.

Helen understood why Mrs. Weber kept Anna at home for a number of years after most girls her age would have married. She was very immature. On the day of Anna's arrival, Helen had been shocked and very hurt when she had asked Anna about her Shoshone family. Anna had looked at her as she might have looked at a true novelty. "Oh *you* are that Indian that came from Washakie's band! Why yes, your mother is dead, I heard. I don't know what happened to her, but she didn't come around and my mama asked about it." Susan gasped at the insensitivity of the delivery of this sad news and embraced Helen, who put her head down and did not speak. Soon, Helen wrapped Sarah in her cotton blankets and tied her in the traditional cradleboard she had made from willow branches, soft deer hide and cotton. She put Sarah on her back and left the house and walked up the road toward the mountains.

Elder Smith, upon hearing of Helen's grief, saddled an extra horse and rode after Helen. Upon catching up with her, he held her and expressed his remorse for her loss. He promised her she could visit her Shoshone family in the next summer. He tried to convince Helen to bring Sarah home. Instead, she took the extra horse, strapped Sarah to the saddle and told her husband that she needed to pray for her mother in the Shoshone way. She promised to be home in a few days time.

Elder Smith was furious with Anna. How surprised he was that this traditional Mormon girl from a good family was such an immediate disappointment, when Helen, who had no schooling or formal religion and knew nothing of their way of life had always been such a pleasure and blessing to the whole family. Anna retreated to her new room alone, to cry into her embroidered pillows.

After this first day fiasco, Amy, now twelve, took over the introductions of Anna to the homestead just as Clarissa had done for Helen. It was planned that Anna would help Amy with the garden, and with washing clothes. Amy was now also responsible for all clean up in the kitchen so the extra hand would be welcomed. Helen had graduated to Clarissa's role as family cook and of course took the primary care and feeding of Sarah.

Anna did not like the idea of allowing her skin to brown in the sun, or her hands to chap in cleaning water. But she and Amy liked giggling together. Anna complained frequently and became a constant negative influence for the impressionable Amy. Susan was at her wits end with the girl and hoped that the marriage, which would happen at the July 4th celebration, would settle this child into a woman. Soon the community of Mormon women united to "influence" Anna and teach her the respectful ways of a responsible wife. Helen, like her father would have done, removed herself from the situation and went about her chores and snuggled with her baby, Sarah, allowing the force of the women in the community to eventually have its way with the difficult Anna.

Part 16. Logan

In the nine years that Helen lived at the Pillar Cache Ranch, she had never been to Logan. Even though they were only fifteen miles away (if they could have gone directly without worry about the crossing of the creeks) the big town could have been another world. Helen was uncomfortable among large numbers of white people. She was hard working at home and did not really want to go anywhere, except into the mountains to pray. The Ranch was enough novelty for her. During the times Helen found herself becoming interested in the world outside the Ranch, her curiosity was usually set aside in favor of a pregnancy or nursing a young child, which made leaving the farm, except for Meeting, too dangerous or ponderous. Helen had two other miscarriages and was careful to do all she could to bring healthy children to term. Happily, six years after Sarah was born, she and Elder Smith welcomed a healthy blue-eyed son they named George, into the family.

In the first year after her marriage, she had rarely left the Ranch, except to go to the Meetinghouse in Clarkston and to walk alone or with Clarissa to the remaining wild places around the ranch. Clarkston was two or three miles away and was a town in its own right. However, it was virtually closed on Sundays; no one lived permanently in Clarkston Utah in the 1880s unless they were Mormon, and therefore present at the Rock Meetinghouse on Sunday. Rock Meetinghouse was an imposing building made of local stone and mortar, with arched stained glass windows and chandeliers inside. It had been built in 1877 by local volunteer labor.

The first time Helen went to town during the week, she saw the ladies and Elder men from Meeting doing shocking things; milling wheat, buying groceries, banking at the Deseret National Bank (owned of course by the Mormon church), operating the telegraph or tending the tithing granary and hay stacks. It took her a while to understand that the people she knew were not perpetually at the Rock Meetinghouse, but had totally separate roles, such as baker, school teacher, sales clerk, dentist, midwife (none of whom ever made it to the Pillar Cache Ranch), ticket seller at the rail station, or blacksmith. The people were kind, helpful and cooperative with anyone who was part of the Mormon community and very standoffish to anyone who may pass through town without ties to the Church of Latter Day Saints.

Clarkston was known for its wealth of grain. Dry land farming had been perfected in the 1870s and the soil and climate were well suited to grow wheat. They also grew barley, sorghum and alfalfa where other parts of the state were too rocky or cold. For anyone without good valley bottom land for farms, sheep provided the perfect income from their wool, which was shipped and sold through the town's wool merchants. Clarkston, Utah was a thriving and organized town with a tight community who knew all about each other.

The Pillar Cache Ranch was to the west of Clarkston, in the Bear River Mountains, the northernmost part of the Wasatch Mountain Range, the only range of mountains in the western United States that runs east and west, rather than north and south. Between the Ranch and Clarkston was Gunsight Peak. Creeks flowed from all the mountains providing wonderful and easy (unless you were the one digging) opportunities for diversion of water into irrigation sloughs and canals. While it was isolated ground, it was optimal for a family run operation. This led to self-sufficiency and diversity of products of the land.

November of 1893 was to be a treat for everyone. Three weddings were planned at the Temple in Logan. Wilford was to marry a pretty girl from Logan and Alvarnus was to marry the baker's daughter from Clarkston. Amy, now nineteen was to become the second wife of a local rancher a few miles away in the Cache Valley. Most of the family would attend the three weddings. Since Helen and Sarah, and Helen's infant son George still did not have a Temple Recommend to enter, they were to wait at the Logan House Hotel with the youngest children for the wedding meal.

The family was to stay in Logan for three nights. The day after the wedding, Wilford and Jane, his bride, would move to a house they had purchased in Logan, where Wilford had a desk job with his new father-in-law, a banker. Alvarnus and Ellen would return to the Ranch and move into the house Orson had vacated when he moved to Salt Lake to open his meat shop. Amy and her husband and new family would be only about five miles away from the Pillar Cache Ranch.

Elder Smith promised that the next day after the wedding, Sarah's seventh birthday, he would bring all of the ladies to the department store, and each would buy a new ready-made dress, proper shoes and a hat. Then perhaps they would have an ice cream and if the weather cooperated, stroll along the paved streets of the big city. The day was to be topped off by a theater production in the luxurious new playhouse.

Susan and Helen were especially excited to see Clarissa, who would take the train from Salt Lake City with her husband and two small boys and Orson and his wife and their three children. It was to be a joyous reunion.

Two decorated wagons rattled toward Logan carrying the Smith family, now consisting of Elder Smith, Susan, and her soon to be married children, Wilford, Alvarnus, and Amy; Thom, Harriet and their five children; Helen, Sarah and George; and pregnant Anna and her twin daughters. Other wagons decorated for the party, carrying Alvarnus' fiancé's family and Amy's fiancé's family, made the trip a joyous caravan.

As they moved along in the sunny November chill, Helen thought of all that had come about in her life since she left her Shoshone family. She had learned so much and had five pregnancies, and two healthy children. Her new family was very dear to her.

Elder Smith's promises that she may visit the reservation had been impractical. There was always so much to be done on the ranch, and health and pregnancy were a concern. There was news in the papers of the dreadful conditions among the Indians, now starving on reservations. The government had attempted to make them farmers and the churches had attempted to make them Christians, but mostly, according to the news, they became drunkards and beggars, always wanting more government gifts. There were frequent runs of disease reported.

Helen did not know if her father was still alive, or if she would even recognize anyone she knew if she went back. She could not imagine the people she knew being confined to one dirty fort town as she knew they were in their hearts nomadic. She remembered the wonderful times in her youth when they went from camp to camp, the elders knowing where good foods could be found, and singing and dancing and living without the constant structure imposed by the Mormon way of life. It seemed a million years ago.

Sarah loved going on the trip. In her mind, any time away from the ranch with its drudgery of chores, was a good time. Attending the one room school, as she did in the winters for three days each week, was her pride. She was the smartest and quickest student in Clarkston. She could read well by the time she was six, and wrote her letters in a steady and clear hand. Mathematics was also easier for her so she tutored even some of the older boys. The teacher, Miss Prentice, hinted that perhaps Sarah could go someday to Brigham Young College, now called Utah State University, in Logan, but likely only for one year, since she was a girl. Sarah sensed there was a wide world away from the ranch. Even at age seven, she wanted to see it.

The trip also had Harriet thinking of traveling. She asked everyone in their wagon to tell stories of trips they had been on. Since Thom was driving the team and could not hear the discussion and she was traveling with only Susan, Helen, Amy, Sarah, George and Harriet's sleeping children in their wagon, no one in the wagon had anything much to contribute. Helen, whose feelings toward Harriet had softened over time, broke the silence to tell of a hunting trip she had been on when she was about Sarah's age, with her Shoshone family.

She told of breaking down the lodges (which Harriet insisted were called "teepees"), and loading the travois behind the dogs and horses and pulling the camp far away into a sacred range of mountains. She used the Shoshone names, so the places sounded mysterious and exciting. The whole tribe had gone and along the way they gathered roots and plants and ate berries. They went fishing in beautiful lakes with hooks they made from special tree branches. They stopped whenever they wanted and cooked what they were able to find and ate and slept and sang when they pleased. Then when they got to the hunting place, the women set up the lodges again and the men left to hunt. They stayed in that place for most of the summer. There was elk meat, bear meat and venison dried over fires. There had been horse races, swimming in water holes, bow and arrow contests and scouting for fine things. Relatives and friends joined the camps and they made big fires and danced. The Shoshone words said by Helen sounded beautiful and romantic.

Everyone was thrilled by this story, but in different ways. Helen had so rarely mentioned her life as an Indian that most of them had forgotten, except for her darker skin and brown eyes, that she was not white. Harriet and Susan were shocked. They had known such things must be true, but hearing it first hand reminded them of how different Helen really was from their ideas of "normal".

Sarah was stunned. She knew she and her brother were half Indian, but since so little mention of it was ever made at the ranch, and Wilford and Alvarnus had threatened to beat up any child at school who called their Indian family members bad names, they did not really believe that they were at all different. Sarah could not wait to ask her mother for more information, but did not want to do it in front of the nosy Harriet.

Once they arrived in Logan, the distractions began. The first thing one saw was the beautiful shining Temple and the tall but still unfinished Tabernacle high on hills in the heart of town. The Temple had been recently dedicated and was the pride of the community. Then there were streets and streets of shops and buildings. There were fancy multi-storey houses with porches and gingerbread woodwork. There were more people than any of the children had ever seen in one place. It was very exciting.

As they passed one open area in the outskirts of town, they saw a number of shacks with outside fires burning and men in dirty shirts sitting and staring. The travelers realized this was a small band of Indians when they saw the "teepee" standing beyond the shacks. Helen could tell they were Shoshone, but did not recognize any faces. Everyone, except Harriet's daughter Julia sat in silence staring at the apparent poverty and filth of the group. Julia leapt up and jumped excitedly up and down saying "Indians! Indians!" Sarah looked with fear and fascination. Helen tried to quiet George so as not to draw further attention. One of the women came running along side of the wagon. She was drunk and begging. Helen could hear and understand her words asking for food and turned away in embarrassment. They did not stop.

Part 17. Discipline

After the trip to Logan, Sarah could not get enough information about her mother's people. Helen reluctantly began telling Sarah small things that Sarah clung to like treasures. Elder Smith discussed Sarah's constant badgering about the Indians with Helen. He felt that it was unhealthy and would lead to wrong and romantic notions. He told Helen to stop answering any questions in this vein. Secretly, he was concerned that opening this door could lead to discontent in Helen, who had become his favorite wife. He did not want to lose her.

It was Sarah, though, that became more and more discontented. For the next few years, she read all she could about Indians, and formed a vast fantasy in her mind about 'her people'. Helen respected her husband and hoped Sarah's ideas, most of which were not accurate, were a phase. Sarah became disrespectful of Mormon teachings. For this she was disciplined with spanking by Elder Smith using his belt. Twice she was briefly locked into the old smokehouse until she could calm down after particularly naughty outbursts.

Soon, Helen decided that this would not do. She told her husband she must talk to Sarah about the Shoshone people. She would answer all her questions in hopes that being open and truthful would satisfy Sarah. Helen expected that soon Sarah would be on to another childish interest.

Then came the day in the spring of 1895 that Anna's mother and father came to visit. Mrs. Weber appeared to be quite old now, but was still of sharp mind. She was delighted to see Anna and the twins and their toddler son. She was also delighted to see Lupineflower, and how she had transformed into the sturdy and practical Helen, but was still as bright and cheerful as when she was a child. Helen had not heard anyone say her Shoshone name since she had left her people. It made her want to cry. Mrs. Weber also told Helen that Slow Walker was now called Trees Told It and he was very much alive. Much difficulty had befallen Washakie's band with frequent breakouts of disease. They were, however, better off than many bands of Indians as they had many horses, good water, land and still places to go into the Owl Creek Mountains to hunt. Washakie was very old, but he worked well with the government agents who ran most of the lives of the Indians, now.

As far as Sarah was concerned, it was the final straw that she had a Shoshone grandfather whom she did not know existed. She begged and pleaded to be allowed to return with the Webers on the train to meet her grandfather. Helen also wanted to go. She had missed her mother's passing and had not seen her Indian family for many years. Elder Smith relented after talking to the Bishop. Perhaps they could use this as an opportunity for a mission.

It was quickly arranged. Elder Smith would not be able to go to the new state of Wyoming, as the farm work was particularly intense this time of year. However, a group of four young men from Clarkston, and Helen and her two children would go to Wyoming with the Webers upon their return. Mr. Weber would be there to lead the group and they could all stay at the Weber ranch and help with his farm work if needed. Helen promised Elder Smith she would return with the children on the train in two weeks, safe and sound.

Part 18. The Mission

On the day Helen Sarah and George were to leave with the Webers and the four Missionaries, Elder Smith held a private family prayer for their safe return.

> I ask that the Lord will kindly preserve the lives of all my family, that they may be permitted to gather to the future home of the Saints, enjoy the society of the people of God for many years to come, and when their days are numbered that their remains may be deposited at the feet of the servants of God, rather than be left far away in a wild country. And oh, Lord, grant this sincere desire of thy servant in the name of Thy Son Jesus. Amen.

Elder Smith gave Mr. Weber a generous sum of money for his family's use on their trip. Susan also gave Helen a pair of the Garments, which were worn by all Mormons who had taken part in the sacred Endowment ceremony. Although Helen had not been Endowed, the protection of the Garment was the least Susan could do to shield Helen from harm on the trip. The Garment was one piece from collar to ankles to wrist. It had a crotch that was symbolically tied with string. Garments had four marks snipped into the cloth, a square representing the justice and fairness of the Heavenly Father; a compass, representing the north star; a naval mark representing strength and a knee mark representing that every knee would bow and every tongue confess that Jesus is the Christ. Of course Helen was familiar with these Garments from so many years doing the laundry and because Elder Smith never took his off, even for sex. She thanked Susan, but privately decided she would not start wearing one now.

The party took the train part way, then went the rest of the way in the Weber's wagon, which was waiting with their team at the livery near the railway station. Helen, Sarah and especially George were very excited to ride a train. The station was busy and the cars were full of miners going to the coal mines in the northeast in Wyoming and copper mines to the north in Montana. One of the miners was Mormon and he and some of the other miners spent quite a bit of time with the missionary boys, filling their heads with frightening tales of the Wild West and the bloodthirsty Indians they were to convert. One of the boys had a cough and a swollen neck, but he was jolly and seemed well enough not to cause worry.

It took three days to arrive at the Weber's farm. Helen remembered the farm well with its garden, barn and front door. It was very odd to be a household guest with a room for her and her children, when she remembered squatting with her mother behind the barn with their horse, hoping to beg some vegetables. The first night she wondered as she looked outside at the full moon, whether she could perhaps see her mother hiding beyond the split log fence.

The next morning was to be Mr. Weber's visit to the reservation. Because the missionaries were not allowed to be there by government rule, he wanted to see if there was a way to arrange a meeting with Washakie's people. Privately, he also wanted to keep Helen and the children from the reservation if the situation were not appropriate due to an outbreak of disease or if some unrest among the Indians could create a danger to those he felt were under his watch. Helen wanted to go with him, as of course did Sarah, but he refused, saying they should rest after their long trip and they would all go the next day.

The next morning, Helen woke early as usual. She could not write, of course, so she asked Sarah to leave a note for Mrs. Weber saying they would walk by themselves to the Indian camp. They dressed as usual and Helen and her children went off across the yard. In truth, Helen knew she could not sit and wait for Mr. Weber. She also did not want to visit her New'e family riding up on a Mormon wagon with stiff missionaries.

Her feet knew the way and before she knew it, she was well on the way to the band's usual camp. They crossed a stream and Helen stripped off her bonnet and loosened her hair. Sarah saw and laughed. This was her real mother! Brown skin, brown hair, and a twinkle in her eye. George was very excited to meet real Indians.

Helen began to tell them how to behave. Do not look at anyone in the eyes; that was considered very impolite. Do not speak unless someone speaks to you; then answer only the question you are asked. If they ask in New'e, Helen would translate. Be quiet and respectful and stay with me. If you are offered food, you must eat some, but not much, as these people may not have very much to eat.

Soon Helen could smell the smoke of the camp. It was such a delicious smell, different from other campfire smells and memorable right into her bones. Dogs barked as they drew closer. She picked up the pace, frightened of what, or who, she might, or might not, find. At the edge of the camp they were met by dogs and curious children. Helen "shooed" the dogs away in the New'e language. The dogs growled at her unfamiliar scent but were confused by her authoritative manner. The children of the band were dressed only in loincloths as was usual on a warm summer day. They hung back, not knowing these strangers in white peoples' clothes. The woman called to them in New'e, and they ran away to tell their grandmother.

Within minutes, an older looking woman came toward them as they reached the first lodge. She was very thin and wrinkled and bore ugly fever blister scars all over her face and neck. She wore a dirty man's cotton shirt and a deer hide skirt to her knees but had beautiful beadwork moccasins. Her hair was plucked in the front and was tied in a single braid down her back, giving her the appearance from the front of having no hair at all. Her skin was very dark from the sun and from the dust circling everywhere in the camp. A number of children followed behind her.

Helen stopped. Then she choked something in Shoshone before throwing her arms around the woman. The woman was clearly frightened but then as she recognized something familiar in the plump, tidy, almost white woman, she stepped back and pushed her away for a better look. They were sisters. This was Bent Foot Healer. She was 43 years old, which was quite old for the reservation. She looked ancient. She had a daughter, Verbenaflower who was Sarah's age. Her son, Rides In Laughter, was out hunting but would return soon.

Soon the whole camp was buzzing with the wonderful news of the visit. Helen and the children, now shyly hanging onto their mother's skirts and completely overcome by the touches and petting of their relatives, were taken to the lodge of Trees Told It. There he was, quietly sewing amid a mound of scraps of hides and tools. In seeing him, Helen forgot about all things Helen, and became Lupineflower again.

Through the morning visitors came and went from the lodge. Soon Mr. Weber appeared with Washakie, who had almost immediately been informed about Lupineflower's return. He should have known he would not control this situation. But to his mind, all seemed happy, and well, so he told Helen he would return in a few days. She would be welcomed to come back to the farm, or stay here. Helen said she and the children would stay.

The first three days of the visit were beyond any happiness Helen could remember. There were some new New'e babies, although many less than one would have expected in a Mormon household. People were very thin and constantly struggled to find enough to eat. Many people bore scars of the many rashes and fevers and accidents that had come and taken so many of the other members of the band. Most had badly rotted teeth and badly healed wounds. There were horrible stories of the government agents and their stupidity and cruelty. Some Indians had taken to drink and were ignored by the others.

However, the New'e laughter, jokes, love and familiarity were wonderful to Lupineflower. Soon Sarah and George were playing with the children. They played as they never were allowed to play in the strict Mormon household. Trees Told It quietly laughed and marveled at Helen's tales of life among the Mormons. They were both glad of the choices they made and much happier now that they were together again.

On the third night, the drums beat to signal the Mormon meeting. Lupineflower thrilled to see the drum's effect on her children, and to remember it in herself. It was the strangest meeting Lupineflower had ever attended. Trees Told It and Rides in Laughter, who had just come from a successful hunt, agreed to come. There were the usual prayers and songs and speeches by the missionaries. Two of the mission boys complained of sore throats, so they did not talk long.

In the end, everyone wanted to hear her story. After much persuasion, Lupineflower stood up and in rusty but clear Shoshone words, told of her good life in Utah. After she spoke, many more Shoshone wanted to be baptized. The first week of her visit ended in such happiness.

But then everything began to fall apart. Mr. Weber came to Helen at Trees Told It's lodge and warned her not to come back to the farm. One of the missionaries had a clear case of diphtheria. His neck was swollen and he had fever and was developing horrible legions on his legs. They were considering taking him to the hospital at Fort Laramie. Mr. Weber just hoped that the boy had not infected anyone in the camp. The people there were already weak from their poor diet.

That hope was soon crushed. Two children, then one man came down with fever and fatigue. Soon Lupineflower felt her own throat become scratchy and the next day she had difficulty swallowing. Terrified of infecting anyone else, she hugged her children then ran as fast as she could to the farm. The wagon was just leaving when she arrived. Mr. Weber was in a panic. He did not know where to turn to for help so he decided to take Mrs. Weber, who was also ill, and three of the missionary boys to the hospital at Fort Laramie. It would be a two-day long ride, but it seemed urgent as the fourth missionary had just died after palsies and an attack left him to strangle. Mr. Weber did not know how to nurse the disease alone. He piled all the ill ones onto the wagon onto blankets. He would drive his strongest team without rest, if necessary. Helen, for the last time in her life, got on a Mormon wagon leaving her home. She died on the second day of the hot, bumpy ride to Fort Laramie.

Part 19. Catastrophe

For the Smith family, the summer of 1895 was a full-on catastrophe.

Six days after Helen left with the Webers, Elder Smith was working alone with an oxen team moving rocks from a new field when he was bit on the thigh by a five-foot long rattlesnake sleeping under a large rock. He immediately moved away from the buzzing snake and pulled a sharp knife from his toolbox in the wagon. The bite area was severely painful and was already swelling and tingling. He took off his pants and cut through his garment so he could slice deeply into the bite and hopefully squeeze out some of the venom. It bled but he did not know how much venom had already entered his body. He knew he had to get to the house fast. Unfortunately, the oxen were very slow and by the time he arrived, he was vomiting, perspiring, and the pain was intense.

Susan, who did not know what to make of her husband driving the oxen to the front door and climbing down from the wagon without his pants. Realizing the urgency of the situation she immediately plastered the bite area with porous mud from near the pump, in hopes it would draw out the poison. While it seemed to be drawing a significant amount of puss, Elder Smith, who was moved to the pallet by the fireplace, was anxious and his swollen leg began to harden. Susan sent Anna to fetch Thom and Alvarnus right away.

They were all with him that afternoon when he struggled to sit up, but fell back in agony, writhing until a few hours later when his heart stopped.

Alvarnus was sent to town to alert the community and to send a telegram to the Webers. Helen and the children were to return home at once! Alvarnus waited in Clarkston but no return telegram came. The telegram did not reach Mr. Weber before he set off in the wagon to take those with diphtheria to Fort Laramie. Alvarnus went back to the farm, not knowing what to think.

The Smiths did not hear from Mr. Weber until two days later when he sent a telegram to them from Fort Laramie saying that Helen and two of the missionaries had died of disease.

The entire community was in shock. First Elder Smith, and then his wife and two strong young men from town, who had been on a mission to serve God! Elder Smith's funeral at the Rock Meetinghouse in Clarkston became a funeral for four, although there was only one body to put into the ground. The others had been buried in a soldier's cemetery outside of Laramie. They were comforted that the Mormon community in Wyoming had come together and sent representatives to their graves to see that they were sent off with appropriate prayer.

Mr. Weber stayed in the fort hospital with his wife and the other missionary, who were treated and recovered from the disease. In reality, the disease may not have killed Helen and the young man, but likely the wagon trip to Laramie, with insufficient clean water severely dehydrated them, hastening their deaths.

Thom, in his grief, decided he must go to Wyoming immediately after the funeral to bring Sarah and George home to the ranch. He left on the next train then hired a horse and carriage once he came near the reservation. He lost two days wandering in the dry Wyoming countryside, not knowing where to find the Indian camp. Finally, some miners working coalfields around Hudson directed him to Washakie. For the first time, driving about the hot desolate unfamiliar country, sorely missing his father and feeling the responsibility as the new patriarch of the family, Thom cursed God.

He did not think it could be worse, until he came in sight of the Indian camp. A drum was beating a slow boom. He could hear wails from the camp that sent shivers up his spine. They could only mean that there was illness and death in the camp.

A soldier rode up to him as he came near. Thom was not allowed to go into the camp, as diphtheria had broken out and was infectious. The camp was under quarantine. A number of children and two adults had died. The outbreak was blamed on Mormon missionaries who had infected the camp. Thom knew that he was in danger of being killed by the Indians if he was associated with those Mormons. How could he go to Sarah and George? What if they, too were sick? The soldier told him that no medical help was to be afforded to the Indians. They would be left to heal their own.

Thom asked after other Mormons in the area and the Evans family homestead was indicated. Thom spent a week with the Evans waiting until he may go into the camp. He felt helpless and horrible and spent much of his time sitting in the barn staring straight ahead when he was supposed to be helping with the Evans family chores.

Elder Evans sometimes employed a local Indian named Joe for day jobs. When Joe came to the Evans farm at the end of the week, he was able to give some news. He knew of the Mormon woman who had come and brought the disease with her. He had heard her talk and wanted to become Mormon himself; but not now. He was glad she was dead as it was the spirits' revenge for making so many others sick. Her son and daughter were both also ill, but he did not know if they were alive or not. At the end of his working day, he would take Thom to the camp to see, but he did not offer any guarantees of his protection.

Thom and Joe waited until dark to go into the camp. They rode to a half-mile away where Thom left his horse in a stand of trees. Thom hoped maybe he could slip in undetected. Already the women's mourning wails could be heard. They seemed to wail after sundown and were quiet during the day. Luckily, the lodge of Trees Told It was near the edge of camp. Joe indicated the lodge and disappeared into the maze of the camp. The lodge vent door was open, as it was a warm night. Suddenly, George ran from the lodge and cried "Thom! Thom!" Next a tall but old Indian came out. He watched as Thom picked up little George and nuzzled him.

"I want my Mommy!" sobbed George.

"Hush now, little one," said Thom, tears rolling down his face.

"Sarah is sick! I was sick too, but I'm better, now!"

Thom turned to the old man. He stood protectively in front of the lodge entrance. Thom saw that it would be senseless to move Sarah or bring her to the Evans' farm. He went to stand before the old man who looked at him but did not speak.

"I will come back in two days, or send word to me through Joe if I should come earlier. Thank you for caring for her."

The old man did not respond. Thom did not know if he understood.

The next day in the late afternoon, Joe trotted up to the Evans' farm on his skinny horse. Thom was outside helping Mrs. Evans with her garden and George was sleeping in the house, still weak from his illness.

"Trees Told It says to tell you that the girl has died."

Joe watched as Thom's face distorted, and a sob broke his composure. He went immediately to saddle his borrowed horse. Mrs. Evans shook her head. What a tragedy for those Indians, and for the Smiths!

When Joe and Thom came near the camp, a high screeching wailing echoed like smoke from the Indian community. Thom looked in alarm at Joe, who looked at Thom, and said simply "Death Songs." Joe escorted Thom to the cemetery on the edge of camp. There, two women and a young girl about Sarah's age were wailing around a wrapped bundle next to a hole in the ground. Thom approached, but one frightening looking old woman with a bald forehead, pox scars and a bleeding arm saw him and stood in his way. He stopped, unsure of what was to happen.

The women continued the Death Song, and left him to stand and watch. Thom's nerves were tightly stretched. He was shaking with the uncertainty and strangeness of the situation and with the underlying the sadness of the last weeks and with an anger he could not place. Now beautiful little Sarah, too, was gone, buried among the Indian people she was so interested to know. Damn these people!

The women put the bundle into the hole and covered it. The ground was swept with a pine branch in an effort to achieve privacy for the dead and the women began again to wail. Thom felt he had no place here. He walked back to his horse to ride away toward the Evans' farm. A part of him wanted to wail like the women, but sensed that this was not permissible for men. Instead he allowed the tears of frustration to splatter quietly from his nose and chin. As he rode by the lodge where Sarah had died, he saw the old man sitting stone-faced outside. The old man looked at him, and Thom paused, but then just tipped his hat with his shaking hand. The old man stared, then nodded.

Thom nudged the horse forward. He wanted to take George home as soon as possible, away from these heathens. The thought of home brought a whole new set of crushing concerns to think about.

The Pillar Cache Ranch house would now be empty except for Susan and Anna and Anna's three daughters. As the two women had never been fond of each other, and because they would need help in running the ranch, perhaps he and Harriet and their children would need to move into the main house. Thom felt the heavy burden of enormous work waiting him. He wondered if he would be able to shake off the sluggish feeling that overcame him. He suddenly wondered if tomorrow he would be able to move one foot in front of the other.

His family had always seemed large and happy and strong. Now it was much diminished to women and children. They were all looking to him for leadership.

How he would miss his strong and kind father. How he would miss the steadying influence of Helen. How he would even miss the spunk and fight of young Sarah! The Pillar Cache Ranch would never be the same.

Part 20. The Trick

From her first step into the Shoshone camp, Sarah felt at home. The scary looking woman, her aunt, called Bent Foot Healer, had a daughter just her age named Verbenaflower. Grandfather, Bent Foot Healer, Verbenaflower and various other relatives sat with her and Lupineflower around the outdoor fire after the welcome feast the first night and talked. Soon, Sarah was sitting in Bent Foot Healer's arms, stroking the woman's pocked skin and listening with adoration to the joyous talk. George fell asleep on a pile of hides inside the lodge. They stayed up all night and no one informed them that it was time for bed. She realized that here, it was time for things when the people wanted, not when custom dictated.

By the end of the first night, Sarah could grasp many of the ideas behind the language, even though she could not understand the words. When her grandfather spoke, everyone listened respectfully. They often laughed together over what he said, even though he looked fierce and stern. A sparkle often entered his eyes and it was clear Grandfather was witty and sweet and much loved. These people were close and relied happily on each other. Verbenaflower taught her the games of chance using sticks and guessing. These activities lasted into the night. It was such fun!

By the time her mother became ill and left, Sarah knew she did not want to leave these people. True, their food was scarce and terrible and sanitary conditions were not what she was used to, but the peoples' relaxed meaningful days and nights of community made up for all the inconvenience. Sarah was thirsty to learn more of these ways and to fit in.

As soon as her mother hugged her and left, Sarah ran to sit before her grandfather. "Oh please, don't make me go! I want, Grandfather, to stay here with you!"

Trees Told It did not respond. His heart was full with Lupineflower's return and the sweet company of this good healthy girl and the playful little boy. He remembered his first family, bloody and frozen and cruelly destroyed at Bear River.

Trees Told It stayed up all night and prayed and smoked. He came to see that the white men owed him his family back. He would wait until Lupineflower returned, then perhaps he could persuade her to stay with these two beautiful children.

Bent Foot Healer could not imagine Lupineflower, now that she was home, would want to go back with those strange Mormon people. She believed that they were home to stay. Rides in Laughter saw danger in his mother's thinking. He warned her, "Do not become to close to her or the children. They will leave us. They are white now. Their white father will come for them and they will get on the Mormon wagon and they will go away to Utah again." For this reason, Rides in Laughter kept his distance after the welcome feast. He thought it would be better to make a family of his own than wish for another man's family. He went hunting to avoid this danger.

After Lupineflower became ill and left, George and Sarah showed signs of becoming feverish. Sarah was sick only a few days and recovered quickly, but stayed in the lodge to avoid spreading the sickness. Then, six days after Lupineflower left, Washakie sent his son to the lodge of Trees Told It. The Indian Agent's soldier had come to Washakie and said that Lupineflower had died.

Oh the wails and screams! Bent Foot Healer dashed slashes onto her arm and began to cry out in screams that lasted the whole night. Sarah, not knowing how to grieve for her mother copied Bent Foot Healer and also slashed her arm. After a night of wails, she found she felt better. When she began to feel hurt, she slashed her arm, again so the hurt was manageable, and wailed. George was ill and slept, not really knowing what had happened.

Trees Told It was internally furious about the death of Lupineflower. If only she had stayed, they could have nursed her and made her well. Now he was sure. He would find a way to keep the children. The white people owed him this family. They were his family and they would not be taken from him like so many were before.

He must plan, because surely their father would come for them. Trees Told It decided that if he had to do it, he would kill that man, and then the children would be his. He was having trouble even walking now, though, so how would he kill him?

Then he began to wonder if it could be much easier. He could say that the children had died, then take them away to the mountains or to the Fort Hall reservation to live with the other Shoshone people, Pocatello's band. No one would know them. It just might work.

Trees Told It comforted Bent Foot Healer and Sarah. He told them of his plan. Sarah was thrilled. Bent Foot Healer agreed. Together they planned.

They would tell the other Shoshone people that the children were very sick. Then, they would prepare two bundles that could be buried when the white man came for the children. Trees Told It would take the children and go to the mountains and when the children were strong enough, he would make his way to Pocatello's band.

The next day, Rides in Laughter returned from his hunt. He had a small deer and many rabbits which he brought to the lodge. Trees Told It pulled him away from the lodge and into the trees at the edge of the camp so that the story would continue that the children were very ill.

Trees Told It was strangely excited. Rides in Laugher had rarely seen him so animated during his entire life. Then he became furious as he heard of his grandfather's outrageous plan. "No, you must not do this thing! They will find out! You will be hanged for stealing white children! You know there is a brutal penalty for this! Someday the girl will want to go back to the white people, and then what will you do?" Trees Told It was not deterred. "You ride away then grandson, and do not come back until the moon is full. We will see what happens then. You do not need to help us. Just leave us the deer."

Rides In Laughter was incredulous. He was considering whether to disobey his grandfather when he saw a white man, presumably the children's father, riding toward the camp with Joe, who worked sometimes at a white man's farm. Trees Told It motioned Rides In Laughter away, and he sprang back to his lodge with more agility than usual. Rides In Laughter rode away quickly but watched the scene unfold from his mother's lodge.

He saw Lupineflower's boy, George, rush to the white man. He saw Trees Told It block the man's entry into the lodge. Then the man left with George.

Perhaps, thought Rides In Laughter, the Great Spirit had found a way for them to get away with keeping just the girl.

The next day everything went perfectly. Trees Told It informed the community that the girl had died. Joe was asked to bring the white man. Rides In Laughter dug the burial hole. He helped his mother and Sarah wrap the remainder of the deer, once they had taken choice parts for eating. Then another woman from the camp and Bent Foot Healer and Ver-benaflower prepared to bury the deer. Just as they were ready for the burial, the man arrived. Trees Told It and Rides In Laughter sat in front of the lodge, with Sarah hiding inside. They watched the show put on for the man. Rides in Laughter began to sweat. He did not want to be part of this crime. He jumped on his horse and rode away. He would stay at the Arapaho camp until all this was over.

Trees Told It thought of the white man, who would loose the girl. But he did not act like a man, crying like a woman. Strangely, he looked younger than when he was here before to marry his daughter. In any event, he did not deserve the girl. So many buffalo, warriors, women, wild places, Indian children, his children, had all been lost to these horrible white men...

That night, when the sky was darkest, Trees Told It and Sarah sneaked out of the lodge with a pack, went to three readied horses, and rode away into the mountains. They would stay near a lake through the summer, then decide whether to go northwest to Pocatello's band or to return.

Within a month, members of Pocatello's band passed through the mountains coming to trade with Washakie's band. Trees Told It helped Sarah, now called Sugar, dress in Indian clothes, put on hair wraps, and darken her face with dirt. Sarah sneaked back into camp. Trees Told It came back alone. Then he made a show in the camp of thanking the confused visitors for bringing his relative. Ah, they thought, he is old and speaks nonsense. Sugar stayed in Trees Told It's lodge and happily learned to be Shoshone. While people in the camp knew something was not as was being presented, they liked the idea of Trees Told It taking back some pleasure after his hard life, and outwitting the white men.

It was a year later that they heard from Joe that man who had come was not Elder Smith, but his son. The Elder had died after being bitten by a snake. Trees Told It decided that this was fitting. White men had killed the Snake Indians at Bear River, now a Snake had killed the white man who gave Trees Told It back a daughter. All was as it was meant to be.

Third Generation Rides in Laughter, Also known by his English Name, Thomas Homena (Born 1876)

Prologue An Arapaho Legend

In the old times, when the whole world was covered with water, a man carrying Flat Pipe, his companion and counselor, walked across the waters for four days and nights.

The man felt respect for the pipe. He wanted to find it a good home. After six days, he determined that the place for Flat Pipe should be a place with many other creatures. On the seventh day the man went to find land with creatures upon it somewhere among all the water. He called to the four directions. Many animal helpers came to him and helped find land with a home for Flat Pipe. Four Old Men were asked to go in each of the four directions to control the winds. The land would be a place to have a Sun Dance celebration.

The man said to Garter Snake, "You will be a great comfort to the people and have a great place in the Sun Dance as the Sacred Wheel to represent the waters that surround this Earth." Then came Long Stick, a bush with dark bark and flexible limbs. He said, "I offer myself for the wheel for the good of all." Long Stick became the ring of the Sacred Wheel, representing a circle that is the Sun. Eagle saw what was happening and offered his strength. "It is great enough to carry me above the Earth and water as I fly on the winds of the four directions. My feathers can be used to represent the Four Old Men." The man was pleased. He told all the creatures that the four bunches of eagle feathers would forever be tied to the wheel to honor the desire of the eagle. It would also honor anyone who would ever offer an eagle feather as a gift.

The man shaped the Sacred Wheel. He painted it like a garter snake. He placed the feathers in the position of the Four Old Men who rule the directions and control the winds: Northwest, Northeast, Southeast and Southwest. He represented the Thunderbird who brings the rain and added groups of stars, painting special images of the Sun, the Milky Way and the Moon. He tied blue beads to represent the sky.

The man carrying Flat Pipe thanked Garter Snake, Long Stick, Eagle, the Four Old Men and all the other creatures for serving his people. The creation of the wheel symbolizes all creation.

Letter to the Editor

June 14, 1933

Thomas Homena
PO Box 749
Fort Washakie, Wyoming

Editor
The Wyoming Post and Herald
Cheyenne, Wyoming

Dear Editor,

I am a Shoshone Indian and a veteran of the United States Army. I served in France in World War I. I am writing in response to the article in the paper of May 28, 1933 titled "Alcohol Problems Rampant on Indian Reservations".

I believe it is time your readers heard from a Shoshone point of view in hopes that this may help them understand how things came to be as they are on reservations. Maybe some of your readers will think twice next time before they say something mean to an Indian, refuse to hire an Indian, or do nothing when the government makes bad decisions that hurt Indians.

I am over 57 years old and have lived on the reservation all my life. I will tell you about myself so you will see that I know about my people, soldiering, and the federal government dealings with Indians.

There are many branches of Shoshone people, whose traditional lands included parts of the deserts, mountains and grasslands of what are now California, Arizona and Nevada, Utah, New Mexico, Texas, Oklahoma, Oregon, Idaho, Colorado and Wyoming. Some traditional Shoshone cultures were centered on hunting, mainly buffalo; some were centered on fishing, mainly salmon; some were centered on farming, mainly corn and some were centered on gathering wild plants and hunting small animals. Even though our people were different from each other, we had the same language and spiritual beliefs and many individuals went from one clan of people to the others through their lives since almost all of the people were nomadic.

Under international law, the Indians have always been separate nations, and were treated as such by the United States and before the time of the United States with the first English pilgrims. This came from a basic international law created by the Roman Catholic Church when the pope established the idea of "worldwide papal jurisdiction" and a "universal Christian commonwealth". When better ships allowed greater ranges of travel for those in Europe, this law evolved into the "Doctrine of Discovery" so discovering governments could expand the Christian commonwealth. Numerous papal bulls, or edicts from the Pope, divided lands among "discoverers". "Discovery" of the mouth of any river gave the discovering government all the rights of "discovery" to all lands drained by that river. The rights of discovery included the exclusive right to buy lands from all "infidels" thereon, but the natives continued to possess the lands until the purchase. In the eyes of international law, natives no longer had the right to transfer lands to any other party except the discovering government.

So in America, different European countries owned discovery rights on different river systems. When the United States was created, the Constitution declared that the lands of the colonies were to be governed by the new government, but the Constitution gave Congress the right to make treaties with Indian tribes. The United States continued to make sales agreements and began making treaties with the many tribes. The United States continued to acquire other discovery rights. For example, the Louisiana Purchase from France was a purchase of the discovery rights of the Western drainage of the Mississippi River, including Wyoming. So you see, treaties are grants of rights FROM Indians, and if an Indian tribe did not grant away rights, it still has them. Unless of course they were stolen from them.

That is why these federal agreements I mention here are "treaties" that are affirmed by the Senate, and not just regular actions of the government. So Indian tribes have a special place in law, with the abilities of governments. Indian governmental rights are not new rights "given" to Indian Tribes. These rights were possessed since the beginning of time and existed before the United States. The Supreme Court calls these rights "inherent sovereignty." However, the rights of tribes as governments have now been whittled from a whole round into a strange skinny shape as the government has forgotten international law and has simply decided to steal what it could. As we speak, the knife of federal and state governments is still whittling!

Early in the government's dealings with tribes, they knew that the Indian livelihood was being taken away. The government decided in treaties and later through court cases that the government owed a "trust" to Indian people. From the earliest days of Indian treaties, Indians were prohibited from taking charge of our most important possessions. These possessions are our remaining land and the valuable things on our land such as timber, water, and coal and even our fish and herds of wild animals. From the beginning, our possessions were mingled with the land, water, and other resources that were controlled by the Army, and later by settlers and rich white industrialists.

The government officially owned and effectively controlled these important possessions. The government made all the choices for infrastructure and how to buy and sell the possessions. This was so plain to the United States Supreme Court that when lawsuits came before them about the theft of Indian possessions, the court said that all Indian possessions were owned by the United States in "trust for the tribes". This trust is just like a trust set up by a rich man for his grandchildren. A trustee is supposed to manage the rich man's money after he has died and make the grandchildren comfortable and wealthy from this money. In our case, the trustee has not done a good job, and many would say that the government trustee used the Indian possessions for it's own benefit, or the benefit of the American public, rather than for the benefit of Indians who are now very poor.

I will tell how I know these truths.

I was born on the Wind River Reservation in Wyoming in 1876. When I was two years old, the Army moved the Shoshone enemies, the Arapahos, to the reservation. My parents were Shoshone but I now have many Arapaho friends. Despite being enemies, one on one, the Shoshone and Arapaho people usually got along.

They counted the people left in both tribes in 1876. There were 1250 Shoshones and 938 Arapahos. Both of these tribes had been decimated in their numbers by recent Army massacres. In the winter of 1863, the Army killed around 450 Shoshone people at Bear River. In 1864, the Army killed around 200 Arapahos and Cheyennes at the Sand Creek. Could you imagine if one fourth of all the people you knew were killed? When they were moved to the reservation, all of these people were still in grief.

My Shoshone grandfather, named Slow Walker, and my mother, Bent Foot Healer, narrowly missed being at the Bear River massacre. That day, they had gone to a private place to pray at the time of the attack. It was a wintertime camp of over 500 people in what is now Utah with peaceful Indian men, women, children and old ones, who had signed a treaty of peace with the United States. The camp was marched upon and attacked by a California Volunteer Militia, who did not care that the people they attacked were peaceful Shoshones under the headman Sagwitch, my great grandfather.

U.S. Army soldiers killed all the other members of Grandfather's first family, even his mother, his twin baby boys and his pregnant wife. Mother told terrible stories of coming back and finding the family and most of the people in the camp murdered and frozen.

I admire them because they did not give up. Grandfather found a new wife and started over. Mother, who was still a young girl then, found it within herself to go on and eventually marry my father, Edward Homena, and have seven children. Over the years, all six of my siblings have passed away. Indian people are strong and resilient, but their challenges have been terrible.

Many Indians believed they should have kept fighting for their way of life, but if so, probably no Shoshones would be alive today. So they did what they had to do for the people. Indian people just want a good and peaceful life, like everyone. What happened at Bear River and Sand Creek was not war, but murder.

I might sound bitter to you writing this, but I know about soldiering since I was myself a U.S. Army Private First Class who fought from 1914—1916 and was injured in France during the Great War. Some are surprised that I could fight for the same army that killed members of my family. But by doing this, I honor the treaties made by my Chiefs.

Except that the Army stopped shooting at us, things did not get much better on the reservation in the 1800s. By the time I was twenty-five years old, there were only 841 Shoshones left and 801 Arapahos. There was so much disease, despair, hunger and many, many funerals. Funerals are one of my strongest memories of childhood.

When I was born I was named "Rides in Laughter" because my mother carried me on a cradleboard on her horse and I laughed when the horse ran. In the early part of my life I lived a traditional nomadic life in summertime, although the first treaties had already been signed and we were frequently pushed to stay on the reservation. Then, things changed and Indians were required to stay on reservations. I went to boarding school. After I was eighteen, I worked, when I could find odd jobs, at Fort Washakie, Wyoming on the reservation. During this time, I married my wife of fifty-two years on the reservation and together we have had eleven children, five of whom are still alive and have given us fourteen grandchildren. I joined the Army when I was thirty-eight years old. I was lucky to survive World War I, where I fought for two years in the trenches and came home after I was shot there. I earned a medal for bravery. Since then I have lived back in Fort Washakie. I worked for a number of years as a schoolteacher before I retired. I read many books about my people and our history.

During our lives we have seen the Shoshone and Arapaho peoples become trapped on a small piece of land after having the whole Western United States as their home. This happened in stages.

In 1851 my branch of the Shoshone people were wealthy and strong buffalo hunters who traveled all across the western plains. In that year, they signed a treaty that promised they would be friendly toward whites and would allow white people to travel through their lands.

The Bear River massacre certainly terrified all the other Shoshone bands and soon after the massacre, Shoshones agreed to the Ft. Bridger Treaty of 1863. In that treaty, the Army promised they would leave the Shoshones in peace in the greater part of Wyoming, Colorado, Idaho and Utah and that they could live on and hunt in as their Reservation. The rest of our previous territory was opened to homesteading.

The Shoshones that wanted peace, or saw that it was suicide to fight the white men, came to that reservation and kept their promises. But the government did not leave them alone. In 1868, the Wind River Reservation boundaries were "clarified" and all competing claims to particular parts of Shoshone land were denied. By 1871, the military camp at Laramie was moved to the reservation and its name was changed to Camp Brown. They built government buildings, or the agency, and the Episcopal Mission and school on Shoshone land. Later, they again changed the name to Fort Washakie, the only Military Base to be named after an Indian.

Under the treaty, the Army was supposed to use these buildings for storing promised food to supplement the Indians' diet, but of course these agencies became a way for the government to meddle in Indians' day-to-day lives. Just a few years later, in 1874, the starving Shoshones, in exchange for cattle and other necessities, agreed to secede the southern third of their reservation and its rich coal reserves to allow mining and white settlement of those lands under the Homestead Act.

Then, in 1878, the government moved the whole Arapaho tribe onto the Shoshone reservation. There was no payment for this act, even though the 1868 treaty required compensation for any new government use of the reservation.

During the late 1870s, about the same time the Shoshones agreed to secede the southern third of their reservation, the last buffalo herd was wiped out. Professional hunters killed the vast herds, millions and millions of buffalo, not for their meat, but to exterminate them. They were killed on purpose so that cows and farms could be brought in and ranches created. You must understand that Indian people, not just my Shoshone people, but also many other Indians, ate buffalo as their main food, and their culture existed around the buffalo. The government knew this and promised to give the Indians food and houses and to take care of them since they no longer had buffalo.

People think that these promises led some of the people to be lazy. I say that culture teaches us how to act, what to believe, and how to sustain ourselves with dignity. For my people, two main teachings of our culture were to be nomadic and to hunt for buffalo. We could no longer do either of these essential activities. Many other parts of our culture did not make sense anymore.

People did not know what to do or how to act! Even if they had known what to do, there was nothing left to do every day under their former culture. They were in grief! They were diseased and hurting! This is not a recipe for creativity and industriousness!

People began to starve. Many did what they could to get by with hunting other game, which was very hard to find. The government said they must become farmers, but this is like telling Wyoming ranchers, who are already ill, that they must move to the sea, build their own ships and tools and become deep ocean fishermen. It was simply not realistic. Many Indian people tried to grow crops but they did not have the tools and knowledge to do this. Even if they had the knowledge, the Indians access to land and water was made very difficult by a whole series of federal government rules and the trickery of white people.

The story of Indian's troubles did not stop with the destruction of the buffalo in the 1880s. In 1887, Congress passed the Dawes Act, or the General Allotment Act. This was during the time that more and more settlers were coming west. Some of the good land on Indian reservations was looking pretty good to those settlers. Since Indians weren't quickly picking up farming, the government thought they could do two things at once, by giving each Indian family 160 acres to farm, and then allowing all other "surplus" agricultural lands on the reservation to be homesteaded by white farmers.

The allotment system was not ready to go at Wind River until 1907. This is because in 1897 and again in 1904 the government took away reservation lands. Because some allotments under the Dawes Act had originally been designated in lands now taken back, new lands were required to be designated, which delayed allotments.

My Shoshone grandfather was allotted 160 acres on the reservation. He was quite old, however and did not move there. My father was also allotted 160 acres but he sold it a few years later for twenty silver dollars and a cow, because he did not want to farm.

I was also allotted 160 acres on the reduced reservation and I moved out to that piece of land with my wife and children, far from my people. It was lonely and we had almost nothing. We had to go days into the Fort when we could pick up the meager government rations that helped us survive. I tried to be a farmer, just as the white men wanted. Of course the land was not irrigated and very dry and the soil was poor so nothing grew despite my wife and sons and me breaking our backs. One fall, our entire harvest was 178 cabbages. We survived on those cabbages and a few cattle that roamed out there that long, cold winter. The cattle were skinny and had little meat, as we had no money to buy hay for them and of course there was no grass. I left when war broke out and I had the chance to join the Army. My wife stayed behind and with my sons tried to continue to farm. I worried all the time I was away that they would die out there.

In the meantime, in 1896, the government had taken away another huge piece of the reservation; the half that contained the hot springs, an important traditional place for our people. Then another land cessation was agreed to in 1904. This was made to sound like a good deal for us. All the ceded land was to be held in "trust" by the government for the tribes. We were to get paid for the timber, grazing leases and sales of lands to white farmers. We were also promised that some of the funds would build an irrigation system for the reservation. These funds were paid to a white man contracted to build the irrigation system. He hired many of the hungry Indians to dig ditches for ten dollars a month. The Indians working on those ditches never saw their paychecks because the man spent the money and went bankrupt. The irrigation system failed because the ditches were unfinished. We did not know where the money from our ceded land went. The local people grew angry that the Indians were "getting handouts".

So in the end, the Wind River Reservation is a small portion of what was promised to Chief Washakie. It's about one tenth of the original reservation, mostly hardscrabble mountainous lands. Of the better bottom lands, there are about 300,000 acres of government "withdrawn" lands for irrigation, meaning that the government flooded it with a reservoir that benefits white farmers, and about 100,000 acres allotted to Indians and 150,000 acres owned in fee by white men. These lands create a "checkerboard" of ownerships and rights that's just really hard to administer.

Then oil was discovered in the Wind River Basin. Many oil wells were drilled on the reservation, but most of them are on white peoples' lands and those white farmers began getting rich. Many now have new tractors and pick-up trucks. Oil companies came to talk to us and they drilled some oil wells on Indian allotments. If any money comes from them this oil, it goes to the government because the Indian lands are still held "in trust". Sometimes those Indian families get small checks but they don't explain the amounts and they aren't close to being enough to buy a truck.

We have seen quite a bit of damage to the land. There are dumps where the oil companies are putting wastewater and who knows what. These dumps smell to high heaven. We know not to complain about it. A driver dumping this waste on tribal lands waved a pistol at me when I stopped to look at what he was doing.

I can tell you what happened to my allotment. When I was away at the war, they actually finished an irrigation ditch that made my land pretty good agricultural property. For one year, my wife and sons were able to grow and sell good crops. Because I had a good job getting shot at by Germans, the Bureau of Indian Affairs deemed that I was "competent" to pay the taxes, and my land was transferred from a federal allotment to fee land under the state's jurisdiction. My wife and I owned it free and clear!

However, the letter notifying me of my "competency" did not make it to me in France, so I did not know that I now needed to pay Wyoming state taxes. My white neighbor paid $14 in property taxes owed to the State of Wyoming. The sheriff came to my wife and gave her two hours to get my kids and all our possessions off the land. Now my good agricultural land is part of that man's ranch.

When I got home from the war I was very angry over this trick. But the sheriff warned me that if I made any trouble, I'd be arrested and put in the County jail. He called me a "red nigger", even though I was a war hero. There was nothing I could do. So my family and I went about our business in the one-room Indian house we shared with my father in the reservation town at Forth Washakie. He died in 1910, so the house then became ours. It seemed to me that while at one time we were allowed to live in dignity, step by step the Shoshone people, and the Arapaho people, were moved into smaller and smaller lives, until there was no room at all left for dignity.

After the war, I was sick for quite some time with what they called "shell shock" and over the hatred of the white people. I had a very hard time knowing how to act when I got home, so mostly I just went to bed. Slowly, though, I got a little better. Because I was a veteran and I could read well, thanks to my relative Sugar Ethete who insisted we all learn everything we could and taught us excellent English, I got a job at the Indian School and worked there until I retired. Because my hearing was mostly gone from all the bombs and guns during the war, all I could do construction and odd jobs. They had white people to be teachers and I was not allowed to talk to the students. I did do many small kindnesses for the students, I think. With this job, I also had the chance to read books in the small school library. This was a joy to me and has helped me teach my children later.

I had gone to that same school when I was young but my memories from there were difficult! It was the Wind River Indian School. When I attended, it was part of an Episcopal Mission. The teacher was an Episcopal Reverend. You see, the government promised different Indian reservations to different religions for conversions and to "civilize" us with Christianity.

I went to school from the time I was 7 years old, until I was 18. It was a boarding school. All children left their home and stayed at school for nine months. Even though the school was only a few miles from the Indian camp where my parents lived, I did not see them at all during school months. Most Indian families did not want their children to go away and be taught by white people. But my father, who was converted to be a Mormon, wished that we learn the white man's ways. So my mother allowed the Reverend to take my brothers and sisters and me to live at the school.

At first there were about 35 boys and 25 girls, many of whom were children of white soldiers who married Indian women. The boys stayed in one dormitory and the girls in another and we had separate classes. The boys learned English, Christian Religion, Reading, Mathematics and Carpentry. We helped build the school buildings. We also did labor around the camp. The girls learned English, Christian Religion, Reading, Sewing and Domestics. They also helped in the kitchens and cleaned the school. So I did not see my sisters very often.

I was very lonely and afraid. Upon our arrival they had cut off our hair, which had a sacred importance to us, but which the whites called "uncivilized". We watched as they took and burned our medicine protections that had been given to us by our families. We were given white men's clothes to wear. They sprayed us with chemicals because they said we were "dirty". We were not allowed to speak Shoshone or pray to our spirits, or even go outside very much to be among nature.

We were told these things were bad and would send us to a white man's hell after our death where terrible devils would torture us. I became very afraid of these burnings and other tortures. I was afraid for my father and other family. I vowed never to act like an Indian again. We were slapped with a long stick in front of the other children when we broke the rules. This was very humiliating and shaming for us. Some boys that were disobedient were beaten quite badly. Others were stripped naked and put in a cold room until they agreed to follow the rules.

Some of the girls became pregnant while at the school. I was too young at the time to wonder how this could have happened as they were rarely around any of the male students. The teachers said the girls had been very bad. I do not know what happened to the babies they had, but I was told they were adopted. Those girls never again had babies. They were told that because they were bad, the government had sterilized them. As this sterilizing happened, our women became afraid to go to the government hospitals. When they went for any reason, they no longer could have babies. No boy wanted to marry a girl who had gone to a doctor.

Later, after the school buildings were finished by our hard work and there was greater emphasis on keeping Indians from their old way of life, the government forced ALL Indian children to move away from their family lodges and come to the school. Both the Shoshone and the Arapaho children came together at the same school. We knew to distrust the Arapahos from ancient times. We were angry that we must now live and study together.

The worst times were the first weeks of school. When the children came in on the wagon, they were separated from their brothers and sisters and held down while their hair was cut off. It was horrible to hear the screaming and fighting of the children as this happened. As an older boy who had been at the school I was required to help. I tried to tell the children it would keep them from being tortured from devils, but I think this made them more afraid. In the first nights the dormitory was silent. Shoshone and Arapaho children were taught not to cry when taken by the enemy, but to be strong. In later weeks, the crying would begin as children forgot their Shoshone teachings and simply began to miss their parents. Teachers were strict and often lost their patience as they had constant care and teaching of the children. Many of these teachers were mean, but some were nice.

We expected that the happiest times would be the short winter and longer summertime breaks from school when we could go home. Our parents would come to the school and cry and dance as we appeared outside, the boys wearing suits and ties and the girls wearing their cotton dresses and pinafores. Meetings became awkward as parents failed to recognize their children, and children behaved in the strict manner they had been taught. Going back to the lodges with these two very different ways of life was very confusing for me and for my parents. It created problems for everyone. Eventually school was made to be five years long with no breaks for the children to go home to their parents.

When I came out of school I moved back to my father's lodge. I had no use for the suit or the reading or the carpentry skills I had learned. I rode about on my horse and spent my time hunting to keep from starvation. The government food rations were only enough to feed us for one day each week. The government policy was officially "work or starve" but I only know of two men who had paying jobs driving wagons for the government to and from the railway station. I grew my hair long again but was too afraid to pray to my father's spirits. My hunting was not good and I attributed this to my failure to pray. I could not use the Episcopal religion for anything and my Shoshone religion was dangerous. I was lost. My brothers and many of my friends died of measles, diphtheria and influenza.

For many years I got by in this strange changing time. My parents were able to move into a government one-room house. We had barely enough to live on. During these years I had nothing. I could not help my family in any way, as hunting was poor and there were no jobs for me.

Other men my age and I would ride our horses aimlessly. We were a bother to the white farmers living on the reservation. I think they were afraid of us. Many of them were violent and if we encountered them, they would taunt us. One time three farmers met me on the road and beat me until I had broken bones. We began to drink whisky. Some of my friends spent much time in jail for being drunk or stealing or fighting. I will not say I did not do these things, but I was lucky never to be in jail for them. I would have died, or become a drunk during those times if I had not found a job breaking horses and doing other farm labor for a half Shoshone friend from school who worked at his white father's ranch. Slowly, I came back to the Shoshone ways. I thank my grandfather, Trees Told It, for teaching me ancient songs and prayers before he died.

Life on the reservation during those times from 1893 to the start of the First World War in 1914 was harsh. We had a constant struggle to keep warm and fed. There was always the need for firewood, which we had to travel farther and farther to find. Our water became polluted and we began to carry water from the white man's pumps. We waited for government food rations or shared in government cattle slaughter days and scrounged for other foods. We tried to carry on some traditional activities. Women wrapped in their blankets did beadwork, and there were always games of sticks and other Indian gambling games. We also had many funerals in those days. They were sad times. People were loosing hope for any good future for our people. People missed their dead loved ones.

Before 1892, some people also followed traditional spiritual ways as best we could with dancing, medicine talks, sweat lodges and other ceremonies. As I lost my fear of being tortured by devils, I began again to participate in these practices again. The elders held a few Sundances, the most important Shoshone prayer. White men did not understand these practices, and the churches did not like them. I believe they saw them as competition for Christianity. So in 1892, our religion was made illegal. Many people continued small versions of the traditional ways, but with the threat of jail or worse, the large gatherings we all so loved ended. Many more people who had managed to remain strong now lost their sprits in this way.

World War I was a way for me to volunteer to be a warrior and to show my willingness to fight for the United States, which is my country. In many Indian societies, men cannot be leaders until first they are warriors. So even though we were not yet citizens of the United States with any right to vote, many Indians, over 17,000 from across the country, joined the Army. This is the same Army that was our former enemy and had killed members of my family!

Even though it was illegal, before I went to war, I went through tribal war ceremonies to prepare me for battle. I knew that war disrupts the natural order of life and causes disharmony. To survive this chaos makes one strong. I needed this strength, as war was more terrible than I could have imagined.

When in France, I met many Choctaw Indians. They spoke their language over the radios in order to confound German eavesdroppers. I was very proud of these men, who helped save my life with their language. Two Indian nations, the Onondaga and the Oneida officially declared war on Germany.

When I came home, the war had affected me very badly. A few old men came to my grandfather's small house one night. They built a fire outside and had me come outside to sit with them and smoke from a sacred pipe. They prayed with me in the Indian way. They honored me as a warrior and gave me a pair of traditional moccasins that my grandfather had made with his own hands many years earlier.

Then they told my wife that we would have a feast where we would bring out a drum kept for special purposes, even thought this was not legal, and healing songs would be sung. The booming of that drum was like the booming of the bombs, but the drum was regular and strong. It replaced the chaos of the bombs into a healing ancient pattern. The singing of the old songs mimicked the screams of the men and the flying of bullets. Those horrible tangled memories of war were contained into the songs, which freed me to once again hear other, peaceful sounds. The power of that beautiful ceremony saved my life. How many other Indians do not have these healing chances that I have been given?

Can white people understand how helpless and hopeless some Indian people feel? As I have told here, our culture was made largely irrelevant, images of our Chiefs and heroes were made a joke by Hollywood stories, our traditional territories were taken, our family land was taken, our people died of disease, we were taken from our families when we were babies and put into brutal and lonely boarding schools, our religion was made illegal and we were taught other religions which made no sense to us, our women were sterilized, our resources were wasted for other's greed, and very few people can support their families in dignified ways. There have been many bad times for Indians.

The most important thing I will say here, though, is that despite all the obstacles, there is so much good to celebrate! I have told you here about my beautiful wife, five strong children and fourteen sweet grandchildren, my proud military service, my and my children's education, our continuing ceremonies, the strength of our community to overcome to survive! Even in lives that contain despair or problems, there are times of beauty and love. The problems are put in the newspaper; the beauty is overlooked!

There is an Indian saying, that in seven generations, our people will come back and again be strong. We are a good people with much to share. We will always start over and we will succeed. My grandfather told me that if you just keep walking, the landscape will change, so as long as you can walk you can find something always better. Maybe in seven generations, the beauty will be in the newspapers, and the problems will be overlooked.

Sincerely,

Thomas Homena

Editor's Note: While Mr. Homena's letter is passionate and well written it is declined for publication. Some of the statements made here could not be verified. Further, it has been determined that many statements are too controversial for our readership.

Fourth Generation Erickson Ethete

(Erickson Ethete, Born 1906)

Prologue Legend of Kettle Falls

(Adapted from Ruth Lakin, Kettle River Country, 1987 Told by Aeneas (Eneas) Seymour, Lakes to Goldie Putnam. Reprinted From: http://www.colvilletribes.com/book_of_legends.php)

I am Coyote, the Transformer, and have been sent by Great Mystery, the Creator and arranger of the world. Great Mystery has said that all people should have an equal right in everything and that all should share alike. As long as the sun sets in the west this will be a land of peace. This is the commandment I gave to my people, and they have obeyed me.

My people ...lived near the Kettle Falls. I gave them that Falls to provide them with fish all their days. The Falls was surrounded by potholes in which my people cooked their food. When the Hudson's Bay people came they called it the "falls of the Kettle." The traders of the North West Company called it La Chaudiere.

Many generations ago my people were hungry and starving. They did not have a good place to catch their fish. One day while I was out walking I came upon a poor man and his three daughters. They were thin from hunger because they could not get salmon. I promised the old man I would make him a dam across the river to enable him to catch fish, if he would give me his youngest daughter as my wife. The old man agreed to this and I built him a fine falls where he could fish at low water.

But when I went to claim the daughter the old man explained that it was customary to give away the eldest daughter first. So I took the oldest daughter and once again promised the man I would build him a medium dam so he could fish at medium water if I could have the youngest daughter. The old man explained again that the middle daughter must be married before the youngest, so I claimed his middle daughter and built him a fine falls where he could fish at medium water.

Shortly after the father came to me and said he was in need of a high dam where he could fish at high water. He promised me his youngest daughter if I would build this. So I built him a third and highest dam where he could fish at high water. And then I claimed the long-waited youngest daughter as my wife.

And now, because I had built the falls in three levels, my people could fish at low, medium, and high water. I had become responsible for my people, and I saw that the fish must jump up the falls in one certain area where the water flowed over a deep depression. I appointed the old man as Salmon Chief, and he and his descendants were to rule over the falls and see that all people shared in the fish caught there.

Party Line

The party line phone rang on the Spokane Indian Reservation on an autumn day in 1955.   After seven phones picked up at the ring, with each person announcing his or her name, a 49 year old army veteran and rancher from Ft. Washakie, Wyoming asked to speak to a woman he had become sweet on at last summer's Indian Days Pow Wow and Rodeo. "Uh. Hi. This call is for Sally Joseph."

Two of the answering callers hung up. Four of the answering callers listened in, nosey. "This is her Papa, Denton Joseph. She ain't here right now. Can I take a message?"

"Yeah. Thanks. Tell her this is Ericson Ethete, from Wind River. My Mom, Sugar, she ... died yesterday. I thought Sally would want to know. They got to be friendly when Sally was down here for the Pow Wow this summer."

"Sorry to here that, son. We'll say a blessing for her. She was that elder lady with the moccasins, enit?"

"Yes, sir."

"Sally wanted you to come up and see us. You come if you want, son. She told us a lot about you and your family."

"I might do that, sir."

"I'll tell her you called."

"Thank you, sir."

Heading North

A month later, Ericson was heading north, toward Browning, Montana, reservation home of the Blackfeet, with his cousin Betsy Old Bear and her son, Milo in their 1940 ford pick-up truck.

In the back was everything Erickson owned: four shirts, three white undershirts, two pairs of work pants, a pistol that he used to kill rattlesnakes when needed, a few personal items, his summer light woven cowboy hat, two novels bought for a nickel each at the Lander Public Library used book sale and a pair of moccasins made for him by his mother. The items were tied by twine into a cardboard box. On his body he wore his rodeo prize belt buckle on his worn leather belt, and his winter grey felt cowboy hat with his best shirt, pants and worn western boots. In his wallet were a few pictures and $76. He had cashed out the box he kept in the ranch tool shed with his share of last year's calf sales money. He had left everything belonging to the family with his son, Michael, at Wind River, including a thick envelope of papers written out in his mother's hand on the backs of old agency paper discards and a really old beaded headband with a nice piece of turquoise. He hadn't had the heart to read the papers yet.

Milo, aged twenty-six, drove. Betsy and Milo had come back home to Wind River to take part in the death songs for Sugar St. James Ethete. Betsy had married a Blackfeet called Crazy Don Old Bear. He was dead now, frozen outside of a bar in Browning nine years ago. But Betsy and Milo worked his allotment land and had some cattle up near the Canadian border on the St. Mary's Creek by Babb, Montana, so they mostly stayed up there. Almost every winter one or both of them came back to stay at Wind River for a while 'to get out of the cold' they joked.

"You heard from Priscilla after the funeral? She get back ok to New York City?" asked Betsy.

"Yeah, hard to believe my daughter is a city girl. Her train got in a few days ago," replied Erickson.

"She should of stayed home. Ain't right for a Indian to be in the city, even if the government wants us there."

"I'll miss her."

"I bet."

"When you're in Spokane will your ex-wife take care of the ranch?" Milo was always fretting about his cattle, and when given a chance, he worried about other people's stock, too.

"Yeah. She and Mikey know what to do."

"Your boy Mikey's ok; but she worries me; in-nair."

"Mikey's almost as old as you, Milo. No different than you and Betsy takin' care of your Dad's place." Milo's jaw muscle clenched reflexively. He didn't like that.

Erickson backed off. "Iris is ok. She talks too much, but she knows how to run a ranch. Mikey will be ok. Time he was the man around there. Been watching me ranch his whole life. Time I got away from there for a while."

Betsy chimed in. "Ain't right living with a woman divorced you. 'Bout time you traveled some. Should of been *her* that left though. Guess she liked her gravy train."

Erickson rolled his eyes out the passenger window. He was tired of all the opinions about how he should live. The Army had taught him to follow orders, but he'd been out of the army for over ten years. For the first time since before the war he was doing what he wanted, not what somebody told him to do.

"More like, she likes her *whiskey* train; in-nair." Milo hated anything to do with alcohol after coming home from boarding school and seeing his father changed and ruining himself. Second to talking about cattle, criticizing drinking was his favored topic of conversation. Iris didn't drink much, but after seeing her have a few beers at the funeral, Milo's imagination had her turned into a drunk.

Erickson didn't answer, but pulled his hat over his eyes and feigned to settle into a nap. It stopped the conversation.

They drove on in silence through the cold evening, warmed through by the truck's heater. Betsy and Milo watched the wind blown dry sage lands rise outside as they passed north of Cody. They could sense the start of the hills that peaked up on the horizon, near the Yellowstone River. They would be back home at the Old Bear 7 ranch before morning, if they stopped only to fill up the gas tank in Billings. In the back they had packed bologna sandwiches, boiled eggs and a thermos of coffee to share.

After a stop to fill the tank, then because the gas station toilets were for whites only, another stop by the side of the road to relieve themselves, Milo began another conversation.

"The two bulls have thick hides this fall, likely be a cold winter; in-nair."

Erickson grinned. "Huh. Ain't this Montana? When's it warm here in winter?" Erickson could tell Milo wanted to talk about his herd. "How many you running now?"

"Forty pairs. Only two calves lost this year. Cow rejected one after it got stepped on and had a broke leg. Seen signs of it after Ma heard coyotes up there. Bear got another one. Plus I got forty-two heifers and two good bulls."

"Your hired guy do ok?"

"Yeah, old man Yellow Owl. He's part blind; in-nair; and lives with his daughter now. Sold all his stock a few years ago. But he likes to get back to the range when he can. Works good for him to come out here and watch the place when I'm gone for a week or so. Don't know I'd let him stay out there much longer and I think he gets tired of eating fried eggs and beans; in-nair. He wants to go home to his daughter's cooking and his four grandkids. Some younger guys around that help at brandin' and hayin' but I don't trust 'em when I'm not here. They drink too much.

"Calves weaned yet?"

"We had good grass this summer so the cows are strong and I got hay put up for a big winter. Planning to separate 'em and move the cows and heifers this week to the south side pastures, and the few I'm gonna sell to the yard here. Leave the calves closer up here on the north side pasture. Bulls are way out by the highway and I can leave 'em there for the winter; in-nair. Mom wants me to get her a milker. Gonna try my luck bringing in a wild cow from the range after we separate out the calves. I got one kinda mellow. Have to warn Mom about her before she tries to get her hands on her teats. Saddle up and help me tomorrow?"

"Yeah. But then I gotta catch a ride on to Spokane."

Wellpinit, The Spokane Reservation

"I made a new dress in case you were coming." Sally Joseph was shy, but Erickson could tell she liked him. She was standing close and they were both wondering how to really say 'hello' now that they were finally alone in her Papa's kitchen after Papa took Sally's two little ones to sleep on their side of the privacy sheets in the second room of the house the family all shared.

"I like it. You sure look pretty in that blue, with that white collar next to your ... kissable neck." Erickson's voice dropped as he touched the brown skin over the bone that disappeared inside the rounded neck of her dress.

Sally blushed, but she pulled the collar of the dress aside and slightly presented her warm neck. Erickson moved closer so he could touch her pulse point with his lips, then brushed it lightly with his tongue.

She murmured, "You can sleep in the boat barn. There's a rolled up mattress and a kerosene heater. Do you mind a sleepin' bag? I can," she licked her lips as he began to suck lightly on her neck, "zip two together?"

"Better than the army way." He took her hand and pulled her in to him. He opened his lips softly into hers. Her mouth responded and her tongue tasted of coffee. She was so soft, so powerful. They adjusted to each other, going deeper. Thus began the slow, relentless exploration that would keep them fascinated throughout the night and for the next many years.

Grandmother Sugar's Story

"I gotta tell you the damndest story my mother told me right before she died." Erickson said softly. They were watching the sun come up through the open door of the boat barn. They were on the cornhusk mattress, wrapped in a quilt, leaning on the hand-carved canoe that had kept them company through the night of lovemaking.

"What story's that?"

"Seems I'm half Arapaho, a quarter Shoshone and a quarter white."

"What? Sugar? She had a white Mama? There ain't nobody more Shoshone than her in this world! Enit?"

"No, she had a white father."

"I thought her father was that elder they talked about at the fire that night, Trees Told It."

"No that was her grandfather. Turns out, Trees Told It was her mother's father. I didn't even know *that* before she told this story. I always knew she took care of him when he was old, but the story has always been that they were only distant relations somehow.   Tribal records say that she had come as a girl from Idaho and just stayed and took care of Trees Told It."

"Yeah, lots of confusing relations from those days. So what did she say? Was her mother raped by a white man or something? Most of the old ones hate to admit to that stuff, but it happened all the time."

"No, even more strange than that." He paused for a while. They watched two skinny young dogs roll and yip on the grass, then one lifted his leg on a weed and peed. The dogs trotted off when a light came on in the kitchen and Papa came out and headed toward the outhouse.

"You always say to everyone you're Shoshone cause you didn't live as close with the Arapahos." There was a pause while they both thought. "Wow. I never kissed a white man before."

Instead of rising to the joke, Erickson said, "Yeah, I know. All these years I hated white guys, and here it is, that ... stupid. Showing up under my own skin."

"Anyway..."

"So..." Erickson sighed, then continued as if to himself. "Funny. Now some weird stuff my Uncle Thomas, they called him "Rider", used to say makes sense. He died last year. He used to call me 'Whitey' some-times, and Mom would get so mad. I thought it was because she hated white people too. He must have known. When he lost at stick games he would sing this little Mormon song and my mom would shush him in New'e and make angry hand signs. It just seemed so odd. But he never told any-thing more. I guess he just liked to jab my Mama with it sometimes... I'll be damned... It's just coming to me; a bunch of puzzle pieces fitting together."

"What does Mormon have to do with it?"

"Sugar was a Mormon."

"No."

"Yes. So, here's what she said. She was born in Utah. I guess her mama, holy shit, my grandmother, who was Trees Told It's daughter from his second wife... Well there's even more to this story. Trees Told It's first wife was killed by the U.S. soldiers at Bear River. The first wife was this famous chief's, Sagwitch's daughter. The old man and his daughter by that wife somehow weren't there when the attack happened and they came back to find the whole tribe, including the first wife, murdered. That first daughter was Rider's mother. So his second wife, my great-grandmother, really raised them. Anyway, my grandmother, when she was just a child really, got married off to a Mormon guy who was passing through. I guess they were really hungry back then and maybe she otherwise would have starved. She gets to Utah and has to be this guy's second wife. You know, they were polygamists. They lived in some kind of commune. That's why my Mom could speak such great English. She always corrected everybody's speech to this perfect form of English that nobody on the rez spoke. I always thought that was odd, you know? Another puzzle piece: she spoke English as her first language! She told me she only learned to speak New'e when she moved back, when she was about 10!

"She said that she lived in this commune with all these other Mormons and went to their meetings and ate their strange food and worked day and night on this farm. She didn't know she was Shoshone until she was about nine, and her Mom was telling stories. She said she knew right then, deep down, that she would leave the Mormons and come home."

They sat for a while, imaging all that. The sun was shining now, warming things up slightly. How those Indians must have suffered to let their little girl get taken away; how Sugar must have had so much courage to become the respected elder she was within the tribe if that was where she began.

"My Mom had a little brother, too. His name was George. The last time she saw him, he was five. He stayed with the Mormons. She doesn't even know if he lived."

"How did she get back to the Shoshones? What happened to her Mom?"

"She said that when she was a young girl, the Mormons came to preach to the Indians at Wind River and her Mom brought her two children back with her, so they could meet her family, I guess. When they were there, diphtheria broke out at the Indian camp and everybody got sick. Her mom died. Her half-brother came from Utah to get my mom and her brother, but Trees Told It tricked everyone by saying that the girl was dead, too. Mom said they had a fake funeral for her and everything, and that her aunt pretended to do the burying. The brother went back to Utah with the half-brother. Then Trees Told It hid my mom out in the woods and later brought her out and pretended that she came from Idaho. The Mormons thought my mom was dead too."

"Well, your grandmother died with her people. That makes me happy somehow."

"Yeah. Me too."

So, as a young girl, Sugar had to go from being a white girl, living on a Mormon commune, to living on the rez in those hard days, and learning Shoshone, and pretending to be an Indian?"

"Well, she was half Indian. But, I guess so."

"Holy moley."

"It makes sense that's why she was so insistent that we always do everything Shoshone. She worked at the agency for a long time so I guess she had access to the records and stuff. She's the reason Trees Told It was one of the first to get an allotment, so it was some of the best land, and just before he died, too. I been ranching on that allotment my whole life. It has good water, soil, some trees. Plenty time white people tried to trick us out of it, but Mom always saw and was smarter than them. One time they wanted to drill for oil. There's oil wells all around us. But she said it would ruin our water, and water was more important."

"Your Mom was a great lady, enit? She should of met my Grandma Winne. Grandma Winne was my Mom's mom and she raised us after Mom died. Now she lives down by the river in a little cabin Papa built for her. I'll take you over to meet her today if you want."

"Yeah. I'm missing my Mom something awful. It'll be nice to hear another elder lady's stories."

It's the River

"It's the river," Grandmother Winne said.

"You have to understand the miracle of the river. Really it's the miracle of water, but here, where we live, you hear the voice of the miracle loudest in the Spokane River. It flows into the Columbia River." Grandmother looked at her granddaughter's new man, Erickson. He was listening patiently. She liked that.

"Imagine the Earth! A hard, dry rock floating around in the universe, held in its place among the stars by forces of gravity from distant planets and energies from different stars. We don't know why our Earth is exactly *where* it is, whirling around itself, in constant motion, and whirling as part of all the cosmic junk but still staying in its place.

"So Earth, anyway, is different from all that other universe material. Each planet and star is alive, you know. They all have different personalities. Mars has red gas. Venus has clear gas. The stars are each swirling dense masses of their own types of energy; maybe not solid at all, but so strong we can see the light given off as part of their energy from so far away!

"What gives Earth it's personality? Water! All the elements that make up all the gasses, solids and liquids of the universe come together in different ways. Somewhere out there is a planet or star that is covered with flowing gold! Somewhere out there is a planet or star that is covered with flowing magnesium!

"But our little planet, by chance or by design, is covered with flowing water made up of hydrogen and oxygen! And our air is full of hydrogen and oxygen, probably broken down from water, and which will reform someday to make water.

People! We are made up of a lot of hydrogen and oxygen along with carbon and lots of other elements. But it's the water that makes us who we are, and not rocks made of dirt.

"So now we know that water is what makes Earth special, and what makes us people. You know that water keeps everything alive, right? People can live in the desert if they can go from wells to wells, or from springs to springs, or know where a river might be. Gardens need water to grow. Have you ever seen grass get green overnight because it rained? Yes! Well that's the magic of water! It makes life! Life as we know it here, anyway.

"Go back again, imagine that Earth. If you could look at it from space. It'd be blue, right? Because there are so many oceans? The blue is *water*! It'd also be white, right? That white is *water*, well, ice or clouds made up mostly of water. If you took all that water away from Earth, it would look gray, or maybe brown. It would be about half its size and shrunken, dead gray. But no! It has water swirling and moving all around it, and interacting with it, and changing forms from wet ocean, to steamy clouds, to ice on the mountaintops and on the top and bottoms of the Earth. There is water under the Earth's surface too! Beings that live on the Earth are partly water! When they die, their water goes back into the sky or onto the ground, where it becomes part of the Earth. It remains the magic! It goes on to make something else live.

"So all our water is *moving*. Aside from constantly changing form from ice to vapor to liquid, it's actually flowing all over and under and above the Earth!

"Imagine that Earth's water is one being! It's a living thing in a dance of beauty! Floating... revolving... lifting... sinking... vaporizing... freezing... flowing. It goes up and down and around us all the time. Go sit in a rainstorm someday. Just sit there. You will feel so much power all around you. You can open your mouth and let water into your body. You can taste that power. You do taste that power every day of your life. But maybe you don't remember that what you're tasting is God!

"Anyway, I got distracted. The river. We might forget that a drink of fresh water is us! Us partaking of the miracle. But you can't look at the mighty river and not see the miracle. First, it's just *BIG*! You can see where it pushed the ground before it, in small ways where banks are eroded, and in huge ways like in the great canyons.

"You can see time itself, in the river. Just by looking, you can tell that it's been there, for almost forever, doing its thing. But the trick is that it's not *this* water. It's the same river with different water from long ago that did this. But *that* water is united with *this* water to make a river that goes back into time, and that will stretch into the future. So you can look in there and see your ancestors, and your children's children.

"And that water is all connected! It's connected to all the other water in the sky, the oceans, and in the glaciers. But it's also connected to the past and the future. Because it's alive. A miracle. Magic. Put your finger into the river and you are touching the whole Earth. You are connected to the

Mediterranean Sea in Italy! You are connected to the Volga River in Ukraine! You are connected to Antarctica! You are connected to your own people, back in Wyoming."

"Ha ha!" Ericson laughed, "My Mom used to say that all the time! She used to say that we need to take care of the waters, because they are connected to everybody everywhere."

"Well of course," said Grandmother, "Indian people know this. Or they did anyway, once upon a time. Now I think most of the young people don't know a damn thing, but maybe I say that because I'm old and when I was a young person I didn't know a damn thing either. Anyway, I was explaining what's different about Spokane country. You felt it, right?"

They younger man nodded.

"So you asked me, 'Grandmother, why is this place so special? Why do I feel like the air is fresher and the grass is greener and the spirits are closer?' So I'm answering you in a big way."

Ericson thought for a while. Slowly, he said, "Grandmother, I never really understood it that way. So is that why you are so upset about the new dam on the Columbia being built?"

Grandmother's face changed from joy to fear. "Hush your mouth, son! That ain't going to happen! Some leaders went to Congress and told them what it would mean. They can't do it now. So don't talk about it. Ever."

The young man looked down, shamed and hurt. All was quiet for a moment while the Grandmother huffed and Ericson breathed as if he might cry. Then, he calmed and decided to speak.

"Grandmother?" He whispered slowly, "I'm sorry, I know it's important, sometimes not to talk about some things. People ask me about the war, and for a long time I couldn't answer at all. I felt like there was an evil spirit right under my skin and hiding in my mouth. It took almost all my power and energy to keep that devil in. If I let it out, or let it have my voice, terrible things would happen. Because when I was there, in the Philippines in 1943, the evil war spirit was at work through me. We were a killing machine that did horrible, ugly things every day. When it was going on, I didn't loose a wink of sleep at night about it. I had welcomed that devil in to let me do the things I had to do.

"But that evil spirit stayed in me when the war was over. Somehow, I thought that he would just go away after the fighting stopped, and I'd be myself again. But even after I got on the transport home, the evil spirit stayed in me. He was mean and violent and wanted me to hurt everyone I came across. So I tried to kill him with my thoughts, but he would not die.

"So I realized I'd have to live with him in me. I knew he couldn't come out. So I held him in. But he was stronger than me, Grandmother, and I knew it. I tried to drown him with whisky, and gin and anything I could get. That worked for a while, but that was a trick, too. Because pretty soon he learned how to make the alcohol his fuel. Sometimes, when I was drunk, he got out. He got out in a way where he didn't leave me, but where he made me like him. Because I liked him, I also hated him, and I hated me. I was tired, Grandmother. I believed the only way to kill that devil was to kill myself.

"I tried to, you know. I took my Dad's gun and I went out to his shed where I couldn't make too much of a mess. I just wanted that devil in me gone. So I laid down and put the rifle up to my neck and tried to figure out how to pull the trigger. I needed a stick, so I got up to go in the house for the yardstick that always leaned by our refrigerator. When I went inside, Dad was sitting there drinking coffee. He looked at my face and he knew. So he grabbed me and hugged me. And he saved me.

Then my Dad had that warrior ceremony for me."

The grandmother was quiet. She drew breath as if to talk, but then only looked up at Ericson. A tear escaped her wet eyes. Finally she said, "Oh son, we have all had so much sadness. But you are right. Keeping our evil spirits in us aint the way. I'm gonna think now, about the river. I'm gonna think about the salmon. Will you come back tomorrow? We can talk again then after I've gathered myself. Let's have a smudge, now. This is important stuff, enit?"

The old lady went to her battered cupboards. On the small yellow Formica top, there was an assortment of items most people would find odd, but were perfectly normal in her reservation house. There were an assortment of chipped, unmatched dishes, a tub of lard, a bottle of Clorox bleach from which drops were added to sanitize the dishwater, a jumble of papers, a wadded bandana, a fishing reel, a colorfully beaded hair clasp, and a bowl with ashes and a half-burned twine of sweetgrass.

The grandmother brought over the bowl, and a silver flip open lighter to the wobbly table where they had been drinking coffee. She filled a half glass of water from the dip bucket. She stooped over the smudge bowl with her eyes closed while Ericson waited. She flipped open the lighter and struck the flame which appeared blue and gold. She held it under the burned edge of the sweetgrass twine and slowly the grass started to smolder. She blew breath over the small flame and snapped shut the lighter. The flame leapt for a quick moment then reduced to a red and black rim on the grass. As the red worked its way into the twine, a sweet and calming scent of earthy smoke rose to the ceiling. Grandmother held the smoking sweetgrass up then down, then turned slowly all around, offering the smoke to the spirits in all four directions. She brushed the smoke to Ericson, who brought it to him with his hands. He breathed in the smoke and breathed out his own good intentions, which the smoke carried up away. The room was cleansed with the lovely scent of the burned sweetgrass.

Grandmother Winne looked at Ericson with pain on her face. "You go now, son, but come back tomorrow. I need to rest. Enit?"

Ericson kissed her forehead lightly and left.

About ten o'clock the next morning there came a knock on Mrs. Winne's screen door. It rattled the bent screen against the smudged doorjam and broke the silence of the musty smelling home. Ericson let himself in, and the Grandmother toddled out from her bedroom wearing her cotton rosy floral shirt and a beaded pendant tied around her neck with rawhide. Her swollen feet were held inside beautiful moccasins that had seen much wear, appearing very much a part of the old woman. Her blue, long skirt was faded but clean. A pot of coffee was ready on the wood stove, drips of the dark stuff already drying on the yellow formica from Grandmother's first cup. Grandmother had eaten. Half of a piece of white bread with a slice of orange government cheese remained at the table.

Grandmother filled their mismatched coffee cups without having to ask whether to do so and put the rest of her sandwich on its plate on the counter.

"You are such a good boy to come sit with an old lady." Grandmother said, in thanks.

"I miss my own Mom. She just passed. I feel her presence here with you."

"Thank you son. For that. I can feel your Mom, too. She has a strength, enit?" Grandmother sighed. She looked suddenly tired; it made Ericson afraid for her. "I been thinking about what you said. I need to tell some stories to you and my granddaughter Sally before I pass." She took a breath and seemed to grow stronger. "I can feel that devil you told about growing in me. For me the devil is anger over what's going on, what has gone on, the whole mess of it all. I can't make any sense any more. Maybe aint nothin' I can do. We all been saying they won't build that dam, but we gotta have a plan, in case they keep going forward." She stopped, "Should I tell you all this?"

Ericson shrugged. Secretly, he didn't know if he wanted to hear this worry, for he sensed it would come with responsibility. Every tribe had big problems. He had just left the ones at Wind River that he couldn't do anything about. He wasn't ready for a whole new set of unsolveable problems. "I don' know, Grandmother." Grandmother looked at him. Ericson felt a nudge within him. Perhaps this was from his mother, the invisible person in the room, who had always believed in him and had been staunchly proud of being Shoshone and had always stood up for her people. He waited, acknowledging all this, then shrugged again with a sigh. "I got no place to go. Maybe you should tell me, Grandmother."

"Are you afraid, son? It's ok. We all gotta be strong. I was thinking last night and I think we gotta plan to do something before they kill the river. Before they kill our ways. I know you don't really know our ways. Sally, she does. But you are one of those horse Indians; with your Arapaho father and Shoshone mother. Maybe telling you will help me think it through. If I was talking to Sally, I wouldn't have to tell the whole story, cause she would know. You need the whole story. Maybe if I think it through, I will know what to do."

Ericson was looking down. He didn't say anything, but he was still there, waiting, so she kept on. "Yesterday you asked me about the dam. I'm gonna show you something."

Grandmother pushed herself up from the table. Ericson saw the pain she felt in her knees, or maybe her hips, in her face. He wanted to help but getting old was another thing he didn't know how to stop. She went to a bureau that had sat next to her sagging couch. She pulled out a bulging black book, held together by numerous rubber bands. Grandmother snapped the bands off the book as she sat down and pulled them over her wrist for safekeeping.

Inside the book were many neatly clipped newspaper articles, along with notes in pencil, written in the grandmother's spidery writing.

"These tell a story. It's a slow tragedy for us Spokane people." Grandmother sighed, then, went on. "It's a triumph of mankind and industry in the eyes of white people, enit? But you know they have been tricked, too. Nature always wins in the end. We know that the end of the salmon means the end of man. It was foretold by our old medicine men. White people don't know what they are doing. And they are doing it to themselves, well to all of us, to Mother Earth. One change is made and its impacts multiply. Then there needs to be more changes, they continue to enforce the machine of the first change and because they get focused on that machine, they don't see or they ignore where it is going. The impacts multiply. One small thing effects and controls and compounds. White people are killing the rivers with their dams."

Ericson was tired of this kind of talk. He had been to war, and had seen the marvels of industry. He was ready to see progress that could make people's lives easier. He liked cars, trains, airplanes, medicines, electric lights and telephones. The bomb had ended the war. So many old people seemed to want to go back to the difficult times before industry, but they forgot about being cold, living in the dark, dying young from small injuries, and traveling on foot. He knew to interrupt was impolite, but he did not want to spend his day on pointless talk about turning the clocks back to 1800. "Grandmother," he said, as patiently as he could, "The salmon aren't gone. We had salmon for dinner last night."

Grandmother looked shocked. Her round, watery eyes stared into him, then into the something else that he had become. Ericson could see that she was thinking he was ignorant, that he was siding with her enemies, that he was her enemy. Her look turned to fear and frustration. She looked away and slumped in her chair and was quiet staring at the floor. Ericson began to be afraid he had deeply hurt her feelings. Then, after a moment, she held up her hand, palm to his face. She said, "This is what I must fight. This is what I must do. Thank you, my son, for showing me."

Ericson was puzzled, but he knew he must now show respect and be quiet; that she would explain.

"Yes, it is good that we still have some salmon. While they are still here, they can heal, they can come back. But you do not understand what is being lost. Tell me, would your great grandfather be satisfied that there are still a few buffalo walking behind barbed-wire fences? After seeing the vast herds that provided everything to the people, would he not fight their destruction because a few ranchers will, in the future, keep a few as livestock?

"What happened to the buffalo is what is happening *right now* to the salmon. Those men building dams are like the buffalo skin hunters with their tommy-guns blasting away at the last of the buffalo. The dam builders are worse because it's not just salmon they are killing." She slapped the table, making the coffee cups jump, "Destruction! I told you yesterday, it is about the river. It is water! It is life! It is all connected! Yes, change can happen, change always does happen, but value must be placed on doing change right. Unfortunately, people are impatient. They want it all, now. But something must slow down the change so people can be educated. So people understand. So people know what they are loosing in their haste for convenience."

Right then, there was a knock at the door. "Grandmother?" said a male voice from outside.

"Come in, Ducky..."

Andrien Winne, known as Ducky by everyone on the reservation, Sally's cousin who Erickson had met the night before, came in bringing the smell of the late morning and pine with him. He was wearing a dusty jean jacket, work pants and boots. There was a wood chip and some saw dust in his long hair and calluses on his hands. Ducky was a woodcutter with hard muscles and a brown face. He had amazing grey eyebrows that jumped about on his face as he laughed and joked.

It took him only a second to assess the situation. "Ah, Horse Indian just stepped into the Fish Wars!" He grinned, showing a missing side tooth, his eyebrows dancing. He poured coffee and sat down, moving a pile of laundry from off the clothesline out of his way.

"Morning Ducky," said Ericson.

"Ducky, what's the biggest salmon you ever caught at Kettle Falls?" asked Grandmother.

"Back in 1927 me and Addy speared a red weighed in at 26 pounds. Enit? For you, Horse Indian, that's a sockeye that swam inland. In those days, we often caught Chinooks that were 75 pounds. It was something to see those big boys fighting up the river. They were so big that their backs got a sunburn and their bellies drug the bottom! Before they made it this far up and fought that hard to loose their weight, they probably weighed over 100 pounds." Ducky grinned.

"Why they call it Kettle Falls?"

"Water been flowing there so long it carved big kettles into the granite, pools three men deep where salmon would get stuck and we could just reach in and get them out, enit?"

"How far upstream from here is Kettle Falls?" asked Ericson?

Grandmother and Ducky glanced at each other. "Kettle Falls was about 40 miles from the Canadian border, north of Spokane, over 100 miles from the sea. It don't exist no more. It's under the lake, Lake Roosevelt."

Ericson blinked; he was starting to get it.

"Ericson, how big was those salmon you had last night?" asked Grandmother.

"I guess the biggest one was about 4 pounds", he answered.

"See, the salmon are changing. They live four years, you know. Born in the rocky shallows in fresh water in the summer, then swimming all the way downstream to the sea. They go on migrating in the ocean for three years, getting fat and strong eating shrimps and planktons, then swimming upstream all the way to where they spawned, so the females can lay their eggs and the males can fertilize them. Then they die right there, making a feast for us and the bears and the wolves. Well, that's how it should be; was since God created them. Now, they can't get back here. The circle is broken. They don't need to be strong to get back, so they can be small enough to spawn down by the ocean. The dams block their way. Grand Coulee dam stopped all the fish, not just the salmon, from getting to a huge part of the river system. One year we had fish like Ducky said. The next year we had no fish at all."

Ducky's mouth twitched. "That was a bad year, enit? I think we all knew that it would happen. When it came time for the medicine men to sing salmon songs, they did it, but no salmon came. The people wanted the First Foods Ceremony, when the first spring salmon came back. We all stood around the edge of the lake with empty baskets and no fish. Lot of our elders died that summer, remember? Bunch of us went to fish downstream at Celilo, but you know that's been the other tribes' fishing site for thousands of years, so we weren't welcome there. Some old guys let us fish for a few hours; felt bad for us, hurt our pride. We brought seventeen fish back when in years past we had seventeen hundred. It was horrible to eat government cheese all winter. We didn't have nothing to do all summer cause we couldn't fish. People started getting drunk a lot more."

Everyone was quiet.

Ducky changed the subject. "Hey Grandma, Emmy says you have that beadwork done?"

"Just a minute, and I'll go get it," she said and pushed herself up from the table and padded across the wooden floor of her cabin to her bedroom.

As Grandmother was out of the room, Ducky said softly, "Thanks for letting her talk about the fish. The men in Council are trying to decide what to do. The old ones have good wisdom. I think this is gonna be a long fight. Tribes downriver are where we were twenty years ago, with the government wanting to build dams and not much we can do."

"You bet, Ducky. I don't have nothing better to do right now, and I want to know about all this. It is like the buffalo all over again," replied Ericson.

"If you're wanting to stay around here and are looking for work, you should think about the new uranium mine jobs. I hear there's a few opening."

After that, their visit was of other, more mundane things. On his way out Ericson said, "Grandmother, can I borrow your news clippings so I can read about the dams?"

Grandmother smiled. "Yes, son, but bring them back to me soon. We need to make a battle plan about these 'fish wars' as Ducky calls 'em."

School

"Hey Lovey?" said Sally to Ericson, "Mom told me that tomorrow Grandmother is going to the school to tell stories to the kids. Wanna go?"

"What time? I'm working late shift, down in the pit."

"It'll be morning; you just want to wake up early."

"Sure. I been wanting to see the school. See where our little baby will go when he or she is old enough." Ericson snuggled into his new wife, giving her growing midsection a tap.

"I like the new school principal. He's letting the kids hear Indian history from the Elders. When I went we couldn't speak our language and had to pray to Jesus. If we did anything Indian we got beat. I hope that is over! These kids can hear Grandmother in school. My, my, my how things have changed."

The next day, they walked from the reservation houses to the small elementary school. There were 8 classes, with 220 kids. Because the weather was nice, they all sat outside, the school children seated on the grass gathered around Grandmother who sat on a chair decorated with a colorful blanket under the shade of the edge of the pine forest. In addition to the children, the ten school workers were there along with a few other adults, many of whom were elders or the disabled who often came to the school to have lunch with the children, and have a free warm meal prepared for them.

Grandmother began to talk and the children listened with respect. They had been taught the proper behavior with elders.

"When I was a little girl, this was back in the late 1800s, there were three tribes of Spokane Indians. We all lived along the River; that one that is flowing right there, to the south of where we are sitting. We have all lived along this river for thousands of years. One group was called the Lower Spokanes, because we lived on the downstream part of the river, west of Spokane Falls. How many of you have been to the Spokane Falls in downtown Spokane?

A number of silent hands went up among the children.

"Those falls were very important to our people. They remain very important to our people. In the old days, before the dams and Washington Water Power, we went fishing there. That's where most of our food came from. We lived on the salmon that swam upstream to there from the Columbia River, or the Nch'l Wana, in our language, from the ocean. Some of our people also fished at Kettle Falls, which is underwater now since the 1930s. We called that place Shonitkwu, which means "Noisy Waters". In those places, when it was time to fish and all our people would come, we had thousands of people. It was a whole city of Sun People, all fishing, and sharing and feasting.

"Another group of our people were known as the Upper Spokanes. They lived at the headwaters of the river, up by Coeur d'Alene Lake. Then there were the Middle Spokanes who lived along the Little Spokane River, to the north and west of where we are now. We all got along and supported each other when there was any trouble. We were three parts of one big family. Then around us were many other peoples. We also got along well with them. We were also very close to the Kalispel People.

"Who knows where our name came from?"

"One little girl in the front row raised her hand. After Grandmother nodded, she said, "We are the Children of the Sun."

"Very good. Yes, our name means 'Sun People'. You know not all of us Sun People came here to this reservation. Did you know that many of the Upper Spokanes went to live with the Jocko People, or the Flathead People in what is now Montana? Some of the Middle Sun People went to live with the Coeur d'Alenes in Idaho."

"When I was a little girl, one of my first memories was moving here to this reservation. This reservation was made by an Executive Order by President Rutherford Hayes in 1881. Many other Indians have reservations made by treaties, but because we didn't have many wars with white people, they didn't sign treaties with us.

"I was a Middle Spokane and we had a choice to move here, or to the Flathead or to the Colville or to the Coeur d'Alene reservation. Our Chief was named Enoch. We were mostly Catholic. My father's people were from here so we came here. The people that were here were Protestant, and their chief was Chief Garry. We all decided to get along and live in peace. So that's what we did." With this Grandmother gave a sideways look to one of the other elders there. Erickson could tell something more was being said than was clear to him.

"Before we moved here we lived in lodges made of pine poles and skins. We also had ceremonial places made of Tule mats. We like the new longhouse, too. Our people traveled around the area, we knew where to find good things every season. Now many of the forest creatures are gone, but we used to have lots of wolves, and bears, and wolverines, and elk, and deer, and coyotes, many other creatures.

I was going to tell you some stories about these creatures, but I decided to tell you a story about our people instead.

"Just two years after this reservation was established by the President, and we had to give up all our other lands, gold was discovered in Coeur d'Alene. Lots more white people, miners and such, came here and the city of Spokane grew very fast. The whole area was growing. The white people wanted our land because it is such a good place. They wanted to make farms here and everybody thought there was gold here too. So soon after, the government, who had agreed to stop taking our land if we would stay on this reservation, decided that these white people should get to come on our lands here, too. They passed a law that said every Indian would get a piece of land then everything left would be for white people to have for free. I actually have a newspaper clipping from 1909 from the Spokane Cronicle that has the headline 'Indians Have Gobbled Best of Spokane Reservation'. Really! Those fools had forgotten that this whole country was ours." Grandmother seemed to realize she was getting worked up, so she paused and took a big breath. She continued more slowly.

"There was another thing. If white people wanted another white person's land, they had to buy it from them. But for Indian land, they were supposed to just come here and take ours for free under the government rules. So of course they wanted our lands.

"Pretty soon, the government said that it was time for white people to come get free Spokane land. You should have seen them all lined up! Over 40,000 applied for land on the first day. The railroad asked for everything left, but because it was plots all over and not so as you could build train tracks, that got denied. The white folks were camping, waiting. Over five hundred men right on our border. They had their shovels and their horses and their plows and their cars. They thought that once the signal was given they could each run or drive onto our land and take whatever they wanted. But the government had not done it right. We had a good government agent, then, one of the few. His name was Anderson. He was not done allotting to the Indians, and he took his time. Those white men got mad! The government had to call in federal police to make them go away. Over 100 police were needed to keep a riot from taking place in the camp. Many of our people, including my Dad joined the police. He had a gun and those police stood on our reservation boundary and no white men dared come in. It was pretty near to bad bloodshed. But a good lesson. You gotta protect what is yours, enit?"

Everyone in the audience was spellbound. Some of the white teachers looked uncomfortable.

"Finally, in 1910 they had finished the allotments. They let white people come in then and look for minerals, but the claims didn't hold because they didn't find no gold, silver, or copper here. They didn't know to look for the uranium that was only found here last year! The government did take a bunch of our land, though, to build Little Falls Dam, which is right down the hill there, and let the river flood part of the reservation. One white man, named David Wilson made $25,000 in that land deal just by claiming the land then selling it to Washington Water Power. We Spokanes got nothing from that.

"Eventually a bunch of white people did come onto our land and get homesteads from the government. Our leaders were smart, though. Once our tribe had some cash from the government selling our timber, the tribe bought those people out. Imagine, paying to buy back our own land.

"Way back in time, before the dams, we used the rivers to get around. We had canoes, you know. We didn't have any roads then. Our traditional canoes could go all over our area quickly and quietly.

"White people used the rivers, too. They had big steamships that brought them from the ocean ports all the way up Nch'l Wana to a place called Cascade where there were small waterfalls where the river dropped down quickly towards the sea. They were mad because at the Cascade there were waterfalls that their steamships could not go over. They had to get off the ships below the waterfall then walk around to the top of the waterfall and catch another ship. Of course Indian people have been doing these portages forever so we know that it is part of life. Then the white people would get on other boats and go from the Cascades all the way up to Celilo, which is still a wonderful salmon fishing place, used by our cousins the Yakima, Palouse, Warm Springs and others.

"Then the white people figured out they could put blocks into the river and make small floods on part of the falls so that their ships could float straight over them! These are called "Locks". So the first locks were made at Cascade and were called Cascade Locks and Canal way back in 1896. I remember my father was absolutely amazed to see those ships going up the river. Then they built more locks at Celilo Canal and Locks soon after 1905, so boats could come way up to Spokane from the ocean and then on to Lewistown, Idaho. Imagine! Lewistown Idaho as a seaport! They called it the "Inland Empire." In 1918 they started cutting down our forests for timber. The government got paid three dollars per board feet of pine and a dollar fifty for everything else. Soon, the animals and birds were leaving our lands because the forests were gone. Spokanes started their own companies to log. If someone was gonna do it, we were gonna do it right.

"Then during World War II, white people knew that they could generate electricity from the water flowing down the Spokane River and the Nch'l Wana. They needed electricity to make the aluminum for airplanes built in Seattle. So they made the locks into dams. The dams weren't so smart though. They stopped the fish from coming up the Nch'l Wana. You know we still have more dams possible...."

Grandmother's voice trailed off. She seemed overwhelmed by the rest of the story she wanted to tell.

A little boy, not wanting it to be over, raised his hand and asked, "Could you sing us the salmon song?"

Grandmother smiled and relaxed. She reached for a hand drum she had tucked under her chair. She centered herself then beat a steady thum, thum, thum. She began to sing in her high voice in Salish. Her song had a beautiful "Oo-ah! Oo-ah!" chorus. Soon the children were singing along. A sad voice joined from deep in the river, where salmon used to swim. Some of the children heard that voice and listened harder.

The Uranium Mine

"Take a break, boys!" called the foreman. All the men were a funny yellow-green from the uranium dust. Yellow sweat dripped from under Erickson's hat and down his neck. Creases around his eyes showed brown skin behind the yellow powder. His black braids were tied together behind his back to keep them out of his way. His gloves were slimy inside from the fine dust and sweat. It was one of the hotter days. The shoveling of the blasted tailings was moving slow. The men gathered around the ceramic water cauldron, taking turns pushing the little lever that released the water into the paper cups. Erickson licked the dust from his lips, happy to drink.

"Fourteen meters that side." Pointed the foreman for the men gathered. "Tansy, you take Chief and the Bird Man to that area." Erickson hated being called "Bird Man", but the foreman had nicknames of his own for all the Indians at the mine. They all knew that the Indians were paid two dollars less per hour, too, but most were happy to have the work so it was accepted. None of them could imagine that they would ever be paid the same wages as white workers. White workers drove the machines. Indians drove the shovels. The jobs for the men of the tribe had been a real blessing. People were building nice cabins rather than living in government houses. The Wellpinit School was full of children as people had hope for the future.

"You workin' Sunday, Erickson?" asked Ron Abrahamson.

"Yeah, need some hours."

"When's your baby supposed to get out of the hospital this time?"

"Doctor says maybe Monday. Sally'll take the bus out here from Spokane, when they let him out, I guess."

"He must be doing better to be getting released, enit?"

"Yeah, but they still say there is something wrong with his kidneys. It's like he was poisoned or something."

"Hope he does better soon."

"Yeah, me too."

"You hear that Ray Garry's in the hospital? Cancer they say."

"Yeah, I heard he was sick, but not about the cancer. That's too bad for Julie. They just got married. She pregnant?"

"No, don't think so."

"Shame, she may have missed her chance. I hope he comes back home here. No sense dying in a damn hospital."

"Time to get back to work you red boys!" Shouted the foreman. Erickson picked up his shovel.

Fish Wars

"I finished looking at your news articles, Grandmother."

"How's little James?"

"He's hanging in there. He is talking a blue streak, now."

"That's good. Teach him some Salish words, maybe some of your Shoshone, too."

"We sing to him every night with traditional songs. He likes that."

"I just hope he's feeling better."

"He's awful yellow colored."

"Sometimes the little ones are stronger than you think. Try giving him a sunbath. That helps with the jaundice."

Erickson was quiet. He knew in his heart that a sunbath would not cure his son. "I'm hoping that the new medicine will help, too, Grandmother."

"My grandfather was a medicine man. When I was a child, at First Fish ceremony, he would hold a healing song for anyone who was ailing. It helped so many people. I'm gonna think today if I can remember some of the words to that song. Maybe we can have a healing song. But it needs some first fish...Maybe son, you can go downriver next month when they will be coming in?"

"I know Kettle Falls is gone, and there's no fish up there now but the trout they are stocking, but could we go there?"

"No Erickson. The healing comes from the power of the salmon, and the many lives he has lead to get back to the place he was spawned, in order to spawn again. A trout ain't the same. Or you could sing all you want without any fish, but the life-circle of the salmon has spirit behind it that the song needs."

"I can get us some salmon from downriver. You know Beak Nose from the mine? He's half Yakima. He said he would give me some fish when they come in. He fishes at Celilo. But, I'm going up there to the Kettle Falls just the same. I want to see it. It's calling me."

Grandmother looked at Erickson. She had not been back to Shonitk 'wu since the day fifteen years earlier when the falls slowly vanished forever as the waters rose behind the temporary structures that allowed for the building of the gigantic Grand Coulee Dam. "I haven't been there since the Ceremony of Tears. After the falls were gone, all the tribes came together for the last time. There were all the Colville tribes: you know, the Lakes, Methow, Okanagan, San Poil, Columbia, Wenatchi, Entiat and Chelan. We also had the Coeur d'Alenes, Kootenai, Kalispel, Nez Perce, Flathead, Pend Oreille and tribes as far away as the Tulalip from the coast, and our old enemies the Blackfeet. The drums beat slowly and loudly. The spirits of the fish could hear our wailing. Even the old men were crying."

"Were there any white people that came around the falls? Did they know what they did?"

"Oh, as more people moved in, yes, whites came to the falls alright. All kinds of folks fished there. There were over fourteen tribes that would come from all around. At first the whites weren't welcome. My mother used to talk about the Catholic mission some Jesuits built there at Shonitk 'wu when she was a little girl. She hated the priest, Father Pierre-Jen. He spoke all French but learned some Salish. He didn't want us living in our way. My mother thought he had lots of nerve to come to a place where thousands of people had been living a good and strong spiritual life for thousands of years and telling them they were bad. Planting shame for our good ways. Telling them they were going to be burned in a fire for this so-called evil. Some people believed him. Most thought he was crazy. He had to be, wearing a long black robe when it was so hot.

That was back soon after they established the Canadian border. Of course, so many of the tribes that came to fish at Shonitk 'wu are now considered Canadians. Back then we were all just cousins. There was no border at all.

Then when I was little there was a big hotel built there. Silly white men came with fishing poles from back East, when you could scoop the huge fish up off the banks with your hands or with nets. I remember seeing them just shaking their heads at the wealth of those millions of salmon that far from the sea and all the Indian people camped there in their lodges and such.

We were a big gathering! People came for the fish, of course, salmon but also the huge steelhead. But they also came for news, to trade, to see friends and relatives from other tribes, to court, and to settle disputes. They used to have special fires where elders would act as arbitrators for problems that would be brought to them. Whatever they decided was the rule. They were very wise. People came and went but everyone tried to be there for First Fish and many people stayed until October.

There were so many fish! You could see them coming, the water boiling with them. They would mill around just below the falls then start coming up. They would bound – high! Out of the water, jumping over a riff of water in rocks. Some were too weak to make it over. Those were the ones we took. We let the strong ones go, and they got to lay their eggs above. Their meat was such a beautiful color."

"That must have been a sight to see! I saw in the news articles that the Colvilles got a government settlement for Grand Coulee. Do you have an article about the Spokane's payment from the government? Wasn't a bunch of Spokane land flooded?"

"They are still negotiating for payment to our tribe, son. In 1940 a law condemned all tribal lands up to an elevation of 1310 feet above sea level. So many people had to move up hill from their traditional homes! And you know we bury our dead along the river. We had long councils that lasted for days to decide what to do. All our loved ones were eventually washed away. We knew the spirits forbade us to pull them from the ground and re-bury them somewhere away from the river. We had big arguments about what to do, but in the end it happened so fast, we didn't have time to decide and the river decided for us. Our loved ones are now under the lake named after President Roosevelt.

"Anyway, under the law a quarter of the lake was reserved for us for fishing and boating for us Spokanes and for all the tribes that make up what the whites call the "Colvilles". Stupid of course because there are no fish and we don't just go boating around for fun. We canoed for transportation. We were supposed to get paid for our land, too. Most of us didn't care about that because the loss of the fish was the loss of the way of life. Many elders said the money was trading our old ways for the white way of money and greed. That money would not buy us what we wanted, and that was to have the salmon and steelhead back. But others said it was the principle of the thing. We could not let the white men steal from us again.

"So a whole delegation of Spokanes were invited to Washington DC in the first week of December, 1941. They left here on the train carrying their full regalia for the meetings in the nation's capitol. Beadwork, head-dresses, shields, jewelry. You already know what happened that week, being a world war veteran. Once the Japs hit Pearl Harbor, the Spokane settlement was not important to anyone. We were promised reparations after the war but nothing has yet to come of it."

"You saw from those news articles, our people follow the white man's rules. We negotiate, we go to court, we speak before Congressional Committees."

"One of the later articles I saw was the Yakimas going to tell Congress not to build The Dalles Dam because it'll flood Celilo Falls. Once they know what it means, Celilo will be safe."

Grandmother was quiet for a while. "They haven't paid for what they already done, son. And they have a fever for electricity and irrigation. They call Grand Coulee the "Eighth Wonder of the World" cause it's the biggest dam and power producer in the world. Why would they not do it again?"

"Now Grandmother. That won't happen. Celilo is too important. It's the last one."

"Erickson, haven't you seen the paper today? It says the farmers need more water for irrigation in Oregon. Where does that water come from? It all comes from the rivers. They need those dams to channel the water into those ditches to take far away to the farms. Well, not to Indian farms, of course." Grandmother was showing her bitterness. She sighed, "Oh son, I'm getting mean as I see these things happen. Don't let this get you mean."

Grandmother, as long as my wife and son are alright, I'll be alright. But I still want to go see the sight of where Kettle Falls used to be. I'll sing a buffalo song there. The spirits of the buffalo and the salmon and the steel-head will hear."

"You do that, son. You do that."

Precious Child

As soon as she heard the news, Grandmother Winne began to walk along the road toward her granddaughter's house. She walked slowly, using her cane. A few cars and some horse drawn wagons passed, but she waved them away when they slowed down to offer her a ride. Everyone knew where she was going, and knew why she wanted to walk. She carried with her a snap shot picture of herself wearing her best beadwork, holding her great grandson, his fat baby smile dimpling his cheeks and chin.

By the time she arrived, almost two hours later, she was walking so slowly and so painfully one of the relatives, Martin Abrahamson, had parked his car and he and his wife Martha were holding her elbows, walking with her the rest of the way.

When they rapped on the screen door to let themselves in with a "Hey 'O!", Erickson jumped up and opened the door wider for them. They hugged and held each other. Then she went to Sally, who sat in her rocking chair holding the still body of her son James. Grandmother put her forehead against her grand daughter's forehead. They both let their tears fall onto the face of the child.

Erickson's work pants were still covered in the uranium dust that floated about the room, sparkling green in the specks that glistened in the ray of sun that came through the window. He had been allowed to leave the mine when news came that his son had died at home that morning.

Peace Children

"Milo, this is Sally, Grandmother Winne, Ducky, Brady, Martha, Tommy, Greg, David, Joe, Fish, Terry, Luanne, Mike, Richard, Mary, and Bill. You know my son Michael and my daughter Priscilla."

"Everybody, this is my Aunt Betsy and her son, Milo Old Bear from up near Browning. Thanks for coming. Means a lot to me you would drive over during round-up."

"Hey, in-nair, Michael, Priscilla, everybody."

"I thought you was Shoshone, Erickson?"

"Yeah, and my Dad was Arapaho. Betsy married a Blackfeet and Milo was born up there. We always been close."

"Warmer at Wind River in winter, in-nair. We go visit every year and stay at the family allotment where Michael ranches now. Runs nice heard of cattle, in-nair."

"Bill was telling us a spirit story."

"Hard when a little one goes."

"Stories help."

"Oh Sally, come here love." As Sally and Erickson held each other and cried softly, Bill, always a leader, took up a song. Everyone that knew it joined in.

When the song was done, Milo surprised Erickson by starting a story. It was not like him to talk to strangers, or to talk about anything not related to livestock. Erickson knew then how much Milo was touched by his son's passing. Erickson felt so much love.

"The Blackfeet; we call ourselves "Piegan", know how hard it is to loose a child, too, in-nair. They say it's the hardest thing in the world. It's a tragedy in James going like he did. My Dad, he told me a story came from his grandfather, Senaeoquoteen. His relation was long ago one of the Peace Children. Anybody ever knew of the Peace Children?"

The assembled group remained silent, signaling no, looking at Milo, respectful of the story.

"This was in the days before the Long Knives, or white men. The Cree and the Sarcee had been at war for hundreds of years. The Bloods, Stonies and Piegans got involved and helped their Sarcee relatives. So many horrible deaths between the Blackfeet bands and the Cree bands. It was hurting everybody.

"Then two old medicine men, one from each tribe, had visions, in-nair. They had their visions separately but about the same time. Then in a raid, these two medicine men found themselves each wounded. Everyone else was dead or rode off so they shared a campfire and started to talk. They made a temporary peace as they both thought they would die soon and neither had a weapon to kill the other in a good way. During a long night, they realized each had the same vision, and that big medicine was working through them. So they decided to live. They were to bring back to that place, in three moons, a group from each of their peoples. Ones who wanted peace, if they could find them.

"So, in-nair, they met again, each bringing a small band of people willing to talk peace. The medicine men laid out their plan. It took a long time for them to convince their people, and most of them did not like the plan. But the medicine men told of something that would happen. A sign that would appear in the sky, a great light with two tails, to show that the plan was needed. They told of the Long Knives that were coming and how the Piegan and Cree peoples would need to work together to defeat the white Long Knives.

"So the people went back and waited for the sign. Then the sign came. A comet with two tails. The people cried and screamed because they did not like the plan. They were convinced, however that they must do this thing to make peace. They went about the rest of their bands and told what must be done. People were so afraid of the comet with two tails they almost agreed. But it was too much.

Then the next sign came that had been told of by the medicine men. It was a whirling wind that killed two children from a small band of Bloods. A similar whirling windstorm chased a hunting party of Cree, and four horses were killed.

"After the second sign, it was agreed that the thing was to be done. The two medicine men met at the designated place on the Bow River. They agreed they needed five and set up a place to make the peace.

"All of the women with little boys under the age of four moons had to come forward. They were told long stories about the honor they would do for their people. The medicine man rattled special bones for each of them, and threw them on the ground before the women. Five were chosen from each group. At the end of the ceremony, each was ready to do what she must and knew what an honor she would make.

"On that day the five Piegan mothers met the five Cree mothers at the Bow River. The medicine men took the five Piegan children, all boys and the five Cree boys. Each Piegan mother was given a Cree child, and each Cree mother was given a Peigan child.

The children were each given a new name. All were to know that their name would forever be "Peace Maker."

"Those bands never fought or made war against the other bands again. They grew to love their enemies' Peace Children, and to wish for the best for the people of those other bands who cared for their own. For they were raising each others' children, and keeping them safe. The Peace Children were honored into old age.

"So, you see, all children are precious. All children have a place in this world. Your child James had his place and his life is not done making peace for you, even though he is gone from you now."

"Aho!" said Erickson softly. He got up and went to embrace his cousin.

Sally did not know whether to be more frightened by this story, or to take it as a comfort as it was intended. She went to lie down. She had disturbing dreams of her son being carried away by another woman, and a strange being crying in James' empty crib.

Kettle Falls

Erickson had a few days off from work after James' funeral. He didn't know what to do with himself. The family had gone and everyone was back at work at the mines, which now employed many in the tribe. Sally wouldn't get out of bed. He had a sweat to cleanse his body and heart.

The next day, he borrowed an old truck from a friend who cut timber for a living. Erickson wanted to go to the site of Kettle Falls. Maybe it would show him some peace.

Kettle Falls was almost directly north of Wellpinit. Stretching right between the two places was a range of mountains. The option was to go to one side or another. Rather than go west and then north along the edge of Lake Roosevelt on the Colville Reservation, he went east, then north up through the beautiful farms of the valley bordered by the Colville National Forest. He could see the water in the alfalfa, potatoes, corn and orchards. These farms were all irrigated by the river. Without the dams these farms would all be dry.

He drove through Chewelah, which in Salish meant "water snake". Then up further into the town of Kettle Falls. It was such a pretty place. Dry air, blue skies, rolling hills of blond grasses framed by green-blue forested mountainsides. Some of the higher mountains still had white snow atop. Coming into town you could also see the shimmer of the lake, a few boats meandering there.

Along the main street small town people stopped to stare at the unfamiliar truck. They either looked away with disinterest or stared with warning eyes once they saw Erickson's long braid and sharp Indian nose. Erickson ignored everyone and followed the signs to "Kettle Falls". He wondered what he would see in that place.

Outside of town there was a parking spot with a historical marker. Erickson pulled over to center himself. Perhaps he was coming to the place. But it wasn't the place, yet. The marker had a map showing the Northwestern United States and the Southwestern portion of Canada. It read:

Columbia River Drainage

  The area drained by the Columbia is as large as the nation of France. From its origins in British Columbia, the river's huge drainage basin serves Washington, Oregon, parts of Montana, and all of Idaho. Some of its tributaries start from as far away as Nevada, Utah, and Wyoming, and many of the larger rivers that feed the Columbia, such as the Snake and the Willamette, have their own drainage basins. All this water ends up in the Columbia as it rolls to the sea. The river's total vertical drop along its 1,214-mile path from its source in Canada to the Pacific is a little more than one-half mile. This may not seem like much, but it's all downhill, and the volume of water coursing down the river is tremendous — it is estimated than every year the mighty Columbia dumps 198 million acre-feet (or 275,000 cubic feet per second) of fresh water into the Pacific Ocean.

Erickson pulled back onto the dirt road and took the first turn to toward the lake. He felt that he should know where to go, though he had not been there before. He saw a sign for Bradbury Beach and turned in. There were a few kids there, enjoying a day playing hooky from school. They looked at him with some concern, but when they saw he was Indian, they turned back to what they were doing. Erickson looked at the beach. It was pretty. It felt empty. There was nothing to show him that the falls may be anywhere in the area. He tried to imagine what it may have been like before the lake. He could not.

He went on to Evans Campground. There were a few campers sitting in their parking spaces, but the place was quiet. At the boat dock, the lake lapped softly along its shore. The water was clear, but grew murky about ten feet out. Erickson could see nothing indicating there was a river there once. He went back to his car and drove to the North Gorge Campground. It was the same. All the pretty recreation places meant nothing to him.

Finally, Erickson pulled over and walked to the edge of the lake next to a car pull out area. The sacred place had been swallowed up by the lake. Erickson wondered if even the old ones could recognize the place where it was. This graveled lakeside would have to do. Erickson was suddenly exhausted.

He sat on his haunches and touched the water with his eyes closed. He imagined his reach through the water going to Italy, where his friend had died in the war; to Russia where the communists worked their evil; and to Sage Creek running through his ranch in Wyoming. He thought of the water touching Kettle Falls, now 90 feet down in the murk, all that water weight crushing down on them. The "kettles" where the fish used to get stuck probably were filled up with silt. Erickson fell back on his butt. He began to cry.

After a few minutes, he began to sing softly the Shoshone Song of the Buffalo. With his eyes closed he heard a deep moaning like a whale's call rising up from the waters. It sang along with him until his song was done. He wondered if that was the cry of the salmon, or maybe his son, answering him.

Erickson picked up a pebble from the shore to remember the voice with and to put in his pouch. He looked at it and realized it was a small arrowhead. It was dull now, but still perfect in shape. Yes, that had been both the cry of the salmon and the voice of his son.

Fifth Generation Priscilla & Jeremiah

(Priscilla Ethete Born 1928 and Jeremiah Smith Born 1922)

Prologue: Shoshone Legend

The people were camped in a good place, but a danger arose and some young girls had to be left behind in hiding. When it was safe, the girls came out of hiding and went to find the rest of the people. They came upon an injured wolf and nursed him back to health. They became adopted by the entire pack of wolves, then. The wolves protected the girls.

Soon the girls' fathers came looking for them. They saw the wolves and not understanding they had adopted the girls, The men killed the wolves. The girls cried and told the fathers of their mistake. The people vowed to honor the wolf as a protector.

This became tradition and remains so today.

July 25, 1945

Jeremiah Smith was on a transport home. The ship, an old luxury ship that had been redone for the war shuddered under him as some change in the engines powered a change in the ship. He could only sit there and wait. It was two months after V-E Day. He saw the worst of it in Belgium, and before that France. For the rest of his life, he would relive it and do his best, at the same time, to forget it.

The wash of the seawater against the ship was not really there. The sun shining on his closed eyelids was not really there. His ass, on the deck chair, was not really there. For the rest of his life, he would be a fraud. The part of him that made him real was back there, in the blood and noise and stench and vomit and smoke from the guns.

The thing he is remembering about his time since leaving the battle-field and while he was waiting for orders was that he had taken a very long bath that had cooled slowly. He laid his head back and floated in the filthy water, truly resting for the first time in, it seemed, years. After a long while, the water became cool and the bathhouse lady had come in to clean. He was roused by her swearing and screaming in Flemish, to get out, to get the fuck out. Didn't she know he had killed so many for much less? But this was different than on the field of battle and he was not to kill this lady, but to mind her and grab his towel, his new clean uniform, given him by the army, and get the fuck out. All he had wanted was an uninterrupted hot bath after four years of being entirely unclean.

Part of him, now, was still in that bath, floating, detached, insubstantial. Maybe the washwoman had let some of his spirit swirl down with the brown water and soap scum that eddied out of that rusty old-fashioned drain. It had maybe gone down into the plumbing to mix with the underground water that carried the dead spirits of the soldiers of all countries that had died within miles from the town where they bivouacked and used the local bathhouse and the other local establishments – the coffee shop, the chocolate shop until it closed, the whorehouse.

The war was over. All the locals were hugging all the soldiers that had freed them and sent the Nazis to hell. Everyone was in a euphoric madness of joy and ending. But it was not really over. He had seen the beginning of the migrations that were to come; all the damaged people who now had to try to go home. He smirked when he realized he was one of them.

The beginning had not yet begun. The soldiers were given orders and then a few days of R&R, then a march to the port where they boarded the militarized luxury passenger ship, now with enormous gun turrets welded to its top deck and sides. The soldiers now just played cards with other men that had cried and killed and bled and destroyed.

They all tried to adjust to not having a gun. He would wake and grab for it and realize he had only a wool blanket, a flat pillow and his canteen. He clenched his metal army canteen even now, not because he was thirsty, but because the reflex to hold a live-saving metal object was so ingrained. He had to think not to curl his right first finger around its lip when he heard an unexpected noise. This was going to be difficult.

They were steaming toward New York harbor. From there, they had train tickets, bus tickets or what the fuck ways to get to wherever they had come from before they left to fight the Nazis. America. He had tears just to think of it. How he never thought he would see his country again. How many others did not.

The incredible mud. He was sorry for the mud that must be drying and solidifying around the faces and bodies of his friends, making a mask mould of their features. He guessed some unfortunate soldier, probably a newby, had the job of digging them all up and putting them in some nicely defined government grave. He hoped they would not put their putrid flesh into boxes and bring them home. There really was no point. They could lie where they were, becoming one, with Mother Earth.

Breathe in, breathe out. Do it again. And again. He was alone.

His comrades in war had already said good-bye. One he could imagine going home to a long discussed but unseen wife in Cleveland. Others, he could not imagine what they would do. Joey, the foul-mouthed sharpshooter who could fart louder than anyone in his unit was an account-ant. A fucking accountant. Would he be back running numbers at his father's firm in Texas this time next week?

The guys he met on the ship looked either about ready to commit suicide or to dance a jig. A few did kill themselves in the last days before going home. Just couldn't imagine what else there was, after that war. One guy hanged himself with shoelaces. What a fucking shame; he should have shot himself in Belgium and his family could have thought he was a hero. Other guys were so excited they couldn't sit still but paced back and forth. Imagining their wives' legs open and a steak dinner. Little kids with chubby cheeks who they haven't seen since they were infants. Mom and Dad slap-ping them on the back and looking older.

Jeremiah did not know where he was going once he got to New York. When he filled out the form he had written "Smoot, Wyoming". His family had a prosperous grocery business in that small, all-Mormon town.

But he didn't want to go anywhere near Wyoming. He would live this part of the war like he had lived all other parts of the war. One day at a time. He fingered his bus ticket in his folio at his side. He got it out and looked at it. He stood up and walked to the edge of the Starboard side, third deck of the ship. He slowly tore the ticket to tiny pieces and fluttered each small piece over the side of the ship, into the cold Atlantic. He would be a New Yorker, at least for a while. Then, he didn't know what.

July 30, 1945

Priscilla Ethete had been in New York City for five days. It was not like Denver. It was extraordinarily bigger, and more hot and humid, and well, the people were *eastern*. They looked only at what was before them. They did not have long distances to see into and know mystery. There were many kinds of peoples: blacks, Jews, Irish, Italians, even Africans that were not black. But she had not seen a single Indian, much less a Shoshone. She could not have imagined a place where this was so.

New York City was certainly not like the Wind River Reservation. It was another planet. Two days before, the war had come to New York. A B-25 bomber had crashed into the Empire State Building in heavy fog. She had heard and seen the crash as she wandered the streets looking at the skyscrapers. The plane had appeared out of nowhere in the fog and had woven its way through the tall buildings. You could tell the pilot was trying not to hit them as he banked and turned. But his luck had run out. He plummeted into the north side of the beautiful building making a hole and huge explosion. Flames had spread down the side of the building as the fuel cascaded out. Many people had burned to death inside the great sky-scraper. Priscilla was frightened. What had she done to come to this place?

Life on the reservation had been bad during the war. Maybe life on the reservation was better during the war than before the war, though. Before the war had been a drought, and government funding for their treaty promises was gone during the depression. People got by on what they could grow and scrounge and beg. One winter her family had eaten fish almost every day to stay alive. When they didn't have fish, they had some government cheese and flour from big government sacks that they made into fry bread with lard and water. Everyone had clothes made of those sacks. It was always a joke.

Priscilla had been sick. She was a pre-teenager with pneumonia, then something else, that had got into her lungs and made her cough and cough. She had woken up one day in a white man's hospital. She had stayed there for a long time. There were other Indians there, and they were all kept in the same big room, most of them coughing, but some with other illnesses or broken bones, or failing livers. The doctors had them sign many papers. She knew many of the other Indians in passing but she wondered where the others had come from.

Priscilla could read some English, but mostly she spoke a mixture of Shoshone slang and English that didn't look like the words on the papers. She signed anyway. What difference did it make if she could stay and become well? She had surgery, but no one had told her why. She had woken up with significant pain in her abdomen. Her lungs had mostly healed. Why had they operated on her down there? Another woman from the reservation laughed at her. She was an old drunk who had been beaten up in Lander and was there for a broken arm and ribs. "They cut out your baby parts," she said. Priscilla did not believe this was so, because it was her lungs that were the problem. But yet…why did she hurt down there…?

When she asked the white nurse about it, the nurse had straightened her upper lip and said, "You have TB. You should not be having children. You asked for this."

"When did I ask for this?"

"You signed the papers. You got sick in the first place. Do you know how much it costs to keep you here? We could be using these beds for other, decent people. This helps solve the problem, long term. Now stop bothering me."

After Priscilla had been released, she waited for the government bus to Fort Washakie, the tribal headquarters. No one knew she was coming, so she waited until a neighbor with a wagon pulled by two skinny horses came through town, hauling hay for his cattle. He had taken her to within a mile of home, so she walked the rest of the way to the small house on the family allotment.

She had been too ashamed to tell anyone that she was not a woman any more. Her difficult life had lost something significant. She could not picture her future at all. For a year she had done her work on the ranch, chopping wood to keep the house warm and cook when they had something to eat. Moving their few skinny cows around to find good grass; hauling water to the garden, watching it run off without sinking into the ground to nourish the plants. In the summer she spent her days working the feed corn, then staring out at their dead stalks later that winter.

She heard of a new program, offered by the Bureau of Indian Affairs, offering bus tickets to Indians who wanted to leave the reservation and go to cities. There were jobs there! Jobs to help with the war effort! You could leave the reservation and assimilate into white society. Priscilla said she was 18 even though she was barely 15 and signed up. She got a bus ticket to Denver and a paper with the address of the Denver Indian Center. There, she imagined they would have a nice place for her to stay and jobs for her to go and eventually a nice house with nice things.

She did it in part to punish her parents and in part because she had no future if she could not ever have a family. She would miss her brother, Michael, though. Michael was tough and wanted to stay on the allotment. Priscilla told Michael about her plan but had not told her parents. Michael had hugged her that morning before he went out to ride fence. He told her to write. He looked very sad.

Her father, Erickson, was a rancher, but not a very successful one. Her mother, Iris, was a horrible woman. So Erickson stayed out on the land, living in an old teepee, as much as possible. When he came home he fought with Iris. Iris had other men. For a long time in her youngest days, Iris would disappear and Priscilla and her brother Michael were left to do what they could. They waited for their father, who at least came home at night. He would heat up a can of beans. They ate a lot of beans and fry bread. Later, Michael would kill birds with his gun or bow and arrows and they learned to dip them in hot water and pluck them and cook them on the big iron stove in the house. Their father would come home and say "Well lookie here! We got us a grouse feast!" But it wasn't ever a feast, just enough to keep them from starvation.

Priscilla knew how to chop wood from the time she was four years old. They had a big wood pile and she would take the ax and swing it to make chips and start the stove, then poke in whatever wood she could find or cut with the sharp ax to keep the house warm. It got really cold in their small wooden house if the stove wasn't going. Priscilla got used to thinking about wood and where to get it and how to cut it and how much they needed. The fire had always been women's work for Shoshones. With Iris gone so much, Priscilla didn't want to freeze.

Priscilla's bus ticket was to Denver. There were other Indians on the bus with her from the reservation, anxious to find a better life in the city. Most were men too old for the war. They all got off the bus together. They looked around. It was madness. Cars, paved streets, lots of white people.

A white man looked at them with distaste. Since their trip to Denver had been in April, he had been wearing a nice wool coat the likes of which Priscilla had never seen. It was blue and clean and had very nice buttons for a man's coat. His shoes had been shiny. Not boots, but shoes! It made her realize right away that she was dressed poorly. Her coat was a sewn up version of a man's coat that had been at the give-away at the Episcopal Church. She had done her best with a needle and thread to make it fit her small frame. Now she was embarrassed. Her moccasins were warm but they were a dead give-away of her Indianness. She wanted shoes. Real shoes.

They had asked the bus station attendant, a black man, where the Indian Center could be found. He looked at the address on Colfax Avenue and gave them directions. He seemed pretty nice. The directions were all about streets and blocks and right and left. Back home the directions related to streams, stars and rail lines. But he didn't call them any names or threaten to beat them up, like many white people had done back home. It was a start.

They had walked almost two hours until they finally found the center. It was dark. Closed for the evening. They looked at each other. Between them they had a few dollars. They divided up the small stock of food they had wrapped in cloths from home and sat down behind the Indian center, in the alley, to wait. They stayed there all night listening to the strange sounds of the city. No one noticed them. They knew how to be quiet.

The Indian Center had been a nice place, with a half Lakota, half Caddo woman the first to arrive. She was tall and buck-toothed. She seemed accustomed to finding a pack of Indians in the alley, waiting. She sat them in folding chairs and said she would start coffee. Priscilla went to help her. She might be a new friend, her first non-reservation person! But she was not very friendly, and kept saying "Oh Dear. Oh Dear. What will we do?" Everyone got a paper cup that burned their fingers once the hot coffee was poured in.

Soon the Indian Center lady, named Rosalee Blue Nose, began a speech that seemed like it had been given before, many times. Half way through the speech, a frightened bunch of Cheyennes came in. They had bundles wrapped in blankets, everything they owned tied to their backs. They were men, but here they seemed entirely overwhelmed and quiet. One still wore his blanket around his shoulders, in the old way. A short, skinny young one about her age sat next to Priscilla but he did not look at her. He smelled of smoke and perspiration. They all listened.

There was nothing for them, but the coffee. They would have to find jobs. Find a place to live. Did they know anyone in Denver? There was the Salvation Army and the Sisters of Charity, and sometimes people came to the front of the building down the street looking for day labor. She warned them about the pimps who came seeking out the young ladies. As she said this, she looked hard and straight at Priscilla. Priscilla blushed. She did not know what a pimp was, but she had an idea that this would be a poor fate. The Cheyenne man next to her looked at her sideways. She did not know if he was a good man, or a mean one. She moved closer to the Shoshones she knew, even though they may not be good to her, either.

They all went out the front door of the Indian Center and looked up the street and down the street. The Shoshones walked back to the alley and sat down to decide what action was best, next. The Cheyennes followed them. Simple introductions were made and they spoke of homes and small things and their bewilderment of this BIA program. The government could still surprise them at the messes they could make for Indians. They all joked and chuckled of this for a while, as Indians did. It was a good way to maintain dignity; to point out the stupidity of others. Their chuckling had a frightened edge.

Another Indian arrived in the alley. He seemed to be from the city. He introduced himself as Joe Curtis, a half Navajo. He knew of a meat plant that was hiring and came to let them know before the jobs were gone. He said the work was dirty and hard, but pay was ten dollars a week and you could stay in the bunkhouse. There were six jobs open. The young Cheyenne man asked about the army. Yes, Joe Curtis knew where the sign-up center was. Priscilla didn't think he was old enough, but maybe he could pass. He left with Joe Curtis. Another group went off to find the meat plant. Priscilla did not want to work at a meat plant. She would starve first. She did not sign up for something terrible. This was her chance to have a good life. She sat by the dumpster all day. That night more Indians came, this time from Southern Colorado. They were Utes. One older lady brought her drum and she sang for them until a policeman came in his car with the lights flashing. They all knew this was dangerous and they scattered and hid as best they could, sometimes just by walking down the streets and pretending to be invisible. Later they came back.

Someone brought out a bottle of bad whisky and a few men began to drink. Priscilla knew what may happen next. She and the lady with the drum, Edna Brown Bird went to the next alley and found a nondescript building's dumpsters where they made their camp between two of the containers that were not too smelly. The next morning, quite early, a big truck came to empty the dumpsters. The two women were startled awake, and moved away from the dumpsters. The truck was driven by a woman! She jumped down and worked the levers that poured the trash into the back of the truck. This gave Priscilla and Edna some hope. During the war, there seemed to be a broader list of things a woman was able to do. The truck lumbered off without the woman acknowledging their camp or even meeting their eyes.

They were hungry and went back to the Indian Center. Rosalee Blue Nose pointed them toward the Salvation Army soup kitchen. As they were leaving a man was waiting outside. He was white, with a nice car and a big hat. He offered them jobs. Priscilla did not like the man, he seemed scary, so she said "no" in hand signs, and moved away. Edna got into the man's car. Priscilla walked alone toward the soup kitchen. This seemed better, as she could look at the soup kitchen and not have to go there, either, if she did not want to do it. But she was hungry and knew she probably would go in. This independence felt powerful, but also very lonely. She could have some soup and would know better what to do next.

The soup kitchen was warm and steamy and full of mostly older people, but a few women with babies. Many of them were quite smelly. Priscilla got behind a black man with grey hair who held his hat respectfully in front of him. They served thin pea soup but it contained some small squares of ham. They also each got a piece of white bread. There was no butter but she saw some people salting the bread from shakers at the end of the line. Priscilla ate her soup quietly, alone and as slowly as she could so that she could continue to sit there a while. She did not know where else to go.

A man sat down beside her. He was nervous and appeared clean, with nice pants, a collar shirt and a grey jacket. She wondered if he was a pimp. He seemed nice. Finally, he said, "Could I ask you something?"

Priscilla nodded but did not look at the man.

"Are you looking for work? Because if you are, I need some help." Priscilla waited to see what else the man would say. She did not know how to talk normally to white men. "I have two children, and my w-wife, well... she is sick. I need some help with my boys, and to watch out for my wife. Are you... do you know anyone... could you... take care of my kids today so I can go to work?" Priscilla did not think this was what a "pimp" would ask her. So she nodded her head, up and down.

The man took a breath, "...I guess I should ask for your qualifications."

Priscilla stared at him. She did not know what to say. "Well, let's start with your name, then where are you from?"

"Priscilla Ethete. I am from Wyoming"

"Does Ethete mean anything?"

"It means 'good morning', in Arapaho."

"Are you Arapaho?"

"I am part Arapaho and part Shoshone."

"Do you know how to take care of children?"

"Yes. I have a brother."

"Could we try it out for just today? I will pay you three dollars for today."

"Yes, I will do it," said Priscilla making the hand sign for emphasis.

"What was that?" he said, imitating the sign.

"It means 'yes' on the reservation."

"Ah. I see. Well, let's go, if you are ready."

And so began the next few years for Priscilla. She felt extremely lucky. She was surprised how quickly your life could go from one thing, to something entirely different, and then to a third thing.

Mr. Engstrom was what he called an "auditor" who worked in an office building. He had very thick glasses and was exempt from the war. He seemed rich beyond anything Priscilla had known. He had taken her to his two-bedroom house with the flushing toilet and hot and cold running water in the kitchen and bathroom. His wife, Anita, had a cancer, and became more and more ill. The two little boys, Richard and Everett were sweet; disciplined and polite. Their house had many rules, which Anita taught Priscilla patiently from her soft chair. There was the rule about washing your hands, about responding to questions with words instead of signs, about how to properly use forks and knives and spoons, about getting up at the same time every day and having meals at the same time and children's nap time at the same time and bedtime at the same time. There was a rule about going to Sunday church (Priscilla was exempt, but did go once,) and a rule about making meal plans and a grocery list and cooking the foods they liked.

The first few times, Anita took Priscilla to the grocery. She showed her what the different foods were. There was lettuce, many kinds of fruit, a whole counter of meats and cheeses. Anita complained that there was nothing available and the ration cards were "so restrictive" but Priscilla could not believe the abundance and ease of the foods they could buy. At home they mostly foraged and fished and caught rabbits and ate government supplies.

Anita breathed through her pain while Priscilla learned to run her house, make the foods that they liked, and love her children.

Priscilla slept in the room with the boys and was given some of Anita's older clothes and a comfortable pair of shoes. She put all the money Mr. Engstrom gave her in a sock in the back of her bag. She would buy herself a penny candy at the grocery, but the other items at the store seemed so intimidating for her. It was the boys, who came with her to the grocery, that talked her to into buying the candy. Her favorite kind was the little cinnamon bears. She also liked the swirls of caramel and white fluff on a stick. She needed to use a sugar ration stamp at the candy store, but this seemed alright, since they did it only infrequently. As she became comfortable shopping at the many stores for the family, she began to dream of the money in her sock, and what she might someday buy. Perhaps a pair of boots, with red designs.

She found it very strange that the Engstroms had no other family or friends, but she learned that because their name was German, and the war was against the Germans, many people would not help them. Their family was far away into the East. Priscilla did not care. Most people would not help her, or talk to her, either.

She went back once to the reservation. She thought she might stay if things had improved, however, once there, everyone asked her for money and commented on how well and healthy she looked. So many were sick and malnourished and drinking there. She left after a fight with her mother over the money in her sock. She was relieved to take the train back to Denver.

Then one day over a year after Priscilla had come to their home, Anita had gone to the hospital and died. Mr. Engstrom came home from there to hug his boys and gave them all the news. He was crying softly. He was quiet, even over the next days when he and the children sat together and hugged. The funeral had seemed very strict and quiet. She had wanted to wail for Anita in the Shoshone way, but did not. The church was dark and smelled funny and made Priscilla want to run away.

There was no mention to Priscilla what Anita's death might mean for her, but she decided that Mr. Engstrom needed her even more, now. This proved to be true, and she became even more a part of the small, sad family during the next year. She loved the boys and imagined herself caring for them until they were grown, and then the boys caring for her as she became old.

She was a servant, though. She was reminded of this when Mr. Engstrom came home one day and announced that they were moving to New York. It was a small town where his sister lived with her family about five miles from "the city". He did not want to be alone any more in Denver with Anita gone. When the movers came to pack, Priscilla packed her bag with her handed down clothes and counted the money in her sock. It was a fortune to her, almost four thousand dollars. But she did not know where to go to spend that money, without a grocery list or an idea of how to live in Denver without the structure of the Engstrom home.

"What are you doing?" asked Mr. Engstrom; "Of course you are coming with us!"

Priscilla had not considered this. Now she did. She would go to New York! She was so relieved not to have to find her way, or go back to the reservation to starve.

The four of them took a train. They seemed an odd little family, with the blond Engstroms and Priscilla with her long, thick braid and dark skin. Many other families seemed to have "help". She softly sang Shoshone songs to the boys who had learned to "drum" along by tapping on the table-top.

Mr. Engstrom's sister's house was very grand, with four bedrooms. Gertrude was single and had a woman that lived with her. Priscilla did not know what her relation was, but she was nice, named Olanda.

Gertrude did not approve of Priscilla, however. She did not want an Indian in her house and on the second day, when Mr. Engstrom was out beginning his new job, Gertrude gave Priscilla twenty dollars and paid a taxi driver in advance to take her to Manhattan. She had given the taxi driver the address of the YWCA, where Gertrude told Priscilla she could stay until she found other work. She told her 'Olanda could mind the boys', wished her 'good luck' and slammed the door of the taxi. She whispered something to the driver, which Priscilla heard, "Don't bring her back."

Priscilla stayed in her bed at the YWCA as long as possible. On the second morning, she took two dollars out of her sock and went to a bar. She was young, but the bartender was friendly and didn't ask questions. Her first beer was bitter, but cold and enjoyable. She felt at home in the

cozy dark pub with the businessmen and sales girls and old men, all minding their own business. The bartender seemed kind. They had a kitchen
that made simple foods. Now she knew what else she could do with her
money.

August 2, 1945

Jeremiah went to a pay phone with a handful of coins. He called his
father, long distance from New York. They had a very short conversation in
booming voices; long distance was expensive. You imagined you needed to
talk very loud to be heard all that way. They were so happy to hear his
voice after four years! Yes, he was safe. Yes, he was back in America.
No, he was not coming home just yet. Yes, he would come home as soon
as he could. Yes, he loved them, too.

He could not explain it, but he thought that maybe he would feel
right enough to go to Smoot, Wyoming and face all the small town normal-
ness and questions about the war if he took a few weeks here, first.

He wandered for a few days around the city. He felt enveloped in
his anonymity. He breathed in the swirl of people, ideas, smells and sounds
of a healthy city. It was beautiful to see buildings that were not damaged by
bombs and streets with functional civilian cars and people with happy smiles
on their faces. The war was over! Everything had the sheen of exuberance
and possibility! He still clutched his canteen.

He bought two plaid short-sleeved shirts and a pair of blue pants.
He even bought new socks and skivvies. He threw away all his army
clothes. He had an uninterrupted bath, ate eggs and real bacon, smoked a
Cuban cigar, and slept in a bed. It had been a cheap hotel, but it seemed
like a fantasy. He talked to a girl with crooked teeth but she had been shy
and he did not know how to begin the process of getting her into bed, so he
had said goodbye. He considered finding a whore but knew this was a sin.
It had not seemed so bad during the war when he was on his two short
leaves, but he did not know if this would be the same here. He was trying to
draw some lines between then and now. As if it would help. It was worth a
try.

After about a week, he began to feel itchy without a routine. He saw
a sign, "Dishwasher Wanted" at a bar and went in. Perhaps if he had a job
doing something normal he would become normal again? He should be
able to handle cleaning plates. Just holding a glass plate and scraping off
the leavings into the trash and washing it clean with hot water seemed like it
might be healing.

It was midday and the place was almost empty. At one end of the
bar slumped an old man and at the other end of the bar sat a very pretty girl
with shiny long black hair. He looked away from her quickly and ap-

proached the bartender. He felt very conspicuous and knew the two patrons would listen to what he was saying to the bartender. Well that would have to be ok.

"I saw your sign. You still need a dishwasher?" He pronounced it "warsher" like they did back home. The girl looked over at him, some connection in her eyes. Their eyes met. He smiled slightly at her. Without returning the smile, she snapped her attention to the square paper napkin upon which her beer rested. She moved her beer and folded the napkin neatly in half. She looked like an Indian. Odd. What was she doing here?

"Job still open!" grinned the bartender. He was chubby with red rosy cheeks and a white haired comb-over. "You applying?"

"Yeah, I suppose I am."

"You a veteran? I ask because I can tell. I got this limp in France in 1918. I'm Bertie Delaney," he said thrusting out a friendly hand.

"Yes, sir. Just home."

"Don't you be calling me sir, now. We ain't in the army no more! Or was you Navy? No, I'm guessing Army. Am I right?"

"Yes, s—; Mr. Delaney."

"Ha ha! Learning already! Don't you worry none. It gets better. You'll be alright, son. Job pays two bits an hour. You are hired if that sounds good to you. If you are ready to start, come on back and I'll show you around. Got a pile of glasses ready to go now. Where you from?"

"Wyoming, Mr. Delaney."

"Well it must be cowboy Tuesday! This gal, her name's Priscilla, she's from Wyoming, too!"

Priscilla looked up, afraid. Again, their eyes met. He smiled. She smiled back tentatively. He put out his hand to shake hers and she slowly reached her hand out, too, palm down. She awkwardly shook his hand, fingers only, lightly. To him, her touch was soft. Nice. To her, his touch was unusual. No one ever touched her. His rough hands seemed warm and strong. She had an odd desire to put his fingertips into her mouth and suck on them. She looked away, began to fumble for her money. She got up to leave the bar.

"Where in Wyoming?"

She froze. "Just north of Fort Washakie."

"The reservation?"

"Yes, but I been in Denver for a few years."

"Can I buy you dinner later?" The question took him by surprise. It was as if someone else was talking for him.

"Ok."

"When am I off, Mr. Delaney?"

"Well I'll be damned! It *is* cowboy Tuesday! All our lucky days! Why don't we say you get off in five hours, about eight? That is if you come back and wash up the dinner service early tomorrow about ten A.M.? And what's your name, son?"

"I'm Jeremiah Smith," he said to both of them. "Is nine too late for you, Maman? Meet you here?"

Priscilla had never been called "Maman" in her life. "Ok." She said. She turned and walked out of the bar. Again, she felt her life had changed. It was bright outside. She decided to go shopping for a nice dress and a pair of pretty shoes; the first she would ever buy in her life.

August 3, 1945

A shaft of sun blazed onto her eyelids. She realized she was awake, in *his* bed. It was a hotel, a nice one. Clean, on the fourth floor, with a man ready to bring up their bags. But they hadn't any bags. They ignored the look of the man who checked them in as he had said this.

The pit of Priscilla's stomach was full of fluttering wings. Morning. What was this she was feeling? Excitement, happiness, anticipation of *more*. They had hit it off. More than hit it off. It was as if they had known each other forever. They had eaten spaghetti at an Italian place. They each had two glasses of sweet dark wine. They had begun to laugh right away. Then they were hungry for more. They had wordlessly gone to a hotel where Jeremiah had almost torn her new blue dress to reach the skin underneath. They had made love madly, beautifully. She had never felt so good, so right.

Now, she wanted more of that connection. It had been so long since she had felt absolutely free to love anything; maybe since she had been a baby. But this was an adult love. Lust. Glorious, fabulous, rock hard sex. The good stuff.

September 1, 1945

Priscilla reminded him that the humidity and heat of New York City would soon begin to diminish with the coming of September. She was *so* good for him. She brought his mind to the here and now. To think about the weather...such a mundane thing! And just to feel her hand, or her kiss, or her body at night reminded him of where he was, and was not.

The past month had been unimaginable. There had been Priscilla. An Indian! With high cheekbones, a long black braid, dark skin, and funny hand signs and strange words for things. Back home a love affair with her would have been unthinkable. Here, now, it was perfect; as another puzzle piece of the fantastic times in which they moved.

A few days after they had their first dinner and lovemaking, they heard of the hideous but wonderful atomic bombs dropped on Japan. Wonderful because they had ended the war, hideous and frightening in all other ways. He hated the Japs, like he hated the Krauts, but he had seen enough of them dead and suffering to know how bad this really was. Then there had been news of the Nazi Death Camps. He had heard rumors of them, but he had still been sickened along with the rest of the American public when they saw the news reels in air conditioned theaters before the Rogers and Hammerstein movie "State Fair". The rural American charm of the show had been a comfort and had almost taken the bile from his mouth.

They had also explored the city. Chinatown, Harlem, Little Italy and Brooklyn were like different cities within the city. They had cheered like crazy people at a Yankees game and had walked the boardwalk at Coney Island on one romantic summer evening.

He had been with Priscilla and two million other people in Times Square at 7:03pm on August 14 when the revolving news sign made the announcement: "Official—Truman Announces Japanese Surrender". The people had exploded in joy! Dancing, kissing, cheering and crying. He had been strangely quiet.

Priscilla sat next to him on a curb and they watched the revelry all around. His mind was reliving a movie reel of some moments of the last four years. What it had taken to come to this moment! He had begun to cry and Priscilla had held him, not asking questions. She was so good at that. Just being quiet but still providing her attention.

After he was done with his outburst, he looked at her and grinned and pulled her into a very public but very dirty kiss. It was the times! Then they had eaten an ice cream cone given away free for the celebration by a vendor on West 34th Street, and had gone back to his room where they had been staying since that first night in the hotel.

They had made love in a frenzy, and then again very slowly and clearly until they were both ravenous for food. They still smelled of sex as they walked to a curry house they had discovered that stayed open until midnight. They ate hot curried potatoes and chicken with rice. It was very New York. They were in love.

Jeremiah was happier than he ever thought he could be. His future began to crystallize for him. They would go to meet his family to Smoot. They could not help but love her, after they got used to the idea of his wife being an Indian. He could see their beautiful children! She would love the house he would build for her. He would get her an electric stove, a new car and anything else she would want inside. They would vacation here in New York City any time they wanted to kindle their romance. It would be so good!

September 2, 1945

Priscilla and Jeremiah were going back to Times Square. Today was the day that the war would officially end by the signing of papers on the USS Missouri, out in the sea by Japan. There was going to be a wonderful party, and they were part of it all!

Priscilla was so proud of her soldier man. She would die for him and never hurt him. It was so good to see him ready to have some fun. The last time they had been to Times Square for the announcement of the end of the war, he had been haunted and sad. She knew how he must have suffered during the awful war. Now she felt powerful. Sex— her sex — and her attention to him had been a big part of the cure! This was where she was meant to be. With Jeremiah.

Energy was in the air. Everyone knew that today was the day. The streets were giddy with dressed up people moving about and laughing. Shops were closed and New York felt like one big neighborhood filled with joy.

They walked north, up 9th Avenue from Chelsea Park where they had rented a small room. They held hands and smiled at the other New Yorkers. Priscilla had woven bright red, white and blue ribbons into her braid and soldiers just home, nurses in their uniforms, and young mothers all noticed and smiled. They turned right onto West 36th Street to get to 7th Avenue so they could walk down that main street toward the lights of Times Square.

Sitting alone in a doorway was a little girl, fat tears rolling down her face. Priscilla stopped. While children played alone in the neighborhoods all the time, this did not seem right. The area was commercial and the girl wore a red and white party dress with a blue bonnet. She was probably about three years old with curly blond hair and chubby red cheeks. Her pudgy little knees showed above her white socks and baby shoes. She was holding a small American flag on a stick.

"*Pehnaho*, little one, you look very sad!" Said Priscilla, reverting easily into Shoshone to talk to a child as she had done with her brother and the Enstrom boys. The little girl looked down and did not answer. Jeremiah moved toward her but Priscilla knew that this might frighten the child. She signed for him to stay back and he watched as Priscilla worked her magic. She crouched down to look into the eyes of the child.

"Did you loose your Mommy?" The little girl nodded up and down.

"Would you like me to help you find her?"

"I'm not supposed to go with strangers." Whispered the girl.

"Well then, we should introduce ourselves. I am Priscilla Ethete. What is your name?"

"Rebecca."

"Where do you live, Rebecca?"

"New York City."

Priscilla smiled at the girl then at Jeremiah. "I live here, too. Near Chelsea Park. Do you have a park where you live?"

"Bryant Park."

"That's a lovely park! Should we go there and see if we can find your Mommy?"

"Ok. My Mommy is going to Times Square for the end of the war."

"Yes, Ohmaa, but she will be looking for you, and maybe someone at Bryant Park will know where she is."

"What is 'Oh Ma'?""That means 'baby' where I am from."

"Where are you from?"

"I am from Wyoming."

"I'm free, not a baby!"

"Of course you are three. I'm so sorry. You are not a baby. But we should find your Mommy. Come, let's go look for her."

Rebecca took Priscilla's extended hand and they both stood up. Rebecca held up her arms and Priscilla swooped her up and carried her. Rebecca put her arms around Priscilla's neck and snuggled in. Her warm cheek was so soft and she smelled so nice. It was lovely to hold a child again.

Jeremiah watched, impressed at Priscilla's patience, charm and motherly affection. He would ask her to marry him, today.

A few blocks from Times Square was a police station. They walked in with the little girl and there was Rebecca's frantic mother sobbing and trying to fill out a form. She had three other children, all of whom ran to Rebecca and claimed their sister from Priscilla's arms as the mother dropped her pencil and crushed her child to her chest.

"Thank you, thank you for bringing back my baby!" she cried.

After a few moments, they walked out, knowing it best just to leave the family to their celebrations. Perhaps the children's father would soon come home from the war, too.

"You were wonderful." Said Jeremiah.

"I am so happy her mother was there."

"You will be a wonderful mother."

This stopped Priscilla in her tracks. She turned away from him. Jeremiah did not see the color drain from her face. He realized this was forward, but they had always been honest with each other.

"I want about ten kids! It's expected in Mormon families, you know. It's almost a religious requirement. I would be so happy if you were pregnant right now! Imagine what our children will be like! I hope they all look just like you, except the boys need to look like me, in, well, the manly ways. They will have dark eyes, black hair, and your long legs. Oh Priscilla, let's get started right away! Let's go to City Hall tomorrow and get married. I love you and want to be with you for the rest of my life!" He had dropped to the ground on one knee. People all around had stopped to stare. They were smiling and a few women gasped in happiness for the lovers.   It was such an exciting day!

Her face was ashen. He thought it was surprise.

For so long, Priscilla had accepted her fate as a loner, one who would never have a family.   Meeting Jeremiah had felt like two loners coming together to keep each other company in their loneliness. Why had she not realized that he wanted a real woman, a whole woman? Babies, family and a happy life?

The world had turned white all around her. She thought she might faint, or explode, or evaporate. A big slow knife cut the air in front of her, separating her from Jeremiah. Forever. She turned and ran as fast as she could.

"Well I'll be damned!" said Jeremiah to the stunned people around him. "I guess she wasn't ready for a proposal!" A few people laughed with him as he rose from the ground, embarrassed. God, why had he been so impulsive? He ran after her.

Priscilla's braid, entwined with red, white and blue was the last glimpse he had of her running down into the subway. He reached the platform just as a train was pulling away. "Dammit!" he cursed.

Priscilla watched him from the other stairs. She almost went to him, but then he began beating his hands – hard – on a trashcan. He did not stop until the can was dented and a subway cop began blowing his whistle.

This was her chance to get out. She ran all the way, adrenaline in her blood; circling back to their room. She did not have much time before he came looking for her. She emptied a pillowcase and stuffed in her money sock, her three dresses, her second pair of shoes and a few other things sitting about. She ran out. Gasping, she went out and ran down the subway stairs. She got on the first one and took it until the end; the south end of Manhattan with a view of the Statue of Liberty from Battery Park. To sit there on a park bench and think and decide what to do next.

September 3, 1945

"Women!" thought Jeremiah.

He got on the next train but soon realized he had no idea where to get off to follow her. He went back to the 47th Street platform where he had last seen her, but she wasn't there either. No sense going to Times Square, it was a madhouse. Frenzied people were everywhere, celebrating. He decided to go back to their room. When he arrived, sweaty and now angry, he was stunned to see she wasn't there waiting for him. He sat down on their bed, where they had made love just a few hours before. He looked around.

Her dresses were gone. Her shoes and few personal items were gone. "What the...?" Jeremiah's anger turned to fear. He didn't know what to do. What on Earth could he have said? A simple "no" or "it's too soon" would have been ok. He sighed and laid back. Certainly she would come back after she cooled off. He would wait for her.

He woke up the next morning and she had not returned.

September 4, 1945

Priscilla had sat on a bench looking out at the Statue of Liberty all night. Her mind was a blank. It was useless to try to decide anything. Around dawn she decided sleep was the best thing for her. She wanted a quiet place. She walked up Broadway until she found a cheap hotel. She went in but they would not rent to an Indian. She continued walking and ended up back at the YWCA. She sat through their talk about Jesus, then thankfully lay down on one of the dormitory beds. She slept soundly until almost midnight. There was still nothing in particular that had come to her about her future. It was as if thinking about Jeremiah was too painful, so she simply did not. Instead she focused on the here and now. She was hungry.

Suddenly she felt like a stranger in "his" town. She did not want to go anywhere they had ever gone or where he may see her. She felt like an intruder where she was not welcome. The bar was out of the question. The curry place, too. She found an all-night diner in a different neighborhood and went in. The pancakes and bacon and eggs and coffee were magical. She concentrated only on eating every last bite.

She looked at her smeared, empty plate. Tears came to her eyes out of nowhere. She was in a corner and the waitress was busy, so she permit herself a quiet cry into the diner's paper napkins. It would be ok to feel sorry for herself for a while. She began to sing a Shoshone song from her childhood. It was comforting.

During the song, she began to think of home: Wyoming. The wind in the grasses, the clear air, her brother, her sweet father, even her some-times funny mother. She had a letter from Michael when she was in Denver. He seemed to be doing well and taking over much of the ranching on the allotment. They had had a good hay crop and their cattle had been sold for a good price that year...when was that, last year? Maybe things had improved? It was time to find out. It felt like the safest thing to do.

Priscilla washed up in the bathroom of the diner, then paid for her breakfast. She would go to Grand Central Station and take the next train to

Denver, then home. She could hide in the train terminal in the meantime among all the people. It was still the middle of the night, so she walked slowly toward midtown. The city was still alive with celebrations, with many people staggering out of the bars, and taxis hurtling past.

The statue of the eagle with spread wings atop Grand Central Terminal greeted her. The eagle had been so important to everything on the reservation. She felt this was a sign to her.

Inside, Grand Central was quieter than the only other time she had been there at rush hour, but it was still open and active. Shops with sleepy proprietors sold junk and magazines. The newsstand was closed and sold out with everyone wanting a copy of the end of war headlines, but soon new papers in bundles would arrive from the presses as life went on. Vendors sold coffee and pastries left over from yesterday. The arching ceiling of the main concourse was awe inspiringly lovely.

She felt so small in that massive room with all those people with someplace important to go. She would miss New York and all the fantastic things she had known there. It had been a little heaven for a short time.

She followed the signs until she found the long distance transit center. She looked at the giant board with names of towns across the United States and Canada. She could go to any of them. This made her even lonelier. Luckily there was "Denver", leaving at 6:45am. She had three hours to wait. She bought her ticket with cash from her sock and sat down on the end of a hard wooden bench next to her things. Eventually she put her head on the pillowcase with all her possessions and dozed off.

"Priscilla! Thank the heavens I have found you! I have been looking for you and waiting for you!"

Priscilla jolted awake. What time was it? Had Jeremiah found her?

Instead, there stood William Engstrom, a ridiculously large smile on his face.

"I have been coming to this train station every day before work and every day on the weekends. Sometimes I bring Richard and Everett and we all look for you. I hoped you would eventually try to go home and I just prayed that you would not take a train while I was at work! Oh Priscilla, I am so sorry for what my sister did to you! Can you ever forgive us?"

Priscilla was entirely bewildered. "I cannot have children," she said. "What?"

"I was sick and they gave me surgery that sterilized me at the white man's hospital."

"How awful for you! But this does not matter to me, or to the boys! We have missed you so, they have cried and cried for you! I have realized how much you have meant to our family! I have informed Gertrude that if I found you and you agreed to come back we would move out of her house immediately. Will you please come back to us?"

Priscilla began to cry. She did not know what to do. Impulsively, she gave the hand sign for 'I will do it.'

Mr. Engstrom, who had always avoided touching Priscilla for any reason now awkwardly reached out and hugged her to him. He picked up the pillowcase with her things and they walked toward the commuter trains back to his sister's house and Richard and Everett.

December 15, 1945

Jeremiah no longer thought constantly about the war, or carried his canteen like a gun. Now he had a new obsession, Priscilla. Where had she gone? What had he done wrong? Was she hurt? When would she come back? He tossed in their bed for hours without sleep imagining all possibilities, and never knowing which was true. Sometimes he was sure she must have been in an accident. He went to the hospitals looking for her. Then he was sure she was married, or had another lover.

But he knew she loved him. What they had was so real. Or was he crazy?

He left the room as little as possible and threw open the door anytime footsteps crossed in front in case she had come back. He went to his dishwashing job and enlisted Mr. Delaney to watch for her in case she came back to the bar. Mr. Delaney just sighed and shook his head. Young love so often came to nothing. He hoped Jeremiah would forget her soon.

Jeremiah ignored the letters and then the telegrams from his family. What did family matter if he could not bring her back to live among them? He haunted every place they had gone together, wondering if it was a dream.

One evening he left his dishwashing job and climbed the stairs to his room, where he was sure tonight she would return. Sitting there, his back against his door and his knees up, was his father, George Smith.

Jeremiah had not seen his father in almost five years. He still had the broad shoulders and muscular hands of a hard worker and the tanned skin that came from the strong western sun. His hair was entirely gray now, even his eyebrows and the hairs coming from his ears. He wore his city suit and held a bowler hat at his side. He looked so much older than when Jeremiah had left for basic training. It was so bizarre, but with his aging face and without his hat, you could almost imagine Indian features. Jeremiah knew he was crazy now, because he looked oddly like Priscilla.

George struggled to stand from his uncomfortable seat on the floor of the hallway. He seemed not to know if the man before him was really his son. Jeremiah realized he probably did not look like the boy he had been the last time they had seen each other. Jeremiah was now much smaller, having lost his rural healthy bulk. He was now also a little stooped, and skinny, though strong. His face showed the aging and scars of four horrible years of battle, and the grief and pain of the past months. Jeremiah did not look well.

George held out his hand. Jeremiah took it. Then they barreled into each other in a long needed bear hug.

"I come to bring you home, son. We been so worried about you. Why have you not answered our letters or come home? We love you son!"

Jeremiah did not know the answers to these questions. But suddenly, he didn't care. Seeing his father had woken him up from a strange spell. What was he doing in New York City?

"I been washing dishes, Pa."

George thought this was very odd. "Well son, we have dishes in Smoot, so we can fix you right up. It's time to go see your mother. She is furious to see you. She and your sisters will have been making potato dishes and baking all week. I have lots of news to tell about all the family. You have quite a few new nieces and nephews to meet. Everyone wants to hear your war stories." George could have kicked himself for this last statement as a darkness passed over his son's eyes. George began to realize that Jeremiah needed healing; he had not simply been living a high life in the city. George was glad he had come to find his son, and wished he had come sooner.

"I could use a potato dish."

"Well let's go get us a steak! I could eat a bear and I'm ready to see New York City! Show me around, son!"

After only one city block with his confident and capable father at his side, Jeremiah began to see himself differently. He was certainly loved. He was certainly a good man.

They went to a grand wood paneled restaurant that Jeremiah had passed but had not entered. They ate outrageously expensive steaks that were worth a week of ration coupons. To celebrate, his father even had a beer, giving Jeremiah a wink to acknowledge the unusual breach of Mormon rules.

George did most of the talking, letting Jeremiah come to saying what he needed to in his own time. He told of the expansion of the family grocery business with the Church's decisions to prepare stockpiles of food in the event of the local needs of war. He told of other boys, home from the war and marriages and babies born. They talked of his mother's feistiness and welcoming warmth. All his brothers and sister's growing up to become adults.

Jeremiah watched his father's face. Again he saw the Indian features from his Indian blood that Jeremiah had never really thought about. Finally he said, "Since I've been stateside, I met a woman. She was a Shoshone, from Wyoming."

"Now that's unexpected," replied George.

"Yeah, I know. We are probably the only ones from Wyoming in this city, but we ran into each other where I work. She ran out when I asked her to marry me. I've been waiting for her to come back. But I guess she won't."

"You know lots of Indians have bad troubles. They had a rough time of it, loosing their spiritual and other ways at the hand of the government. Many of those people are pretty damaged. I'm sorry, son, but it's probably for the best."

Jeremiah felt a huge flash of anger. A stubborn piece of him wanted to scream that "IT WAS NOT FOR THE BEST!" but his soldier's calm took over. Instead, he did as he had been trained to do; he waited for the right opening to respond.

Instead his father surprised him. While Jeremiah knew he had Indian blood, his father had never before talked about his own mother. They had always heard of the big family with multiple mother figures. "I vaguely remember being a child and going to the reservation with my mother and sister. Those people were really something. So different from our own, but of course just the same as you and me. They were happy and free in a way we will never be. They laughed all the time and played tricks on each other even though they had only snakes and gofers and weeds to eat. People were in pain from broken bones that weren't being attended and big sores that had maggots in them. Many were sick all the time, but they sang their songs with all their beings and told stories about the living rocks and stars and the buffalo, even though the buffalo were long gone."

"I didn't know you had a sister."

George got a far away look in his eyes. "Yes, I never told a soul about this. I guess to protect her, but she might still be alive and living out there. I want your promise you'll take this to the grave."

"I promise."

"When my mother died when we were there for a visit, our grandfather, an old man named what amounted to "One Who Walks Slow", I can't remember now how they said it in Shoshone, but he took care of us. Him and his other daughter, a crazy looking squaw with hair only on the back of her head. I don't remember her name, but she was a strong lady. I can remember her bossing all the Indian kids, including me, around, but having a heart of gold. Well, they wanted us to stay with them, not go back to our Mormon family. So they told people we were dead. Being young, I forgot this when I saw my Brother Thom come for us. I run out of that teepee to hug him. So I guess they couldn't pretend I was dead. Brother Thom took me home but he didn't know my older sister, Sarah was there in the teepee, alive. She always wanted to be an Indian, so I didn't say anything. Even when they had a funeral for her, I thought it was too late and I didn't know what to do. So she never came back to us. I don't know if I did the right thing or not. Poor thing probably died of starvation or something worse out there."

"Did you ever want to go find her?"

"No son. What is done is done. I advise you to put your Indian gal behind you too. Let's go on home. You are gonna forget about her when you see all the pretty girls back home waiting for the soldiers to come back."

Faced with his father's strength and goodness, Jeremiah could almost believe that.

December 20, 1945

Priscilla and William Engstrom were married at their local city hall the week of Christmas 1945. He had asked her after Gertrude continued to demand that she leave her house. William determined that Priscilla never leave them again. So they married and moved to their own home on Long Island. While she felt comfortable with quiet and stable William, with him there was no great passion. But he was good to her, and she was good to him. Priscilla loved Richard and Everett. She thought it was so odd how her life had turned out so different and so far from home.

Not until years later would Priscilla go to Wyoming. She went to her mother's funeral on the Wind River Reservation. A part of her never forgot who she was, even though she was now in a whole new world.

She would occasionally visit her father and his new family in Wellpinit Washington, on the Spokane Indian Reservation.

She and Michael wrote to each other all their lives. She was proud of her brother Michael. He was a successful rancher on the family allotment, originally allotted to Trees Told It. Michael married a happy Navajo lady named Anna and they had twin sons, Timothy and Mike Ethete. Sadly, Anna had been killed in a car accident when her boys were just starting high school. When her nephews graduated from high school in 2005, they became warriors, together joining the United States Marines.

Sixth Generation Timothy & Michael Ethete

(Timothy and Michael Ethete Born 1977)

Prologue : Part of the Navajo Creation Legend

The Twins, sons of Changing Woman, went to the east to find their father, the Sun. They wanted his help in slaying the monsters that had come to destroy them and kill the Dine' People. On the way, the twins met Spider Woman who taught them many things and gave them a Sacred Hoop and Sacred Words to say during their journey to the Sun. After many adventures, they came to the turquoise palace of their father, the Son. He made the twins pass many tests before he would believe that they were truly his children.

Their father agreed to help them. He gave the twins helmets and shirts of hard flint scales, chain lightening arrows, sheet lightening arrows, and deadly sunbeam arrows. He gave each a stone knife with a hard blade and a stone knife with a broad blade. The next day, the Sun took the boys through a hole in the top of the sky to travel to the home of the Dine' People. The Sun saw their home. "My sons, you will succeed in your war with the monsters. And in this war, you will make a passage from boyhood to manhood."

Explanation

After the attacks on the United States of September 11, 2001, aerial bombing of Afghanistan started in October of 2001 to destroy terrorist training camps. Soon, American and other NATO troops were on the ground in the Global War on Terror. From December 2001 to February 2002, the 26th Marine Expeditionary Unit (MEU) reinforced the 15th MEU who had conducted the seizure of Camp Rhino (previously a drug distribution center for the Taliban) and Kandahar International Airport. Both MEUs worked together under one command. By December 7, 2001, the Taliban leadership no longer controlled the government of Kandahar province but American and NATO troops carried on active fighting in the area.

"Atsili" means "Younger Brother" in Navajo. "Anaai" means "Older Brother" in Navajo. Michael and Timothy are twin brothers, born in 1977 to Mike Ethete of the Shoshone Reservation. Anna Begay, their Navajo mother, died in 1996 after a car accident .

"MRE" is a meal, ready to eat. This is food for soldiers in the field.

"ANSF" is a member of the Afghan National Security Force.

Email #1

FROM: Ethete, Michael E-3 USMC MAGTF 15 LCE <michael.ethete@FOBKandaharA.mil>
SUBJECT: 10 DEC 01
DATE: December 10, 2001 04:15:33
TO: Ethete, Timothy E-4 USMC MAGTF 26 MEU <timothy.ethete@FOBRhino.mil>
- 1 Attachment, 1.2 KB

Atsili-

Hey got our internet and emails working last night. The techies got er done. Coming to you from satellite, I guess. I'm hearing yours is up too. So hope this gets to you. Guessing on your address. Nice the censors don't fuck with our .mil to .mil emails.

Will send generic greeting to Dad later. Funny to imagine him typing on a computer.

Been here 11 days. Flew by copter over 400 miles from the base ship out in Arabian Sea. Probably the same for you in the 26th as it was for me in the 15th. We got here a few weeks before you! Kandahar Airport bombed to hell when we arrived. Chased out the rats. Using an old warehouse for our mechanics shop – it's set up and cooking. Broken vehicles started arriving yesterday. What you grunts doing to these machines? Got a huge line of repairs in mechanics bay. Not much sleep to keep up. Got the boys and girls working all hours. Coming in faster now but we'll get them going back out. Gotta be jack of all trades. I can see I'll be making parts out of scraps. Sand fucking everywhere. Most of problems just parts gummed up oily sandy mess. Some huge rebuilds where hit by mortars-those can wait.

Making progress against Hajji. Imbedded journalists are saying Kandahar fell a few days ago. Seems the same to me here at Kandahar Airport. Hope you are watching their asses as they run away or else eliminating them out there in the suck.

Kill Osama for me, ok? Ooh-rah.

Anaai

Email #2

FROM: Ethete, Timothy E-4 USMC MAGTF 26 MEU <timothy.ethete@FOBRhino.mil>
SUBJECT: 10 DEC 01
DATE: December 10, 2001 10:24:45
TO: Ethete, Michael R. MSgt USMC MAGTF 15 LCE <michael.ethete@FOBKandaharIA.mil>
- 1 Attachment, 1.2 KB

Anaai-

In base for a hot meal and a night on a cot and got your message. Been sleeping on the rubber bitch on the ground and eating MREs for 19 days straight. Mess here better. Eggs for breakfast! Happy to have you at base cleaning up our Cadillacs.

What can I say? Signed up for just this. Nonstop action in the suck. So far unit is well-oiled and following procedures. Seen more of the bum-fuck rocky hillsides and small desert villages of this country than I expected. Mostly copters get us around but some hikes into positions. Turning over rocks but haven't found Osama. Plenty of other nasties though.

Bit by giant spider on the wrist. Ugly thing with red belly which I tried to swat when I woke up from a hard sleep against a wall but it got me. Hand swelled up and got a needle from a medic which cured it but for a mighty itch.

I'll also let Dad know I'm good.

Yeah. Running the bad guys out of Kandahar Province. They were surprised and totally out done as we came at them after dark. Whole nests of them routed and killed. They used to fighting when they can see and snoozing at night. We got them out of nowhere from the black. Night-vision, spy equipment and air support indispensable. They are running to the mountains and we'll follow them. Ooh-rah.

Atsili

Email #3

FROM: Ethete, Michael E-3 USMC MAGTF 15 LCE <michael.ethete@FOBKandaharA.mil>
SUBJECT: 14 DEC 01
DATE: December 14, 2001 15:20:05
TO: Ethete, Timothy E-4 USMC MAGTF 26 MEU <timothy.ethete@FOBRhino.mil>
     -        1 Attachment, 1.4 KB

Atsili-
Little rattled today.   Doing repair on a couple Humvees.   Not really much wrong on one but it saw a bad casualty.   Inside covered in blood and specks of Marine.   Worst part of the job was hosing it out.   Shit's fucked. Hope you are good.
Anaai

Email #4

FROM: Ethete, Timothy E-4 USMC MAGTF 26 MEU <timothy.ethete@FOBRhino.mil>
SUBJECT: 19 DEC 01
DATE: December 19, 2001 02:43:41
TO: Ethete, Michael E-3 USMC MAGTF 15 LCE
michael.ethete@FOBKandaharA.mil
- 1 Attachment, 1.2 KB

Anaai-

You know that Navajo story Mom used to tell us? Bout the twin warriors? You'll know if I'm hurt or down. Just like I know you are tired. Get some sleep.

Atsili

Email #5

FROM: Ethete, Michael E-3 USMC MAGTF 15 LCE <mi-
chael.ethete@FOBKandaharA.mil>
SUBJECT: 21 DEC 01
DATE: December 21, 2001 07:04:55
TO: Ethete, Timothy E-4 USMC MAGTF 26 MEU <timo-
thy.ethete@FOBRhino.mil>
-           1 Attachment, 1.4 KB

Atsili-

Imbedded CBS journalist did a video message for everybody in the shop here home for Christmas. Will email Dad and tell him to watch the news. They'll show mine in Wyoming and Arizona since we have family in both places. Easier to get to us on good video here at the airport base and mechanics shop than you guys out in the suck. We have showers now too so stateside they can see we are fightin the fight but standing tall with the stink washed off. We were getting a little ripe after unknown days since the last warm shower. Guessing you wiping down your ass with cold canteen water.

Kill Osama for me. Ooh-rah.

Anaai

Email #6

FROM: Ethete, Timothy E-4 USMC MAGTF 26 MEU <timo-
thy.ethete@FOBRhino.mil>
SUBJECT: 24 DEC 01
DATE: December 24, 2001 12:50:40
TO: Ethete, Michael E-3 USMC MAGTF 15 LCE <mi-
chael.ethete@FOBKandaharA.mil>
- 1 Attachment, 1.2 KB

Anaai,
Merry Christmas. Much to tell. Later.
Ooh-rah. Love you.
Atsili

Email #7

FROM: Ethete, Michael E-3 USMC MAGTF 15 LCE <michael.ethete@FOBKandaharA.mil>
SUBJECT: 24 DEC 01
DATE: December 25, 2001 20:04:55
TO: Ethete, Timothy E-4 USMC MAGTF 26 MEU <timothy.ethete@FOBRhino.mil>
- 1 Attachment, 1.4 KB

Atsili-
You are freaking me out asshole.
Merry Christmas.
Love you.
Anaai

Email #8

FROM: Ethete, Michael E-3 USMC MAGTF 15 LCE <michael.ethete@FOBKandaharA.mil>
SUBJECT: 25 DEC 01
DATE: December 25, 2001 22:14:22
TO: Ethete, Timothy E-4 USMC MAGTF 26 MEU <timothy.ethete@FOBRhino.mil>
- 1 Attachment, 1.4 KB

Atsili-

Alright. Nice surprise seeing you walk into the shop this morning. I let Dad know you were here and we got to see each other for ten minutes on Christmas. Good thing your copter landed near the shop for fuel. You couldn't of made it here in time before you took off if you landed on the usual copter sites! Shit. Best present I got. Other guys were jealous – not many of us get a minute with family here. You are looking rough. Six pack abs the both of us. But your shoulders must be six inches wider than mine. Plenty of packing shit around where I'm just leaning over these metal hulks all day. Where are the ladies when we are buffed up?

Saw something in your eyes. What up? Guess I know but don't really. If you got it in you – I'm here.

Ooh-Rah.

Anaai

Email #9

FROM: Ethete, Timothy E-4 USMC MAGTF 26 MEU <timothy.ethete@FOBRhino.mil>
SUBJECT: 29 DEC 2001
DATE: December 29, 2001 12:50:40
TO: Ethete, Michael E-3 USMC MAGTF 15 LCE <michael.ethete@FOBKandaharA.mil>
- 1 Attachment, 1.2 KB

Anaai-

Yeah, shit's up.   Ugly out here. I'm writing thoughts onto a paper – it's in my helmet. Anything happens to me, my buddys got instructions to get it to you. Don't show Dad.

Atsili

Email #10

FROM: Ethete, Timothy E-4 USMC MAGTF 26 MEU <timothy.ethete@FOBRhino.mil>
SUBJECT: 29 DEC 2001
DATE: December 29, 2001 12:59:02
TO: Ethete, Michael E-3 USMC MAGTF 15 LCE <michael.ethete@FOBKandaharA.mil>
- 1 Attachment, 1.2 KB

Anaai-
Ok I'm stupid. Disregard the last. Burned the paper.
I'm ok. Let me get some sleep and I'll give a report. Just a little whacked right now.

Atsili

Email #11

FROM: Ethete, Timothy E-4 USMC MAGTF 26 MEU <timo-
thy.ethete@FOBRhino.mil>
SUBJECT: 30 DEC 2001
DATE: December 30, 2001 2:43:02
TO: Ethete, Michael E-3 USMC MAGTF 15 LCE <mi-
chael.ethete@FOBKandaharA.mil>
- 1 Attachment, 1.2 KB

Anaai,
Slept well for a full six and felling better.

Probably seen four major fights last week. Usually about two to three a
week- Hurry up and wait, but been crazier lately. Two day rest here at
Camp Rhino now. When we're on patrol, things go from sitting around with
our rifles to running our ass across a bullet line to thumping along in a copter to sitting again to pitch black time to attack with all hell breaking loose
when we are ordered to go. They evacuate the wounded (ours first and any
prisoners next) and a day later, which seems like ten minutes, it's getting
dark again and we are on the move, ready for the next night fight. We gear
back up, reload. Then if we aren't on watch, sleep for a few hours during
light. They do a good job with intel. I always know exactly where I am on a
map and where the relief is. Can't tell you how many hajjis I killed. First
one gets you in the gut. So do all the others- later.

No civilians involved so far, but I hear other patrols been getting confused with human shields. Women sitting outside a tent full of Taliban.
They say you can tell because they are just sitting stiff as boards, not cooking or tending kids or animals. Assholes using their daughters for cover.
Felt sorry for the daughters until I we got approached by a woman in a Hajiib
who pulled her scarf aside to show a bomb strapped to her neck. Shot her
before she could detonate. Who knows, maybe it wasn't her choice? But
probably was. I keep wondering why she showed us?

I used to love to walk and explore, climb trails and get a good work out.
I will never hike again. Crossing a landscape is now a task in need of great
skills and better luck. Perilous, horrible, dangerous, echoed noise in my
head, tricky. From a trek to a patrol.

Atsili

Email #12

FROM: Ethete, Michael E-3 USMC MAGTF 15 LCE <michael.ethete@FOBKandaharA.mil>
SUBJECT: 31 DEC 01
DATE: December 31, 2001 02:00:54
TO: Ethete, Timothy E-4 USMC MAGTF 26 MEU <timothy.ethete@FOBRhino.mil>
  -          1 Attachment, 1.4 KB

Atsili-

Just got all three your emails. Been tough here but not that tough. We were bombed twice last week but casualties kept to 2 ANSF. Other side of the base from our shop but still louder than hell. Loyal Afghanis are still in training. They don't know what to do in an attack. Staff Sgt working with them says their instincts are a long way from ready for the battles but they been in this war for how many years? Works in your favor. Use it. Shit hole country.

Keep your procedures. We are the best trained in the world. I know you are doing us proud.

When we get home -no hiking for sure. Let's get beautiful Native wives and fuck them all night and wake up only to eat roast beef and fry bread and drink cold beers. I used to want to go to Vegas when we got home but after all this fucking sand, let's make it a trip to a lake in Wyoming. I want to float lazy and look at a blue sky full of white clouds. Ride a good horse.

In the meantime, you're doing good, killing Osama – remember why we are doing this. Keep America safe.

Anaai

Email #13

FROM: Ethete, Michael E-3 USMC MAGTF 15 LCE <michael.ethete@FOBKandaharA.mil>
SUBJECT: 8 JAN 02
DATE: January 8, 2002 08:10:04

TO: Ethete, Timothy E-4 USMC MAGTF 26 MEU <timothy.ethete@FOBRhino.mil>
          -            1 Attachment, 1.4 KB

Atsili-

Not heard from you. Did hear your unit had some big action and a few guys were through here that knew you. I went to see them in sick. One guy, named Tubbs, said for me to tell you he's going home- they took his leg in an emergency surgery here. He was pretty bad shot up and also lost a finger and an ear and had a bunch of serious bruises. They said he'll get a new leg in Germany but he'll be ok. He's mad about getting injured and leaving the Marines that way. He told me you were a fucking rock. I knew that. I'm proud of you Atsili. It should be me out there in the suck. You here fixing trucks. I spend my day bossing around little pukes who cry baby over long hours. I tell em to man up. I don't want to see any mistakes because you guys are relying on us to have the equipment perfect.

Dad says they been having bad weather in Wyoming. Lost a few cattle but the horses are all ok. Good water for next spring with lots of snow in the mountains. He said he got an email from you around Christmas. I email for both of us when I get a chance to be here at the IT tent.

Anaai

Email #14

FROM: Ethete, Timothy E-4 USMC MAGTF 26 MEU <timothy.ethete@FOBRhino.mil>
SUBJECT: 9 JAN 2002
DATE: January 9, 2002 23:30:02
TO: Ethete, Michael E-3 USMC MAGTF 15 LCE <michael.ethete@FOBKandaharA.mil>
- 1 Attachment, 1.2 KB

Anaai,

Supposed to be at base the next few days for R&R but just found out it's ending early. Heading out again in a few hours. I almost hate R&R because I have time to sleep but can't and when I get up all I can do is think. Thinking bad. Better to be doing. We are all big jumpy. Barbequed burgers for us but ruined the feast right in the middle with news of an emergency briefing about something big.   One more short brief coming and we go out again.

Funny how some of the guys I didn't like as much during training have come to be the most reliable.   One guy, Enis, from Arkansas called me "Chief" once in the beginning. He now pays full respect. He signed up same year as us, 1995, right out of high school. Do you still think the way we did?

Atsili

Email #15

FROM: Ethete, Michael E-3 USMC MAGTF 15 LCE <michael.ethete@FOBKandaharA.mil>
SUBJECT: 11 JAN 02
DATE: January 11, 2002 11:30:22
TO: MarineDaddy@wyoming.com
        -          1 Attachment, 1.4 KB

Hi Daddy.

I got a visit from the Chaplain last night.   He came to the Mechanics Shop with my CO. He said I should email you today. But I already knew. It happened at about sunrise. I saw Tim. He said goodbye in a dream. I'll tell you all about it- it was absolutely real.

I'll be coming home. I have two weeks leave. I don't know the details yet of my flights, but I'm leaving for Germany in an hour. Things are moving fast.

I love you.
It should have been me.
Mike

Email #16

FROM: Ethete, Michael R. MSgt USMC MAGTF 15 LCE <michael.ethete@Lageune.mil>
SUBJECT: 10 JAN 06
DATE: January 10, 2006 07:15
TO: MarineDaddy@wyoming.com
  -            1 Attachment, 1.4 KB

Hi Daddy,

I'm mustering out tomorrow. My last day as Active Service is the Fourth Anniversary of Tim's death. First thing I will do is go to see Tim's grave.

Another big deployment of Marines out of here last week. This time it's to Iraq. Brother marines coming back from Afghanistan, too, on the same day. I been stateside for seven months and after three deployments I've seen enough of the world. Put on my civvies and come home to Wyoming. Can't wait to see you. I wish Mom was alive. I miss her and can't believe she'll be gone 10 years this fall. I'd like some of her mutton stew and yeast bread. I bet Tim is having some now with her.

It was good seeing Mom's Dad here at Camp Legeune over New Years. He's getting old but still a spark in his eye. He said to tell you "Ya'ta' hey". When my CO found out he was a code talker in WWII they invited him to give a talk to some of the new recruits. Most people here thought I was a Pilipino and now they look at me different. He enjoyed the attention and tour of the base. He was based here in '42.

My shoulder is healing up pretty good from my injury. You'll see that I can't do much with my right arm right now though. When I was in sickbay they put me through a psych program. They are recommending some treatment for PTSD. I'm thinking about it. I'm gonna try without for now. Once I get home there's not much I can do anyway unless I drive to Warren Air Base. Seems stupid to drive hours to talk for one hour to a shrink. You have the Veterans there ready for me, to do the soldier ceremony, right? That's what I really need. Part of being home.

My thoughts on war have changed since we signed up. You know that's the last thing Tim ever asked me, whether I still thought the same about it as before we went in.

War is a trick of the Devil. To a young man, war promises glory. This is a job where you kill people for a living. What possesses people to apply for that? It's not the paycheck but the promised glory and importance. The thrill of making that ultimate difference either by killing or dying.

Despite the promises, war first delivers oblivion. We disappeared into the United States Marines. All we needed was the fundamentals and procedures they trained into us. We were blessedly no longer accountable for anything we did. We wrapped ourselves in the isolation of the lack-of-responsibility-blanket. It was invisibility. We expected it to be lonely but that was ok since we thought we would be safe and together inside that protective skin. We thought that from the blanket we would emerge at the end, whole, wiser, maybe sadder as a witness of beautiful tragedy without really having been a participant. Somebody with good stories. Now it's just me. Timothy's gone.

So other deliveries, after the oblivion, have been unexpectedly arriving to me. Into the space under that blanket came a fear I can't put down. A curtain to the world was pulled closed into my own chamber of fear. No one can look in. I cannot cancel this delivery, like a wrong order from Amazon. I wish I could. I am in too deep to stop it. Other deliveries I don't know will keep arriving in the future.

Some of the deliveries are for me. I know now that some are meant for others. You got an especially cruel package. My wife, if I ever have one, will probably get a load of shit. Timothy got death, which maybe he understood, since he understood the enticement of glory that started the whole thing. My only hope is my country will be made better.

Strangely, maybe even my enemy will be made better. You know, I see now how we are all the same. Just like the army killed our Shoshone people, I'm now in the army. And just like we shoot at the Afghanies, they are all just people too. Some of them a pure evil and stupid and do more harm than good, most of them just want to keep the strangers off of their lands. Maybe we helped them understand how to keep law and order, and now it's time for us to get off their lands.

In the beginning I refused to dishonor tobacco by using it as a crutch for courage. It was all crap. I smoke two packs a day now. I gotta quit when I get home.

It's all just a rifle range and training and ooh-rah until you point a loaded gun at their head and kill in silence and darkness. I have fired into the yellow eyes of war. Dad, the moral ambiguity of what I did is killing me. One way or another, my part is soon over, my relief begins with the next man to stand up. I wish they would stop standing up. It's a trick of the Devil.

Love you and see you next week at home.

Mike

Seventh Generation Tweak

(Rose Old Bear "Tweak" Born 2000)

Prologue : Myths and Realities

From the Website of the Confederated Tribes of The Colville Reservation
http://www.colvilletribes.com/myths_and_realities.php

(These rules generally hold true for all tribes and Indian people.)

Property Taxes

MYTH: The Confederated Tribes and individual Colville Tribal members never pay property taxes and all of their properties are held in trust for them by the federal government.
FACT: In a few instances, the Confederated Tribes and in many instances, individual Colville tribal members, pay property taxes in the respective counties where the property is located. Only lands presently located within the boundaries of the Colville Indian Reservation, land which was located within the boundaries of the former reservation, commonly referred to as the "North Half" of the Colville Reservation, and lands known as allotments (parcels) that are owned or were owned by members in areas on and near the present Colville Indian Reservation qualify for the "trust" status.
Example: A Colville tribal member who owns property in west Coulee Dam, Grand Coulee or Electric City (or any area that is located outside the boundaries of the Colville Indian Reservation) will pay applicable property taxes even if the property is purchased from another Colville tribal member.

Other Taxes
MYTH: The Confederated Tribes and individual Colville tribal members never pay sales tax, federal income tax or other taxes.
FACT: The Confederated Tribes and individual Colville tribal members are not required by federal law to pay state taxes on goods and services purchased within the boundaries of the Colville Indian Reservation and/or delivered to them on the reservation. All Colville tribal members who earn income pay federal income taxes; the only exception is for Colville tribal members who earn income from their own trust allotments. However, the Confederated Tribes pays applicable taxes in conjunction with operating businesses such as the Keller Ferry Marina and Seven Bays Marina, which are both located off of the reservation. Individual Colville tribal members who own "fee status" property pay applicable taxes and members who own and operate businesses located off of the reservation pay taxes. In addition, the

Confederated Tribes and its members pay sales tax when purchasing goods and services that are not deliverable to the reservation.

Example: A Colville tribal member who chooses to shop in Spokane, Washington will pay Washington State sales tax plus an additional percentage or 8.1 sales tax total. Also, members pay taxes applied locally for lodging, food or whatever.

Per-Capita Payments

MYTH: The Confederated Tribes finances its periodic "per-capita" payments with monies received from the sources such as federal, state and local funds.

FACT: Per capita payments are funds strictly from the Tribes own resources and are primarily generated from the sale of timber and wood products.

Housing

MYTH: Adult Colville tribal members living on the reservation are all eligible for a free home such as a HUD home or some sort of free housing.

FACT: Some Colville tribal members in low income categories may own or rent HUD homes located on the reservation, however, housing for the elderly, individuals on fixed incomes and those classified as low income is terribly inadequate and constitutes a chronic need. Most tribal members have to take care of their own housing needs with \ minimal or no assistance from the Tribes.

Example: Some qualified tribal members can get home loans from Colville Tribal Credit, the Tribes' loaning institution. Not everyone qualifies.

Free Money from the Tax Payers' Pockets or "Welfare for All"

MYTH: Every enrolled Colville tribal member gets "a check in the mail" from the federal government every month simply because they are members of a federally recognized tribe; and this so called "welfare" payment is financed by taxing American citizens.

FACT: Not true. American Indians can apply for welfare just like everyone else.

Tweak, Wind River Indian Reservation, 2013

I woke up suddenly this morning from a dream about a bicycle. I was riding it effortlessly away from this reservation. It was windy in my dream. I could feel a striped shirt I was wearing billowing and flapping sideways as I rode along, feeling hopeful. I had covered a lot of ground in my dream. Then, as my mind came to being awake, I realized the flapping sound was just the tarp on my Mom's trailer roof. The roof leaks sometimes so yesterday me and my sister, Della put some tarps up there and covered them with old tires to hold 'em down on the corners. I guess we need to put more tires up there.

We rolled these from over by our uncle's. Della didn't want to roll hers because it had too much dirt inside that we couldn't scrape out and it was lopsided and too heavy for her. So she trailed along after me as we made four trips and I rolled them over here. We got pretty dirty. It took a while to pull 'em up on top of the trailer with a rope but it's better than getting dripped on at night and laying in a wet mattress that stinks after a while. I have to keep my eye out for more tires within rolling distance of home. Maybe we could put some big rocks up there. Well, I'll think about that. I don't know how to tie a rope on a rock to lift it up.

It's summertime and there's no school. My Mom's been gone to town for a while, maybe four days. She has to work at the convenience store. (More like an inconvenient store for us. AaaYa!) But she knows I'm here to take care of Della and I'm responsible and creative. Besides, my Uncle Tall Elk is over the way if I need him.

I'm thirteen years old now and I know how to get along out here in the country where we stay on the family allotment. We got a trailer from a government program when I was little. Before that we lived in a house from old days that's now just fallen over. Sometimes we pull boards off it to burn if we are cold and the power is off. Our water and power are both on right now and Mom has her job in town so we're doing good. She comes home for a few days after four or five days of shifts and bring us the things we need.

I'm a writer and artist. I got double gold stars on a story I did for 8th grade fair! So now I think, and then I ponder, and then I daydream so I can write with convincing. I mostly like to think and write about the past. It was interesting times then. But, I have trouble sitting still to actually get it all down on paper.

For a while this year, I have imagined that I am my grandmother Edwina's spirit reborn. My Mom (Edwina was her Mom) said Edwina died the year before I was born. So I figure she would want to come back to the family as me? I am gonna write a story about that anyway.

Grandma Edwina was a Blackfeet Indian from a reservation in Montana. I never got to go to Montana but Mom went for the North American Indian Days in Browning when I was eight. She left me and Della here with Uncle Tall Elk because she said we were too little to go. There was giveaways and a pow wow and specials.

Anyway, Edwina married my Grandpa Milo who lived at Blackfeet then moved here and became a official tribal elder at our rez until he died when I was 6. I used to sit next to him. He said I asked too many questions. Grandpa Milo ended up here after Grandma Edwina died because *his* mother was from here. Her name was Great Grandma Betsy and she married a Blackfeet named Crazy Don (he was a rodeo bronc-rider.) They all moved to my Great Grandpa Crazy Don's Montana ranch at the Blackfeet rez where my Mom was born. Even though they lived at Blackfeet, Milo was a Shoshone from his Mom and so after Edwina died, the whole family came back here and I was born on this rez and I'm a registered Eastern Shoshone tribal member even though I could be a Blackfeet if I wanted because my Mom is registered Blackfeet.

I feel that Grandmother Edwina knew how hard it would be so she came back as me...for two things: to give me her strength so to make my life easier and to also get to be me and live the life she wanted but couldn't have back when she lived on that ranch.

Grandma Edwina was married young. She was 16 (that could be me in three years but it won't) and Grandpa Milo was 30 when they got married. Mom says Edwina and Milo had nine children, seven who lived. My Uncle Tall Elk says his father, Milo, was a hard worker and loved his cattle. My grandfather would stay out on the ranch with his cattle and Edwina stayed at a BIA house in town where she had a sewing business. He wondered where all the children were coming from but knew they were his because when he visited town he saw her pregnant and the new babies all looked like him. He would take the older ones to the ranch and they helped him with the livestock and they learned lots of traditional ways.

Edwina sewed a lot, of course, because this was her job. My Mom was her last child so Mom stayed in town. Edwina named my mom "Barbie" after the new doll that came out the year Mom was born. This tells me that my grandma wanted things, beautiful things from the white world. People think that my Mom has a different real name but her real name is truly Barbie.

I can imagine what Grandma thought while she sewed. Her kids would bring her things to sew and mend from the white neighbors and coins after. My Mom's older brothers knew how to live and get by in the old ways and also with white man's work. But my Mom didn't really learn the old ways.

Edwina's kids grew and she sewed and thought. She made beadwork designs on things they wore at home so her family would be beautiful in the Indian way. My Mom used to help her sew sometimes, but Mom says it was boring so now she works at the c-store where she gets to hear what's going on.

Sometimes old voices talk to me. Not like I'm crazy or anything, I just know things that seem to come from old people gone by. I feel like I'm making it up, but I'm not. I can hear the old ones' inflections and tones. Spirits, friends: they come to visit. Very real while they're here and we bond right away and I don't forget them. They are now my old friends. My own voice sounds funny and tin if I try to talk during their visit and it hustles off my friend. I have to *let 'em*. *Know* 'em not to go, that I still want to visit.

They tell me stories, if I ask. I like people telling me stories. Sometimes they are shy and it takes a while to get started. I heard a story about the wind one day from one of them. I was just thinking and all a' sudden I realized they weren't my thoughts because they were all brand new to me and fully formed. It was something like this — about the wind.

There was once a crow who forgot he was not flying. He was standing on a post and he had his wings out facing into a fierce west wind. He looked out at the grass and sage and highway in the far-off and they were all moving...coming under him in waves. Bits of trash were skittering by beneath him. Then the crow remembered where he was and fell off the post. He was laughing at himself after he got up off the ground!

Wind is like inspiration from somewhere else, breathed in and out. It's a good thing I like the wind, because there's a lot of it here.

My Mom was married to an Blackfeet guy but they didn't have any kids and Mom took her name back to Old Bear, like her parents. Then she met my dad at a pow wow when she was about 30. My Dad was at the pow wow from Canada. So she moved up there with him for a while and got pregnant with me. Then when her mom (Edwina) died she went back to Montana and ended up coming with the family back here to Wyoming just before I was born. So I'm half Cree but I don't really know much about it up there.

Hearing those voices doesn't scare me. They have never been what people call evil. I think I would know if there was danger. This knowing about the voices is the exact opposite of the idea that: thunder never hurt me, but sometimes I'm scared of it. With the voices, I hear them, but I'm not scared at all. Weird.

My Uncle Tall Elk says it's a old Indian saying that if you walk far enough, the landscape will change. I also think that if you wait long enough your life will change. I want mine to change because this life can be bad.

I'm in junior high school. I'm proud because I'm doing good in school. Every year about five people from here go to college. Most of 'em come back a few months or maybe years later as drop outs happy to see the rez again, or in a military uniform, or even as graduates living back here in a trailer. But not me. I have a responsibility for Grandma Edwina that I need to have a good and exciting life for Grandma to live her dreams.

Uncle Tall Elk is a man who when he sees something beautiful does not mention it. But I always know a moment to remember is upon him because he opens his palm, closes his eyes and gathers up time in his hand and cups it up to his heart. Like when an eagle flew over. He is a sculptor and maybe some of these pictures in his heart end up in his art.

Everybody here on the rez is related and you can spend all day talking to folks and hearing disputed interpretations of the relations and sometimes bits of truth that nobody will directly say. It's a given that the ones who know ugly things won't tell unless they are drunk and then it comes out mean and can sting you to know things about your relations and therefore about yourself.

It's easy to let yourself believe that those ugly things make you ugly. You have to fight that sneaky sense of dread and shame and remember *on purpose* some of the good stories. The old people like me because I collect these thoughts and stories and I don't let them make me lonely and mean, and I'm usually ready for more. And the spirit voices supplement. People get surprised by some of the things I know.

The old people like me, but the other kids think I'm weird. Even Della walks off sometimes when there are kids around or when she sees I'm thinking she will roll her eyes or pout her lip at me. She just seems to somehow know better about the world of friends and music that's popular and how to laugh easy and be welcome with tough kids. Part of me doesn't care about this but part of me hates myself for being like I am. My Uncle says some people live best when they are young, but that *I'll* live best when I'm older. I'm counting on that.

Next time Mom comes back I gotta give her a letter. All the family are getting government letters about drilling for oil on the family allotment. It's maybe a way to get money but mostly a way to reinforce our feeling about how the government is a manmade machine trying to act like a natural force and how they have messed it up since white society tried to organize life the Indians always let organize itself. We all said little jokes about the letters but mostly they will just sit in a pile of papers and trash on people's counters, and eventually get moved to a drawer or someplace for serious papers or just get lost with old newspapers or garbage.

We all laugh when the serious government letters come because we remember everybody's right names. My Uncle Big Boy's white name is Melvin. For a day after government letters come you know they are here because people will snicker and call you "Lester" or "Eugene" or "Belva" instead of "Chunk" and "Rail" and "Oma". My name on my official papers at school is Rose. But I've always just been "Tweak" to everyone.

Della's given name is "Rodella" so she makes sense that way. I don't know where Mom got this name, maybe from Della's father, but we don't know for sure who that is. With Della, Mom just came up pregnant with no real man around. Maybe like an earthworm she just split a part of herself off and made Della.

Some people here say my Mom is a drunk. But she isn't, well not always. Most of the time she is wonderful. Being a Blackfeet and then living in Canada gave her some knowledge. I think her exciting life so far made my Mom restless and she comes and goes. Since I am half Cree and half Canadian, maybe it explains my likelihood to dream and hear voices.

I just want to be older so I can leave and get to the part of my life when I am living best. I study my schoolwork hard and I have almost $18 saved up from gathering cans and taking them to town in big garbage sacks. These odd ways will be useful to me I know.

Here is another story told to me by spirit voices:

> There were these two boys. Brothers who loved each other very much and who were important just because they had each other. There was a war and they were fighting in it. One brother saw his Mom get killed with a gun. The other brother took a hatchet and killed the soldier who shot the Mom. The first brother then saw the second brother who had just hatcheted the soldier get killed by a close up shot that sprayed his blood out onto white snow. The brother was too stunned and layed next to his brother and died when more soldiers came.

I don't know where this violence came from, but it reminded me of stories I heard told about soldiers killing Indians in the old days. Dumb boys. Girls don't do this kind of violent stuff. Well not usually. It's the girls in the family and tribe who always just carry on. And the girls who move us forward. Like I will.

Barbie Old Bear, Border Town, 2013

"I'm part Indian, you know."

That's what this dumb ass said to me at Doubies' Water Hole yesterday. God, I shoulda scratched him. What's I supposed to say? 'Oh, welcome back to the tribe! We been waiting for you!' Jerk wad. Middle aged white guy with red hair; fat belly, all wiggly and shit. "Really," I say.

"Yeah, way back, though. I'm Mormon and you know…back then they tried to bring the Indians back to … well to make 'em Mormon."

"I thought Mormon's don't drink? What's that, root beer?"

"Well, I gave up on some of the Mormon stuff. I like my coffee and a glass of wine sometimes."

I just stared at the idiot. He probably wanted to see if he could impress me and I'd show him a good time. I was deciding how pissed I was gonna be, then Meadow came over. Probably thought I was getting a free one from this asshole.

"What you say, Red! Buy us a drink!" slurred Meadow. The white guy paused and looked at her. She hadn't had a shower in probably a week and she stunk. Her hair was recently cut. She did it herself when she was drunk, I'm sure. Looks like she got stuck too close to a fan. Her tube top was slipping too low and she yanked it up so her nipples wouldn't show while at the same time pushing out her chest so the guy would know she was bait. She ran her tongue over her chapped lips.

He raised his finger up and wagged it for Doubie. Doubie gave me a look.

"I'll buy these ladies each a drink, please."

"You lost or something, Red?" This was Meadow. He looked a little frightened.

"No, I'm looking for some folks who live around here. I wanted to just see the town, first."

"Well, we're in the town." Meadow can be pointless. Doubie set down the two new drinks. She stirred her new vodka with her finger.

"I think my ancestor was from here."

"Maybe we're cousins," I said. He looked at me funny. "What, not what you expected?"

Right then Melvin Sunningboy came up. I could tell he was fingering his knife. He liked to scare people with it. He didn't like strangers, either. If he wasn't drunk, he would of been afraid to come near the flabby white guy. Melvin looked strange at him, kinda deciding.

"This here is Melvin. Be careful or he'll mess you up," stated Meadow, leaning hard into Melvin.

The white guy was in over his head. He backed up, kinda smiled. He threw down a twenty and a five and nodded at us. He got up from his barstool and grabbed his coat, started to walk toward the door.

When he got far enough away Melvin said, "Stay out of here white man." He showed the white guy his knife blade. The white guy looked more scared and hurried out.

We all laughed. Meadow took the five off the counter and put it in her pocket while Doubie was looking after the white guy. She said to me, "Who was he? Barbie, what was he saying to you?"

"Nother wanna-be. Says he had a Indian princess grandmother. Shit. Do we go up to white people and say, 'I got a white man in my family tree.' Hell no. Ass hole. White men fucked everyone, blacks, Indians, Mexicans. Now their grandkids show up here and act like their grandmother was doing something important for her people by introducing the old fat white man to our holy ancient ways. Stupid idiots."

"I fucked a white man. He had a small dick." Meadow put her pinkey in her mouth and moved it in and out. Melvin laughed and brought out his big knife. We all laughed like it was the funniest thing we every saw. Doubie yelled, "Put your thing away Melvin." We laughed some more.

Meadow brought out the five. "Three more, Doubie! Make it quick!"

Daniel Smith, Riverton Wyoming 2013

It might have been a mistake for me to come here to the Wind River Reservation. However, I have been curious for a long time about my ancestry, and about Indians in general.

A Smith family legend is that in the late 1800s, when the Mormon pioneers practiced polygamy, my great-great-grandfather had an Indian wife. She died, but my great-grandfather, George Smith, was a surviving son from that wife. Sure enough, when I did a high school project in genealogy class, I discovered that this was true!

The LDS church has always had a fine appreciation for genealogy. Basically, we want to make sure that all our relations are properly baptized into the faith so that we can be reunited in Heaven. There is even a strong program for baptism by proxy.

This makes us the best in the world at keeping track of our ancestors. The whole Mormon ancestry thing has always stirred in me a great curiosity about "my" past.

Every so often in Mormon schools students are assigned to research an ancestor so that we are all familiar with doing research in the genealogy database. I chose as my assignment to research the Family Indian Legend (as I like to call it.)

In the past, in one of my school assignments, I had determined that our Smith family name did not in fact come from the Prophet Joseph Smith, but that our third-great-grandfather was actually a blacksmith from England! He was a true pioneer, though and still very worth my reflection.

The Indian story was fascinating but the hard facts in the ancestry database left quite a number of questions for me. I was able to find that my ancestor George Smith married a woman named Helen who was identified as "Shoshone from Wyoming" and that she died along with her daughter, Sarah, in 1895. I don't know how she came to have been married to my great-great-grandfather, or how she died. They were polygamists back then and some of the later wives' lives were not fully documented, especially if a surviving wife was the one doing the documenting.

I was also unable to locate this Indian wife or her daughter's gravestone in the family cemetery at the Pillar Cache Ranch, so that was odd for our family too. A number of these questions have languished since my school years. Now I am 38 years old and have a wife of my own and three little girls so I want to be able to pass on more information to them. I always wanted to research it further some day.

Then the letter came. It came to Grandfather, as surviving heir to great grandfather, George Smith. Grandfather gave me the letter last time I had visited him because he knew it was something interesting to me. It was a letter from the Bureau of Indian Affairs on behalf of an energy company. It was signed by one "Lou McNulty", a "Landman". The letter states that as set forth in Bureau of Indian Affairs land records, my great grandfather, if he is a tribal member, retains an interest in an Indian Allotment on the Wind River Reservation in Wyoming; that this interest is a fractional interest along with many other members of the descendents of someone named "James (Trees Told It) St. James". The company wants to drill for oil on that land and wishes for signatures of any such tribal members.

Well that was fascinating! We are not tribal members, to my knowledge, so I doubt we have any monetary interest in this property. However, I decided that it was worth asking some questions. Perhaps we really can be members of an Indian Tribe! After phone calls failed to provide answers for me, I took a few days off from my grocery company to travel to Fort Washakie on the Wind River Indian Reservation to look at those records for myself. I want to see if I could track down some answers.

My daughters wanted to come on this trip, but they are in children's soccer leagues back in our hometown of Logan. I did not want them to have to miss their practices! So I decided to come by myself. It will be easier for me this way if I spend my time in dusty records rooms.

Upon my arrival, I checked in to a Best Western in nearby Riverton, Wyoming. The reservation boundary is a short way away, and the Indian Agency in Fort Washakie is about a forty-five minute drive north.

I don't know what I was thinking but on my way to Fort Washakie I saw a tavern and decided it would be nice to see the local flavor and maybe ask around to see if anyone knew anything of Trees Told It St. James, or Teton Energy. It was a rather bold thing for me to do, as I don't frequent taverns and only rarely have a forbidden alcoholic drink, and this was on a Tuesday afternoon! But I was on vacation, so I went in to see what I could learn.

Good God! I was not prepared for drunken Indians in the middle of the day! One of them pulled a knife on me and I realize now I better be careful about where I go and to whom I speak. It was frankly frightening. I don't feel like I'm really in America, but in some foreign place. As I said when I started, maybe I should not have come here.

I pulled over and sat in the car a few miles up the road from the bar to get my wits back. It was ridiculous. I am perfectly free to go look at the public records. I just don't need to be going into any more strange bars. That had been foolish. Perhaps I won't mention it to my wife, Karen.

I pulled back onto the highway and headed up towards Fort Washakie. I was thinking while I drove.None of us know our history. We don't know what our ancestors lived through or may have done. And really, it's all so complex, anyway.

My Mormon family sees history as being made today, so we keep track of our stories. I recognize that the Mormon story that I've been told, and taught to believe, is really only just some peoples' ideas. They think they got these ideas from God, but aren't all ideas with love and goodness at their base from God?

In families, we know our recent history best, but the more generations you go back, the more is conjecture, rumor, tales, and confused ideas been passed along. If a person wrote it or told it or said it, it's what they think they know. So it's all certainly worth considering, but just maybe, not really "truth".

The other trouble with family history is that the more generations you go back, the more people there are to keep track of. Surely a good number of those people are sons-of-bitches, and then naturally their mothers were bitches. I laughed at this private joke inside my head.

"Official" history is probably wrong too. As they say, the victors write the history books. None of the losers get their stories told. Even the victors were likely pretty shitty sometimes. The victors don't brag that they were plunderers, rapists, or cruel.

In our own families, we have both victors and losers. We prefer to imagine our ancestors' place as that of the valiant, the achiever, the progressive, the devout, and the good.

What white southerner pictures her family's part in the relative poverty of the people of Haiti? What Catholic pictures his church's genocide of the California Indians? What son of a pioneer pictures his family's land stolen because it was promised by treaty to an Indian tribe? What Sioux imagines his ancestor as having post-traumatic shock disorder and clinical depression? What merchant using rail to ship his goods knows that rail line's contribution to the destruction of the North American buffalo herds? And yeah, what Mormon imagines his ancestors' culturally destructive ways for these tribes?

I guess I can talk with some authority about that if I am, indeed, part Indian.

The Family, Wind River Indian Reservation, 2013

"Old Mike is having a 49!" Screeched an excited Tweak as soon as I walked in the door, two days later.

I have been gone, working at the c-store almost a week, but my brother Tall Elk has been looking in on the girls. Thank God I have four days before I need to be back at my job. I am glad to be home to rest and see my girls. Since my car broke down; it needs a new water pump, I have to rely on rides from others who are going the forty miles from work to my trailer. I can't hardly afford the gas anyway. If I don't have a ride, I just have to stay in town! In the last hour of my shift today, my brother, Big Boy came in to the c-store and offered me a ride home. I suspect Tall Elk had sent him to get me. I hurried and gathered up some groceries for the girls and left work a few minutes early. This time I was glad Big Boy came by. I usually stayed at my friend Meadow's trailer in Fort Washakie if I didn't have a ride, but I missed going home and I had four days off which I didn't want to spend sitting at Meadows or at Doubies. I know the girls need me, but they are old enough to take care of themselves and Tall Elk is here, anyway. When I don't have a way home, rather than being bored at Meadow's, I'll take a ride into one of the nearby towns for some fun. Someone's always going to the bars and asking me along.

I used to be a real partier, but now, I'm mellower. I was beat up pretty bad and raped about five years ago after a day at a bar. But that happens to lots of us Native women. Not like the law did anything but take my statement. A tired looking FBI agent had come by the hospital and wrote down what I said. It's stupid that the FBI handles major crimes on the rez, rather than the tribal police. That makes for so much more violence. Since I wasn't sure exactly who jumped me, he didn't seem too concerned about further investigation. So I am getting over it. Slowly. I still have nightmares. I didn't tell the girls or Tall Elk. It wasn't like they would find out when an arrest was made. We don't expect the law to be on our side. I'm more careful now, and I try to keep my kids at home as much as possible. I worry about what will happen when they are old enough to leave our sheltered trailer home. Tweak is so trusting and a little dense about people. Della is pretty and social. I don't want them to have this shit happen to them. I need a better job where I can watch for them. But there's nothing else on the rez. I might have to go back on welfare. It's almost the same as what I make anyway.

So when I get a ride to my trailer, I go and I'm thankful to be home. It will be good for me to go out to the country and stay away from the bars for a few days. Not that I'm a drunk! Believe me! I know *lots* of people who are drunks and who have died from the booze and from drugs. I *only* party a few nights a week, now. But this week had been pretty crazy and I am glad to see my girls.

"Why would Old Mike have a party?" I asked. "And quiet down, you don't need to scream, I can hear." I saw the reflection in the window of me looking tired with my cigarette bouncing on my lip. A few cans of beans fell onto the floor from the sack of groceries I was carrying. "Damn! A can fell on my toe!" I stopped listening to Tweak and rubbed my foot.

Della came in from the bedroom. She was spending too much time there. She watched hours of television every day. The muffled voices of canned laughter came from inside the other room. Della hugged me with a big smile. I could smell her musty scent combined with a floral hair product she got from God knows where. She loves me and I know she misses me when I'm gone.

"Hi Baby," I said, giving her a hug. We stood that way for a while, affectionate.

Tweak was always different, though. She wasn't touchy-feely like Della and came out of the blue with really odd statements. She can talk your head off and asks more questions than any person could possibly stand to answer. I'm used to this and love Tweak very much, but I know you need to respond differently to her than to Della.

When Tweak was in first grade, the school called me in for a meeting. The teacher and the school nurse were there. They told me that while Tweak was very bright, she had some problems. The school nurse had the nerve to tell me that Tweak was an "FAS child, however it appeared to be a mild case". I had to ask what "FAS" meant. They had looked at me like I was stupid and said it meant "fetal alcohol syndrome". I was so mad I stormed out. Sure, I partied a lot when I was with Tweak's father in Canada, but not so much that it would hurt my baby. Tweak was just a unique little girl with lots of big dreams and funny ways.

"Old Mike told Tall Elk about the 49-party and Tall Elk told us. It's next Wednesday. Old Mike's sister is coming to town and he wants to have people come out to the ranch and visit her!"

"Aunt Priss is out home?" I am really happy about this.

"Who is Aunt Priss?"

"Old Mike's sister. She is the one from New York with the white husband and those lawyer boys."

"Have I met her?"

"No, I haven't seen her in about 10 years. She doesn't come out home very often. She must be in her 80s. She used to be pretty famous here and with Indians all over the country. She is the one who joined all those Indian rights protests and helped get some of the bad laws changed for tribes in the 1970s. Most of the older ones couldn't stand up to the government, but she and people her age did it. She inspired a lot of kids in those days to stand up and fight for our rights. Her boys are both lawyers now in Washington DC. I guess her husband must be dead."

"Why does she live in New York, instead of here?"

"I don't know, Tweak. You can ask her."

"So we can go? YEAH!" shrieked Tweak, as only a teenage girl can do.

"Of course. I want to see Aunt Priss. I used to love listening to her and her stories."

"Can we go to Wal-Mart to get a new outfit for the 49? My jeans are too short and besides, they are out of style now," stated Della.

"Oh crap, Della. If I can get us a ride into Riverton. I just got a paycheck and it has some overtime on it. I'll see if Tall Elk can help me pay the power bill. I wasn't sure it would still be on."

"It went off day before yesterday and I got Tall Elk to pay already," beamed Tweak.

"You're a good girl, honey."

Daniel Smith, Riverton Wyoming, 2013

Daniel Smith stretched out on the bed. He didn't like the jaunty floral polyester covering over the hard bumpy mattress. He lay there and wondered who had done what on it since it had last been washed and had therefore left their germs on the bedspread. He got up and went to the bathroom. He unfolded a thin white Clorox smelling towel and draped it over the area where he was to sit, sat down, then leaned back in again, relaxing. He wished he had thought to bring a feather pillow in a clean case from home as his neck pressed down against the flat rectangle they called a pillow.

Today he had driven around the reservation. He felt oddly singular in his car looking out on the broad vistas of prairie surrounded by mountains. Lonely; but not wanting to call home. It was as if he had been in a bubble of his own world, in his four-door sedan, looking out the window at a very foreign place, like a sneaking, peeping tom. Now he was back in the cheap Best Western, with it's thin walls, strangers walking around outside on the landing, and diesel farm trucks belonging to nice cowboy families clattering in the parking lot. He was trying to process his day.

It had been beautiful outside: sunny, a little breezy, perfect temperature. There were fields of wheat blowing waves in the slow wind, forming quiet ripples of beauty. He had gotten out of his car and had watched the sun play on the shimmering, undulating surface of the field. He wanted to run through it and touch the budding ends of the crop as he ran, feeling himself a part of the dance. He imagined it and then imagined how ridiculous it would look by anyone watching. It would probably also cost the farmer some money by maybe messing with his bushels per-acre if he knocked a fat path through the immaculately planted rows. He had shaken his head and got back in the car. More than once today, he had these kinds of silly thoughts.

He had seen an Indian child, probably a little boy about eleven, wearing jeans and a tee shirt and tennis shoes riding a painted horse expertly bareback through a sage covered field. A mangy looking dog had been following the child, padding along with its tongue lolling out, but seemingly happy to be along with the boy. Daniel wondered where the boy was going and felt a little jealous of this free idea of childhood.

He wondered why no one took the time to clean up. It was so beautiful with a brilliant turquoise sky, soaring mountains in the crystal distance, jagged bluffs on the near horizon, rugged landscapes of rock and scrub and wildflowers always at your feet! But the beauty was marred by many muddy beer bottles along the road, "big gulp" soda cups, occasional articles of clothing and nasty looking road kill, some of it small, rabbits or snakes, and some of it large, dead dogs and deer carcasses. A chaotic mix of all kinds of plastic and paper trash had caught on the sage and barbed wire fences.

Then there was the long-term trash, like the rusting 1970s dodge dart, the old tires, a refrigerator without a door, and a car that looked like it just needed basic maintenance sitting with three flat tires next to the road. These bigger items let the casual observer know that the small pieces of garbage all around were not merely the unfortunate recent result of someone's trash can blowing over on a windy morning. This was the local "normal". It was frightening and ominous to Daniel.

He stared at the houses. Clearly of the same government design, it was a sad bureaucratic attempt at a neighborhood. Some attempts to distinguish each had been made: exterior walls painted bright yellow, blue, or gold. Many had one or more broken windows covered in flapping plastic. Some had sagging roofs and a few had recently been on fire, but were still standing. Many of those he thought must be abandoned had new looking satellite dishes.

There were no garages or sheds around the houses so miscellaneous junk sat around outside of each. Small tractors with flat tires, sorry looking horses standing still in small pens, children's riding toys, small campers hooked up to large rusty propane tanks. About half the homes were trailers. Some appeared new, others quite old. They often lacked the dignity of the bottom skirts that gave the impression they were permanent, so that now you could see the wheels underneath that made them "mobile" homes. They sat in mud or on well-worn dirt tracks. Some had plastic and tires on the roofs. Why did people put tires on their roofs?

There were some beautiful ranches on the reservation, too, where healthy herds of cattle and horses grazed. The chaparral marking the entrances both invited and threatened a stranger who might wish to enter over the cattle guards through the barbed wire fencing toward the private properties of these ranches. Daniel wondered if these were Indian ranches, white ranches, or fancy dude ranch second homes owned by rich men as hunting spreads.

Oil and gas were being produced, too. From the highway you could occasionally see large dirty looking tanks sitting on bare patches of ground. Pipes connected the tanks to the Earth. Here and there, a few pump jacks moved lazily up and down or sat still at various odd places in the landscape. Decked out "Halliburton Services" pickup trucks driven by white looking men in baseball caps or cowboy hats passed Daniel on the road. Now and then an oil tank truck lumbered along with the farm trucks and beat up sedans. At the little "Shoshone Gas" convenience store, the pump had a hand written sign "You Can Now Buy Gas Made From Local Oil Stolen From Indians." Daniel did not like the victim mentality behind the sign.

Daniel felt the need to spend a few hours with a lawn mower and a weed whacker when he got out of his car in front of the building labeled "United States Department of Interior Bureau of Indian Affairs – Realty". Was this messy dump with the gravel parking lot really a federal facility? It was a small clapboard house on an overgrown, weedy lawn. Dirty windows hid a forbidding looking basement. Although the building appeared to have been recently painted, window trim and all, it was that strange shade of government green, the sickly color of Forest Service trucks.

Clearly, the federal standards for the "BIA" were different than those of the officially proud brick of the Riverton Post Office, where Daniel had stopped this morning to mail a postcard reading "Riverton Wyoming" home to Logan. The standards here were even farther from the marble federal buildings with impressive flower planters serving as traffic barriers that he was used to at the majestic federal buildings at home.

The woman inside the creaky door of "Realty" had looked up as he entered. The room smelled of stale coffee and dust. She had been doing some kind of needlework behind her metal government desk. She was an Indian woman and appeared alone in the office. Daniel felt self-conscious before her. Her eyes had been distant and her face unsmiling and blank as she asked, "Can I help you?" Daniel felt the distance of generations of mistrust as he cleared his throat.

"Yes. I was hoping you could help me find the records for an allotment. My grandfather received this letter." As Daniel held it toward her, she glanced quickly at it and Daniel saw a flash of recognition on her face.

"Which allotment?" she said glancing at a pile of cardboard file boxes stacked beside her.

"Uh, it says here, it's Number 9052343, and has the name 'Trees Told It St. James'.

She did not answer, but paused. She then turned, stood and opened the top box and slowly began to look at the files. After a maddening few minutes during which Daniel wondered if she had forgotten him completely, she extracted a file and pointed to a folding table surrounded by mismatched office chairs. "Don't remove any of the papers, but you can use a sticky and copy on my machine for ten cents a page." Without smiling, she handed him a raspberry colored small pad of sticky notes with the thick file.

So far Daniel had not done well with connecting with the locals. He decided to try. "What are you working on there?"

She looked at him for a few seconds. "Beadwork."

"Can I see it?"

"It is not for sale."

"No, I didn't … I just wanted to see it."

She slowly handed it forward without a word. It was a round piece of cotton with thin thread and a sharp needle waiting for a tiny bead. The pattern was a delicate detailed rose of pink and red with green leaves. On the back it showed a meticulous pattern of tiny stitches holding the colored beads in place.

"It's beautiful. How did you learn this?"

"My grandmother." She took it back but her look was less frosty than before.

Daniel nodded and sat with his back to her at the folding table so that he could review the file. He read for almost an hour, sometimes marking a page with a raspberry sticky for copying. At the end of the file he saw a thick batch of letters just like his, all with names of others in the solicitation. These people must all be his relatives. He did not want to copy them all, so he just copied one, marked "Current resident". It read "Michael Ethete."

He also marked many of the early papers, the original allotment document to "Trees Told It St. James", and an early list of his offspring. There, he saw the names, in formal pencil script: "Lupineflower (Helen) Smith—D", "Sugar St. James, Fort Washakie, WY", and "George Smith, Cache Valley, Utah". He moved his finger over these pencil notes. They had come all the way through the years from the hand of some government scribe. He had not seen the name "Lupineflower" before. Did "D" mean "deceased"? This must be his ancestor George's mother.

He found other more Indian sounding names such as "Bent Foot Healer" and "Rides In Laughter". A thrill went through him as he imagined these long-ago, far away, strange people. A whole list of strangers populated the files. He wondered if he should copy it all, but decided he could come back another time, if needed.

The magic light shone through the dust mites on the glass and burned the past onto new paper. He gave $1.60 to the Indian lady after he made the 16 copies from the file on the old machine. She took back the file and watched him without speaking as he began to walk out. He looked back, nodded and smiled. "I like the rose" he had said.

She had smiled and said, "thank you."

"Do you know where this is?"

"What is?"

"This land. The allotment. The property they are talking about in the letter."

"It's up by Gypsum Spring. About 20 miles away. If you ask at the Malco they can tell you."

"Malco?"

"It's a little gas station on the north highway."

"Ok. Thanks again." He wondered why anyone would call a business 'Mal Co'. His knowledge of Latin root words told him that 'mal' meant "bad". Seemed a poor start to a business to call it "Bad Company". He guessed a lot of English words seemed equally wrong to the Indians.

When Daniel pulled up to the Malco he was glad to see the working gas pumps and the single garage door of the old-fashioned station open. Someone was moving around behind a car with its hood up.

Daniel walked in to the edge of the garage and interrupted the person bent into the hood with an, "Excuse me!"

The face that appeared out at him from behind the car was a movie-star handsome Indian face of a youngish man, complete with a long thick black braid and clear brown eyes. He smiled a white perfect teeth smile and said, "Yeah?"

"I'm looking for Michael Ethete's place, could you give me directions?"

"I'm Mike Ethete," he said coming out into the sun, his smile fading and a distance appearing in his eyes.

Daniel smiled, trying to make a friend of his likely cousin. "I have just come from the BIA Realty office and..."

Mike broke in. "We are not gonna approve the drilling. So get back in your car and don't try to feed me your crap about my income from the oil or send me another one of your deal men, or ask for the right to come over and look around. The answer was 'no' last month, and it still is." He waived his wrench toward the car and motioned as if the car were disappearing over the horizon.

It occurred to Daniel that he had a lot to learn about his letter, and what it meant for these people. He also realized the lady at Realty had left a lot of information unstated about this Malco stop. He felt very much an outsider and a fool. "Can I show you something?"

"I'm not interested!" stated Mike firmly as he turned his broad back and walked back toward the garage.

Daniel quickly went back to his car and shuffled through his papers on the front seat and brought out the letter addressed to Grandfather. He felt silly but slammed the door and ran after the disappearing back of Mike Ethete, waving his letter. "Wait! Wait! I think I am related to somebody named 'Trees-Told-It St. James!"

Mike stopped and looked a bit confused. "Where are you from?"

"Logan"

"No, I mean which tribe?"

"I, uh, don't have a tribe, but I think my great, great grandfather was from here. We got this letter."

"If you are not a member, you don't get a say on this oil matter."

"Grandfather might be a member. The letter came to him. I'm trying to track down what's going on." Daniel would have been surprised if Grandfather was a member of an Indian Tribe, but he didn't know the rules, and maybe he was?

"I thought you were from the oil company. They are greedy bastards."

"I'm Daniel Smith, from Logan, Utah. Grandfather got this letter and I am here to research what it means. I went to the BIA Realty office and copied some of the file. I think I know how we are related. I want to help. I don't want anything but just to know about my family's roots."

Mike still stood with a stony face. But he surprised Daniel by saying, "Maybe you better meet my Dad. He lives on the allotment. He's called 'Old Mike'."

"I would appreciate that, if it's not too much trouble. You could give me directions..."

"I'll take you," said Mike picking up keys and walking to one of the dented pickups on the side of the Malco. "Follow me."

Daniel wondered if he would lock up the station, but he didn't. He started up the pickup and bounced over the potholed driveway and out onto the highway, not looking back to see if Daniel was following, or likely wondering if his gas station would be robbed blind.

Meeting at Trees Told It's Allotment, 2013

They drove for a few minutes on the paved road, then turned into a nondescript dirt road leading through a hay field where four old mailboxes marked the entrance from the road. After a half mile, the hay crop ended and a pasture with a number of healthy looking paint horses, which Daniel always thought of as 'Indian ponies' began. The scene was lovely with high bluffs in the background and yellow and red wildflowers blooming. They drove on and came to a small rundown house sitting amid huge cottonwoods near a small creek. There were three older cars parked askew in the front of the house. A picnic table needing paint sat among weeds under one of the massive trees. One of the windows in the house was cracked and the blue paint was peeling, but overall, it appeared comfortable.

Old Mike was sitting on a lawn chair on his front porch. The porch appeared to be a fairly recent addition made from plywood. He had a wrinkled but handsome face that was lit up in a happy smile. His short hair was white and stood straight up from his head. Even from the distance across the yard, Daniel could immediately see the family resemblance between Mike and Old Mike.

Daniel thought that they both looked like stereotypes of Indians from an Old West poster, brought into a modern context. They had high cheekbones, brown skin and prominent noses. Daniel was aware his thoughts flagged him as a prejudiced fool and he vowed not to say anything that would insult them or sound stupid.

As Daniel was parking his car, he saw Mike jump down from his pickup and begin talking to Old Mike. Daniel wanted to give them a moment so he took his time stepping outside and walking toward the two men on the plywood porch. As he approached, Old Mike stood up, leaning on a gnarly wooden cane, and smiled warmly holding out his hand to Daniel. Mike stepped aside. "Hello, I am Old Mike. Welcome to the paradise!" The old man said.

His handshake was rough and strong but his joints were twisted. He was probably in his mid 70s. His gaze showed he was very sharp-minded. "I was just sitting here watching the warblers. Do you see the male, there in the willow thicket? Their nest is in that cottonwood. The female is around here somewhere. They flick their tails and hop around looking for bugs to take to their chicks. Their little ones will fledge soon, if I haven't already missed them. This is my paradise, you know."

"Hello sir. I'm Daniel Smith."

"Come in for coffee," Old Mike said without question. He turned and opened the squeaking screen door. Mike, and then Daniel followed him inside.

The interior had a musty smell mixed with old coffee. A light was on in the kitchen, which was to the front door's left. The kitchen showed ancient cupboards seemingly recently painted with the federal green color and new looking red-checked curtains over a small side window. The kitchen still held an antique wood stove, upon which sat a porcelain coffee pot and a cast iron skillet. Above the stove hung a number of other dented pots and pans. The sink and small refrigerator were 1950s vintage. Everything in the kitchen was tidy with one corner stacked with canned goods and a huge old-fashioned cotton sack mostly full of "white bleached flour". Mismatched dishes were drying on a rack next to the sink. A tattered dishtowel hung neatly on a cupboard handle.

The small square house appeared to be about 800 square feet with the kitchen and living area in the front. There were two identical doors next to each other opposite the front door in the center of the bigger main front room. The doors presumably led to two rooms in the back of the house, perhaps a bathroom and a bedroom. To the right was a sagging couch and battered chair. Next to the chair was a large pile of newspapers. Over the television was a large picture of a soldier with a folded American flag. Daniel thought the soldier was younger Mike, but then he saw a photograph of Mike and someone who looked exactly like Mike, arm in arm, both wearing the uniform of the United States Marine.

"I should tell you about Angela!" Said Old Mike. "She was my dog. Little mutt but boy could she do some tricks! One thing was she would bring me tools from the shed back of the house. She got hit by a car and died last year." There was a long pause as Old Mike poured the coffee from the steaming pot and Mike arranged another chair at the table. "Hope she's keeping company with Timothy. That's my son, his picture. Killed in action in Afghanistan. Mike's little brother by four minutes."

At first Daniel had thought Old Mike must be a little off talking about the dog. Then he realized Old Mike was finding a good way to bring up Daniel's noticing of the photograph of his son.

"I'm sorry to hear that, sir," said Daniel. "About your son, and about Angela." Daniel felt his face flush with embarrassment for putting the dog and the man together in one statement, but Old Mike saved him with a smile.

"I used to be a son-of-a-bitch. I was mean to everyone. Then our boy was killed. I decided it was time to turn around and act for good. Stop frowning and start smiling. For his sake, live a clean life where I'm making up for being a grouch when he was alive. It's been eleven years and I have smiled every day." Old Mike put a cup of black strong coffee in front of Daniel's new spot at the table.

Mike took all of this without comment and changed the subject as they all sat down. "So your relation got one of those oil company letters about drilling on the allotment?"

"Yes, here it is. We had a family story that we had an Indian grandmother ancestor but nobody really knew anything about it. I was always curious but could not find many records. Then this came and I decided to come out here, to the reservation, and see what I could find. I went to the BIA Realty and copied some documents about the allotment if you want to see them. They are in the car."

"I'm having a doing here on Wednesday evening. It's kind of a 49. Why don't you come?" Old Mike said brightly, seemingly out of the blue.

Daniel was frustrated that the old man was not listening to him and did not want to see his documents. It also seemed odd to him that Old Mike was planning to entertain. Again, Daniel wondered about Old Mike's sanity. "What's a 49?"

"Oh it's just a Indian party. Usually after a pow wow, but that's what I like to call it."

Mike brought the subject back around. "Look, you should understand our point on these letters. The oil companies have been stealing Indian resources since the 1930s. There have been all kinds of legal ways. Mostly in the old days it was just the BIA leasing out our lands and resources without the tribe or anybody's approval. The tribe was supposed to get a royalty, usually 12% of all the revenue made, but until the 1980s the payments were on the 'honor system'. So we got almost no money and had oil people all over our reservation with their water pollution, waste oil dumps, oil trucks ruining the roads, and no enforcement of the laws or leases. No Indian has ever seen any benefit from those oil leases, only ruined fields and roads, water pollution and dumping of god-knows-what on our lands. There was violence in the 1970s. You carried a gun if you wanted to keep people out. Then oil companies got bigger guns and goons to beat up anyone who asked questions. We finally got some laws changed, but they didn't go far enough.

There's a big new play now and the oil companies are leasing up all the non-Indian lands on the reservation. But there's a big block of us tribal members that have allotments right in the middle of what they think is a pool of oil. So we decided to say no to the oil company. But the damn BIA can still approve the leases without us, if less than 50% of us agree. Deal men been coming around bugging the elders and asking them to sign. I ran a man off my auntie's place just last week."

"I understand why you don't want this development, with the possible environmental damage. Do you have environmental groups helping you? I'm a member of the Sierra Club and I could call someone," said Daniel helpfully.

"No son, you don't understand," said Old Mike. "We want to develop this oil. We just want it to be done right; by the tribe, or at least by somebody working under our rules and with our negotiated terms. We'd appreciate it if you would leave your Sierra Club friends out of it. We'll be just fine on our own."

"We are pretty sick of you outsiders telling us how to live. And pushing your ideas on us like we need your help. Outsiders' so called 'help' never did us a damn bit of good, and mostly ends up stealing whatever they came to help with." Mike said.

"Don't you like your coffee?" asked Old Mike; again wavering from the subject.

"Oh, it's fine. I just don't drink much coffee. I'm Mormon."

"Ahh," Said Old Mike. Then after a strange pause he continued, "Yes. Why don't you come back Wednesday, about dinner time."

"I'm really sorry Mike, Old Mike. I don't want to be a bother about this and if we have any say here, we'll be happy to say no to this drilling by sending a letter back to the company. Is that what we should do?"

"You just come back Wednesday, ok?" said Old Mike. Both of the Indians looked at Daniel. Not knowing what to do, and feeling like he had been dismissed, Daniel got up from the table.

"Ok, I'll see you then. Should I bring anything?"

The men looked at him oddly. Finally Mike said, "Like what?"

"Well you know, when I go to a church meeting or social gathering, my wife usually brings potato salad or something."

The Indian men began to laugh. Daniel wondered what kind of mistake he had made.

"Watermelon. Bring a watermelon." Said Old Mike kindly, drying his eyes after the merriment.

Daniel had gotten into his car and bumped back to the highway, then driven an hour carefully back to Riverton, past the fence posts, broken down trailers, power lines and oil jacks moving slowly up and down in the beautiful landscape.

Tall Elk, Wind River Indian Reservation, 2013

Tall Elk put down his tools. He stretched his back and looked up from his work and out the window at the sunshine on the leaves. He always got lost in his carving. Sometimes when he looked up after what he thought was a few hours he would see that it had become dark. Talk Elk counted himself a lucky man. He had everything he could imagine wanting.

He loved his trailer on the reservation. He had a pasture for his horses and a place by the river for his sweat lodge. He lived solo and liked it that way. He had girlfriends that stopped by sometimes, and he had women he visited, too. Then of course there was his crazy group of brothers and sisters and their kids. That was enough for him.

One summer, a white schoolteacher who had come to the reservation for her training had spent the summer after school ended at his house. They liked each other but it did not work. She wanted him to mow the grasses outside his trailer. He explained that they were fine as the Great Spirit had planted them. She gave his dog a bath and brought it into the trailer. He explained that dogs were animals and had always lived outside and did not take baths. He wanted him to go with her to the gym to work out. He explained that he had plenty of exercise doing his art. She wanted to "discuss" the "dysfunction" among his family. He explained that he accepted his family as they were. It seemed she was always seeking ways to make life more difficult and further from the natural order of things. He kissed her goodbye very happily when she moved back to Ohio.

Out back he had converted the old horse barn into his carving studio. It had nice light and a big door for moving his finished pieces out in the back of his pickup. His place was off the highway and hard to find unless you knew where he was. He liked being left alone, except by the people he knew well. He liked having a small circle of people he could count on and who could count on him. The world could go to hell.

Sometimes people from the art community wanted him to do something particular, for their taste or to make a statement, or to get a higher price. His work sold just fine. If he could make more doing something he didn't want to do then they could keep their money. He did what he wanted.

Tall Elk's expenses were minimal and if he sold three or four pieces a year he was comfortable. He usually sold quite a few more than what he needed. He had never worried about money or getting by. He kept a nice savings account at the Riverton Bank. He helped out his family when they needed him, but they would be surprised to know how much he had put into the bank. It didn't matter in the least to him. The elders often said money was bad. Tall Elk thought he knew what they meant. Money was an expression of value far from what the elders valued. To him it was a tool, not a means in itself. People got confused; he decided he could use the tool, and not act contrary to his culture. Tall Elk thought some people stayed poor because they hated money, they did not know how to think of money. In their traditional culture, this tool was now known.

He went inside and opened his refrigerator. He realized he had forgotten to eat today. There wasn't much there. Maybe he would go to Riverton and get a burger and fries. He hiked up his jeans that were slipping down his waist and flipped his ponytail to the back. He guessed he should put on a clean shirt to go to town. He would go see if Barbie wanted to come and bring the kids. They just didn't get out much in summer when the school bus didn't roll around every day to take them to Fort Washakie.

Right then, as if brought in by his idea, Tweak's face materialized in his window. She smiled when she saw him and he waved her in. "Can you take us to town? Mom says we can go to Walmart before Old Mike's 49 on Wednesday."

"Sure, Tweak, I was just thinking I'd go in for a burger. Go get your Mom and Della and hurry it up."

A half hour later the three came trudging down the path from their trailer. Della carried a big laundry basket full to the top and Barbie carried a second bulging sack. Tweak had a bargain tub of detergent in one hand and a plastic bottle of fabric softener in the other. Tall Elk saw that his trip to town would be a long event.

"I thought I'd do my laundry. I haven't had a chance for two weeks. The girls are wearing their clothes backwards to show the clean side. Do you have quarters? I'll throw yours in too if you want." Said Barbie as greeting.

"Ok, but I want to eat first," said Tall Elk grabbing discarded clothes from his floor to add to the basket. They put the laundry in the back of his truck and piled in to the cab. Tall Elk's grubby little nameless yard dog followed along wagging his tail. "Remind me to get dog food," said Tall Elk. They headed off to town.

Daniel Smith, Riverton, Wyoming, 2013

Daniel decided to extend his stay in Wyoming so he could go to the Wednesday night party, or whatever it was. He was nervous about it and wished his wife could be there too, but she was not feeling well in the first part of a pregnancy she had just announced last month and he didn't want her traveling. He was always better in groups if he could hold her hand when he walked in a room full of people. He was afraid this "doing" would be a disaster, and he would be entirely out of place. His curiosity made his decision, though. He had not come here not to see this through. He called his wife. He could tell she was beginning to wonder about his odd adventure to the reservation, but all she said was "You need to tell me all about this when you get home, ok?"

He had a few days so he decided to go off to visit Teton National Park, which was only a few hours away. He had been there before, but as a child, then with his wife right after they married. It would be nice to see it by himself, so that he could enjoy the quiet and look at the views with his own thoughts in mind. Daniel wondered what was getting into him. He had not done anything like this before.

Priscilla and Gabriel, Denver, 2013

Priscilla's plane landed at Denver International Airport at 2:00pm. Her grandson, Richard's third boy, Gabe, had taken time off from his law practice to escort her on this visit home to the Reservation. Funny, it was not home, but of course in many ways it still was for Priscilla. Especially as she got closer to being called to the Spirit World, she yearned to go back to see her family, especially her brother Michael. He had done such a good job maintaining the family roots and teaching his boys. Priscilla had not seen him since Timothy's funeral. She had vowed that she would go back for something other than a funeral next time. Now she was going to spend a week. She wanted to talk and talk and talk and listen and listen and listen. They had missed out on so much.

Her adopted sons Richard and Everett and their families doted on her in her old age, especially since their father had died eight years ago. She could not have asked for better sons or daughter-in-laws or grandchildren, even if they had been her own by blood. They all lived in a wealthy suburb of New York City. Her grandchildren were lawyers, doctors, stockbrokers and school administrators. But they had all learned Shoshone songs as children, and they all accepted Priscilla's values as their own.

She was always the strange looking one in the group. Priscilla maintained her beautiful long black hair, now gray, all her life. She was the picture of an Indian woman. He dark skin contrasted markedly to the blond square-jawed European look of her husband and sons. Through their lives she had frequently been mistaken for a Mexican family servant. Priscilla had just shrugged. She had started out in that role, so why bother to care what people thought? She had so many other, more important issues to battle.

She didn't know where it came from, but in her thirties, after the boys had gone off to college, she could no longer stand the government's legally enforced bigotry. In the early 1960s, much to her husband William's initial confusion, she had joined the civil rights movement and went to meetings and sit-ins and events on college campuses. She loved the intellectual importance and freedom of saying what was true and right.

After a few years, though, it left her feeling like something big was missing from her efforts. Then as the American Indian Movement began to gain traction, Priscilla found her place. William, always the calm and steady hard worker, caught on to the excitement of helping Priscilla come to terms with the injustices she had seen all her life. Shy Priscilla began by writing letters and opinion pieces. Then she found a community of Indian people who shared her revolutionary ideas in upstate New York. Priscilla had learned much about peaceful change from the civil rights community. She helped to apply that in the sometimes radical and impatient movement for Indian rights. She became a leader for Indian rights, always backed up by William, and then by her two sons, both of whom decided law school would help them make a difference. They volunteered and worked for changes in Indian laws. After years of work, they saw successes with the State of New York and with the federal government.

At one point, though, as she grew older, Priscilla realized she had traveled much too far from her people; the people she had grown up with and been part of on the Reservation. Her ideals and efforts were based on philosophies and laws and social planning all coming from her comfortably remote wealthy home. She wondered if her efforts if had been for good at all or if she had become so detached as to be ridiculous? She disappeared from the movement when she became a grandmother to Everett's daughter. And now, decades had since gone by. She was 84 years old and needed to go home.

"Grandmother, I have your bags in the rental car. Are you ready to go?"

"Yes. Isn't the air clear and the sky blue here? I love the western states for that." Priscilla had been waiting on an outdoor bench looking out at the sky.

"It sure is pretty. I got navigation on the car so we won't get lost."

"Oh I think I can get us there. But good thinking." Priscilla smiled and Gabe helped his grandmother into the car.

"Are you tired after the flight?"

"No, I'm excited to be here. Did I tell you about coming to Denver from the Reservation, on the Greyhound bus in 1945?"

"Tell me again, Grandmother. That's how you met Granddad, right?"

"Yes, it was. It was."

Daniel Smith, Teton National Park, 2013

Teton National Park
A Poem
By Daniel Smith

I made a journey to a sacred place.
The remote valleys were still pure and magical as in the days before people.
There, I learned a song to help me celebrate!
Who we were, who we became, who we will be.

Sip the air. It is quiet of judgment.
Clear, crisp, lonely, independent.
We are among stars, among creatures, among spirit, among Earth as made
by God—As still being made by God.

Witness the creation around you!
These people, like rocks, will be worn from sharp to perfectly oval gems of
many colors.
New and old: changed.
Healed: different and the same.

Change at peace with itself; no emotions attached.
Perception, consciousness can only understand the present.
Breath of ancients in the wood and loam, and bark.
All dampening and becoming Earth.

Spider's silk, granite, water, ice!
Breeze, leaves, pine winds; our favorite sounds,
Complex and simple and true.
Reminding us, if we need it, of where we are.

Birds busy with their doings.
Mountain presence high and vast, in silence.
Abundance sustained; Blessed with experience.
Love of life without greed for more of it.

Waiting at Trees Told It's Allotment, 2013

Old Mike was so excited to see his sister. She still called him "Michael" rather than "Old Mike". It had been since Timothy's funeral, and Michael had not been able to enjoy her company much then. His bond with his sister was special. They understood each other as best as two people who had lived such different lives could. He wondered how it would be if she had stayed. Would they not talk to each other after a fight over some small thing, like so many other siblings he knew of here?

Old Mike had many young family members, but very few who were his age or older. His mom, Iris was long dead and his father, Erickson, and his second wife, Sally had each died of cancer in the 1970s up in Spokane. Erickson had worked at the uranium mines before they took even the simplest of precautions. Lots of people from there were still dying from unchecked radiation poisoning.

It seemed most of the others of his generation from the reservation died in their 40s and 50s. Health care was pretty poor at the Indian Health and of course many had lived very hard lives. There had been drinking problems, accidents, poor nutrition, bitter cold, and just poverty. His favorite cousin, Milo Old Bear, who lived up at the Blackfeet most of his life, was an exception and had come to this rez in 1999 when he was almost 70. He lived to be 76 and Michael still really missed sitting on the porch watching the birds with him.

Old Mike didn't know why the Creator had chosen to keep him on the Earth, especially after the Spirit People had taken his son Timothy. Michael decided it was for a reason, and he wanted to make the best of every day. Michael had started teaching culture classes at Fort Washakie Head Start. It was the littlest ones that needed their language and the old Indian teachings the most.

Today's problems, drugs, especially meth, diabetes, family violence, suicide, and the ever-present poverty overwhelmed Michael. There was a new understanding of the emotional problems that had come from the generations of hardship. How does a group of people heal from 200 years of harm? He didn't know. He did know that the old lessons had mystery and power. He would plant the seeds of the songs and stories he knew and he hoped they would grow.

Michael sat on his porch and waited. It was a beautiful day.

A vehicle pulled onto his road. He saw it was Mike and Anne, his wife, and their three-year-old daughter Neka.

"What you have there?"

"I made bread. And chili beans," said Anne. She was Navajo and loved to make their spicier food.

"I have a kettle of stew."

"Well you can't have too much food. You have a crowd coming tomorrow, and people will be stopping by."

A shiny new blue sedan was turning into the last stretch of road. Michael got up, leaning on his cane. He slowly made his way down his steps toward the dirt yard where the car would park. Ah! There was his sister, a big familiar smile on her face. A handsome young man was driving the car. He pulled up and turned the car so Priscilla could get out and be almost in her brother's arms. They hugged. Tears were on both of their faces.

The 49, 2013

Daniel didn't know what time to go to the party. He decided 6:00pm would be safe. Old Mike had said "dinner time". He was becoming less worried about what he was doing. He had written a poem for goodness sakes.

He stopped by the Safeway and selected the biggest watermelon they had. He circled his cart around. Finally he picked up a few canta-loupes, too. It couldn't hurt.

Daniel slowed as he drove past the Malco. It was closed and locked up, but it appeared people could still use a card to get gas because two beat up old cars were filling up, their drivers laughing with each other at some-thing. He looked hard for the turn but passed it and had to turned around. He followed a pickup with a young Indian family down the dirt road. He could see the man and the woman's long dark braids and the shorter head of a child between them, bouncing on the bench seat. He was nervous.

The yard was cluttered with about ten cars and pickups. A fire was smoking from the area near the picnic table under the trees. A large slab of meat was roasting over the fire. A few long tables had been set up and were surrounded by a mixture of folding chairs, plastic chairs, and camping chairs. Even the sagging couch and armchair from inside had been moved out and sat at the head of the party area, their faded floral pattern looking silly among the grasses and wildflowers. People were sitting and visiting. Children were running about, their small leader waving a stick in the air. It looked almost like every Mormon picnic he had seen.

A deep booming drum started from a place under the trees and some people started to sing in a high voice. Not like the Mormons, after all, thought Daniel.

"Hello, I'm Daniel Smith." said Daniel to the people getting out of the pickup. He shuffled the watermelon and held out his hand.

"Hi. I'm Sylvester. This is Judy and Bailey and Jonnah." He said, bouncing a sleeping round-faced baby. The parents were in their late 20s. Sylvester was heavy with his pants worn low. Judy was wearing a beautiful beadwork necklace and carried a large flat box of cup cakes. Daniel was relieved he thought to ask to bring something. Daniel could tell they won-dered who he was, but he decided to let Old Mike explain.

"What the hell is he doing here?" asked Barbie, who was sitting at the table, talking to her brother and watching his teenaged kids texting on their phones. Everyone looked up.

"Watermelon salesman?" suggested Big Boy. The assembled group giggled.

Mike came outside carrying a pan and long knife. He met the new-comers half way greeting the Indians with "Go put those inside and bring out those pitchers of Kool-Aid to the tables, will you? Jonnah is getting fat! You too Sly." Sly smirked and lumbered past. Mike looked at Daniel. "Oh brought the watermelon, I see. Ok, put that inside, too. Old Mike is in there." Mike walked away toward the roasting meat.

Daniel followed Sylvester and Judy inside. Bailey had already run off to join the pack of kids.

"Who is he Mom?" asked Tweak, now too old to run around after the boy waiving the stick. She was sitting with the adults and other teens.

"I don't know. Some guy I met in town."

"He your new boyfriend? You dating the melon salesman?"

"Shove it, Big Boy." Everyone giggled again.

"I think I saw that on Facebook." Barbie rolled her eyes. "Yeah, there was a picture of you with a guy holding two melons."

"Not funny brother. Watch yourself." But everyone else was laughing.

"Mom, can we get Facebook?" asked Tweak.

"Sure. When internet comes to our part of the rez."

"I just want a cell phone." Said Della.

"Maybe next year."

"Want to play with my phone?" asked Jeannie, Big Boy's oldest daughter. She was in high school, a star of the basketball team. All the girls looked up to her.

"Yeah!" The kids huddled around Jeannie and the phone while she tapped and explained its options.

"Oh yeah. The meat is just about done," said Mike.

Laughter came from the area of the drum. A few random "boom, booms" filled the air as the song had ended. At least eight men sat around the big drum, each holding a drumstick. They chatted as they decided what to sing next.

Inside, Daniel stood awkwardly at the door with his watermelon. A broad shouldered blond man stood with his back to the door at the sink, his arms bare and wet as he washed methodically through an enormous pile of pots and pans, a few clean ones resting on a towel on the other side of the sink. There was Old Mike, stirring a giant pot of something on the old stove. A white haired lady stood leaning on a cane next to him, peering into the pot. Old Mike gave her a taste from a bent spoon. She smiled happily, saying "Oh, that's really good!"

Sylvester and Judy went out past him carrying plastic pitchers of sloshing red Kool-Aid.

"Hi everyone," announced Daniel. Old Mike, the blond dishwasher and the grey haired lady all turned around.

"Mr. Smith! Come in!" said Old Mike. "He's our new friend from Logan. I'm going to introduce him around."

"Hi, I'm Gabe." Daniel put down his watermelon and shook Gabe's hand.

"Dan."

Priscilla thought she might be going crazy. Maybe she was having a stroke? She blinked and shook her head. There, before her, appeared to be her lover from over 60 years ago, Jeremiah, as if he had not aged a minute. What on Earth? What had been conjured in this trip into her past? She stumbled a little, holding tightly to her cane and the windowsill.

"Grandmother! Are you ok?" Gabe said, rushing to her and holding her arm.

Priscilla needed to sit down. "Oh, yes…maybe help me over to the chair."

"We took all the chairs out. Here, sit on the bed." Gabe opened one of the doors and Daniel saw a small room heaped with laundry baskets and a cheap dresser. Twin saggy beds sat on each side of the room. Priscilla was helped by Gabe over to the nearest one and sat down. Through the door she looked up at Daniel.

"I'm sorry son, just a little dizzy. Now, who are you?"

"I'm Daniel Smith, Mamam. I'm err… I'm maybe a relative from a long way back and Old Mike invited me to come to the party today. I'm Mormon, from Logan Utah."

Priscilla stared at him.

Old Mike broke in. "I'm gonna sit here with Priss. You two boys go on out and see if Mike needs anything. Take that elk stew out and put it on the metal stand over the fire."

"You ok Grandmother?"

"Yes. Gabriel. Just give me a minute and I'll be out."

Gabe and Daniel looked at each other each wondering what was going on. They moved back to the kitchen. Old Mike closed the door to the small bedroom.

"Wow, that was weird. Grandmother acted like she saw a ghost when she saw you."

"I'm sure I've never met her. Who is she? Do you think she is ok?"

"I'm not sure. I'll come check on her in a few minutes. She's my grandmother. Her name is Priscilla Engstrom. She was born here and married my grandfather after World War II. They lived in New York ever since, except when she came back here to visit."

"You don't look Indian."

"I'm not. My Grandparents married after my real grandmother died of cancer. But Priscilla pretty much raised my Dad. She was, well *is*, really influential for the family. A really wonderful lady."

"So have you been here before?"

"No. I just started a law practice in New York and am taking some time off to travel with Grandmother. I am just meeting these relatives of hers. Well they are mine too, I guess. I think they like me. They are teasing me and calling me Old Mike's Rent-a-Maid. I guess because I've been doing dishes since I got here. Grandmother said that if they teased me, they like me."

The men carried the heavy kettle of elk stew across the lawn.

"You find another white guy to join the maid service? I thought he was a watermelon salesman!" said a large Indian man Daniel had not met. Now it was time for Daniel to be surprised. Sitting next to the man was the rude woman from the frightening bar in Riverton. Next to her was a large group of teenage girls. The woman was now drinking what appeared to be red Kool-Aid.

Mike saved the moment. "This is Daniel Smith. He got one of the oil company letters and came out here to check it out. He's probably related from someplace far back. Old Mike wanted him to come out. Daniel, you introduce yourself around. But that's Big Boy and Barbie for starters."

Daniel sat down nervously at the picnic table. He was disappointed to see Gabe head back to the house.

"Nice to see you again," he said to Barbie.

"Yeah," she said.

"Hi, I'm Tweak. How do you know my Mom?"

"Tweak? Um well, I was stopping in a place for a snack and she was there. We just met briefly."

"Oh. So are you related to us?"

"Hush now Tweak."

"Darn girl, you could talk the feathers off a bird flying past."

"Thank you Uncle Big Boy."

"Uncle?"

"Yeah, he's my Mom's brother. Over there, that's my Mom's other brother, singing at the drum. He's Tall Elk. Mom had three other brothers and a sister but they already died. And this is my little sister Della and that's..."

"Enough already, Tweak."

The drum started up again with regular beats played in unison by each drummer from his position around the large circle. A song began in a high warbling voice, seeming to be a language Daniel did not know. A group of similar voices answered the song of the leader. You could not sit there without tapping your foot, or somehow following the beat.

"So what does the song mean?"

"It's a round dance song. It's social; just a fun melody to sing along with. It doesn't *mean* anything," answered Barbie.

"What are the words?"

"This one talks about missing a girlfriend who is in Canada."

"Oh." They listened for a while and soon more people arrived. Then more tables were set up, more Kool-Aid and coffee were served in paper cups, and people chatted and laughed and ribbed each other. Daniel noticed there was a lot of teasing.

"You going on vacation Adam? I heard you got scheduled for your bikini wax in Riverton." Everyone including Adam laughed; Adam was obese and very rough looking.

Soon Gabe, Old Mike and Priscilla came outside. They chatted with the newcomers for a minute and then sat in the places of honor on the sofa and chair.

Mike walked over to the drum under the trees. He asked the drum for a prayer and everyone quieted. They waited and the drum started. A little slower and more determined. Everyone stood. A different singer began, his voice lower singing Shoshone words. He sang for a while, repeating a chorus four times, turning to the four directions. Others joined in, singing or beating out the rhythm with their feet or hands. At the end, the drums beat rapidly four times. The sun seemed just a little brighter in the new quiet.

The young girls got up and began filling plates, which they served to the elders. Then, people got up as they wanted and helped themselves to paper plates and bowls for elk stew with potatoes, roasted beef, potato chips, watermelon, and an array of store bought and home made foods. One lady sat before a big hot kettle of lard over the fire. She patted dough balls from a big cooler into flat rounds and forked them into the oil. The dough puffed into delicious fry bread pillows. People did not wait for them to cool but poured stew and beans over the hot bread.

People ate and chatted and teased each other. The kids began to run around again. Someone brought out a guitar and began to play pop and country songs. The teenagers resumed their interest in their phones. Even though there must have been six babies there, Daniel did not hear one of them cry the whole evening.

Tweak was sitting between Priscilla and Gabe. Tweak had an adoring look on her face. They had been talking all through dinner. Barbie and Della joined them and they all laughed together listening to Priscilla's stories.

Daniel listened to the chatter around him, mostly in silence. He answered questions when anyone asked him, but mostly people avoided looking at him. Daniel felt like an outsider, and was embarrassed to look toward the woman from the bar, but he relaxed with some small welcomes, like the sharing of some smiles. He also felt happy as he laughed at the ribbing people gave each other.

One middle aged Indian man teased a younger man. "I heard you got kicked by that mare. Got an astronaut badge for the trip you took, I hear."

"Yeah" said another man, "You going into the satellite business, enit?"

"Well, you aint getting' a discount from me on your TV service."

"Discount! Hell I won't pay my bill anyway! Only show on your system will be 'Easy Rider.'"

"No, he'll have 'Black Stallion' too."

"My Friend Flicka!"

"Seabiscuit!"

"All the Pretty Horses!"

"Hidalgo!"

"The Electric Horseman," added Daniel. Everyone laughed.

Out of the blue, everyone noticed that Old Mike was talking about something. It seemed important. They stopped and strained to hear.

"...so I have this long written story from 1909. My Dad gave it to me before he moved up to Spokane in the 1950s."

"Can I read it?" asked Tweak.

Tall Elk inquired loudly, from the other table. "Old Mike, what you saying?"

Mike interrupted. "Hey everybody, come over here. My Dad has something to say."

The guitar stopped and a hush fell. Slowly, everyone abandoned their plates and cups of Kool-Aid and got up. They moved to stand or sit on the ground around the old man and his sister on the floral couch under the shade of the cottonwoods. Some brought their folding chairs and everyone waited quietly, respectfully. There were probably over a hundred people there. Old Mike appeared to be in prayer, or gathering his thoughts. Priscilla held his hand. Daniel stood near the back, but so he could see the old man's face and hear his words.

Old Mike started his quiet voice. He spoke a few sentences in Shoshone, then switched to English. Daniel felt the ghosts of long tradition; people gathered around elders to hear of important things. There was power in this and Daniel felt awed. He wondered if the others felt the same or if they were used to this.

"Back in 1940, you know, before the war, the tribes had some of their elders go back to Washington DC. These elders testified before the United States Congress about what was going on here. One of our Congressmen, William F. Warren, you know, the Air Force Base now is named after him in Cheyenne, invited them. He was trying to do something good. Back then, we had lots of white people stealing our lands in bad ways. There was lots of violence. Indians didn't go out at night if cars were on the roads, or into town alone. We were beat up. Indians in town were put in jail for nothing. People were really poor. It was after the great depression and things were a big mess. These elders told Congress how it was. The white people around here didn't like it at all. Two of the three elders that went back there were murdered, you know. One of them..." Old Mike shook his cane at Barbie, then Tall Elk, then Big Boy. Then at Tweak and Della. "... was your great grandfather. His name was Thomas Homena. His mother was the daughter of the man who was first allotted this land. That's why you kids got those letters from the oil company about this place and drilling here. That's how you are related to this place. My Dad told me all about Thomas Homena, because they were cousins and real close. He was a war hero from World War I. He was a smart man and had good English for the times. His allotment, what's now part of big dude ranch on the edge of the reservation, was stolen from him. But Thomas was real smart in lots of ways. He was elected to one of the real early Arapaho Tribal Councils. He worked hard to get some justice here on the Reservation."

Mike paused and was quiet. A breeze blew the leaves of the cottonwood.

"My Dad and Thomas's wife and kids was told by the BIA police that Thomas Homena was found drunk in a ditch. Froze to death they said. But my Dad told me that they didn't believe it for one minute. His daughter, Betsy, she's your grandma, Barbie—well, she went north after her Dad died. That's when she married into Blackfeet.

When I was young, my Dad would not say what he thought about Thomas's murder. He would get real quiet about this part. But you know, when he was dying of cancer and I went to see him, he told me to take care of this allotment. He told me people had died to protect our land. When I asked him who had died, he kind of laughed. He said lots of people, our elders, those who came before. He then told me, real softly, that Thomas Homena was murdered for speaking up about what was wrong. He said the family had gone to get his body to be buried in the Arapaho cemetery. He had two gunshots, one that took half his skull off, and the other through his neck. Both shots were from the back. He had been executed and dropped in a ditch. They found another guy who had gone to Washington dead, too. He was stabbed in the jail in Riverton. They said nobody knew who did it, but how could they not know who was with him at the jail? Of course, these murders were never solved.

"So we got to take care of this land. We can't be fighting about it. I know some of you was mad that I live here, and when I'm dead I don't want any fighting about who moves onto this land. There is enough for everybody! Mike and Anne and Neka will get the house. After that, you got to share. Take care of each other. Promise that."

Everybody was looking down and nobody answered. Daniel realized there was a strong undercurrent of this family's dynamics he had not dreamed of. He suddenly saw how people with very few possessions could fight hard over the ones they had, and how families could be cut apart with the death of an old one.

"What's the papers you talked about?" asked Tall Elk.

"My grandmother was Sugar St. James. She was the first one to live out here. She lived with her husband, John Ethete, after the original Indian owner, her grandfather, died. His name was Trees Told It and he was really old when he got the allotment. He died soon after. I remember Grandmother Sugar well because I was nine years old when she died. She was very particular about all our education. She and her husband built the house here. That's her stove in there. I can still see her feeding wood into that stove to warm us up on cold mornings. My Dad was born in that house. So were me and Priscilla. So was Mike, for that matter."

"Sugar had wrote up her grandfather's stories. It's the whole life of Trees Told It, told in his Shoshone words from 1825 until 1901. She was an interpreter for the whites at the Agency and she translated his whole life story. It's written in pencil on the back of thrown out government papers she got from the agency trash. It's a powerful story and I want all you to read it. You'll know who died for this land."

Old Mike had started to cry. He brushed his tears away and sat quietly.

"I have a paper, too," said Barbie, into the silence. Everyone's eyes turned to her in surprise. "Before she died, my mom gave me a letter written by her grandfather, Thomas Homena. It tells his story, or the first part of it anyway. I have it somewhere at home.

"I remember that letter," said Big Boy. "Mom made me read it when I was a kid. It seemed like a bunch of boring ancient history then. She never told me he was murdered."

"Sometimes it takes a while to understand things," said Priscilla. "Maybe tomorrow, we can go to town and get some copies made. Barbie, will you look for your letter? We can come by and pick it up in the morning."

"I think I know where it is."

"There's something else was in Grandmother Sugar's stories." Old Mike looked at Daniel. "You might be wondering who this white guy is whose at this 49." There was general nervous laughter from some. Everyone else was silent. "Sugar tells in her writings about how her mother was Trees Told It's daughter. Her mother went with a Mormon in Utah and they had a son and a daughter. The son stayed with the Mormons and Sugar came home. I think that son is Daniel-here's ancestor. Since Sugar worked at the Agency, she put the son's name in the paperwork and now he has a letter about the allotment."

"Oh my God," said Daniel. "I have copies from the BIA file with the names "Trees Told It", 'Lupineflower' 'Thomas Homena', and others, all the way to Old Mike."

"Maybe we can make copies of those, too?" asked Priscilla.

"Of course," said Daniel, relieved someone finally wanted to see his documents.

With this, his eyes locked with Priscilla's. The regal old Indian woman had such a strange look on her face.

Old Mike was standing up. He reached for a paper sack on the table and walked with it over to Daniel. Everyone watched as Old Mike pulled a small bundle from the sack. It was a rabbit skin wrapped around something. Mike gently unwrapped the skin and handed the item to Daniel. In his hand, Daniel saw a large oval turquoise stone, set in silver and sewed onto a beautifully beaded band. It appeared to be very old. "I want you to pass this around. All of you take a look at it. This belonged to the mother of Trees Told It. It must be from the 1700s."

The item felt heavy to Daniel. He stared at it in wonder. This had been his great-something grandmother's. She must have cherished it. The beadwork was fine and the leather onto which it was sewn was soft and bore the dark smudges of long use. His imagination glimpsed this woman riding a horse with a child in a cradleboard, wearing this charm. He reverently passed it to Tweak, who had run to his side to see it. Her eyes were huge as she stroked the blue stone for a minute then passed it along.

Tall Elk had gone to the drum. He began a slow, deep beat. Other men got up and joined him. The drum grew louder as they joined and everyone stood. The singers began in unison a song everyone seemed to know. Daniel felt the drum in his heart.

Good Night, Trees Told It's Allotment, 2013

The party was breaking up. The moon had risen. With only it's pearl glow through the trees and the leaping fire the world looked magical.

Priscilla was tired. She yearned to go lay on the soft twin bed in the house built by Grandmother Sugar in which she had been born. Gabe had brought her coffee. It was helping her to stay awake long enough to say goodbye to everyone. She knew there was unfinished business.

One by one, the guests came to her and Old Mike. She held all the family members' hands in her gnarled old fingers and looked into each of their eyes. The eyes all held the future and reflected the past. This had been a wonderful party.

When the white man, Daniel came up to say his thanks, Priscilla knew she must say something. She could not let him drive home to Logan tomorrow without speaking. She held his hand. Her mouth would not move.

"What is it, sister?" Said Old Mike, in Shoshone.

"Old times." Answered Priscilla, looking away from Daniel, and turning to Old Mike. They looked at each other, knowing something was important.

"You must tell him what you want to say, sister," said Old Mike.

Priscilla looked back to Daniel. She still clasped his hand. "Tomorrow will you be here?"

"Well, I would like to get copies of the stories and the letter, so yes, I can come by."

"Maybe we will come to town, you can ride with us to the copy place."

"Ok, I'm staying in Riverton at the Best Western," said Daniel, puzzled.

"We can pick you up, say about ten?" said Gabe.

"Yes, that will be fine. Good night now. Thank you so much for having me here."

"You are family. It's right and good that you came. The Creator brought you here. We are blessed that you shared this day with us," said Old Mike.

"Bye, now," said Daniel to the others.

"Thanks for coming!" yelled Tweak.

Making Copies, Riverton Wyoming, 2013

The next morning at 9:55 Daniel sat in the lobby of the Best Western. He had checked out and his suitcase was in the trunk of his car. Before him sat his file of papers. He was waiting, having a friendly chat with an older man who worked at the bank in Cheyenne. Soon Gabe's rental car pulled up. On the passenger side sat Priscilla, and out of the back jumped Tweak. She ran to the door. In the car was Mike and Tweak's sister Della.

"Damn Indians!" said the banker from Cheyenne to Daniel, noticing the car. "Buncha drunks! Look at that car! They are all rich on casino money."

Daniel looked at him with shock. He guessed people really did think that way. "Think twice before saying something ugly like that again, friend. They are my family!" said Daniel, turning his back on the banker and walking out to meet Tweak. She greeted him with an enthusiastic wave and got back into the car. Daniel walked around to the other side with his file of papers and they drove off. He saw the banker standing in the window with his head tilted in confusion, his face red.

They drove to a small print shop in downtown Riverton. As they started to get out, Priscilla said, "Now Daniel, maybe you could stay here and keep me company?"

"I would be happy to do that, Mrs. Engstrom. Here's my file, Mike. It has all the BIA records I thought were important."

"Can I stay too?" asked Tweak.

"No sweetie, you go make sure they get me a full copy of those papers, ok?"

"Ok Auntie!"

They lowered the windows of the car and sat in the shade of the building. Priscilla turned around. "Are you, by any chance, related to a Jeremiah Smith?"

"Well, yes, he's my grandfather."

Priscilla felt like she was talking to a ghost. It was surreal. "Well, you see, you are his very image. I knew him in New York City, right after he got back from the war. We were probably the only ones there from Wyoming at the time."

"He's the one who received my letter from the BIA."

"Oh, my! He's still alive?"

"Yes Mamam. He's in the Veteran's Home in Logan. I visit him pretty regularly. He's still pretty sharp. He just had his 91st birthday. I was wondering what it was on your face when we met. Yes, people do say I look like him in his younger days. I have a picture of him in his uniform and it's pretty amazing."

"Oh dear," said Priscilla. She seemed to be upset.

"I will be sure to tell him you said hello!" continued Daniel, trying hard to say the right thing.

"I'm not sure I want you to do that, son," said Priscilla softly. "You see, we didn't part in the best way. I believe I owe him an apology."

Daniel was at a loss. "What can I do to help, Mamam?"

"Tell me he had a good life. That would be nice."

"Oh he did. He was married to my Grandmother for over fifty years before she passed away. They had seven children and they have about forty grand children. At his 90th we counted over a hundred great grandchildren. He ran the family grocery business and expanded it to Logan. Everybody in town knows him. He's very well respected."

"Oh my. That's good. Very good. So he was never an unhappy person?"

"I don't think so. Of course, I've only known him in these last 38 years of his life. But I never heard of anything."

"Good, good." Priscilla sat thinking for a minute. "Maybe you could give him a letter from me. Could I send it to you so I have time to write it the way I want?"

"Yes, I'd be happy to do that. But he'll be wanting to hear from me as soon as I get back. He was pretty excited about me coming here."

"Well then I better get working on that letter. Give me your address and you'll have it from me real soon."

Priscilla Engstrom, 2013

Dear Jeremiah,

How I have thought of you over the years. You were in my prayers many times and I always hoped you had a wonderful life. I have met your Grandson, Daniel now. He is a good man. This tells me that you did well for yourself and that all is as it was meant to be.

This does not mean that I feel good about what happened between us when I left you in Manhattan in 1945. I owe you an apology for that I know.

I am so truly sorry. I wished I had the maturity and strength to face you with the truth, rather than just running away. I know that must have been very hurtful for you. The last thing I ever wanted was to hurt you.

I was such a child. I was 17 years old then. I had very little training or example in how to handle difficult things. I was so ashamed. Although now I know that my shame was misplaced. None of these terrible things are an excuse. I am so sorry. But I must explain.

You see, when I was barely a child I was sent away from home because I had tuberculoses. Home for me was a small house on the reservation. Times were very hard then, in the depression. Hunger, difficult family life and serious health concerns were common on the reservation during the 1930s. I was in the Indian hospital in Rapid City for some time, alone, away from my family. My condition cleared but while I was there the Indian Health Service gave me a hysterectomy. This was often done in those days for Indians with health conditions. I could not bear to tell you that I could not have children. I know it was important to you. I did not want you to know my shame; that the white world had found me unworthy to have babies. I thought that you, and your people would come to feel the same way. So I ran.

I don't believe I told you how I came to be in New York City. You asked, I know, but again, I was not able to tell you the whole truth. Now I will so you may understand me better.

Our reservation, and a few others around Denver were a part of a trial program by the Bureau of Indian Affairs around the end of the war. There was so much poverty and suffering on the reservations and workers were needed in the cities. The government was also transitioning to a new policy called "Termination" where they wanted the Indian tribes to assimilate into white culture. So they offered young people like me the chance to move to the city. I lied about my age and joined the program.

We were given a bus ticket to Denver and not much more. Later, when the program became institutionalized, the government started offering services to those in the "relocation program". However, I was not fortunate to have any of this assistance. I arrived in the city never having been away from my sheltered life. I spent my first night away from my family in the city terrified and sleeping behind a garbage dumpster.

I was fortunate to quickly find work for a family as a housekeeper and caretaker to two small boys. They were good to me. I was so homesick for the reservation and transitioning to their way of life was very confusing and difficult. The mother of this family, a true friend to me, was very ill, however and she died after a few months. I stayed on with the family when they moved to New York. Soon after arriving there, though, I was asked to leave by a member of their family who did not like Indians and I again found myself alone in a very strange city.

Then I met you. Those days were magical and the best of my life. I recall everything very fondly.

After I ran away from you that day, I bought a bus ticket to go back to the reservation. The father of the family I had worked for found me at the bus station and brought me back to care for his boys. We married later that month so that I would never again be asked to leave their house. He was always very good to me and I have had a good life. My husband passed away a number of years ago but his boys are my sons now and with a strange turn of fate, I am now blessed with wonderful grandchildren and great grandchildren. I realize that all people are the same, only different in beautiful ways.

I was also honored to eventually contribute my time and efforts to help Indian causes and people and to fight the federal government's efforts to "terminate" Indian people through relocation, sterilization, sale of Indian resources and other government policies.

I do not know that I would have been in a position to do that if we had married. Nor would you have had your beautiful family. So I suppose the Creator has had his hand in all of this.

If you will forgive me, perhaps some day we could speak on the phone. Or if you would like, I can come to see you while I am in Wyoming this summer. My brother's phone number is listed below if you would like to call. If not, I hope that you recall me fondly and that this letter finds you a happy man.

                                                                    Priscilla

Tweak, Wind River Indian Reservation, 2013

Della's staying over at Tall Elk's for a few days. She was sick with a fever. Before Mom went to town to work for a few days, she asked if Della could stay over there. I said I wanted to stay home. It's understood that I will be going over to Tall Elk's place when I'm ready to watch a movie or something. Or Tall Elk will check in on me if I stay over here by myself too long. I am alone in our trailer.

I have been reading the copies of all the old stories. The best stories were told by the lady, Sugar in spidery old handwriting that I sometimes can't read well. But those stories still carry a mystery of the old times that's strangely reflected in the places and people I am so familiar with today. It's like having the voices talk to me in a whole new way. I'm trying to figure it out.

I'm feeling scared about all these terrible things that happened in the stories. Those old Indian people were tough.

Terrible things are still happening. Yesterday I heard about two girls and a boy from the high school that were smoking meth together in the BIA housing. They had a fight and all three of them are dead now. Somebody had a gun and I guess it got out of hand and one of them, they don't know which one, killed the other two and then committed suicide against their self. I knew them all, but not really well. I think one of them was related to Big Boy's girlfriend. Stuff like that is always happening around here.

I kind of wonder when I'll be walking along minding my own business and I'll fall into a hole of evil just like they did. It could happen any time to anybody. I don't think we're safe here.

But we're better off here than out there in some other strange place. I like being Indian and living here. I love my family.

My people are Indian and they are strong! My Mom is tired all the time but she works hard and takes care of us. My father was a Cree from Canada. I don't know anything about him or those relatives but I bet they were fierce. My grandfather was half Blackfeet and half Shoshone and he was a rancher. My great, great grandfather a war hero named Thomas Homena who was murdered after people stole his land; and when he was a baby, he was named Rides In Laughter. His mother was named Bent Foot Healer and helped her niece to escape from the Mormons. Her father was a buffalo Indian named Slow Walker and Trees Told It who lived through an army massacre and walked away into the Owl Creek Mountains to die when he was old. His mother from the 1700s had a really pretty turquoise with a beaded band that has been passed down through many hands until today, so that I got to see it.

All this makes me strong. All these things make me proud. I wonder who I will be when seven generations from now, they are reading my story?

I will not be perturbed by these new and strange ways.
My great, great, great, great grandpa said that. I like it!

That is all.

Margaret Martin lives in Boulder, Colorado with her husband. She practices energy law for Indian tribes. Her clients are tribes and tribal businesses across the United States. She has over twenty-six years of legal experience. She has spent most of her career traveling to client locations, often staying for long periods of time on Indian reservations. Mrs. Martin has adopted families from the Navajo Nation and Hopi Tribe. Her family of birth is originally from Montana; her father's family having settled the first homestead in the state, prior to statehood, in 1876 near what is now the Crow reservation. This is her first novel.

The author can be available upon request, to address educational classes and participate in book club discussions. Please email the author at margaretmartin-books@gmail.com.

Author's Discussion Question Suggestions

Seven Generations

1. A common, summarized and short version of "seventh generation" philosophy derived from the Constitution of the Iroquois
   Nation is, "In every deliberation, we must consider the impact
   on the seventh generation... even if it requires having skin as
   thick as the bark of a pine." What lessons can be taken about
   the making of decisions when things change so drastically in
   seven generations?

2. What did you think of the nature of the characters' names, and
   how they were free to change their names over time?

3. Each chapter was written in a different style. How did this
   help or hinder your understanding the perspectives of the various characters?

4. The development of natural resources was a theme in many of
   the chapters. How did development help and hurt the characters and what philosophical struggles were highlighted by the
   need to use resources?

5. How did the characters inherit from previous generations?
   How did the physical objects and the passed down sayings reflect the psychological inheritances?

6. Which of the characters likely suffered from what we would
   now call "depression" and how did they, over time, find hope?
   How did their depression affect how white people may have
   seen them?

7. Which characters did you like best? Why?

8. Native Americans are more likely than any other ethnic group in the USA to join the military and their history in services that were very recently their enemies is rich. Why do you think this is so?

9. What role did the various religions play in the lives of characters? What surprised you about this?

Different chapters characters referred to previous chapters' characters. How did the later generations thoughts of the earlier generations impact your understanding of the characters and their growth over time?

CPSIA information can be obtained
at www.ICGtesting.com
Printed in the USA
FSHW010948040221
78341FS